The Bobbin Girls

Sunday Times bestselling author Freda Lightfoot was born in Lancashire. She always dreamed of becoming a writer but this was considered a rather exotic ambition. She has been a teacher, bookseller in the Lake District, then a smallholder and began her writing career by publishing over forty short stories and articles before finding her vocation as a novelist. She has since written over forty-eight novels, mostly sagas and historical fiction. She now spends warm winters living in Spain, and the rainy summers in Britain.

Also by Freda Lightfoot

Lakeland Sagas

A Champion Street Market Saga

A Salford Saga

The Poor House Lane Sagas

FREDA LIGHTFOOT

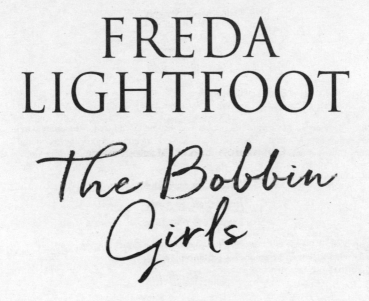

The Bobbin Girls

1️⃣ CANELO

First published in the the United Kingdom in 1998 by Hodder & Stoughton

This edition published in the United Kingdom in 2020 by Canelo

Canelo Digital Publishing Limited
31 Helen Road
Oxford OX2 0DF
United Kingdom

A CIP catalogue record for this book is available from the British Library.

Print ISBN 978 1 80032 209 7
Ebook ISBN 978 1 80032 062 8

Look for more great books at www.canelo.co

Printed and bound in Great Britain by Clays Ltd, Elcograf S.p.A.

To Darley Anderson for his belief in me, and to my editor, Sue Fletcher, for her continued support and advice

Prologue

1916

All the windows of the house were ablaze with light as the young girl dragged herself on leaden feet down the seemingly endless driveway, though she guessed her deathly tiredness made it seem longer than it actually was. The farm or manor house, whatever it may be, was by no means grand. Solid and square and grey in the evening light, there was a bare, unloved quality about it that chilled her. Yet since it was the first glimpse of civilisation she had seen for miles in this bleak Lakes country, she kept her eyes fixed on those lights like heavenly beacons and, gritting her teeth, plodded steadily onward.

The wind moaned through a thicket of trees, making the boughs creak and grind together as if they might at any moment tumble down upon her. Rain-soaked hair whipped like a lash against her frozen cheeks but she did not trouble to wipe it away. Once her hair would have borne a sheen as fine as that of her short silk dress; now it was tangled and dirty, uncombed for days, just as the dress was torn and spoiled. Even the thin wool coat that was meant to keep out the bitter cold did no such thing, since it too was soaking wet with mud or blood, or both. It had been bought not for any practical purpose but to conform to the vagaries of fashion. She had no thought now for such niceties.

Not that she had any right to complain. Men were dying in worse conditions on the battlefields of France; dying in a war not of their making. But then she hadn't committed a sin against mankind either, only against society.

It occurred to her that the bewildering number of lights could indicate that the people within were entertaining guests; they might not take kindly to being interrupted by a bedraggled ragamuffin covered in mud, shivering on their doorstep in her sodden clothing. She should perhaps seek out the kitchen door or servants' entrance, beg a bowl of hot water from a house-keeper or maid so she could wash before making her request. Mama would wish her at least to present herself well. The thought, coming so unexpectedly and automatically, made her almost laugh out loud, but then the pain gripped her again and she gasped, falling to her knees as it knotted her spine, straddled the swell of her stomach and dragged piercingly down into her groin.

She clutched at a nearby drystone wall, her fingernails breaking in the rough lichen. How much longer could she bear it? As the worst of the pain ebbed away, she pressed her heated brow against the iron-cold stone. Was this how death felt? Was this how it came, with red-hot pincers?

What if they – the people at this house – refused to give her shelter? They knew nothing of her and her troubles, so why should they agree? Where then would she go? How could she survive yet another night in this wild, empty country? Her time was near.

With the last dregs of her energy, the girl pulled herself upright and, redoubling her efforts, reached a low flight of stone steps that led up through a wide storm porch to a solid oak door. She doubted her ability to climb them, let alone reach the high polished brass knocker. Her feet slipped on the rough stone chippings and she half fell, half sank thankfully upon the lowest step with an agonised cry, as the pain sliced through her backbone once more with merciless precision.

It had barely passed, loosing her momentarily from its grip, when the front door crashed open and light spilled down upon the steps. There was the ringing of a boot heel against stone then a man's voice, harsh and unforgiving. 'If that's you, doctor, then bloody well get in here, man. Must we wait all night?'

2

There was a deathly, awesome silence in which the girl was acutely aware of the man standing a few steps above her, looking out into the blackness of night, knowing she must reveal her presence but unable to speak against the overwhelming agony that swamped her. As she fought to recover her failing senses and breath enough to speak, she became aware that the light was slipping away and the darkness once more threatening to engulf her.

'*Sir!*' she cried, in a last desperate effort, the word cut off instantly by the scream she could not stifle as the jealous pain returned to claim her. She was so cold she felt frozen to the step, her fevered shivering making her teeth rattle in her head, and then the rain started again, warming her as it washed over her legs, cleansing her body of its burden. At least she thought it was the rain.

Chapter One

1930

His first sight of them brought the blood rushing to his head. He could actually hear it pounding in his ears.

The golden light of evening bathed their milk-white bodies in an almost ethereal glow. They had lit several candles on the shingle beside the tarn, since it was both Hallowe'en and the boy's birthday. The flickering flames were reflected a hundred times in the ripples of the water as they splashed and dived beneath the sheltering willow and alder trees. Their laughter drifted across to him on a wayward breeze, bounced back by the surrounding Lakeland mountains, and fear rose in his throat like bile.

A rope hung from a tree down into the water and the girl's head came up beside it, shaking the sparkling water from the copper locks of her long hair. Then she dipped once more beneath the ripples, twisting her slender body up and over, again and again, like a young otter at play, or some kind of golden water sprite.

When she climbed out of the tarn to run along the tree branch, as graceful and slender as a gazelle, he saw how the young breasts were already budding with promise, the swell of her hips and a small triangle of curled hair indicating the first signs of womanhood. She showed not the slightest sense of embarrassment at being naked before the boy, proving that this was not the first time they had swum together thus.

James Hollinthwaite lifted his hand from the rock he had been holding, and found it starred with blood.

4

What a blind fool he'd been! Why hadn't he anticipated this? Done something about it.

Because, like a moth attracted to lamplight, he could not resist keeping her in his sight.

But then to be fair to himself, he'd thought of them still as children. Yet they were fourteen, with childhood almost gone.

He stepped back into the shadows, anxious not to be seen, knowing they should not have come to the tarn without supervision, that some ill could befall them if he didn't send them off home at once. But he did nothing.

He had never thought himself a coward. In all his forty-five years he had faced many trials and tribulations, lived through a general strike and a World War, and met and dealt with them all in the certain knowledge that he was a man in control of his own destiny. He owned a profitable farm, a bobbin mill, and a large parcel of woodland which supplied all the timber it needed. He must be one of the biggest employers of labour in the valley, if not the whole Furness peninsular, thereby gaining himself a position of respect in the community.

He would survive this recent depression better than most. New York might crash and shares fall, but since he'd had the sense to put his money in land, which they'd never be making any more of, he'd do all right. Land would always go up in value, if one bided one's time, and he had every intention of coming out of this financial crisis with his fortune not only intact, but increased.

He possessed a wife, beautiful and talented, if not so compliant as he would like her to be. And, most important of all, he'd got himself a son.

But now, for the first time in his life, he felt matters were out of his control, a state of affairs he abhorred.

Turning his gaze back to the two bathers, ignorant still of his presence, he was forced to admit their air of innocence. But how long did such innocence last? His thoughts grew darker, soured and curdled like bad milk in his mouth.

'Catch me, Rob,' she squealed, as once again she jumped into the water. Dragging his gaze back to the boy who ran close behind, reaching for her just a second too late, James saw for the first time that his son too was near manhood, and the expression in the boy's bright eyes as he leapt after her told all.

Blind anger erupted, raging through him like a summer storm. The pain of it spread through his chest and ran down his arms like fire. For a moment he thought he might actually pass out. The urge to pull the heedless, ignorant boy from the water, cart him off home and thrash the life out of him, was almost overpowering. James clenched his two great fists, managing by dint of enormous willpower not to hammer them into the trunk of a nearby alder. He wanted to slap the wanton girl for this flagrant breach of convention, her lack of propriety and shamelessness. Instead he stood transfixed by her beauty, making not a sound as she skipped and ducked and ran between the flickering candles, leaping in and out of the water in a hectic game of tag. He became bewitched by the mounting excitement that flowed between these two young creatures who stood on the brink of adulthood. Sweetly innocent they may be as yet, but for how long? Dear God, how long before this magical, breathless aura of gilded youth changed to something much less wholesome, far more potent, and a thousand times more dangerous?

Why did he hate her so? Because she was rebellious and undisciplined, or simply a burr beneath his skin that would not leave him alone? Already there had been times when she had looked at him with something like insolence in those damned fine eyes of hers. And she had a brain far too agile and knowing for a child's.

Even as he fought the urge to bellow his fury at them, the girl raised her arms above her head and, lifting her hair from her neck in a languid gesture, let it tumble down loosely over her bare shoulders. It glowed like molten fire in the dying sunlight as she walked on sure feet along the tree branch. James heard her gurgle of laughter, saw that the simple action held the boy's gaze spellbound; saw her raise herself high on her toes and dive cleanly into the pool, a perfect arc formed by a perfect lithe body. When she surfaced she was laughing, her lovely young face bright with joy – and something else. Knowledge. Power. The age-old wisdom of all beautiful women.

An urge to turn and run hit him for the first time in his life. His entire body began to tremble at what must inevitably happen next.

But he was wrong. The pair stood inches apart in the water, not moving, not touching, simply gazing at each other as if they had made a tremendous discovery. It seemed worse, somehow, than any fumbling adolescent caresses.

It was then that he made his decision.

–

Alena Townsen burst into the small kitchen like sunlight breaking through thick cloud. The woman standing hunched over the table turned at the sound of her running footsteps and, quickly pushing the letter she was reading into her pocket, lifted a face carefully smoothed clear of worry.

Her smallness was more than compensated for by an air of calm capability. Her hair was light brown, and though it bore a natural curl, was cut short and sensibly clipped back from a thin, delicate face. Her blue crossover pinnie had been recently starched and pressed and she slid work-worn fingers over the fabric, as if smoothing it down, while checking that no sign of the paper peeped from the pocket.

'Someone sounds in a hurry,' she laughed. 'You can't be hungry after that tea you must have had?'

'We had a wonderful tea but I can smell ginger parkin.' Alena put her nose into the air and sniffed. 'Oh, I knew you would make some today! Didn't I say so, Rob?' She launched herself at her mother, wrapping two thin arms about the slim figure in an exuberant hug of delight.

'It tastes better if it's been in a tin for a day or two.'

'We can't wait *that* long.'

Laughing, Lizzie Townsen reached for a knife to cut two large slabs of the still warm cake, face softening as it always did at sight of this precious daughter of hers. That tip-tilted nose, the almost boyish grin and teasing blue eyes in a perfect oval face… it was a wonder to Lizzie that anyone could deny the lass whatever she asked for. Certainly not the boy who stood, as usual, so compliantly beside her. Their friendship sometimes troubled her. They'd always been close, happen a bit too close, and although he was a grand lad, who could not in any way be blamed for the sins of his father, she wondered sometimes if she should put a stop to it. But that would break the child's heart.

She slid a piece of cake into each outstretched hand. Only then did she register their appearance. 'Your hair is all wet, the pair of you. Have you been swimming in the tarn, when you know full well…'

'Oh, Ma, stop fretting! We both swim like fishes, you know we do.' Alena flung a damp arm about her mother's waist while, mouth full of cake, depositing a sticky kiss upon her cheek. 'Not on Rob's birthday.'

'Did you have a nice party then?'

'It wasn't exactly a party, Mrs Townsen. Mummy doesn't like too much noise in the house, but Alena and I had a scrumptious tea, and Miss Simpson let us play Newmarket.'

Alena continued to talk between mouthfuls of cake, despite disapproving glances from Lizzie. 'I can't believe we are fourteen. When we were babies, which of us was the most beautiful? Was it me, seeing as I was older than Rob by a whole day?'

'You were both grand babies.'

'Did you expect me to be big and blonde and a boy, like my brothers?'

'I was just glad to have you.'

'When you and Mrs Hollinthwaite were both, you know – pregnant at the same time, did you go on waddling walks together?' Alena giggled while Lizzie merely looked nonplussed for a moment then, laughing, slipped the cake into the tin to hide her awkwardness.

'Impudent madam! No, we did not.'

'Did you both wheel us out together in our prams then?'

'Not that I remember. Mrs Hollinthwaite had a nanny.'

'But you must have admired each other's babies, living so close in the same village? Did you compare notes: how much we weighed, what we ate, sleepless nights, or if we were sick? Didn't you become friends?'

'Questions, questions. Don't you want this turnip you asked me to get for you?' Lizzie handed it to her, thankful for the distraction.

'Oh, yes, please. Can we make a lantern?' Alena wiped her sticky fingers on her mother's apron and, grabbing a knife, eagerly began the arduous task of carving eyes, nose and mouth into the tough vegetable. The job took longer than expected. When it was hollow, Rob lit one of their remaining candles and set it inside. 'Can we take a walk around the village, Mrs Townsen? I'll look after Alena. See she's all right.'

'I don't need anyone to look after me,' she hotly protested, but if Lizzie had been about to refuse, the arrival of Jim and Harry, her two eldest sons, home from the mill and anxious for their tea, quickly settled the matter. They came in on a blast of cold air, filling the small cottage kitchen with their thickset bodies and booming voices. Harry, not quite as broad as his younger brother, but taller by a couple of inches, and with a thatch of hair as thick as corn, settled himself in the fireside chair, slid his feet out of his clogs and rested them upon the fender with a grateful sigh.

'Like blocks of ice they are,' he groaned, half to himself.

'Where are the other two, and your father? Supper's ready,' Lizzie said, her eyes on the door.

Jim, the biggest and most soft-hearted of her sons, rested a gentle hand on Lizzie's shoulder. 'You can guess where our

Tom is, but Kit's had a bit of a shock today. Sally Marsden has dropped him so Dad's taken him for a quick pint.'

'Oh, no,' she sighed. 'Not another.' Kit's lack of success with women was legendary, but for all she thought him the most good-looking of the four, she knew him to have the quickest temper. Too like his father.

'Ma,' Alena persisted, afraid her needs were about to be forgotten as Lizzie was already reaching for the oven cloth to fetch the steaming tatie pot she had ready and waiting in the oven for her menfolk. 'Can I go now?'

'Let her, for pity's sake. She'll come to no harm.'

'Aye, give us a bit of peace,' Jim agreed, ruffling his sister's hair.

'Would she listen if I said no? She never has yet. Take care now. Don't get up to any more mischief. And be back by eight, not a minute later. D'you hear?'

Their promises were lost in the sound of running feet and bubbling laughter.

—

This was one of Alena's favourite nights of the year. She envied Rob being born on Hallowe'en, though because their birthdays were so close, they always celebrated them together on this day.

She loved Christmas best, of course, and the pace-egging that they did at Easter. When she was small, she'd loved to dance around the maypole, and even enjoyed the rushbearing cere-mony her mother took her to each year at Grasmere, though she had never been chosen to wear the special green and white tunic and carry the linen rush-sheet herself. But then she did not live in Grasmere. She lived here, in the village of Ellersgarth, in this beautiful valley of Rusland. Between Coniston Water and Windermere, it was full of twisting lanes and fine old beeches, green fields and deep, mysterious coppice woods. Secret places where a person could hide themselves for hours, perhaps days.

A little further north it merged into the thick forests of Grizedale where you could lose yourself forever if you didn't take care. Alena never tired of exploring the woodlands, for all she was not officially allowed to venture far. She found following rules and regulations a great nuisance, preferring to work on the principle of what her mother didn't know, wouldn't hurt her. Swimming in High Birk Tarn, for instance, which was but a short, steep climb from the village and had become one of her favourite pastimes. There was little else to do in this quiet spot, and Alena felt sure that she was perfectly safe.

'Will we knock on old Jessie's door?' Rob's voice broke into her thoughts. He was swinging the lantern tied to a stick and as he looked down at her, waiting for her reply, the light sent odd shadows across his face, causing the gold flecks in his brown eyes to glint and sparkle. In that moment he looked much older than fourteen and Alena's heart swelled with pride that he was her very special friend. She hoped he would remain so when he really was old. Life without Rob seemed impossible to imagine.

In that peculiar moment of intimacy at the tarn, between one heartbeat and the next, she had longed for something she couldn't quite put a name to. Had known instinctively that Rob felt the same way, almost as if they could read each other's mind.

But then, she had loved Rob Hollinthwaite for as long as she could remember. He was a part of her life, a part of herself. Since her own brothers were so much older, he had been the constant companion of her childhood. As children they had played together in her cottage, on the village green or in the cold waters of the beck.

'Only if you can run away quickly enough. It's no fun if we get caught,' she reminded him.

Sometimes Alena had been allowed to share his lessons, which were taken at his home, Ellersgarth Farm. He'd often begged to go to school, as other boys did, or as Alena did in the village, but he was never allowed. Rob being an only child and, his mother insisted, rather delicate, he'd received his education at the hands of Miss Simpson, his nanny turned governess. Alena hadn't minded the extra work involved when she joined Rob at his studies. For all she fussed too much, Mrs Hollinthwaite had been kind, lending Alena books and even teaching her a little mathematics and French; encouraging her to make something of her life, perhaps one day become a teacher. Alena doubted her family could afford such grand ambitions. Not that it troubled her, she cared only about being with Rob, but being quick and eager to learn, not soft and silly like other girls, she was happy enough to go along with it.

And she could stand her own corner when it came to pranks. Four brothers had taught her that much, if nothing else. They teased her for being a tomboy, of course, but then expected her to stand up for herself. When Jim put a frog in her Wellington boot, she would put a toad in his. If Harry left a dead spider by her breakfast plate she put frogspawn in his bed. Kit and Tom, being the two younger boys, would chase and wrestle with her, as if she were one of them. Yet she knew that if any outsider were to threaten her, her brothers would be the first to stand up for her.

There was nothing Alena loved more than a bit of fun and mischief. And mischief was what they were about now. Which was another reason she so loved Hallowe'en.

They scurried along Birkwith Row, flicking every knocker, rattling every dustbin lid, then stifling giggles behind their hands they melted swiftly into the darkness just as doors opened and light spilled out on to the pavement.

Mrs Rigg at the village shop caught them just as they were about to rattle her letterbox. She pounced before they could hope to escape and, with an ear belonging to each of them grasped firmly between fingers and thumbs, took them right into her kitchen where she made them fill all her coal buckets. Then she gave them each a sticky toffee and sent them on their way with what she called 'a flea in their ear'.

'I'll have that kind of flea any time,' mumbled Rob through a mouthful of caramel.

'Me too.' And they grinned at each other in perfect companionship.

'Does she sit waiting for us, d'you reckon?'

'I think she must.' The idea of Mrs Rigg with whiskers on her chin and her pink floral pinny wrapped tightly about her skinny body, sitting behind the shop door in wait for them, made them laugh. But she'd always been a good sport. In all the years of rattling her letterbox, she'd never failed to catch them, make them do some task or other, and then produce a reward as if they'd done her a favour, at the end of it.

Next door to the village shop stood The Golden Stag, which seemed half empty this early in the evening, though it would no doubt fill up later when the workers from the bobbin mill had eaten their supper and came out for their usual pint, and perhaps a bit of a sing-song.

They peeped in through the door and saw Jack Turner, the pot-bellied publican, shake a fist at them. He'd come back from the Great War to find his wife had run off with his best friend, so had never been quite so amenable as Mrs Rigg. They backed quickly away, taking no offence since this was their village and his irascibility held no threat for them. They ran around the back of the public house and headed towards Applethorn Cottages, just beyond Ellersgarth Green.

'Let's go to Hollin Bridge instead,' Alena suggested, dragging Rob to a halt.

She knew that the Suttons lived on Applethorn. Dolly Sutton had once been a close friend but the friendship had faded. Two years older, Dolly thought herself above hanging around with schoolgirls now that she worked at the mill and had money in her pocket to spend. She wore lipstick, marcel-waved her hair and always had a string of boyfriends in tow.

'We'd best not touch Dolly's house,' Alena warned. 'She'd half kill me.' And think her such a child.

Rob raised an eyebrow at this sign of weakness. 'I thought you weren't scared of anyone?'

'I'm not.'

'Well then?'

'I'm no fool neither, Robert Hollinthwaite. Dolly Sutton is bigger than me by a mile.' And tough with it.

'So you'd run a mile from her, all the way to Hollin Bridge?' It was dark down there, and there was talk of a ghost; a pale lost maid who wandered that part of the woodland, weeping and wailing for her lost love. 'It's getting late. We'll have to be going back soon. I promised your mam.'

'You're scared.'

'I am not.'

They stood on Ellersgarth Green with the lantern between them, and argued. It was always so. If one said one thing the other would say the opposite. But it made no difference to their closeness, only emphasised it, for they both knew that in the end they would do whatever Alena had decided, as they always did.

–

The clock in the hall chimed eleven as James Hollinthwaite climbed the stairs later that evening. Following the revelations at the tarn he'd walked for miles, going over and over everything in his head. Had he made a mistake? When? He didn't usually. Except in his marriage.

He entered his wife's bedroom without knocking and looked down upon her with something very close to contempt, the whole arrogant stance of him silently protesting at having to be in the same room as her, if only for a moment.

She sat propped up in bed against embroidered pillowcases and beneath starched linen sheets, swathed in a nightgown he knew reached from chin to toe, revealing not a glimpse of flesh between these two extremities. Even the rich sheen of her hair was denied him. It hung in a solid plait over one slender shoulder.

Never robust, years spent in trying to produce a healthy child, her naturally nervous disposition, and a growing disillusionment with life in general and himself in particular, had all taken their toll. Olivia Hollinthwaite was no longer the woman she once was, now spending more hours than was healthy in contemplation of her lot. In James's opinion this was a pity, but surely it was entirely her own fault if it resulted in depression. After two miscarriages and one stillborn boy, she'd finally performed what she considered to be her duty. But following that long and painful birth on a stormy night fourteen years ago, his wife had done everything she could to avoid this aspect of married life, even to insisting upon separate bedrooms. If only she didn't appear so distant, so entirely unreachable, they might have been happy enough. Even now she was reading a book, as if she really didn't care whether he were home or not.

'You were not at dinner,' she remarked, in tones that to James's sensitive ear sounded cool and indifferent. 'The Cowpers and the Tysons were rather put out.'

He'd forgotten about the dinner party. As a good Christian woman she would never have held such an event on Hallowe'en were it not her son's birthday. It had always seemed an odd quirk of fate that the most momentous events of his life had taken place on this night.

'My apologies.' He was perfectly genuine. He shouldn't have forgotten. It didn't pay to offend people, even pompous fools like George Tyson. Who knew when they might prove useful?

Olivia lifted her gaze from the book and rested it upon the ceiling. Like a martyr, he thought. 'I made excuses for you. Some pressing problem you'd been called to deal with at the mill.'

'Thank you.' Annoyed at finding himself in the wrong, he could barely keep the irritation from his voice. 'Ask them again next week.'

'Oh, that would be too soon. I couldn't.'

'Yes, you could.' He had flustered her, which was rare, and he revelled in the sense of power it gave him.

When he had married her twenty-two years ago, Olivia Leck had been the handsomest, most elegant woman imaginable, for all she was three years older than he. Coming from a respected Lancashire family, she'd naturally brought money to the marriage, and a very useful parcel of woodland not too far from his own valley. But most of all, she had possessed that precious commodity – style. He'd admired that in her more than any other quality. Her dress, her grace, her manner, – all had indicated the impeccable training she had received at the hands of her own formidable mama.

She could decorate and lay a table in white and gold, and make it look as if it had just dropped from heaven. But that had been in another age, Edwardian and leisurely, before the war, and infinitely more elegant than this one. In those early days, she had made it seem as if her one desire was to please and pamper those fortunate enough to be invited to sit around her table, lifting her new husband and his humble farmhouse to the echelons of the middle classes, where by rights James considered he should be. Even now she could somehow manage to get all the right people to her dinner parties. Surely a great asset in any wife.

'They are busy people and may not wish to risk the humiliation again.'

'Ask them.' For a moment he saw the familiar rebellion flicker momentarily across her beautiful face. He hated unpleasantness and rebellion of any sort, so said it again, in more forceful, commanding tones. 'Do as I say, Olivia. Ask them.'

She sighed with a tremulous sadness, as if he had wounded her. 'As you wish.'

He had won, yet the exhilaration quickly faded, leaving him feeling flat and faintly foolish. It was ever so. He resolved not to remain in her company a moment longer than necessary, but James liked to be seen to follow the conventions, even when in reality he flouted them at every turn. It seemed correct for a man to bid goodnight to his wife, so he did so. Now he turned to go, his eagerness to quit the suffocating sweetness of the room making him momentarily forget what had occupied his thoughts all evening, and been the cause of his neglect. Turning abruptly he saw her cringe away from him. Even now, after all these years, it had the power to infuriate.

Never, in all their married life together, had she welcomed him with anything approaching desire. He might have been willing to show more consideration towards her had she made the smallest effort to please him.

He could not deny that she carried out her wifely duties without protest, when called upon to do so. But he was a man who demanded passion, for God's sake, not duty. Yet she had the effrontery to complain about *his* lack of sensitivity! Olivia should consider herself fortunate he preferred not to risk a scandal by taking a mistress, which would do neither of them any good. In his younger days he'd once had a fling of sorts, but it had caused as many problems as it had solved. But had he the time or inclination for dalliance, he could still have any woman he chose. He thought of himself as a well-set-up sort of chap, not overweight, with a fine head of dark brown hair, good teeth, and rather splendid patrician features. Yet apparently he repelled his own wife.

But what did she have to complain of? She had money and status, a cook in her kitchen, a governess for her child, the use of a motor to take her to coffee mornings, charity functions and whatever committee she was currently serving upon. He made very sure that her diary was kept full. What more could she need? James liked an ordered life, and had always made certain that he attained one. If that meant supervising his wife and son more than they might wish, that was something they must both learn to tolerate. Which thought brought to mind the real purpose of his visit. 'I saw that child this evening – Alena Townsen.'

'Oh?' Olivia closed her book and showed interest for the first time. 'She is hardly a child, very nearly a young woman.'

'So I noticed. She was with Robert. They were swimming together in the tarn. Naked.'

'Oh, dear.'

He stared at her. 'Is that all you have to say. "Oh, dear"?'

'They are young, and very fond of each other, I know that. They've grown up together, so I don't see a little nakedness as a sin.'

'You've been too soft with both of them.'

'A person needs love. It is an essential part of life.' She looked him directly in the eye as she said this. How was it she could always twist every conversation to his disadvantage? If she was not openly criticising him for having offended yet another of their oversensitive neighbours – as if it were possible to make money without treading on someone's toes from time to time – she was regarding him in silent, condemnatory reproach. He was never sure which he hated most.

True, the folk who lived in this village were practical and hard-working with a natural feel for the woodlands and the wildlife that lived within it. But their country ways, superstitions and slow acceptance of change were constant sources of irritation to him. James Hollinthwaite prided himself on being a far-seeing man; one poised to exploit the future, if he didn't have one foot in it already. The last thing he needed was a difficult wife or disobedient son.

'You'd best speak to the boy. We don't want any – accidents.'

She gave a half-smile but said no more, and fury shot through him, hot and fierce. Drat the woman! Why must she always give the impression of being superior? As if she knew something he didn't, or understood people better than he did, which couldn't be the case. In point of fact, he was more in control than she could ever imagine. But then, he had always been willing to do what must be done.

'It's time we settled that boy's future. Come to my study tomorrow at ten.' And having issued his wife with this order, James strode from the room, certain he had finally succeeded in showing he was the one who made the decisions in this house.

Chapter Two

The next morning when the inhabitants of Applethorn Cottages were busily righting their dustbins, which they always had to do following Hallowe'en, Dolly Sutton had her head in the scullery sink.

She wasn't sure whether this queasiness she felt was the result of eating too much supper or stemmed from a more sinister reason, one too frightening to contemplate. In case it were the latter, she had, over the last several days, jumped off every stair from as high up them as she could manage. She'd taken a dozen baths, whenever her mother was out, most of which had been stone cold because she'd used up all the hot water from the back boiler, but all the more painful for that. She had also taken more than the odd nip of her mother's gin. But despite all her best efforts, there was no sign of her monthly visitor. What she longed for more than anything right now was that familiar dragging pain in her belly. Instead of which all she felt was a ball of breathless fear in her chest.

She remembered reading in some newspaper or other how even the Archbishop of Canterbury himself had given the go-ahead for contraception, so long as it wasn't for selfish reasons, which seemed a bit contrary to Dolly. The only trouble was, the article didn't explain how you went about it. And she'd never dared ask her mother.

She stared into the grubby medicine tin which bore a picture of Queen Victoria's Jubilee on the lid, no doubt indicating the age of its contents, in the hope of salvation. Fenning's Fever Cure. Dolly shuddered. Kill or cure, more like. It would take the coating off her tongue, and even if she was prepared to suffer it, she doubted it would solve her problem. Vick's Vapour Rub. Fat lot of good that would do. And a bottle of Indian Brandee, good for bellyache caused by a period. But would it bring one on?

She heard the back door open and her mother's voice raised in argument. What was wrong now? That old nosy parker from next door causing trouble again?

Dolly's head ached abominably and she laid a cold flannel against it with tender care. Perhaps that third nip of gin had been one too many and that was why the top of her head felt as if it were being screwed off like the stopper from a stone ginger bottle.

Mrs Sutton's voice rang out. 'I wish I'd done it meself, you nasty old witch!' Then the kitchen door slammed, reverberating throughout the small cottage and doing no kindness to Dolly's headache.

If only she were older, she thought, after retching another thin stream of bile-like liquid into the sink. It wouldn't have mattered so much then. She might even have been pleased, on the basis that Tom Townsen would have to marry her. But although he was near enough twenty, she was only sixteen, for all she'd be seventeen come February which was only four months away. Not that being seventeen would help in any way with this problem.

'Are you all right?' Mrs Sutton asked, as she watched her daughter peck at a slice of thin toast. Not known for being picky with her food, Dolly usually demolished two or three thick slices in five minutes flat. Her mother's face cleared. 'Ah, you're on one of them newfangled diets, is that it? To go with the shorter skirts.'

Dolly looked at her uncomprehendingly for a moment since nothing could be further from the truth. Admittedly she was not a small girl: well built some might say, plump certainly, voluptuous being the kinder term. Her face was pretty and she was pleased enough with that. Her hair was thick and brown and lustrous. She had good legs too, with dainty slim ankles, and was never short of admirers. So if the rest of her wasn't quite what it might be, it certainly didn't trouble Dolly.

But right now it seemed easier to agree with her mother that, yes, she was on a diet. Better than answering more probing questions about her pallor.

'Got to rush, Mam. Been on the last minute a bit lately and the foreman is watching us like a hawk.' She stood up and, taking a quick sip of tea, held the half-eaten slice of toast in her mouth as she shrugged on her coat. It was only as she went out of the back door that it occurred to her that such an admission would affect what was produced for her evening meal and every meal thereafter. Dolly groaned. If there was one thing she hated it was lettuce leaves, and that would be what she'd get from now on. The thought added to her depression, which worsened as she ran her gaze up and down the row.

There'd once been one long communal garden behind Applethorn Cottages, though any sign of the apple trees that might have served to christen it had long since vanished. Instead there were patches of rough grass, small vegetable plots and the occasional lilac tree, interspersed with ramshackle outhouses and hen huts that leaned into the wind; even the odd pigsty with its grunting occupant. The saving grace of all this muddle was the view. The cottages faced open countryside: thick woodlands and undulating fields criss-crossed with lichen-covered drystone walls, all lit on this particular morning with bright autumn sunshine.

But something was wrong. Frowning, Dolly tried to work out what it was. By every back door stood a dustbin, and each one had been upended. 'Ah,' she said, to no one in particular. 'So that's what all the row was about. Hallowe'en.'

At that moment Betty Thoms from next door came out, waving a shovel at Dolly. 'I'll knock your block off if I get my hands on you,' she shouted, false teeth clicking with fury.

'What? You don't think I did this?'

'Funny yours weren't touched, don't you think?' The old woman nodded meaningfully at the Suttons' dustbin, lid still firmly in place and not a scrap of litter around it. 'Young hooligan! That's what comes of having no faither.' It was her favourite method of attack when something had displeased her, and always set Dolly's hackles rising. This morning it unleashed every ounce of pent-up emotion so that, for once, she hit back.

'You bad-mouthed old woman! What's that got to do wi' aught? Anyroad, they would've married, only me dad died fighting for his country before they could. Not that it's any o' your business.' Instantly she regretted parting with this piece of private information.

'That's what she told you, is it? That he died a bloody hero? Run off more like. She always did have a romantic imagination, did Maggie. Ask her what she gets up to on a Friday night, and see what she has to say about that. Pieces of muck, you Suttons! But then if you're born wrong, you live wrong. Bastards, every one of you.'

White-faced and trembling, Dolly faced her with stubborn defiance. 'Mam's right. You *are* an old witch. I hope you go to hell.'

This is all your fault, Alena Townsen, Dolly thought, as she marched stiff-backed down the lane. I'll get my own back on you for this, madam, see if I don't.

—

'Are you going to tell me what you're up to then?'

Alena, coming out on to the landing in pyjamas and plaid dressing gown paused as she heard these words; filled suddenly with a childlike curiosity to hear what it was adults talked about when they were alone, she slid into the shadows and listened.

'I thought I'd make a few enquiries, that's all.'

'What sort of enquiries?'

She peeped between the rails of the banister. The kitchen door was flung wide open, and through it she could see the lower half of her father's back and legs. Ray Townsen was leaning over the table, waving a paper, a letter perhaps, in Ma's face. 'Well?' he barked, in a tone of voice she knew well.

Lizzie folded the breakfast cloth with painstaking precision and put it in the drawer. 'We haven't time to talk about it now.'

'When will we talk about it then? I asked you last night and you were too tired. I ask you this morning and you're too busy.'

'This isn't the moment. We both have to get to the mill.' Lizzie was buttoning her coat, tying a scarf around her hair and feeling in her pockets for her gloves. She hadn't been sleeping too well lately, too much worrying, and felt tired and weary, like an old woman, though at forty-six she was far from that. She wasn't surprised by her husband's persistence, rather she'd been amazed how long it had taken him to discover what she was up to. She'd been writing letters for weeks now. All in vain.

'It's about our Alena, isn't it? I thought I told you not to interfere.' And Alena watched, appalled, as his hand lashed out, slapping Lizzie across the face so that she fell awkwardly against the table, the corner of it jabbing into her side. Alena felt her palms grow sticky with sweat as she ached to run down the stairs and defend her beloved mother. It wasn't the first time she'd seen such a thing happen. Ray Townsen had a quick temper, everybody said so, but would the next instant be as sweet as pie with his poor wife, kissing her better and making cups of reviving tea. Alena had long since vowed that no man would treat her so roughly, however sorry he might be afterwards.

Lizzie recovered her balance in seconds and, hand to her cheek where the livid marks of his fingers were already beginning to show, hissed back at him under her breath.

'Will you hush? Do you want the child to hear?' She made no reference to the slap. But then she never did, accepting it as her lot. 'We'll talk about this later, I tell you.' She really didn't want to talk about it at all, but supposed he had the right. Lizzie came out into the hall, still searching for her gloves, to stand unknowingly below her daughter, hiding above on the landing. Ray followed her and Alena sank further into the shadows, praying they wouldn't see her, or hear the thud of her heart.

'She's been asking a lot of difficult questions lately, and I'm running out of ways to avoid answering them.'

'You should never have lied to her in the first place.'

'I didn't lie! I've never lied to her. I simply haven't told her everything, that's all.'

'You don't know everything.'

Lizzie turned on her husband, eyes blazing with anger. 'I know I don't, you daft 'aporth. That's why I'm trying to find someone who does. Without much luck, I might tell you.'

'And what difference would it make if you found your answers?' he persisted.

By way of reply Lizzie went to the bottom of the stairs and called: 'We're going, love. There's some porridge on the stove. Don't be late for school now.'

'I won't,' Alena called back, trying to make her voice sound far away, which wasn't too difficult since she felt as if she were choking. She didn't move until the slam of the front door told her they were well on their way. Even then she stayed where she was, shivering with emotion and something cold and hard in the pit of her stomach that felt remarkably like fear.

'Eavesdroppers hear no good of themselves.' Tom's low voice in her ear made her jump. She hadn't even heard him approach.

'I wasn't eavesdropping.'

'Yes, you were.' His wide infectious grin seemed to stretch from ear to ear, and even as her mind struggled to make sense of what she had just heard and seen, Alena couldn't help thinking it was no wonder her brother was so popular with the girls. He really was a handsome, devil-may-care sort of fellow, with his fair hair and melting brown eyes. But then she adored him too. The youngest of her four brothers, Tom was her favourite.

'Ma and Dad were quarrelling. Did you hear?'

'Not a word.'

Alena met his gaze directly and for the first time in her life knew that he lied.

'Have you had your breakfast, child?' he barked, in a fair imitation of Ray Townsen. And when she flung one leg over the banister rail to slide headlong down it, he thundered after her down the stairs. 'If you don't get a move on, you'll be late for school – then I'll tickle you to death as punishment.'

–

By a miracle Alena was not late for school, but the day seemed endless. The teacher's voice grated on her nerves, the rows of chalked sums on the blackboard seemed blurred and meaningless, and she hadn't any interest in playing Piggy-Jack-Fly in the playground at break-time.

She couldn't get the overheard conversation out of her mind, it kept on going round and round in her head. Who could her mother be writing to? Why had her dad accused Ma of lying? Why had Tom lied about hearing them? Alena hated the thought of lies, particularly told by people who claimed to love one another. Tom must have heard, despite much of the quarrel being conducted in angry whispers. Fierce and furious but generally short-lived, the whole Townsen family had grown used to them, and knew that although their parents' marriage may not be perfect, they still loved each other, in a robust sort of way.

But what could she do? Alena knew she couldn't ask what was going on without confessing to listening in to a private conversation. What disturbed her most of all was the pitiful sadness in her mother's face as she had called up the stairs.

She was still puzzling over it later that afternoon as she walked through Low Birk Copse, looking for Rob. She had on an old pair of shorts, long since discarded by Kit, a sweater that had seen better days and, to please her mother, a soft green beret pulled down over her wild curls. But the ribbon Lizzie had tied them back with had got caught up in a hawthorn branch, where it now flew like a bright red flag.

Rob was late, which annoyed her. She'd waited impatiently by the ancient oak, their usual meeting place, for almost an hour but he hadn't come. The tree had stood sentinel in that clearing for a hundred years or more, surrounded by bluebells at the right time of year, its huge trunk pitted with rabbit holes and knotted with galls. She'd climbed to the top of its crooked branches so she could look out over the smaller trees as far as the mill leat that cut its way down the hillside; she'd swung from the knotted rope they'd tied from one thick branch many years before; walked fifty times one way around the circumference of the great tree, and fifty times in the other. But still he hadn't come.

Now she followed the narrow forest rides that wound between the tall beech, sycamore, oak and ash trees, under-planted with the quicker growing birch and hazel, and called his name. Sometimes he played games on her, jumping out from behind an old hawthorn bush. Not tonight. Just when she needed him most, he'd let her down. So lonely did she feel, it was almost a relief to meet Dolly Sutton.

The girl was sitting under a birch tree, a pile of purple-black berries cradled in her skirt which she was eating one by one, her face screwed up in agony. When Alena asked, with some curiosity, what she was doing, Dolly flew instantly into a rage, yelling about dustbins and how the blame for Alena's Hallowe'en prank had been laid at her door. Then before Alena could reply, or even apologise, since she was indeed guilty of the offence for all she'd thought she was doing Dolly a favour by not tipping over her dustbin, the other girl burst into noisy tears.

Alena was shocked. 'Heavens, it's not that bad, surely? They're only dustbins. And there wasn't much rubbish in any of them.'

'It's not the dustbins,' Dolly said, in between sobs. 'I-it's me.' And away she went again.

Alena sat down beside her and, putting an arm rather awkwardly about the plump shoulders, patiently waited for the crying to abate sufficiently to risk probing further. She had a long wait. It was quiet in the woods, and the crying seemed to swell and echo, shattering the peace in a most disturbing way. Where was Rob? Alena wished he would come and free her from embarrassment, yet knew that if he heard this din, he'd keep well away. He hated any show of emotion.

At last she felt it safe to ask, 'Why are you eating sloe berries?'

Dolly's surprised eyes appeared above a grubby handkerchief. 'I'm not.'

'Yes, you are.'

'These are juniper berries. They're supposed to be good for—' She couldn't say it, couldn't say how she hoped they would bring on her period.

Alena picked up a berry. Squashing it between her fingers, she licked the juice. It was sour and sharp. 'That's a sloe, Dolly Sutton. Soak it in your mam's gin with a touch of sugar, and it'll be delicious. Eat them like this and you'll get a bellyache you won't forget in a hurry.'

'Is that why my mouth is all dry and horrid?'

'I'd say so.'

'Oh God, I can't even do that right.' And she burst into fresh paroxysms of crying.

Little by little the story came out between Dolly's gulping sobs. When it was told, Alena could only stare at her in awed silence. It seemed unbelievable, that Dolly Sutton, who was only two years older than herself, had actually done the unmentionable, when she, Alena Townsen, hadn't even been kissed yet. She felt an urge to ask what it had been like. Had she enjoyed it? Was it as exciting and earth-shattering as everyone said? How had she got over the embarrassment of taking her clothes off? And, most important of all, *who* had she done it with? But it didn't seem quite the right moment for such questions.

'Go on, say it.' Dolly's voice was bitter. 'Tell me I deserve it. That I've got what's coming to me. That's what Mrs Thoms next door will say. I can almost hear her saying it.' And Dolly told Alena of their exchange this morning. 'That was bad enough. Heaven knows what foul words she'll use when this comes out.'

'I'm sure she won't...'

'Won't she just! You can get away with anything, Alena Townsen, with a mother and father who care about you, four brothers to spoil you, proper family and all that. Me, I'm just a little b—'

'Don't say it, Dolly.'

'Why not? It's true. And it's true what she said about my mam. She has got a fella. I think it's the chap from The Golden Stag. She spends enough time there.'

Alena was enthralled by this piece of news. 'Mr Turner? Hasn't he still got a wife somewhere?'

'Yes.'

'And I thought he didn't like women any more?'

'He likes my mam.' Dolly almost giggled, then seemed to remember her troubles and started snivelling again, loud, gasping sobs into a none-too-clean hanky.

'Oh.' Alena could see how that would be embarrassing. She would hate it if her own mother did anything so shocking. 'And she never did marry your father then?' Yet another revelation.

Dolly shook her head. 'Mam says he died at Ypres in the Great War, just after I was born, though he'd promised to wed her when the war was over like. She never had a dad neither, so it makes sense, don't it, that I'm having a little bastard of me own?' And as the tears gushed afresh, Alena wrapped her arms tight around her one-time friend, rocking her gently to and fro.

Rob never did appear, despite his promise, but Alena was too busy mopping up Dolly's tears, cleaning her skirt of sloe juice in the cold waters of the beck and talking her into believing that her period was simply late, to make much of it.

'Don't let yourself think of it for a whole week. Every time it comes into your head, do something else to take your mind off it. Go for a walk, read a book, or go to the pictures. You like going to the pictures.'

'It was going to the pictures that got me in this mess!'

Alena was stunned once more into silence, mind boggling with the implications of doing *It* while everyone else was watching Marlene Dietrich or Greta Garbo.

'Cause of that long walk home from the ferry,' Dolly explained, and they both giggled this time. The nearest cinema was in Bowness-on-Windermere, and you had to cross the lake to get to it. 'So walking wouldn't be a good idea either, would it?'

Alena laughed. ''Course it would. Best thing in the world.'

'Depends who you walk with.'

Again the unasked question hung between them. Dolly said nothing. She hadn't told Tom yet, and really had no wish to break the news to Alena before she did so. What would she say, if she knew it was her own precious brother who'd put Dolly in the club?

Surprising really that Alena had been so kind, when she usually gave the impression of being a bit stuck-up. The way she talked, with scarcely any sign of a Lancashire accent, always having new frocks to wear, and a brand new bicycle bought her last Christmas. Ma Townsen spoiled her daughter, everybody said so. Short of nothing of what she's got, that lass. And never away from Ellersgarth Farm and young Robert Hollinthwaite. Thought she was somebody because she was friends with the son of the mill owner. Huh! Such niceties didn't cut any ice with Dolly. Her mam said the Hollinthwaites might have a lot of fancy goods on show in their shop window, but a lot of dusty goings-on in their back store rooms that didn't bear the light of day. Dolly still hadn't managed quite to discover what she'd meant by this description, since the Hollinthwaites didn't own a shop, but it sounded intriguing, and not quite proper.

Anyroad, those two were nobbut a pair of li'le bairns, Dolly thought, rather condescendingly. Why bother about them?

'We could go for a walk on Saturday,' Alena was saying. 'I could do with a bit of company myself just now.' And she smiled such a winning smile that her lovely face lit up and the last shreds of Dolly's resentment faded away. No wonder she got away with all sorts of mischief. What a cracker she was, and no mistake. Why was it some girls had everything? Wasn't bloody fair. Like this Hallowe'en business. Most folk would simply smile and say, 'Ah, it's only Alena up to her mischief.' But when her neighbours thought she, Dolly Sutton, was responsible, then it was a different story. Just because her dad hadn't made an honest woman of her mam. What did marriage matter anyway?

It just did, she thought bleakly. For all her mother had lost her man in a war, she'd grown lonely and bitter as she'd suffered the stigma of being a single woman with a fatherless child. Dolly hated the idea of ending up like that.

'What do you say?' Alena persisted. 'A walk would be good. We could take a picnic and go as far as Devil's Gallop or even Esthwaite Water.' That would show Rob Hollinthwaite she had other friends she could call upon, and didn't have to wait on him.

Dolly, far from keen on walking at the best of times but unwilling to give offence, hesitated. Yet there seemed no help for it, and the exercise might solve her problem. Or better still, it might solve itself and things be different by Saturday, back to normal like, and then she could change her mind and go and have a cuddle with Tom instead. She might even get round to telling him. By, he were such a good-looking, big-hearted sort of chap with half the village girls after him, she wondered why she was worrying at all. 'All right,' she said. 'Why not?'

–

'Where were you? Why didn't you come? I waited hours and hours, every night this week.' Alena stood with arms akimbo, fists bunched into her waist, lovely face tight with her fury.

'I couldn't.'

It was late Friday afternoon. School was over for the week and really she was itching to tell Rob all about Dolly's revelation, but meant to make him suffer for his neglect before she did so. Then it occurred to her that he wasn't suffering at all from her show of temper. There was an air of suppressed excitement about him. With his brown hair sprouting in every direction, checked shirt buttoned up wrong as if done in a great hurry, and his skinny legs protruding from long grey shorts, he seemed to be bubbling over with some secret he could barely contain. 'What is it?' she asked, abandoning her stance. 'What's happened?'

'Guess?'

'Oh, if you're going to play silly games, I'm not interested.' She flounced away to scramble up into the old tree and sit hunched upon a crooked branch, hurt by his attitude. There were no sounds in the woods but the carolling of a lone blackbird. It sounded so melancholy and forlorn it almost brought tears to her eyes. She certainly wasn't crying over Rob Hollinthwaite.

'You couldn't begin to guess,' he said, eyes glittering. 'Not in a million years.'

Alena gave a long-suffering sigh, and a teasing smile tugged at the corners of her mouth. 'Your Aunt Maud has bought you a new top and whip?'

He snorted and started to toss acorns up into the high branches to show he really didn't care whether she guessed or not. 'Don't be soppy. Anyway, I haven't got an Aunt Maud.'

Alena rolled her eyes, as if pretending to think, but with her mind still on Dolly, she said, 'Old Simpleton is having a mad passionate affair?'

'That'll be the day. But you're getting warm. It is to do with Miss Simpson.' He could keep it to himself no longer. He came

31

to lean with studied nonchalance against the trunk of the tree, hands in pockets, and looked up into Alena's questioning gaze. 'She's leaving.'

Her mouth literally dropped open. This was indeed the last thing she had expected. The governess doted on Rob, adored him, had lived and worked at Ellersgarth Farm since he was a tiny baby. Nothing but a disaster of cataclysmic proportions would drive her from his side. '*Why?*' She dropped down from the branch and together they sat in their favourite place between the roots of the great tree as, with arms wrapped about her knees, Alena prepared to listen to his tale with breathless anticipation.

Rob dragged the suspense out for a moment longer, until she was almost bouncing with impatience and begging him to get on with it. 'Because I'm going away to school. What do you think about that?'

It was only as he watched her face turn deathly white that the full implications of his news hit home. Of course, it would mean that they wouldn't see each other any more. Why hadn't he thought of that before? Because he'd been desperate to go to school for so long, he'd been thrilled when his father had told him. Even the loss of good old Simpleton, of whom he was really quite fond and would miss hugely, had paled into insignificance beside the prospect of this new adventure. Now he wasn't so sure.

'When?' Alena's voice sounded all fuzzy and wobbly, like the wavering image of her pale face.

'Soon. After Christmas, I imagine. I'll be home every holiday, of course, and we get weeks and weeks so...' He let the sentence hang unfinished. Excitement had died in him and unease began to grow. He changed tack and started to talk about the 'new opportunities' that were waiting for him. 'Rugger and soccer,' he explained. 'The school has its own swimming pool and running track. There'll be lots of work, of course, exams and such, but...' He pulled a face, and once again his voice tailed away as he watched the changing expressions on Alena's face. Her white skin seemed to be going all red and blotchy now, right before his eyes. Hardly surprising since a surge of fury, so hot and fierce she couldn't hope to contain it, was coursing through Alena's veins. She felt sick, was sure that at any moment she would throw up all over his stupid feet. How could he look so pleased with himself? How dare he be so *happy* that he was going away?

'You're too old to go to school,' she said with great scorn. 'I'll be leaving soon, starting work and earning money.' This was far from true. Hadn't she promised to stay on, to take her school certificate, which everyone thought she could get quite easily?

'I'm not too old.' She had hit upon Rob's greatest worry: that it was too late for him to go to a proper school, that he'd be too far behind the other boys. The nickname 'Simpleton' suited Miss Simpson rather too well. She wasn't the finest teacher in the world, not by a long chalk, but she had brought joy and enthusiasm to her lessons. Perhaps the new schoolmasters wouldn't. He almost hated his father for leaving it till the last minute like this. Rob struggled to recapture his earlier pleasure as the worries rushed in. 'Age doesn't matter. Being a boarder is different.'

'I hate you,' said Alena. 'I hope it's a stinking school and you're miserable as hell in it.' And she turned and ran away through the woods as fast as she could.

Chapter Three

She stormed angrily back and forth in the small overcrowded kitchen. A clothes maiden of steaming damp laundry stood in her way and, half blinded with tears, Alena pushed against it, sending it toppling. 'He can't do it!' she cried. 'He *can't* send Rob away. I won't let him.'

'I doubt you'll have any say in the matter.' Having righted the laundry and rescued a bowl of starch which looked like going the same way, Lizzie attempted to calm her irate daughter. The chances of her survival had once been so poor they'd had her christened within days of her birth. Jaundiced and unable to suckle properly, it had seemed a miracle when against all the odds the weakly infant had thrived. Lizzie had marvelled at the time on the mysterious workings of God and nature, and still did so today as she looked on the girl with wonder.

No tears brimmed in the sparkling blue eyes, only a hot dry anger. Not naturally uncaring, this recklessness was born from very real misery. Bright hair flung back, face pinched with a resolute fury, she'd been a difficult baby, a wilful child, and had now grown into this strong-minded, beautiful young woman who would prove a formidable adversary for anyone. Even James Hollinthwaite.

'Have you no thought for anyone but yourself?' Lizzie gently chided. 'Did it not occur to you that he might enjoy it, that it might do him some good?'

'I suppose you're going to say it'll make a man of him?' Alena's voice was hard with desperation.

'Happen it will.'

'Well, it won't. He'll hate it at that awful school. Rob is sensitive, quiet and shy.'

'Happen it's time he learned not to be.'

'He'll hate being away from Ellersgarth.' Alena wanted to say that most of all he would hate being away from her, but that sounded rather overdramatic so instead she struggled to express her thoughts fairly and calmly. 'He's used to being on his own. He isn't made to cope with the rough and tumble of a load of uncaring toffs. I just *know* he'll hate it.' She'd forgotten about meaning to keep calm.

Such vehemence, Lizzie thought. Had it not been so sincerely felt, she might have laughed. But she could remember her own youthful passions and knew that for some reason Alena felt things more keenly than most, certainly more than any other member of this all-male household; more than was good for her at times. Lizzie turned away to stir some life into the glowing coals, trying to summon up sufficient heat to dry her washing on this dismal November day.

'He'll be with right-thinking people. I'm sure it will be a good school, and you'll see plenty of him in the holidays.' But the girl did have a point, no doubt about it. Robert was a shy boy, a loner, happy to follow where Alena's more vigorous enthusiasms and imagination led him. 'And happen it's time you made other friends too, young lady,' Lizzie said with feeling. 'You'll be a woman soon.'

'Oh, for goodness' sake, now you sound like his father.'

Lizzie pursed her lips. 'Well, mebbe he has a point. It don't do to be too narrow-minded where friends are concerned. The more the merrier, that's what I say. Now set that table and stop fretting. The subject is closed.'

When her mother spoke in that tone, Alena could do nothing but comply, but the subject, so far as she was concerned, was very far from closed.

—

As soon as school was over for the day, Alena made her way to Ellersgarth Farm like a homing pigeon.

The house stood four-square at the edge of Hollin Woods, its grey slate walls seeming to have grown out of the ground itself. A dour, drab building, rather like its owner, Lizzie spoke of a time when it had once been almost derelict. She told how Mr Hollinthwaite had spent a small fortune restoring it: putting in new windows, repairing the traditional circular chimneys and building on a new porch over the front door. Its starkness was softened by a garden thick with weigela, climbing roses and honeysuckle at the appropriate season. Winter jasmine now brushed against her cheek as Alena made her way round to the back.

She hadn't seen Rob for nearly two weeks. Alena had waited for him every evening by the oak tree, but he hadn't come. They'd gone for a few days without speaking before, but never this long. It was unbearable. She had to find him and apologise for the terrible things she'd said. Even so she felt certain he would have long since got over his fancy for going away to school. She meant them to put their heads together and try to think of some way of making his father change his mind. Rob could come to the local school with her and they'd be as happy as Larry together. Which was why she had decided to see Mrs Hollinthwaite, who would surely be on her side.

'Hello, Alena. How lovely of you to call.' Olivia was standing at the stove stirring soup when Alena burst through the back door, as usual without knocking. Ellersgarth Farm was like a second home to her, and she'd never been told that any formality was necessary. The kitchen was warm and cosy on this brisk autumn day, the smell of herbs and vegetables deliciously appetising.

Rob, it seemed, was not in. He had been taken by his father to visit the new school, which was in Yorkshire, so they wouldn't be back until the next day. Alena wondered why Mrs Hollinthwaite hadn't gone with them but was too polite to ask.

Olivia insisted that she stay and drink a cup of tea with her. 'I was about to put the kettle on anyway. Let's be cosy and chat, or have a bit of crack as they say round here.'

This was one of the things Alena liked most about Mrs Hollinthwaite. She wasn't a bit stand-offish. And despite having a cook-general, the redoubtable Mrs Milburn, she was not above doing kitchen tasks herself. She was an excellent cook and proved it now by bringing forth a plate of freshly baked scones and a jar of home-made blackcurrant jelly. Alena chose a scone, slit it in half and spread it thickly with the jam.

'Hmm,' she mumbled through the crumbs. 'Delicious. How do you find the time?'

'Heavens, my life is easy compared to most. Ask your mother how she manages to keep house for a husband, four grown sons and a daughter, and still hold down a job as canteen lady and general factotum at the bobbin mill?'

Alena couldn't help but smile. 'She'd say it's because she's a woman.' And Mrs Hollinthwaite laughed. It was a lovely, tinkling sound and Alena realised she didn't hear it very often.

'I'm surprised Jim and Harry aren't married. Handsome blond giants the pair of them. Even Kit must be nearly twenty-one by now, mustn't he? And Tom not far behind. It's a wonder none of them has been snapped up.'

'Ma says they're too comfy at home, but she lives in hope.' And they both laughed. They gossiped about neighbours and village life; the Harvest Supper and the new vicar – latest in a long line since few of them seemed to take to the peculiar isolation of the parish, and how Mrs Rigg at the village shop had promised to get in some of the new lightning zip fasteners as soon as they became generally available. They discussed the tragedy of Sir Henry Seagrove being killed during an attempt to beat the speed record on Lake Windermere in June when his boat *Miss England* overturned. And, inevitably, they got on to the depression and the increasing number of unemployed which everyone was concerned about. Alena always enjoyed chatting with Olivia, since she talked to her as if she were an equal.

'And what are you going to do, young lady, when you leave school?' It was a question adults loved to ask, Alena had noticed. 'I'll probably work in the mill too,' she said, a hint of defiance in her voice. She'd somehow lost all interest in teaching.

Mrs Hollinthwaite seemed disappointed. 'Well, I'm sad about that, Alena. You're bright enough to do better. And with women gaining the vote two years back, I would've thought you'd be keen to make your mark.'

'There's naught wrong with working in the mill,' she said, rather heatedly, knowing it was once the last thing she had wanted. But now somehow she craved it, as if to compound her misery by such sacrifice.

For a long moment Olivia Hollinthwaite sipped her tea and said nothing. Then, very quietly: 'You'll miss Rob when he goes.'

It was a statement, not a question, and another reason in favour of going to the mill. Without Rob, Alena felt she would need the comfort of familiar folk about her.

'Yes.' Tears sprang to her eyes but she tightened her lips and ground her teeth together, determined not to give way. If sometimes Alena found her more feminine side in conflict with her tomboyishness, that was a problem she had learned to hide. Rob would think her soppy if she cried.

'He'll miss you too. I know he's very fond of you. We all are. And we'll miss seeing you here every day.' Their eyes met in a long glance. Mr Hollinthwaite wouldn't miss her. He barely spoke to Alena, unless he happened to bump into her by mistake. She thought him very full of his own importance.

'Yes,' she repeated. Then swallowing the pain in her throat, 'Is it definitely decided then? Will Rob go whether he likes the school or not?'

It was a long moment before Olivia answered. 'I'm afraid so.' Another pause and she added more brightly, 'I'm sure it will be good for him. He probably should have gone years ago, though I'm rather glad he didn't, aren't you?'

'Why didn't he?'

'My fault, I suppose. I enjoyed having him at home. What is the point of bringing children into the world then sending them away? That's what I always said. Though I never had as much time for him as I would've liked, so perhaps...' She was frowning now, as if trying to puzzle something out.

'And Mr Hollinthwaite thought the same?'

'What? Oh, yes.'

'Then what changed his mind?' the girl was eager to know. 'Why is he sending Rob away now? Why can't he go to the local school with me?'

Olivia Hollinthwaite looked into the girl's bright blue eyes and admitted to herself that she had wondered the very same thing. It couldn't be entirely due to that silly swimming incident, surely? She'd decided not to mention it to Alena, so as not to embarrass the girl. Fourteen was such a self-conscious age.

She rather thought her husband had developed grand ambitions for Robert. Several years at a worthy university, followed by marriage to some horse-faced female with land. This was no doubt what James had in mind for his only son and heir, so he'd want to cool this particular friendship. Olivia couldn't help but smile. Hadn't he always underestimated Rob? There was much more to the boy than James gave him credit for. But then, Rob wasn't easy to get to know. For all she'd kept him at home, and their perceived closeness, there were times when his reticence, his quiet stubbornness, left even her perplexed. She was never entirely sure what he was thinking. Which made her wonder if perhaps her reasons for keeping him at home were perhaps a touch selfish, and that it was time to cut the apron strings.

'I'm sure he feels it is for the best,' she said briskly. 'Making friends among boys his own age will be good for Rob. Another scone?' But Alena shook her head. She hadn't finished the one on her plate. Her bitter disappointment at finding Mrs Hollinthwaite was not to be the ally she had hoped for, had made it go all dry and lumpy in her mouth.

'I think I'll go now, if you don't mind. Will you ask Rob to meet me tomorrow, as usual? He'll know where.'

'Of course. I'll show you out.'

'It's all right, I know the way.'

'No, I want to.' At the door, Olivia put a hand upon the girl's slender shoulder. 'You are growing up fast, Alena. One day you will be a very beautiful young woman. Don't be in too much of a hurry to grow up though, will you? Sometimes, life – adult life – isn't all that it seems. People – people aren't always as happy as you might imagine. Enjoy your youth. It is all too pitifully short.'

Alena looked into the woman's tired, if once pretty face, and dutifully nodded. On the way home she thought about these words, but could make no sense of them. Being fourteen wasn't much fun either.

–

Alena decided to announce, quite dramatically, this very evening at supper, that she meant to leave school as soon as possible and take a job in the bobbin mill. She wanted to prove how desperately she needed Rob and how her life would be ruined without him. Her mother, she knew, would be disappointed by this news, as she echoed Olivia's hopes for her only daughter.

But as the family gathered for the evening meal it soon became apparent even to Alena that there was a strange atmosphere which had nothing at all to do with her own problems. There was none of the usual joking and hectoring. Her mother was banging supper dishes on to the table with uncharacteristic vigour, not even noticing that Alena was fidgeting with the salt, making little heaps of it all over the cloth. And all four brothers were unusually well behaved. Tom, in particular, sat tight-lipped and pale, with everyone glancing at him in a funny sort of way from time to time. Her father glowered more severely than ever, and worst of all, a deep, heavy silence persisted throughout the meal.

Even so, Alena was determined to make her point. She glared accusingly at the Yorkshire pudding steaming on her plate. Filled with a rich onion gravy, it was usually one of her favourite meals. The very smell of it set her mouth watering but she merely stabbed at it with her fork, eating none of it. How could she? The food would choke her, and she was desperate for someone to understand the very real misery she felt.

Why could no one see how important this friendship was to her? Rob was like another brother to her, wasn't he? No, more than a brother. One day last summer they'd taken a picnic and as they lay together on the crisp grass of the Furness Fells, watching the buzzards fly, Alena had sworn, on her living soul, that she would be with Robert Hollinthwaite till her dying day. He had made the same vow. They'd written the promise out on a piece of paper, folded and sealed it with red sealing wax borrowed from James's office and, having each made a fingerprint upon the seal, had later hidden it deep in the earth beneath their special oak. This simple act had symbolised their pact of friendship.

Oh, yes, he needed her. Rob had made that clear in a thousand different ways.

Like when his father tried to make him study serious books on politics, or to drum geography and mathematics into him till he grew confused and filled with a sense of failure. Rob was no scholar, but nor was he weak. He simply wasn't the son James Hollinthwaite wanted him to be which, in Alena's opinion, made him all the better for that. Rob's skills lay in his hands. He could make anything out of nothing, but for some reason James thought this degrading.

His father had once destroyed a drey that Rob had worked on for weeks. He'd fashioned it with his own hands, and nailed it high in a tree so that he could watch the red squirrels come and go as they set up home in it. It had broken his heart to see it torn down and be instructed to stop encouraging vermin. Alena had hugged him to her and let him cry as if he were a child. But she knew that he wasn't a child, he was very nearly a man. And one day soon she would be a woman. They cared for each other in a very special way. Dare she call it love? To herself at least. A love that one day, she hoped, would blossom and develop into something wondrous and enduring.

Now he was to be sent away, her dearest friend, and they would be separated whether they liked it or not. Alena thought that Mrs Hollinthwaite was wrong about not rushing to be grown-up, believing, as all children do, that adults could decide their own future without interference from anyone.

At last she was gratified to find that her father had noticed she wasn't eating.

'What's up wi' you then?'

'Rob is to be sent away to school.'

He stared at her silently for a moment, as if she spoke a language he didn't quite understand. Alena was slightly nervous of her father. He was a thin wiry man with bloodshot eyes and an uncertain temper that erupted all too frequently from fists like sledgehammers. He claimed that with four sons to keep in order, these were the best tools for the job. To Alena he'd always seemed dark and forbidding, a distant figure who rarely had much time for her, being usually either working in the mill or out in the woods, poaching half the time she shouldn't wonder. He had once been employed as gamekeeper in Mr Hollinthwaite's woodlands but, for some reason unknown to Alena, had left.

'I'm to lose him, d'you hear?' she shouted, feeling the tears spurting afresh. 'My very best friend.' Everyone stared at her in horror for breaking this terrible silence.

'For God's sake, child, we've no patience with your little dramas this evening.'

'But what will I do without him? I'll have no one.'

'Don't talk daft. You've plenty of other friends.'

'Not like Rob.'

'Heaven help us, what's the matter with this family? Have they all gone mad? Life is full of disappointments – some of them, believe it or not, far more important than losing a friend. I lost a good job I once had with the Hollinthwaites, didn't I? You can't trust that lot an inch.'

'You can trust Rob. He's different.'

'Eat up your supper.'

'I couldn't…'

Her father picked up her plate, making them all flinch as he leapt angrily from his seat. Then he opened the back door and threw it outside. They all heard the pottery smash as it hit the stone flags. 'If you don't want it, then the dogs can have it. Now go to your room. I've more than I can cope with already this evening.'

'But…'

'Now.'

Alena went.

–

It was as if a second World War had broken out in the Townsen household. Over the next few days voices were raised in anger, Lizzie went about her work stone-faced, the three elder boys were notable by their absence, and on one terrible occasion, Tom and his father actually came to blows. Ray Townsen took the leather strap down from where it hung behind the back door and thrashed his son as if he were a boy still and not a grown man of nineteen, nearly twenty. Alena felt certain poor Tom might have been killed had not her mother finally managed to wrest the strap from her furious husband's hand.

After that came endless discussions. Much of the conversation took place with the kitchen door firmly closed, and Alena had very little idea what was being said within. But every now and then the odd phrase would break out from the tight confines of the room and reverberate throughout the house.

'What were you thinking of?'

'Have you no sense?'

'She's little more than a child.'

'You're a damn' fool.'

Alena crouched in misery in her room, as she always did when her father was on the rampage, feeling very sorry for herself. Her mother too had been offhand with her recently, avoiding answering her questions even more than usual, as if having a curious mind was a sin. Besides which, Alena could hardly bear to see Tom so white and distraught.

It had soon become clear that her brother's anguish was connected with Dolly's problem. He was the one responsible for the girl's condition, and since she was far too young to marry, no one quite knew what to do about it.

So engrossed was the family with the magnitude of this problem, that even when Alena finally told Lizzie she'd made up her mind to leave school as soon as possible, her mother barely listened. She merely nodded, her sad grey eyes fixed upon the potato she was peeling.

'Won't you be disappointed if I don't become a teacher?'

Lizzie, her mind on her beloved youngest son's future happiness, forced to marry a girl he didn't love because of sowing a few too many wild oats, could barely concentrate upon her daughter's troubles which seemed childish by comparison. 'Of course, love, but it's your life. You must choose.'

At which point Alena flounced out of the house in high dudgeon. She went at once to take out her grievance upon Dolly, and give her a piece of her mind for ruining her family's, and in particular Tom's, happiness. She found her buying pear drops in Mrs Rigg's Village Shop. Alena didn't even have a halfpenny to buy a stick of liquorice but she waited with strained patience until the treasured two ounces of sweets had been wrapped in a cone of paper and handed over to Dolly. When the two girls got outside, she was to wonder how her life could go so wrong, so quickly. Far from having the upper hand, it was Dolly who turned upon her.

'I don't know who the hell you think you are, hoity-toity little madam, looking down your nose at me! Not only did you get me into trouble over those bloody dustbins, but you were seen swimming with Rob Hollinthwaite. In the buff, stark naked, so I'm told.'

Alena stood open-mouthed with shock, hearing with growing alarm that it was James Hollinthwaite himself who had seen them swimming together.

He had seen her naked body!

The very thought made her want to *die* of humiliation. To think that while they'd been happily swimming in all innocence, that dreadful man had stood watching them without saying a word. Where? Why? How? From behind some tree or rock? What a despicable thing to do. She shuddered with revulsion.

Word had apparently spread quickly as Mrs Milburn, cook-general at Ellersgarth Farm, had overheard some private conversation. Listening at doors being one of her hobbies, according to Maggie Sutton, who was told the titillating tale while standing in the meat queue at the butcher's. Dolly, sucking on a pear drop, and still smarting from the leathering Maggie had given her when she'd learned of her daughter's predicament, took great pleasure in outlining all of this to Alena and seeing her discomfiture. She left the girl in no doubt that it would be all around the village in no time.

Embarrassment overwhelmed Alena.

How would she ever be able to face anyone again? How would Rob? It'd been her idea to swim in the tarn, of course. He'd skin her alive for this. But was it her fault if adults always looked at things in the worst possible way?

She saw now why the hasty decision to send him away had been made. Mr Hollinthwaite thought they were up to far more serious mischief than upending dustbins.

–

Alena knew as soon as she looked into Rob's face that she couldn't tell him they were the subject of village gossip. He had more than enough on his plate already.

The day in Yorkshire had been a failure. He did not like the school and no longer had any wish to go to it. It took no time at all for him to make that fact quite clear, and any exultation Alena might once have felt at this discovery, quickly evaporated as her heart filled with pity. The awfulness of their quarrel was forgotten as she saw that all the happiness and delight he had first shown at the news had leeched away, leaving him pale and drawn.

They'd given him several tests, it seemed. On arithmetic, geometry and algebra, which Rob hated, and one comprised entirely of questions such as: If there are five people sitting at a table and John doesn't want to sit next to Mary, Mary wants to sit next to Susie but not next to David, where would Jane sit? Miss Simpson hadn't done those kind of silly tests. Where was the use? She'd spent most of her time telling wonderful stories from history, or about Greek heroes, such as how Horatio held a bridge against his enemies, or how Helen of Troy had caused a war because of her beautiful face.

Consequently Rob had panicked, earning a stern reproof from the examining master who told him that he was in dire need of some proper education. He hadn't liked the sound of that one bit.

'And the school buildings were awful. Not a bit like I imagined. All faded and old, with the paint kicked off the doors and bare little rooms with hard beds. Freezing cold.'

'What about the wonderful swimming pool?'

'Like ice.'

They walked deep into the woods, silent in their misery. They could hear woodsmen sawing and chopping and every now and then the sound of a tree crashing down. Autumn was always the time when undergrowth was cleared and the felling began. They reached their favourite oak and sat side by side between the embrace of its huge roots and Alena listened for more than a hour to his mournful tale. When he had done she said, 'So tell your dad you won't go.'

He looked horrified. 'I can't do that.'

'Yes, you can.' But she knew he was right. Rob Hollinthwaite could no more stand up to his father than a lamb could lie down with a fox, even before what had taken place at High Birk Tarn. Not because he was a coward, but because he worshipped the man and wanted, desperately, to please him.

'I don't want to go, Ally.' He hadn't used her childhood name for years. It seemed to emphasise his vulnerability and filled her heart with new sympathy for him. 'I've been thinking about it a lot since we well, had that bit of a spat. I don't want to leave Ellersgarth either.'

Alena recognised these words as a code, meaning that it was really she whom he didn't want to leave, though he was too proud or embarrassed to say so.

'I asked Father if I could go to your school instead. I've never seen him so angry. He ranted on for hours about how I should make something of myself and not turn into a fool. All about how difficult it is to get a job these days. How I must buck up and get properly educated if I want to take over the farm and mill one day, and be able to manage his thousand acres of woodland. I said I wasn't sure if I wanted to manage all of that. So he hit the roof again and said didn't that prove how stupid I was? I daren't ask him again, Ally. He even said you were a bad influence and it would be better if I didn't see you at all!' They gazed at each other in silence, aghast at such a prospect.

She had to tell him then. Better it come from her, she decided, than some nosy old gossip in the village street; or be faced with James Hollinthwaite's scorn. As she did so, she watched a red flush creep over his face.

'They make it sound so – so *dirty*!'

'I know.'

'And it wasn't.'

47

'No.'

'They won't believe that.'

'But we can't let them separate us.'

'No.'

'I'd die.'

'Me too.'

'There's only one thing to be done then,' she said.

Rob looked at her in silence, the anger burning in his eyes the only indication of his feelings.

'We'll have to run away.'

Chapter Four

They left before dawn on Sunday, each with a change of clothes in a bag and whatever food they'd been able to steal from their respective pantries.

It was still dark, with a hint of rain in the air, as they traced by instinct the way through the woods. The smell of damp moss and earth was strong in their nostrils, their feet slipping on stones slimy with lichen. Hours from now when her heels were rubbed raw, Alena would wish she'd put on an extra pair of socks, or worn her clogs, but for now she was glad of the Wellington boots, and certain they were doing the right thing.

The sun came up all pink and red and gold, spearing the woodland with shafts of light in which dust motes danced and leaves floated like brilliant jewels, causing them to marvel at its beauty. Sunlight and shadow ribbed the path they followed, rust brown from years of autumn leaves being crunched underfoot. As the morning wore on the path wound its way between long grasses for mile upon mile. At one point it divided, one fork breaking off to the left, the other climbing steeply uphill. They took the right-hand fork, not certain where it led but fearful the left might take them back home.

The path narrowed and filled with a network of roots and stones, ready to trip tired feet. Thickly covered in moss, proving it was not often used, bilberry plants grew alongside and they ate a few berries as they plodded silently onward. They paused from time to time to drink water from a beck, nibble at bread or crunch the apples they had brought with them. Sometimes they even talked and laughed, as if they were on some jolly picnic.

In the afternoon they slept for a good two hours. It gave them the strength to go on. The first flush of excitement had long since died and now each was wondering, in their different way, what the future might hold. Alena decided that since her family was so unfeeling, she didn't care so long as she was with Rob, while he felt perfectly at home in the woods, in charge of his own life at last.

They came to a tree stacked about with cut poles and he hurried her quickly away from it, in case people were working nearby.

The late afternoon sun was slanting golden rays among a lattice of hazel, rowan, slender oak and birch as they entered a part of the forest they did not know. It seemed to stretch for yet more miles ahead, on and on over hills and valleys they had never trodden.

As they plodded onward, their progress slowed as the woods seemed to grow thicker and the silence deepened. It grew colder and they hunched their chins into their warm scarves. From time to time they glanced back, anxious their fathers might even now be in hot pursuit. They stopped and looked about them for a moment, feeling quite alone in all the world, vulnerable and afraid. A rustle in the undergrowth set both their hearts racing. Then a pair of pheasants burst from under a blanket of bracken and galloped away, clacking noisily with fright. It made them both laugh, breaking the tension and shaming their nervousness.

When the thudding of her heart had eased a little, Alena ventured a quiet question. 'Where will we go?'

'We'll find somewhere safe, don't worry.' Rob sounded more confident and sure than she had ever heard him. Perhaps more than he felt.

They could see that this part of the forest had been coppiced, as each tree had thrown up several new stems from the stool, which showed the results of previous cuts. These stems were now perhaps ten or twelve feet high and would likewise be ready for felling in a year or two. Here and there was a fine standard oak or ash, deliberately left to grow and form the higher canopy of the forest. 'I can hear a stream. Let's go and drink, cool our feet and rest.'

They did so, eating the last of the bread and cheese they had brought with them. The long walk had made them hungry and they could have eaten twice as much. A depressing thought. What would they do tomorrow, and the day after that? Alena thought of the good hot food her mother would even now be placing upon the table at home. Or perhaps Lizzie couldn't eat at all, for worry. She pushed the uncomfortable thought away.

Afterwards, refreshed, they sang for a while as they walked on, to break the deafening silence of the woodlands.

By nightfall they had seen no one all day and were exhausted. They found shelter beneath a fallen ash that arched over the path, pulled bracken and branches over themselves to gather what warmth they could, then fell asleep instantly, wound together like a pair of dormice.

When they woke it was pitch dark. Alena had never known a blackness so complete. It lay heavy and impenetrable upon her. In the dim light that did filter down through the high branches, she caught a glimpse of bats on their evening search for insects, though there were few about at this time of year. From somewhere in the depths of the trees came the hoot of an owl. She was used to country sounds but not at such close quarters. There were unexplained rustlings, squeaks and whispers, and once an owl swooped blackly down into the undergrowth, the squeal of its unfortunate victim making her shudder.

She tried again to sleep, but couldn't. The cold of night seeped into her bones and, stricken with new fears and hunger, Alena felt a surge of self-pity for the first time in her life.

'If only we'd lit a fire, we could at least have kept warm.' She'd brought a bag of oatmeal which she'd found in her mother's pantry but however hungry they were now, she decided it would be more prudent to save it for breakfast. They would need sustenance even more then, to give them the necessary energy to go on.

'I'll make a trap tomorrow,' Rob promised, his breath a warm whisper against her cold ear. 'And we'll catch a rabbit for supper. We can live off the forest, I'm sure of it. I'll build us a shelter, make us somewhere cosy to live.'

It all sounded so wonderfully romantic and she was so desperately tired that for once Alena didn't attempt to argue. Looking into his handsome young face, alive with the excitement of these new plans, she truly believed him.

'Sleep, Ally. I'll keep watch for a while.' And reassured by his confidence, she rested her head against his shoulder and let her eyes close. In moments she drifted into sleep. Feeling the tickle of her hair against his chin, Rob was afraid to move for fear of waking her, yet his disturbed thoughts, at variance with his brave words, greatly troubled him for some time before he too was overwhelmed by exhaustion and finally slept.

They woke shivering in a cold clear dawn with hunger sharp in their bellies. Even so Rob insisted they put more miles between them and home before risking a fire to cook the oatmeal. They got to their feet and blundered tiredly on. It was some two hours later that they saw the smoke. And then they saw the man.

–

He swung the axe with economical, effortless strokes, taking away chips of wood neither too large nor too small and always in exactly the same place, opening a deep throat in the stem of the tree. Then, with one mighty swing, he cut behind and as the throat closed the tree fell cleanly without damaging itself or knocking against any other. Two or three small boys and a couple of women immediately set about taking off the smaller branches, twigs and leaves at the top of the tree – the 'brash' as it was known locally.

Without pause he started on the next, nor did he allow his helpers to pause either. When one boy whispered to a companion, the man cuffed his ear, sending him rolling amongst the twigs and leaves. It was perfectly clear that the day was for working and earning a living, with no time to waste in laughter or song.

A dog lay some way off. A deep golden tan, he was almost indistinguishable from the bracken in which he lay. Of indeterminate breed, with perhaps some border collie in him, his long nose rested upon his paws, and not for one moment did he take his eyes off his master save when tiredness weighed his lids almost closed. But only for a snatched moment. If the man's rhythm changed only slightly, the dog would be instantly aware of it and ready to react.

The man swung and cut, swung and cut, a ceaseless rhythm that seemed so at one with his surroundings that a robin pecked up the grubs that fell by his feet. Alena and Rob, mesmerised by the scene, crept nearer.

He must have become aware of their approach, however soft-footed. almost at the same instant as the dog, which rushed at them, barking.

'That'll do, Bracken. Down, boy.' The dog obediently dropped to its belly and the man wiped the sweat from his brow with the back of one hand, leaned on his axe and confronted them.

'Now then,' he said. 'What have we here? Mice, is it?'

The pair stood as if paralysed, petrified by the mere sight of him, for a sight he surely was. He wore a jerkin over his ragged shirt, dark trousers tied with string below the knee, and on his feet a pair of huge black clogs. His face was dark as the bark of a tree, criss-crossed with a thousand lines and topped with thin black hair plastered to his head with sweat.

Riveted though she was by the man, Alena could not fail to notice that although the children cast curious glances at these strangers in their midst, they barely paused in their labours; the women not at all. It wasn't hard to guess why. For all the glint of humour in his dark eyes, the powerful build and sheer brutish strength of the man would not encourage waywardness. She reached for Rob's hand and felt a reassuring squeeze in response.

Alena realised at once that this would be a group of coppicers. Gangs like these moved about the forest, spending as much as a year in one place cutting and harvesting the timber, at an agreed rate with the owner, before moving on to the next. They never returned to the same part of the forest until the trees had had sufficient time to rejuvenate themselves, which could be as much as twelve or fifteen years. And this fearsome giant would undoubtedly be their leader.

She was amazed at how confident and strong Rob sounded, even if he did have to clear his throat before he spoke. Nodding in the direction of the children, all busily breaking and piling twigs on to a hand cart, he said, 'Good day to you, sir. We're needing food and would be willing to work for it.'

'Would you indeed?' The man ran his eye over them both, lingering over Alena the longest.

Frank Roscoe considered he had an expert eye for women, almost as good as his judgement of horse flesh or a well-bred cur. He believed likewise he could make an infallible assessment of character, and never forgot a face. This lass wasn't yet full-grown but all the more tantalising for being as yet untried. She had about her that mysterious and complex mix of innocence and instinct and, he'd guess, she'd have a fine temper on her as well. That would be a grand sight to see to be sure, when her dander was up, with that wild copper hair and those brilliant eyes. Didn't he always admire a bit of spirit in a woman? See how she met his inquiring gaze with defiance. Wore pride like a mantle, she did. A rare beauty indeed. Sure and back home in his native Ireland, they'd say such a colleen had been kissed by the fairies.

He chuckled on a burst of humour as she stepped closer to the boy, little more than a pup himself. They weren't mice at all, but children. Babes in the Wood, that's who they were, and he threw back his head and laughed out loud, causing everyone to pause in their labours and wait for him to share the joke. But he only shouted at them to stop wasting time, wasn't he paying them good money to work, and not gawp at folk?

'How old are you, lad?'

'Sixteen.'

Roscoe smiled at the lie. 'Have you done such work before?'

'No.'

'A fine strong lad like you, yet you're a nancy boy who's never used an axe or saw?'

'I have. Once or twice. And I'm a quick learner.'

'This one o' mine weighs seven pounds. Could you even pick it up?'

Without a moment's hesitation Rob stepped forward and did so. For all his confidence the weight of the axe surprised him, and he had to tense every muscle to hold his resolve not to show any sign of weakness. He took up a safe stance, swung back the axe with every ounce of his strength, and cut into the tree very nearly, but not quite on the right spot. Roscoe smiled but lifted his eyebrows as if acknowledging a good effort.

A pair of runaways to be sure, he thought. Some poor soul would be hunting high and low for them, no doubt, at this very minute. Wouldn't he be doing everyone a favour if he packed them off home? But then he'd have to make sure they went, wouldn't he? See they didn't wander off getting even more lost, and him being held responsible if they died of starvation, or caught double pneumonia with the damp.

And if the girl stayed? Tempting morsel, aye, but a mite too tempting mebbe. Wouldn't she only cause trouble when young Mickey got back? Was she even old enough to be allowed out, let alone dally with his son?

Yet her virtue and this lad's lies were none of his concern. He must consider his own interests. He did need more help and the boy showed promise, no doubt about that. Roscoe returned to his chopping. 'I'll take you on. The girl is no use to me. Women and bairns I have in plenty.'

Rob stepped quickly forward. 'It's both of us or neither.'

Dark brows raised in surprise, the axe poised for a moment in mid-air, he examined Rob as if he'd grown a second head. Frank Roscoe was not accustomed to having his decisions challenged. Then he set it down with a shout of laughter, though since this added not a touch of warmth to the wizened face it brought no lessening of the tension. 'Are you in a position to make terms, laddie, on a hungry belly? Where is it you're going? Where have you sprung from, eh?'

Alena felt herself go hot and cold all over. The man was far too shrewd for comfort. Before the thought had properly formed in her head, she burst out, 'I can learn to use an axe too.'

'Can you indeed?'

'Yes. I can do anything Rob can do.'

This seemed to add to his amusement. 'I doubt you can,' he said. 'Rob is it? And what is your name, pretty maid?'

Alena quaked and felt a cold shiver down her spine, making her feel slightly sick. If he discovered their names, all would be lost. They would be sent home, she was sure of it. But before she could reply, Rob continued with his bargaining.

'I'd say you look to be in need of a strong pair of hands to help you. Alena won't get in the way, I promise. She's a good worker.'

Oh, now you've done it, she thought. Now he's got both our names. And the sickness grew worse.

Once again the man curved his lips into what seemed like a parody of a smile though it might have been genuine amusement, she supposed, if somewhat sardonic. It was perfectly certain he was playing with them, entertained by this diversion they had created. Not an unhandsome man, his dark eyes glinted speculatively from beneath narrowed lids as he considered her, and Alena worried over what he might be planning.

'Plunged into the forest on a whim, have you? Like many before you. And now you don't know how to get out of it.' He fell silent again, rubbing one hand over the rasping bristles of his chin. Who would want to know where they were? he wondered. Somebody must. And mebbe pay for the information?

'You'd say your hands were strong, would you? Well, for your interest, I've a boy a year or two older than yourself who helps me here in the forest, though only at the weekends admittedly. He works at the local bobbin mill during the week.' Frank Roscoe did not miss the quick glance that flashed between them. 'Cobham Bridge. D'you know it?'

They shook their heads, saying nothing. But was it relief that had flickered over the girl's face? They knew of a bobbin mill then. With thirty or more in the Furness district, it was hardly surprising. But which?

'Fine strong lad is Mickey. But you're right, we could always use a bit more muscle.' He held out a hand. It was stained a dark blue which Alena later discovered came from the sap of the oak trees. 'Roscoe is the name. At your service, as they say.' He sketched a mockery of a salute which neither of them dared to return. 'Give us a taste of what you can do then. Show me your worth and happen I'll feed you. But she goes.'

'Let 'em be, Frank. They're nobbut childer. Let her stay for a day or two at least.' One of the women had come to stand beside him and, wiping her own blue-stained hands on the skirt of her dress, said to Alena, 'Take no notice. So long as you do as he says and don't come up on him sudden like, he's harmless enough.'

It was not somehow a comforting thought. Alena kept silent.

'Have you eaten yet today?' the woman asked, and when she shook her head, turned and called to the other children: 'Come on. Breakfast. It's time we all stopped for a bite, I reckon.'

And without demur Frank Roscoe laid down his axe and followed her. The matter seemed to have been settled, for the moment at least.

The smoke they had noticed earlier, they now discovered, spiralled upwards from a small stone building, hardly worthy of the name cottage, being more in the nature of a rough hut. One of several exactly the same, it comprised three rectangular walls topped by branches, sods of grass and bracken, the end wall consisting of a circular stone chimney which clearly kept the hut warm, if somewhat smoky, and where food was perhaps cooked in bad weather. This was evidently the coppicers' camp.

Today was cold but sunny and fine, with only a whispering breeze hushing through the treetops. A huge iron pot straddled a small fire in the clearing and the gang gathered round, patiently waiting for the porridge to be served out and handed round. A group of women who had been sitting making swill baskets and besoms, set aside their work for a moment to share in the meal.

The breakfast of oatmeal was hot, filling and reasonably plentiful, more than welcome to Rob and Alena, for all it was somewhat thin and watery. But something about the man alarmed her and she pleaded with Rob in urgent whispers between spoonfuls to move on. He stubbornly insisted they'd be safe enough here and should stay, for a day or two at least.

'He doesn't want me around.'

'He'll change his mind if you impress him with your hard work.'

'One day only then, to give us time to rest. Then we go on.'

'We'll talk about it tomorrow.'

And so they stayed, and one day stretched into two and then into three. Each of them was allotted a space in one of the coppicers' huts. They were given a blanket and told to gather their own bracken to make up into a bed each evening.

'And see you roll it up each day. We don't want no vermin in the house,' the woman, Kate, informed them. 'Any more'n you want folks tramping their wet feet all over your bedding.' This seemed a sensible precaution which they dutifully followed.

'This is better than any old school. A real adventure,' Rob said, face shining as if it were all something out of a *Boy's Own* magazine. Alena sighed, wishing she could share his enthusiasm, but much as she loved the woodlands, she worried about the wisdom of staying with the coppicers. It seemed too near to home for comfort. And what would they do when winter came?

The fire was damped down at night, which gave some relief from the smoke, but fortunately there was never any danger of anyone feeling the cold. Bodies were too closely packed together for that. It was at these times that Alena suffered odd little pangs of guilt and sorrowful longings. She thought about her brothers, and the fun they'd always had together. She pictured her mother worrying and looking everywhere for her, and began to wonder if they'd been wrong to run away.

But her mother hadn't been interested in her troubles, had she? Only in Tom's. And her father had been hard-hearted and callous, as usual. As had James Hollinthwaite with Rob. Nobody understood how they felt. Even so she longed for the warmth of Ma's arms about her right now. She'd always smelled of baking, of floor polish and soap, and *Ma*. It made Alena homesick to remember all of that now.

But then she didn't like to think what her parents' reaction would be when they heard the full story of the swim that the entire village was gossiping about. It was all too shaming. At least this way she and Rob could be together. And so Alena slept with a glimmer of excitement in her heart and tears on her cheek.

–

For all his blunt and sardonic manner, Roscoe turned out to be not half so fearsome as he had at first appeared. He was willing enough to pass on his skills to Rob, teaching him how to hold the axe correctly, how to use the saw without damaging it, which trees were marked for cutting, and which needed to be left as standards to grow on. It was explained to him how coppicing kept the woodlands alive, how regular cropping prevented overcrowding, and brought light to the woodland floor to encourage new growth and wildlife. And if Rob, in his eagerness to acquire these special skills, talked more of himself than he should, encouraged by Roscoe's offer of friendship, the boy saw no harm in that. He surely told him little of any value? Besides, home and its problems seemed very far away. Of what possible interest could they be to this man?

Alena was allowed to follow with the other women and children when they went to the felling, but as she collected the brash, her unease grew as she watched the friendship develop and felt Roscoe's eyes rest reflectively upon her more often than was quite comfortable.

She decided to try once more to persuade Rob to move on.

'I like the work, Ally,' he stubbornly protested. 'I want to stay. And it'll give us time to decide what to do next.'

'No, we should go.'

'Where to?'

'I don't know. Somewhere. Anywhere. He knows our names.'

'So what?'

The familiar bickering continued but, unusually for once, Rob refused to back down. And then the weekend arrived. Roscoe took himself off home on Grizedale Moor for a rest, and his place at the camp was taken by his son.

But Frank Roscoe did not go immediately to the comfort of his own fireside. Instead he drove his battered old truck up and down miles of twisting lanes, as far as Ulverston in the south and Cockermouth in the north, asking questions, making enquiries.

The youngsters could have their fun for a week or two, but wouldn't they tire of the harsh life soon enough? If he found their families, he thought, he could at least put their minds at rest, without spoiling the adventure too much. And perhaps do himself a good turn at the same time.

Mickey Roscoe was as unlike his father as a son could be, at least in Alena's opinion. She hadn't been more than five minutes in his company before she was changing her mind about leaving the coppicers.

He made life seem fun.

If Frank's ways revealed a quirkly sense of humour and silent watchful ways, Mickey was lively and impishly charming, making it clear he liked her, and welcomed her friendship.

Smaller and thinner than his father and, at nineteen, showing little sign of Frank's powerful build, he wore his black cap of hair slicked down with Brylcreem. Foxy rust brown eyes, set wide apart beneath winged brows, carried a glint that gave the impression they missed little of life's pleasures. He had ears that lay flat against the sides of his head, and a mouth that had a slight curl at each corner as if he were perpetually smiling. This gave a puckish air of attractiveness to his face, Alena decided, even if you couldn't for a minute call him handsome. He walked with a swinging gait, rolling on the balls of his feet, hands usually thrust deep in his pockets, shoulders held back as if challenging you to declare him unequal to any task.

Best of all, he treated Alena as if she were a grown-up and not the child that everyone else saw her as, which made her feel warm inside.

For his part, he looked upon her lovely face, burnished to a glowing pink from her days out in the open and polished by the warmth of the fire, now laughing delightedly across at Kate, and fell instantly and completely beneath her spell. Alena Townsen, he decided in that moment, was the girl for him.

So taken was Alena by Mickey's sympathetic charm that she confessed to him her feeling of nervousness when Frank was around.

'Don't you mind him none,' Mickey reassured her. 'He thinks well of himself, 'tis true, believes in hard work, and above all else will let no man be his master. But then he's Irish. I'm not. I was born in these parts, as was my mother.' And she listened with aching heart to the sad story of Mickey's childhood; of how his mother died when he was only a few days old and how he was brought up by a series of women, handed from one to the other depending on which happened to be in favour with Frank at the time.

Alena's eyes grew round with pity. Missing her own mother as badly as she was, she could barely comprehend the awfulness of never having known one at all. She couldn't remember a time when Lizzie hadn't been there with warm reassurance for some childhood disaster, a pair of comforting arms or wise advice. In that moment her longing for home became overwhelming and, to her horror, Alena found her eyes filling with tears. In seconds they were running down her cold cheeks and Mickey was aghast.

'What have I said? Have I hurt you?' He put an arm about her shoulders, patting her, making little soothing noises and being more kind than she could ever have expected.

'No, no.'

'That silly lad shouldn't have brought you into the forest. It's no place for a lass like you.'

Alena hastily brushed away the tears and straightened her shoulders. 'I'm perfectly all right. I *like* the forest.' What was the matter with her? A little sympathy and she was bawling like a baby. Even so, she might very well have confided more of her troubles to him had not Rob chanced upon the little scene and put a stop to it.

'Come on, Alena,' he said. 'We have work to do.'

Mickey, however, kept his arm about her waist. 'She'd do better to stay here wi' me. She wants to, don't you, love?' Alena found herself flushing at the endearment, for all it was common enough and surely meant nothing. Perhaps this was because of the way he leaned his face so close to hers as he said it, lowering his voice in an intimate way. She could smell woodsmoke on his skin and the headiness of it excited her.

'No, she doesn't,' Rob insisted, and taking her arm in a firm grip, led her forcibly away.

'What was all that about?' she stormed at him, the moment they were alone.

'I don't like him. He's smarmy, and he makes you talk too much.' Disapproval made his voice sound tight and hard. 'Too much talk could be dangerous.'

'For goodness' sake, he was only being friendly, as Frank is friendly with you.' Alena shrugged her arm free and marched off, head held high. They didn't speak for the rest of that day, retiring to their respective beds still in a sulk. It was just another disagreement between them, she told herself, except that somehow it felt different.

On the Sunday evening, Mickey departed so as to be ready for his work at the mill the next day.

'Frank will be here by morning,' he told them. Only he wasn't. Roscoe did not appear that day, nor the next. Kate didn't seem unduly disturbed, explaining that he sometimes took it into his head to go off some place, perhaps to drum up more business, or check out a stand of trees for next year. But the work went on just as if he were there, issuing his staccato orders.

Chapter Five

James Hollinthwaite glared at the man before him as if he would like to strike him dead on the spot. 'I blame you for this, Townsen. If you'd brought that child up with any sense of discipline, we wouldn't be in this pickle.'

Ray ground his teeth together, determined, at his wife's request, to hold on to his own temper. 'I'll admit she's overly sensitive. Girls are, but she's not a bad lass.'

'We've only your word for that. But you didn't see her in this damn' tarn. I did.'

They stood on the shores of it now, the night wind buffeting them, fuelling their anger. They had searched every cottage, barn and outhouse, scoured the village and the woods to within two miles of both homes, but they'd found no sign of the youngsters. They'd returned time and again to the tarn, as if to the scene of a crime, certain this was where it had all begun and only too keenly aware that less than a mile away, in Ellersgarth farmhouse, the two mothers sat together for once, brewing endless cups of tea while they waited for their menfolk to solve the problem and bring the silly pair home.

'So I hear. I never thought of thee as a Peeping Tom, Hollinthwaite.'

James flinched. 'I could have you flayed for that.'

'You and whose army? And thy lad is innocent, I suppose?'

'Robert is a soft fool, but I can't help that, can I?' His gaze bored into Ray. 'I've heard one of your own sons is making an idiot of himself over a young lass.'

'Leave Tom oot of this.'

'And you lay off Robert. He's a son to be proud of.'

'Then be a faither to him, why don't you? Then he mightn't be such a noddy.'

'I'm doing my best but it isn't easy, and you aren't helping, man.'

The two men glared at each other with such ferocity it seemed as if each could barely keep from throttling the other. Then, mindful of Lizzie's wishes, Ray made a move to go. 'Laiking aboot 'ere having a slanging match'll do no good. Her ma is half demented wi' worry. It's time we set up a proper search party.' His face creased with concern, and not a little guilt. Was it his own harsh treatment that had sent her off? Lizzie had scarce spoken a word to him since. 'But that'll happen cost money. Folk'll have to stop off work and we can't be expected to mek up their wages.'

'So it's money you're really after, is that it? As usual. You don't give a damn about Alena. You never have.'

Ray clenched his fists, making it perfectly clear where he'd like to put one. 'That's rich, that is, cooming from thee. I seem to remember you were the one who worshipped brass as a god, not me. But then, for a man who's never been known to keep his word, that's not surprising, is it? Scruples is summat you're a stranger to. Backtracking on agreements – putting a man out on t'street who's suffered near death fighting for king and country, wi'out being troubled by conscience – that's the sort you are.'

James, glowering throughout this litany, now jerked as if he'd been struck. Here was one mistake he should have dealt with, right from the outset. Not that he would admit as much now. He took a step nearer. 'I seem to recall you weren't above taking a handout yourself, once upon a time. So I recommend you take that back, Townsen, or you might regret it.'

'Why don't you mek me?' Ray lifted a hand by way of invitation. 'I'll tell you why. Because for all thoo's a bully, Hollinthwaite, and think you can taak a banty cock into layin an egg, thoo's also a coward. You're reviled in these parts, and know it. Where thoo's not a laughing stock, that is.'

It was too much for James. One fist went out, then the other. Blood spurted but, for all he was smaller and lighter, Ray was certainly no coward. He landed a punch in the softness of Hollinthwaite's belly, and while James stood winded from it, doubled up with agony, Ray bunched his bony fists again and popped another on his chin.

'That'll bloody show you!'

James retaliated in kind and within minutes the two men were grappling on the ground, feet, fists and knees flying with more fury than effectiveness. A light appeared, footsteps on the shingle as the two women, bringing what they believed to be good news to their menfolk, now struggled to separate them. Frantic hands pulled at their clothing, a scolding voice telling them not to be bloody fools, that this wouldn't help. But the pair were too far gone in their anger to pay any heed. Somehow they were both in the water, still grappling with each other, still throwing punches. Ray was a keen if undisciplined fighter but James, being the larger, stronger man, had the advantage. And then there was only the sound of Lizzie's crying.

–

Alena and Rob settled with remarkable ease into the daily routine of woodland life. A favourite part of Alena's day was to take a walk alone in the early morning. She would dress in one of Kate's long skirts, her warm coat and scarf, and stride out over the frosted grass, loving the crunch of it beneath her boots and the crispness of the clear air that made her skin tingle. She loved the silent stillness of the forest, sometimes hearing nothing but the sound of her own soft breathing before the birds awoke to fill it with their first joyful songs. She loved too the sheltering protection of the trees, and the rich scents of moss and damp earth, and the drift of woodsmoke as the breakfast fire was stirred into life back in the coppicer's camp.

She watched redwing, tits or a pair of thrushes in their winter plumage. She thought once that she followed the trail of a badger, though never quite caught sight of it. One morning she stood quietly by while a stag rolled itself in a patch of soft black peat and then stalked off with a self-satisfied gait, as if it were all a part of some prearranged ritual. Laughing, Alena went off to her breakfast.

The atmosphere always lightened once the main party had gone off for the felling. When they were alone the women would sing and laugh, exchange gossip and offer each other advice in the age-old way that women do: on how to catch a man, rear children and keep themselves young, attractive and healthy.

'Is young Rob your boyfriend then?' they asked, eager to know all about the newcomers.

'Are you in love?'

'Will you marry him?'

And as Alena sat flushed and tongue-tied, not quite knowing how to answer, she was grateful when Kate stepped in, telling them to 'stop ganging up on the poor lass'.

Then Kate would go on to tell them stories about how she was often mistaken for a gypsy. With her long black hair worn frizzed out about a face that was somehow bright and knowing, as if she could tell a score of secrets should she have a mind to, Alena didn't wonder at it. A natural born storyteller with a wry sense of humour, her stories kept everyone amused while they worked.

'Some townsfolk can't make us out, d'you see? Don't know what coppicing is, so how can they understand what we do?'

On these occasions, as they talked, Alena would be shown how to prepare the spells and taws which, she discovered, were the names given to the flat strips of oak needed for the making of the coracle-shaped swill baskets. The women worked on smaller baskets, but these others were a skilled craft, produced by one or two of the men sitting astride a swill-horse. Finished, they were practically unbreakable and useful for carrying logs, bobbins, fish or any manner of goods, even being used by colliers down in the mines. For this reason they were an important source of income for the coppicers.

Her hands were chapped from being constantly in water, soaking the pieces of oak to keep them more pliable. Blisters appeared and her fingers became sore from the hours spent splitting or riving the oak poles, then shaving them into the necessary thin strips. But for all it was hard work and tiring, Alena found it surprisingly satisfying.

'I tried to explain,' Kate said, 'but this woman was so set on the fact I was a gypsy, she crossed my palm with a silver sixpence.'

'Did you take it?' someone asked.

'Course I took it. How many sixpence's d'you reckon I see? I told her she was going to meet a dark, handsome stranger, live to be a hundred and die in her bed.'

Alena giggled. 'And did she believe you?'

'Indeed she did. That's what they all want to hear, ain't it? So that's what they get told. Is it my fault she wouldn't believe I weren't a gypsy? Anyroad, if it turns out wrong and she doesn't live to be a hundred, she can't come back and complain, can she?'

And everyone laughed, including Alena who wiped tears of merriment from her eyes.

In the evening when the day's work was done they would sit around the fire and eat rabbit stew, roast venison, salmon or trout from the river, that had been wrapped in wet leaves and slowly baked in the hot ash. Alena never dared ask how this delicious food came about, nor was she ever told. She found a wonderful sort of freedom living and working out here in the forest, and if sometimes she thought of home and her family with a wave of nostalgia, she tried not to dwell upon it.

-

By Thursday everyone had ceased to expect Roscoe, and on Friday evening Mickey came back. He hadn't heard from his father either, but didn't seem in the least concerned.

'Like I said, Alena, he's his own master. Freedom to move is his right. Now let me see those poor fingers of yours. Are they sore?' He picked up one of her hands and, turning it over, began to examine the calluses and blisters that had appeared, smoothing them tenderly with the tips of his fingers. 'You need something on those, and I have the very thing. Arnica cream. I bought it for a strained shoulder but you can have it.'

'Oh, Mickey, no. You mustn't give it to me.' But she was grateful. Some of the skin had split and she worried about it becoming infected. The heel of her thumb felt badly bruised and an ache spread right up her wrist and forearm.

His eyes flashed. 'You're very important to me, Alena. Haven't you realised that by now? While you are in our care, we must look after you.'

She found herself blushing as she allowed him gently to smooth on the cream, then wished she hadn't when she saw Rob hovering close by, a scowl upon his face.

Oh, dear, what had she done now? She'd said nothing untoward to Mickey, scarcely a word about herself, in fact, so what was the problem? She loved Rob with all her heart, but he could sometimes be far too serious for his own good. He rarely smiled these days, and the arrival of Mickey seemed to have worsened rather than lightened his mood.

'Are you coming?' he asked, sounding even grumpier than usual.

'Where to?'

'With me, of course?'

Heavens above, she thought, startled by her own perspicacity. He surely couldn't be jealous of Mickey Roscoe? The very idea made her want to laugh out loud. Oh, but she shouldn't laugh. If he was jealous, then that wasn't funny at all. It was perfectly dreadful. But what could she do about it?

Rob sometimes found it difficult to express his emotions, and the last thing she wanted to do was to embarrass him. Perhaps if she made some casual remark, let him know in a roundabout sort of way that he was the only boy she *really* cared about, that might bring the smiles back? But even as these thoughts flew through her head, Mickey spoke up before she could find the right words to express them.

'No, she isn't. Can't you see she's talking to me this evening, for a change? At least I take care of her.' From the bag slung across his shoulders, he dug out a small jar. As he handed it to her, he continued, 'If you want anything else, Alena, you've only to say the word and I'll get it for you.'

'Thank you.' And before she could protest, Mickey took her by the arm and began to lead her away.

'Now we'll have that walk by the beck, eh? It's a grand evening for a stroll.'

'Yes, it is.' And then as if as an afterthought, half glancing back over her shoulder: 'Coming, Rob?' But he only mumbled something she couldn't quite hear and stumped off. Alena watched him go with regret, recognising the slump of his shoulders so expressive of his hurt feelings. Although she was sorry about that, she had to admit that it was flattering to be courted by two such good-looking young men. It made her feel all warm and excited inside. But she'd seek an opportunity to put Rob's mind at rest, first thing tomorrow.

–

The next day, which was a Saturday, Alena didn't see Rob. He wasn't in his hut, nor did he put in an appearance at breakfast. When she enquired, she learned that he'd gone off early with some of the men to fell one particularly large tree. The day stretched out long and lonely ahead of her, with nothing to occupy her but her own hands. She wished now that she'd not allowed Mickey to hurry her away the previous evening. By doing so, she'd only made the situation worse. What must

Rob have thought of her? Why hadn't she settled the matter there and then? Jealousy could be painful, and the last thing she wanted was to hurt him. As the morning wore on, her worries grew and festered, and a kind of self-loathing built up at her own apparent callousness. The feeling became so bad she was forced to speak quite sharply to herself.

'I've done nothing wrong, for goodness' sake. A chat and a stroll by the river, that's all.' If Rob had taken it into his head to be foolishly jealous that was his problem. And Mickey had been kind, giving her the ointment. She could feel the benefit of it already. Alena struggled to stop brooding and concentrate on her work.

This morning she was being instructed in the making of besoms that would be used by housewives as sweeping brooms. She had learned how to gather together a tight bunch of twigs and tie it in three places with hazel withies. Then, taking a length of birch pole already stripped of its bark, she would knock it into the bundle, and peg it to keep it in place. The task wasn't as easy as it looked and she marvelled at the speed and dexterity of the other women, who could make as many as thirty dozen besoms a day, for which they might be paid a halfpenny a dozen for their efforts by Frank Roscoe. What he would be paid later when he sold them on, nobody dared ask.

Despite herself, she was surprised and almost glad when Mickey came to sit with her as she worked.

'You're doing fine,' he told her, and Alena flushed, either because of the compliment or because he sat so close. She was surprised how much Mickey Roscoe's presence flustered her, despite her best efforts not to allow it to. He held the bunch of twigs for her, giving the withy an extra firm tug and a quickly tied knot to hold it in place. Alena tucked her hands hastily away on to her lap as he did so, concerned that they might brush against the tough strength of his.

'Now you do the next.'

The fire in her cheeks warmed further as her fingers fumbled beneath his steady gaze.

'Your hands would harden if you did this regularly, and you'd soon become quick and skilled,' he said, smiling down at her, evidently proud of her efforts. He watched how her cheeks glowed, how the wind lifted her hair, bright as copper beech leaves, from her slender white neck, and how the tip of her tongue crept out at the corner of her mouth as she concentrated.

She half glanced at him from beneath her lashes and wondered if this was to be her lot in life. Would she stay here forever with the coppicers and acquire more of their woodcraft skills? Alena decided it might be quite pleasant, if only she could persuade Mickey and Rob to be friends. The tranquillity and slow rhythm of the forest were already seeping into her soul, making her feel as if she had always been here and time no longer held any meaning. Rob would surely be pleased if she could only banish this lingering ache she still carried for abandoning her mother, and agree to stay in the woods for good. She was the one who'd made the decision to run away in the first place, so she should stop looking back and harbouring nostalgic longings for the past, and look to the future. But how would they get through the harsh months ahead?

As if reading her thoughts, Mickey said, 'Are you cold?'

'Of course not.' She could no longer feel her feet.

'We don't live here all year, you know. We do have homes to go to, and when the worst of the winter sets in, we go to them. That's the time the women catch up on their indoor jobs. Making more of the besoms, for instance. The men make the swill baskets and ship's fenders, sell firewood, do odd jobs, see to their tools and so on. Then, at the first sign of spring, we're ready to pack up and be off again.'

'But I thought you worked in a bobbin mill?' The worry over what she and Rob would do when the coppicers all went off to their real homes niggled unpleasantly at the back of her mind, though now didn't seem an appropriate moment to bring out the subject and air it.

He grinned. 'I'm good at my job so I stick with that. Besides, I need the money. There isn't enough in coppicing for both me and Dad, not nowadays. But I help when I can.'

'Are there many gangs like this in the forest?' Alena asked.

'Not so many as there once were. All the more work for us though, eh? There isn't the same demand for coppice timber as there used to be, not since the iron forges started to use water power or coke instead of charcoal. Not surprising, mind, considering the way the forest was near decimated at one time. There were once pitsteads and iron bloomeries all over the Low Furness Woodlands and more charcoal burners than they could rightly support. Thriving industry, it was once. The forest is better managed these days but we still send charcoal to the gunpowder works, and the larger timber to the bobbin mills. Have you met old Isaac, our friendly charcoal burner?'

Alena shook her head and Mickey's eyes twinkled more merrily than ever as he grinned from ear to ear. 'Now there's a treat in store. You think we live simply, you should see old Isaac's hut. Real hermit he is, but a man of great character and intellect, as he will tell you himself. No flies on him.' He pegged the birch pole into the besom for her and set it to one side, his eyes never leaving her face. He wanted to keep her here all day talking to him. And he would if he had any say in the matter. Which was why, in his position as deputy to his father, he'd been able to send young Robert off into the depths of the forest, leaving the field clear for himself. 'Where was I?'

'You were telling me about the timber you send to the bobbin mills.'

'Oh, aye. Might be five or six inches in diameter, or nearly a foot. They slice the bigger pieces like cake so they can stamp out cylinders for the small bobbins from them.'

'Oh, yes, I know about that, my...' Alena stopped, appalled. She'd been about to say her brothers worked at Low Birk Mill, and could have bitten off her own tongue. One careless word could ruin everything. She felt herself start to tremble, struggling to think of something else to say in its place and cover up her slip.

Mickey, pretending not to notice, continued with his tale. 'They'll always need bobbins, I reckon. Mind you, some of the greedier landowners have planted larch and other quick-growing conifers.' He shook his head, pressing his lips together with disapproval. 'Not good for our line of business. Gloomy dull place is a larch plantation, and doesn't grow well here. Not native timber, d'you see? We worry that coppicing might die out altogether one day, which will be the death of the forest and woodlands.'

Recovering her composure, Alena listened enthralled, drinking in every word. Afterwards she told Rob all that had been said, and how she had almost blundered. 'But I don't think he noticed. I mentioned no names.'

He said nothing.

'Perhaps Mickey's right and it won't be so easy for you to get work, after all?' she suggested, but Rob seemed certain that he could, once he'd honed these new skills he'd acquired.

'Mickey Roscoe doesn't know everything. I can do this work. Besides, it's better than doing geometry and algebra far from home, in the freezing bare classrooms of a new school, I can tell you.'

Yet strangely enough, it was he now who talked of moving on. He was distrustful of the attention Mickey gave to Alena, though not for the world would he say as much. Rob noticed how much time Mickey spent demonstrating some skill or other to her, which she already understood perfectly well, and he found that he didn't much care for it. 'Soon as we've learned all we need to know, we'll find somewhere better. I'll see you want for nothing, Alena, but I've decided we'd be better away from here, soon as we can manage it.'

'*You've* decided?'

'Aye, I have.'

'And when did you decide?'

'Last night.'

She bunched her fists on her hips and glared at him. 'And don't I get a say?'

He scowled at her, wishing for once she'd not argue but seeing the familiar stubbornness set in. 'It was your idea in the first place that we keep moving. That was what you wanted, wasn't it?'

'Well, I've changed my mind. Why can't we stay? I like it here. I thought you did too.'

In the silence which followed, Rob's face became more serious than she had ever seen it. 'You do realise they're probably looking for us, Ally? My father will get up a search party and be scouring every inch of these woods by now. It's right what you said before, we have to get further away. Miles and miles away from Lancashire. Perhaps as far as Scotland.'

This new idea came as such a shock to her, and yet was so eminently sensible, that, stuck for a reply, Alena sat down in a huff and began to pull off her Wellington boots. Her mouth set in a furious pout as she wriggled her freezing toes, wishing again for warmer footwear as a tumult of confused emotions ran through her. She wanted to go with Rob, of course she did, but she also wanted to stay here, in the forest. She'd heard that Scotland was beautiful, with perhaps even more magnificent mountains than the ones in her own Lancashire Lake District, but it sounded a very long way from home. A flutter of unease grew in the pit of her stomach as she recalled the warmth of her own fireside and her mother's home-baked bread. What should she do? She longed in that moment to lay her head upon Lizzie's soft breast and ask for her advice.

'We'll have real skills and experience to offer,' Rob was saying. 'Who knows where that could lead?' His whole face was alight as he talked, gold flecks seeming to dance in his brown eyes. 'I always wondered what I would do with my life. I knew I didn't want to go to university, but nor did I want to work on the farm with my father or have to take over the mill one day. Now I know exactly what I want. Now I know where I belong – in the forest. This is the life for me, Alena. I don't care which forest, or where it is, I mean to be a woodsman.'

She looked up at him then, responding to the thrill of his voice, and her heart swelled with a sudden rush of love for him. The feeling was so unexpected it left her quite breathless, banishing the last of her doubts. Where else would she want to be, but with Rob?

She pushed her feet back into the boots and stood before him. 'What about me?' she quietly asked, struck by a sudden and unaccustomed shyness. 'We won't always be fourteen. We won't always be like this, a boy and a girl. What then?' She looked at him from under her lashes, trying to imagine him as a grown man, fearful he might no longer need her then.

Somehow he had moved imperceptibly closer, so close she could feel the fan of his warm breath upon her cheek, trace every beloved feature of his face, see the satin smoothness of his skin. Was he going to kiss her? In that heart-stopping moment, Alena knew that was exactly what she wanted him to do. She held her breath, swayed slightly towards him, waiting – hoping – longing for the touch of his lips on hers. When the kiss came it tasted as sweet as honey. Just as she had imagined it would. Within a moment it was over, the merest whisper of a kiss, a promise for the future.

'I thought – I thought you might want to be with me,' he said. 'But if you'd rather stay here, with Mickey...'

'Oh, no,' she breathed. It was enough. They looked deep into each other's eyes, and after a moment Rob gave a lopsided little smile and Alena grinned with impish delight. There was no need to say more. They understood each other perfectly. She still had her darling Rob, and now a planned future together. What more did she need? It was the fulfilment of all her dreams.

And then, on the Sunday of their fourth week in the forest, James Hollinthwaite walked into the clearing with a group of men hard at his heels, and Alena knew that their idyll was over. The search party had arrived and nothing would ever be the same again.

Chapter Six

Low Birk Bobbin Mill was a remnant of another era. It had changed little, if at all, since Victorian times. Various owners had used it in an effort to make their fortunes but, once the height of the cotton boom had passed, few had succeeded. The textile industry remained an important outlet but bobbins for copper wire and cable and in a whole variety of other shapes and sizes were made there now, with strange names such as ratchet or spout, number 24s or three and three-quarters. The mill also produced such things as tool handles, toggles, axe shafts and similar products.

All about the outside of the mill, in and around the drying sheds, were stacked the long poles of birch, ash and sycamore. The bark was peeled and the wood allowed to dry at its own pace over a twelve-month period, sometimes finished off in the drying kilns. These were considered to be ready when only a slight dampness remained in the centre, which made them easier to drill. They would then be cut up into slices, like a loaf of bread, and the bobbin-making process begin.

When her shift finished for the day, Alena left the mill as always with mixed feelings; glad to have finished work, yet dreading returning home.

The weeks following Rob's departure for his Yorkshire school had proved to be the bleakest of her life. She'd wondered at times if she would survive. All the purpose of her life seemed to have departed with him.

On their return from the forest, she'd learned that her father had suffered a stroke as a result of an accident at High Birk Tarn.

No one said it had happened while he was looking for her, but they didn't need to. She could see it in the way her brothers avoided her eye, villagers stopped talking when she walked by, and her mother kept on assuring her that she mustn't in any way feel responsible. She knew there had been a fight. He and James Hollinthwaite were old enemies, and because of her flight with Rob, it had flared into something evil and dangerous.

Ray Townsen had laid unconscious in the cottage hospital for four weeks after they'd dragged him out of the icy water. Now he lay in a bed specially installed for him in his own front parlour, barely aware of his family creeping in and out with bowls of vegetable broth or cups of tea. Their efforts were more often than not rewarded with a sour grunt or even a flailing left hand, that being the only limb he could move, knocking the contents all over the eiderdown so that cloths had to be fetched, the mess mopped up and the bowl or cup refilled for the cantankerous patient.

'He finds it frustrating,' Lizzie would say, always ready to excuse her irascible husband. 'He's always hated staying in bed.'

Whenever she herself nursed him, the result seemed to be even more traumatic. Ray would rant and roar at his poor wife, saying that it was she who'd chained him to this dratted bed; that he wouldn't be here at all but for her.

'Didn't I give thee four fine sons?'

'Of course you did, and don't I love you for it?'

'I took care o' things.'

'You've been a good husband to me, Ray. No woman could have wished for a better.'

'Fought a war for the likes of that bastard – and he robs me!'

'Hush, Ray. Rest now.'

None of his ravings made much sense to Alena, but they so upset Lizzie that Ray's four sons and one daughter shared most of the work between them, with as much patience and good grace as they could manage. If only for the sake of their long-suffering mother.

The worst of it was Alena's sense of guilt. Not simply because of her own part in his predicament, but also because she could feel no real love for him, not even now when he was a pathetic wreck of the man he had once been. The distance that had always existed between father and daughter, now caused her more distress than it ever had before. She wanted to grieve for his pitiful state, for his ruined life and the loss of his functions, as her mother did. But she could not. She could only be grateful for the fact that there would be no repeat of the slap she had witnessed, and that the belt hanging behind the back door would never be used again.

In January, almost as soon as Christmas and the New Year festivities were over, Rob had gone from Ellersgarth. He had been allowed to come and see her to make his farewells. That was the first and last time she had seen him since they'd been brought out of the forest, and they'd stood together, not knowing what to say or how they should react. An awkward silence had hung between them, their shared experiences and raw youth making it impossible for them to express any of the emotions that churned within.

In February, as soon as Dolly turned seventeen, the family surfaced sufficiently from their troubles to agree to Tom's marrying her in the little parish church up on the hill. Not a moment too soon since she was already five months gone with his child and as 'big as a cow's backside', in her own choice words.

So far as Alena could tell, there was little sign of its being a love match. The ceremony had been performed as quietly as possible, with little celebration, then Tom had reluctantly moved into Applethorn Cottages with his new wife and mother-in-law, and somehow the light and joy that had always been a part of his boyish nature seemed to fade and die as his new responsibilities weighed heavily upon him.

But if life with her family was difficult, those first weeks at the mill where Alena now worked were even worse.

Inside, the stark lofty rooms were crowded with men and women at their machines. Long slapping leather belts hung from the rafters and flew at a speed that could scalp a careless worker in seconds if concentration wandered. The wooden floor was largely invisible, being knee-deep in wood shavings and sawdust, and Alena, like the other women, wrapped sacking about her legs in a futile attempt to keep out the cold. Since they were now in the midst of a freezing cold March, the girls also wore fingerless gloves, coats and scarves over their pinnies, taking it in turns to sneak into the boiler room and warm themselves, or their bits of sacking, on the pipes whenever the foreman wasn't looking.

The hours were long and the work hard, the only respite being a short break for a brew of tea morning and afternoon, and a half hour for the midday meal, taken in the canteen which was little more than a cottage kitchen. This would normally be where Lizzie worked, warming the girls' soup, brewing tea and providing a simple but substantial meal for those with money to pay for it. In her absence, the girls had to bring sandwiches or a cold meat pie from home, and one of them would brew the tea, with the usual comments that it had been made out of dish cloths.

'Are you coming to the canteen with us?' Deirdre Swainson, a raw-boned girl of about seventeen, asked on Alena's first day. She had already formed the opinion that Deirdre was rather simple-minded, since she spent much of the time giggling over nothing in particular.

'Yes, of course.'

But Alena soon discovered the cause of the giggles. She found a dead mouse in her bait can, reposing beside her jam sandwiches. Although it had turned her stomach and forced her to go hungry throughout that long day, she'd been proud of her own reaction. She hadn't screamed or wept or complained to a soul. She'd merely smiled wryly, tossed the mouse away and closed up the tin again, making no comment whatsoever.

Her workmates, however, seemed disappointed, perhaps wishing for a more dramatic reaction. The next day she found a cockroach, very much alive and working its way through her cheese sandwich.

Alena had been grateful in those early days for having been brought up with brothers. Tricks and jokes were apparently commonplace amongst the girls, in particular against newcomers, but no worse than she'd experienced on a day-to-day basis at home. Certainly there were plenty more played on her, most often, she suspected, by Dolly Sutton, who still seemed to hold some sort of grudge against her despite now being 'family'.

Once while she was away at the lavatory, someone put grease on her machine handles; a dangerous if fairly common prank, making Alena's hands slip the moment she started to use it. Fortunately, she simply ruined one bobbin with no other damage done before she realised, and laughed with the best of them as she cleaned the stuff off.

Aware the other girls were watching her and still weighing her up, she knew that the important thing was to take it all in good part. Life in a mill could be monotonous without a sense of humour and, despite her misery at losing Rob, she battled hard to keep her own intact.

Very little effort was made by the foreman, a hard-faced man called Stan Renshaw, to explain the work properly to her. One of the girls would sometimes be deputed to give a short demonstration of some process or other, and then she'd be left to get on with it. This was apparently the way things were done. She spent a good deal of time on what was known as the apprentice machine, so-called because you put two bits of wood on and took two off. It took thirty seconds to learn but having to do this repetitive task for nine hours a day nearly drove her mad with boredom.

Dust matted her hair, flew in her eyes, clogged her throat and rubbed against every part of her skin.

Another day she was working on a machine that bored the blanks before they were sent to the roughing lathe to be shaped into a small bobbin or, more correctly, a reel. She was cold and hungry, looking forward to the sandwiches that hopefully this time would not be contaminated. She'd taken particular care to keep the box in her sight at all times this morning. Perhaps if her mind hadn't been so occupied, she wouldn't have been so easily distracted.

'Look out!' a voice cried, slightly muffled against the noise of the machinery but close enough to make Alena half turn, startled by the unexpected sound and alarmed at what the problem might be. The spindle, left spinning free, missed her arm by a half inch and Edith was on to her in a second.

'You daft lump! See what you nearly did? You should never turn away like that. You could have ended up with a hole in your elbow instead of in that bobbin – and at four thousand revs a second there wouldn't have been much of it left. Keep your wits about you, girl, if you want to stay in one piece.'

Alena glared at Dolly but saw no point in trying to pass the blame on to her, certainly not in public, for she'd only deny any part in the accident and make Alena look stupid as a result.

So as the winter days dragged on and work in the mill grew colder and harder, Alena gritted her teeth and got on with it, knowing that any complaints would only make matters worse. She rose at six thirty, ate her breakfast, made up her sandwiches, then dressed warmly in thick jumper and skirt, long scarf, woollen socks and boots, with one of Tom's old caps pulled down over her curls, she rode to the mill before it was light on the precious new bicycle bought for her last Christmas by her brothers. Alena came to appreciate this gift more and more. She polished it carefully, oiled and greased it, learned how to cope with a slack chain and mend punctures. And she always made sure that her lamp worked properly, because of the darkness of the twisting lanes. There was nothing she loved better than to join the stream of workers on that early morning ride to the mill each morning; watch the world wake up, the navy blue of the sky lighten to paler blue or soft lemon, hear the birds shake out their feathers and herald the new day with a song. And, best of all, she loved freewheeling back down the hill again each evening.

It was always important to get home in good time. Lizzie would be waiting for her, knowing that the moment Alena arrived she could take a break from the claustrophobic sick room, brew a cup of tea, and put her feet up for a while. Mother and daughter had grown closer as they shared the onerous task of caring for Ray.

So on the evening Alena discovered her tyres had been slashed, she did not see the joke at all. She stood in the mill yard glaring at the damage, quite breathless with rage. Stamping her foot and kicking the offending article did no good either, and she knew well enough that whether she stopped to change the wheel, or set out to walk home, she was bound to be late and Ma would worry and grow even more tired and irritable.

'Damn and blast them!' she yelled, only to be rewarded by laughter as Billy Warren came rumbling by at precisely that moment.

'Oh, aye, they did that to me once or twice,' he said without pause as he cycled past.

'I'll have their guts for garters!' Alena shouted after him, shaking her fist, but that only made him laugh all the more.

'Waste of time. They'll only do it again.'

She saw then that Billy's own tyres were flat as pancakes, the wheels bumping along on their metal rims. Soft in the head, Billy was. Too easy-going for his own good, people said. But Alena Townsen wasn't soft. Oh, dear me, no.

It was time, she decided, to retaliate.

–

A few discreet enquiries brought blank stares and amused shakes of the head but Sandra Myers, a quiet, thin, softly pretty girl who'd rarely spoken a word to Alena thus far, whispered the name of the culprit while they were having their half-hour dinner break. Dolly, as suspected.

'I saw her checking out your bike in the sheds last night. Told me if she had to walk, why not you? She also said as how you might find a rat in your bait tin next time,' Sandra concluded, voice raw with horror.

Alena went white at the thought. A mouse, or even a live cockroach, was one thing; a rat, of which there were undoubtedly plenty around the mill and the mill leat, was another matter entirely. If one got inside the mill buildings, a trap had to be brought in and everyone put on their guard – another reason for the sacking tied so tightly around legs, since vermin could so easily hide in the deep shavings.

'We'll see about that.'

She tackled Dolly on the subject that very evening. Wheeling her bike home, with the rubber tyres flapping, Alena came upon her looking like a round ripe apple in the last months of her pregnancy. She denied the accusation, of course, but then Alena hadn't expected anything different.

'I know it was you, Dolly.'

'Somebody been telling tales?' she asked, looking annoyed.

Alena said nothing to this.

'I've enough on me plate. What would I be doing, bothering about you?' Eyes widening in false innocence.

'Exactly what I'd like to know. You seem to have a personal grudge against me, Dolly. You're not still peeved about those dustbins, surely?'

'Don't be childish.'

'So what is it?'

'I haven't a bloody clue what you're talking about.'

'Oh, yes, you have. You've all had your bit of fun with me. First the livestock, then the grease. Good laugh all round. But this is more serious. Have you any idea how much tyres cost?'

'Like I said, I don't know what you're talking about.' And, smirking, Dolly tossed her head and walked on, lips pressed

85

tightly together, one hand shielding the rounded curve of her stomach.

–

The next morning Dolly was set to demonstrate to Alena how to operate the pressing machine. The larger bobbin barrels, already bored through the centre following the grain of the wood, had to be glued on to the ends or flanges, then pressed firmly together on the press. After that the edges were rounded off on the rounder and drilled on a V-borer with two or more holes, so that the flanges could be pegged securely on to the barrel.

Alena, usually quick to learn, pretended not to understand how to feed through the squares of wood, or put the glue in the top roller. Then, in her clumsiness, she 'accidentally' dropped the pot of glue. It splashed down Dolly's legs and rivers of it ran into her clogs. The expression on the girl's face was a picture, while all the other women in the room roared with laughter at the state she was in.

'Yer one of us now, lass,' said old Edith, grinning from ear to ear. 'You all right?' she asked of Dolly, who insisted with a grim smile as firmly stuck to her face as her feet were stuck fast in the evil-smelling stuff swilling around her feet, that yes, she was very well, thank you very much. So desperate was she to pretend there was nothing wrong, she refused even to take off her clogs and clean them out.

'Eeh, I laughed till I cried, I did that!' Edith kept saying for days afterwards. 'How she got her smelly socks off when she got home, I daren't think. She must've had to cut 'em out o' them clogs of hers.' And off she'd go again into great gusts of laughter.

Alena had no more trouble after that, and Sandra became a firm friend. Even more so when the girl admitted that she'd long since developed a crush on Alena's brother Harry. 'Not that he's ever noticed me. Never spoke a word to me, in fact.'

'Then it's time he did. You'd best come and meet him prop-erly. I owe you that much at least. Only you might have to wait a while,' Alena cautioned. 'Things are a bit tricky at home right now.' And Sandra nodded in sympathetic understanding.

Oh, yes, thought Alena, life wouldn't be too bad in the mill. In fact, it was picking up nicely. And she took great delight in describing this success in one of her regular long letters to Rob.

'*I hope you like your new school*,' she wrote. '*You say very little about it in your letters, except how you hate rugby. What do you do? What are the masters like? Have you made lots of new friends? It's been difficult getting used to my new job in the mill, and I miss having you to talk to, of course.*'

She was a little afraid that he might have made too many friends, and forgotten all about her.

–

Nothing could have been further from the truth. School had turned out to be every bit as awful as Rob had feared. Cold, depressing, and deadly lonely, with each passing day he came to hate it more and more. The first few weeks had been the worst when he'd never seemed to get anything quite right. He'd done exactly as he was told: got up at seven thirty, eaten his breakfast, made his bed and tidied his already neat locker, knowing he must be ready for lessons at a quarter to nine. But even on that very first morning things had gone wrong. For some reason his pillow had disappeared while he was at breakfast and Matron, on her dormitory inspection, had not been pleased.

'This is not a good start, Hollinthwaite,' she'd boomed in a voice that soared over the top of her pouter bosom.

'No, Matron,' he'd agreed, addressing the bare sheet where the pillow had been when he'd gone for breakfast.

'I shall look for an improvement tomorrow.'

'Yes, Matron.'

After that he'd asked a boy the way to his first class, somehow mixed up the directions and ended up in entirely the wrong place. By the time he'd found his way to the right room he was twenty minutes late. Only the fact that it was his first day saved him.

The next lesson had been French, and since his mother had been fluent in the language, he faced it with a degree of equanimity. Unfortunately, though the master was pleased with his translation skills, his schoolmates were not.

'We don't like swots,' one whispered fiercely in his ear.

'Or sucking up.'

This was a remark which at first he did not understand but was to become all too familiar. By the end of that first long day, not a soul had spoken to him.

The biggest humiliation came when they found one of Alena's letters. Colin Briggs, a fat boy who liked to throw his weight around – literally - found it tucked inside Rob's pillowcase and read it out loud to the whole dormitory, making particular fun of her parting words.

'She says she misses him,' Briggs announced to guffaws of laughter.

Rob tried to reach it but was held back, so could do nothing but listen in impotent rage while everyone made fun, jeering at him for getting a letter from a *girl*!

'Just proves how soppy you are,' Briggs said.

Rob finally managed to snatch the letter and put it in his pyjama pocket, then curled up in his bed, red-faced and smarting with embarrassment, as the laughter bubbled around him.

–

Life at number 14 Birkwith Row fell into a depressing and mind-numbing routine. Each day Ray seemed to grow physically weaker even as his temper grew shorter. It was a relief when he slept, though it never seemed to be for long. His loud, complaining voice would call out for a drink or his medicine, or to be turned over because of some ache or pain, at all hours of the day or night. His speech had become confused, the words often jumbled or unclear, but the Townsen family learned to understand his every word. He'd shout that someone had left a ton weight lying on top of him, which would turn out to be his arm, though not for the world would any of them dare tell him so.

Lizzie, forced to give up her work in the mill to stay and look after him, suffered the brunt of his ill temper, and eagerly looked forward to hearing the day's activities from her family when they returned home. But she grew lonely as well as exhausted.

'I've allus worked,' she explained to Alena. 'I miss the companionship of the girls at the mill – making their brews, warming their soup, listening to their troubles and so on. And who'll mend their cuts and sores now I'm not there? I can't see Mr Hollinthwaite paying someone to do what I did for naught. Has he got someone else to mind the canteen?'

Alena shook her head. 'The girls are taking it in turns till you can come back.'

A smile flickered fleetingly over her mother's face, making her look younger, if only for a fraction of a second, as she thought of her job still open for her. By rights, Hollinthwaite owed her a favour. It was as much his fault as anybody's that Ray was like this. 'And a right mess they're probably mekking of it, an' all,' she laughed.

'Even James Hollinthwaite wouldn't be so cruel as to give away your job with Dad like this.'

'Aye, well, let's hope not.' But the worry still showed in her fidgety fingers and puckered brow. 'Though when I'll get back, God knows. Who else could I persuade to look after your father? Only, I do miss having money of me own in me pocket. Money we need. I know the boys do what they can but they have their own lives to lead, and their own futures to save for. I can't be dependent upon them.' And no matter how much Alena or her brothers assured her that they were willing and eager to pay to keep her at home, Lizzie became more and more despondent. But then Ray Townsen was hardly an ideal patient. Alena could think of little worse than being shut up for twenty-four hours a day with her father at the best of times, let alone in his present mood.

And her mother's worries were in fact justified. Jim had confided his intentions of marrying Ruby Pratt come the summer, his long-time sweetheart. Tom had already gone, of course. Kit at twenty-one didn't earn much, and with his bad chest spent as much time off work as in it. As for Alena, she couldn't even keep herself on the money she got. So that left Harry, and it didn't seem quite fair to expect him to keep the lot of them.

'Times are hard,' Lizzie insisted. 'What if the mill should go on short time, or one of the boys be laid off or become sick?'

Harry wrapped his big arms about his mother in a huge bearlike hug. 'Or the whole village go up in flames, or the vicar run off with the organist to a desert island? Aw, come on, Ma, haven't we enough worries to be going on with, without thinking up things that haven't happened yet?' And smiling shamefaced at her grinning son, Lizzie allowed herself to be comforted.

Jim set down his newspaper and picked up his fork. 'Ma's got a point, though. Look what's happening to steel, coal and shipbuilding, not to mention cotton, which most concerns us. Production is half what it used to be, and exports are well down, so a man has to look after hissel these days.'

A fact with which Lizzie couldn't argue. She just wished her family wasn't always so beholden to James Hollinthwaite. She had this prickly feeling between her shoulder blades that he'd take any opportunity to be rid of the lot of them, favour owed or not.

'There's talk in the papers that the country might go bankrupt. If that's true, then it's survival of the fittest, eh?' Jim said, stabbing at a plump sausage and making hot fat spurt everywhere.

'Now who's talking daft? Who ever heard of a country going bankrupt?' Lizzie was laughing as she dabbed at the spots of grease on the clean cloth. 'Eat your tea, and don't count on things till they happen, like your brother says.'

–

Alena was bitterly disappointed when Rob didn't come home at Easter. He'd talked of little else in his letters for weeks. She'd marked the days off on her calendar in red pencil, her stomach churning with increasing excitement. Spring lightened her heart and softened the Lakeland air. Ox-eye daisies, red campion and ragged robin starred the hedgerows. She'd made an Easter card for him, which she'd painted herself using an old childhood paintbox, ready to give it to him personally, under the old oak.

But two days before Good Friday she saw Mrs Hollinthwaite strolling through Low Birk Coppice and eagerly ran to meet her, hugging her like the old friend she surely was.

'How are you, my dear? You never come and see me these days,' Olivia smilingly complained. 'You really must. I miss not having young people around.'

'I'm a working girl now.'

'Of course you are.'

Olivia made polite enquiries about the new job at the mill. Family health and fortunes, Alena's father, even the weather were discussed in a general sort of way, but when Alena anxiously broached the subject of when exactly Rob was expected to arrive, the woman's face took on a faraway look.

'Oh, dear, didn't he tell you? We've decided – well – James thinks it best if he stays at school for this first holiday.'

'*Why?*' Sick disappointment swamped her.

'Because coming home so soon after he's started might unsettle him again.'

'But he's been away *months.*'

'I know.'

'He's been homesick, hasn't he? I knew he would be.'

Olivia nodded, uncomfortably avoiding the girl's intense gaze, only too aware that her own eyes were still puffy and red from the tears she herself had shed on hearing the news that Rob was not to be allowed home after all. 'Yes,' she admitted, in a bleak little voice. 'He has rather.'

But Alena was too concerned with her own disappointment to notice Olivia's. 'And you think keeping him away from home during the holidays will make him better?' There was angry disbelief in her voice that she failed entirely to suppress.

'James thinks it will. He is more knowledgeable about a boy's emotions than I am, I suppose.'

Alena managed, somehow, to bite back further protests, realising that she couldn't say anything more without sounding rude, or shamefully giving way to tears. To be fair, Olivia probably had no more say in the matter than she had. James Hollinthwaite was a selfish brute, everybody knew that. But somewhere behind her breastbone, a piercing pain told Alena that her heart was breaking.

They'd planned to meet again in their favourite place and talk about old times, might even have boiled a couple of eggs in onion skins and gone pace-egging, as they'd used to when they were children, just for laughs. Now all her carefully prepared plans had crumbled to dust.

How would she *bear* it?

'We're going to see him, of course. On Sunday, to take him out to tea,' Olivia eagerly assured her, and then wished she hadn't as she saw hope flare and instantly die in the bright young face. She would have taken the girl with them, of course she would. Only James wouldn't hear of it, so there was no point in asking. 'I'll give Rob your love, shall I?' And the young girl and the woman regarded each other with something very close to despair.

Then Alena turned on her heel and ran, crashing deep into the woods, as if by doing so, she would find Rob there waiting for her, as he always had been.

Chapter Seven

It was in late April that Dolly lost the baby. The child was born seven weeks premature with the cord tight about its neck. It lived barely ten minutes. Tom took one look at his tiny son and walked out of the house.

Alena found him sitting by the beck at Hollin Bridge, having desperately scoured the village for him. 'Leave him be,' Lizzie had told her, but she couldn't.

They sat in silence for some time watching a clutch of water-hens paddle about in the clear spring water, then Tom spoke in a low choking voice. 'I only married her because of the bairn. Now she's lost it. So it was all a waste of time. A bloody waste of time!' And her big nineteen-year-old brother burst into tears and cried like a baby on Alena's shoulder.

Dolly took two weeks off work and then came back, pale-faced and quieter than usual but otherwise recovered from her ordeal and perfectly well. The girls at the mill were sympathetic about her loss, assuring her that there was no reason why she shouldn't have any number of babies in the future. She was young and healthy, after all. It was simply bad luck. And she had that lovely young husband to console her.

'Yes,' Dolly agreed, not wishing to admit that the young husband in question was far from consoling. In fact, he could barely find it in his heart to remain in the same room as her for more than a minute at a time.

Most nights of the week he was to be found in the snug of The Golden Stag, not so much drinking as escaping from her. Or he'd go back to Birkwith Row and have supper with his family. She'd trapped him, he'd said, and now they were stuck with each other.

The Townsens seemed to think they were a race apart, altogether better than the likes of her. And Dolly decided she hated the whole bloody lot of them.

–

Rob told himself that the other boys were in established groups that had grown up over several years. Fitting in as a newcomer, so far into their school careers, was bound to be difficult both for them and for him. But even now, months later, he'd made few friends, and felt very much the odd one out.

He'd expected tricks to be played upon him, of course, and had been determined to take them all in good part, but what he hadn't been prepared for was the sheer vindictiveness of it all. He'd almost come to dread the arrival of letters, constantly worrying in case one from Alena should fall into the wrong hands. This fear so entirely ruined his pleasure in receiving them, that he began to write back less often. And he knew where to place the blame.

Colin Briggs – otherwise known as The Boss, a name he had devised for himself which meant that he had to be obeyed. He was the one that the other boys looked up to, the one to decide who was to be favoured with friendship, and who wasn't. He was Captain of the Lower School Cricket Team, Head Boy of the dorm, added to which his father made vast contributions every year to the school fund.

Briggs it was who encouraged the other boys in the dormitory to do the usual silly things like apple-pie beds and pillow bashing. Rob's natural tidiness seemed to irritate them and, following the success of the lost pillow incident other, more personal items such as shoes, socks or school tie started to go missing, which got him into yet more trouble with Matron.

Once the other boys learned that he didn't like, and couldn't play, rugby – that in fact Rob found team games of any kind to be anathema to him – his life was made a complete misery. He could never quite predict where the ball should go, and if he was unfortunate enough to catch it, would be flattened in seconds, kicked and butted black and blue by a mass of bodies, fervently wishing that he'd let it bounce past. He became convinced that he suffered harsher treatment than anyone else on the pitch, and took to avoiding being selected for a team by any means he could devise, while hating himself for the seeming cowardice. But the more he struggled to fit in, the more he was made to feel the odd one out.

Yet sport was apparently so important that it took place every afternoon between two o'clock and tea at four, after which came the final session of lessons which he welcomed almost with relief. He opted, whenever possible, for hurdles, athletics, or better still cross-country running, which he loved. But even this earned him more brickbats than accolades. It appeared that actually running on these cross-country outings was considered soft. The idea was to get well out of sight of the school and any masters, then smoke an illicit cigarette behind a tree. The fact that he didn't smoke, actually enjoyed running through the open countryside, and usually finished in the first half dozen, only proved that he was trying to suck up to the masters yet again.

The other boys seemed to resent his self-sufficiency, his quiet, thoughtful nature. Even his very real interest in nature and science became a subject of ridicule, and carefully collected specimens of fossils and stones, fir cones and feathers which he kept on his bedside locker, were broken or stolen.

Rob had simply committed the offence of being different.

He often thought longingly of those peaceful weeks in the forest, and missed Alena's cheerful chatter and bossy ways more than he would ever have imagined. There were moments when he'd consider running away, yet he knew that was no answer. It would solve nothing. Besides, he was determined to face up to his problems, finish his education and somehow learn to stand up to his father. He knew what he wanted to do with his life: he wanted to work in a forest, with trees. All he had to do was explain this and everything would be fine. Miles away from James Hollinthwaite's anger and power, such a decision seemed easy.

And some aspects of school life weren't bad. Under the skilled tuition of the masters, he'd discovered that he wasn't such a duffer as he'd thought. At first he'd spent hours longer than everyone else at prep, desperately trying to catch up. But slowly, bit by bit, the work began to make sense to him. Rob began to find the lessons interesting, the masters not in the least threatening and keen for him to learn. Once he'd got the hang of it, even mathematics was a revelation, a logical progression through a set of rules to arrive at an end result. The excitement of realising that he could actually remember and carry out these rules, and bring about the correct conclusion, excited him so much that he didn't care if it earned him yet more accusations of 'sucking up' to masters.

His marks improved steadily, for all they would never be high, except perhaps in science, which somehow made most sense to him. It was when he gained an A minus for a botany project on seed propagation, and was cited as an example to the whole class, that the bullying really began.

One night, as he prepared for bed as usual, there seemed to be a tension in the air, the kind of eerie silence that comes before a summer storm. Trying to ignore it, Rob pulled on his pyjamas and climbed into bed. Seconds later, the covers were yanked off and he found himself surrounded by a circle of scowling boys.

'Get up!'

'What?'

'It's time for your penance.'

'Don't talk rot.' Rob could feel his heartbeat quicken but had no intention of letting anyone guess as much. He glared from one to the other of them. 'John? David? What is this? What's going on?'

David, one of the few who had made any attempt at friendship, looked shamefaced and apologetic. 'Boss says you've overstepped the mark. Sorry.'

'What mark?' A movement near his locker caught his eye. 'What the hell are you doing? Leave that alone.'

Colin Briggs was pulling his schoolbooks out one by one, and as Rob leapt at him to grab them back, hands held him down, pinning him to the bed. Impotent with fury, he could do nothing but watch as Briggs tore out a page here, scattered a few ink blots there, bent corners and generally left his usually neat books looking as if a dog had chewed them up or walked all over them with ink-covered paws.

'When the science test comes up next week, make sure you fail it. I'm usually top, for your information. And I intend to stay there. Right, lads, let's go. Lesson over for tonight.'

The result of this 'lesson' earned Rob one hundred lines from the mathematics master, detention, a telling off, and a chunk of the Old Testament to learn by heart from others.

The science test, however, was perfectly straightforward and Rob sailed through it, beating Colin Briggs to first place by one mark. No other boy came anywhere near and he wondered if perhaps this was a deliberate strategy on their part.

A few nights later, they turned their attention upon him again.

On this occasion, Rob took the 'punishment' without a word of protest. There was little he could do to prevent it as he was held down by Briggs's henchmen while he did the punching, with a few kicks thrown in for good measure. The bruises were cleverly inflicted on ribs and flank, so that when Rob dressed the next morning, not a single mark showed. Over the next few days, so long as he gave no indication of the pain he felt as he moved, and made some excuse as to why he couldn't take part in the cross-country running for a day or two, no one was any the wiser.

But he swore never to let it happen again. His father might bully him. but he certainly didn't intend to allow anyone else to do so.

For his next homework he worked even harder and gained a straight A.

This time they brought a weapon. Rob blinked in disbelief as he stared at the riding crop held high in Colin Briggs's hand.

'You can't seriously mean to use that?'

Briggs laughed. 'Spare the rod and spoil the child, isn't that what they say? And we think you're in grave danger of being spoiled. Not a single master has thrashed you yet, so we thought we'd rectify that omission.' The other boys giggled nervously and Rob turned upon them, hot with anger, which at least helped to disguise his fear.

'And are you lot going to stand by and let him? What are you, bloody sheep? Would you jump off a cliff if he told you to? It'll be one of you next, if you let him get away with this.'

But he knew, even as he spoke, that so long as it wasn't one of them, they would do whatever Briggs instructed them to do. That was their means of self-protection. He was the misfit, not them.

They held him face down on the bed. Two boys pinioned his arms, another two held down his feet. In that moment it all became too much. The slights and pinpricks of boyish bullying had grown to represent all that was wrong with his life. Hadn't his father constantly told him he was a useless failure? Hadn't he strived to make a life for himself and Alena in the forest and failed even at that? And here was the proof of his inadequacies. Anyone could batter Rob Hollinthwaite, and he wouldn't say a word.

The first lash, artfully administered on top of his pyjama jacket, 'So as not to break your tender skin,' as Briggs calmly informed him. whipped every ounce of breath from his body.

Perhaps it was this that galvanised him into action: Briggs's laughter, or the fact that the shock of it caused the other boys momentarily to slacken their grip. But somehow Rob managed to free himself, snatched the crop from the other boy's hand and, snapping it in two, set about Briggs with his fists. It was as if he were pounding his own father for all his unfeeling harshness over the years, or back in the forest showing Frank Roscoe he could chop down a tree with a seven-pound axe. He punched and struck in a ceaseless rhythm of uncontrollable rage. How long he might have gone on in this rare gesture of defiance it was hard to say, but suddenly hands were grasping him, voices screaming for him to stop. Doors were banging, and then the crackling starch of Matron and her high-pitched cry of horror.

Both boys were taken to the sanatorium, but although there was the red stripe of a bruise across Rob's back, Briggs asserted it had been administered by one of the other boys, meant only as a lark or rag, in which he had taken no part at all. His face, on the other hand, was a sorry state indeed, with blood from his nose leaking all over his clean pyjamas, and so his explanation of the dispute was accepted.

Rob's parents were instructed to come and collect him from the school with all speed. He was to be suspended for three months for breach of discipline and lack of team commitment. He had, the headmaster stated, constantly let the dormitory down with his slipshod ways. Nor had he ever taken a full part in games. At the end of three months, he might, on receipt of a written apology, be considered for readmission.

James, however, decided that no son of his should carry such a black mark against his character and withdrew him the very next day. For once Rob warmed towards his father. Now all he could think of was that he could go home. Tomorrow, he might even have the chance to see Alena.

–

One morning a day or two later, Lizzie, coming out of Mrs Rigg's shop, almost ran into James Hollinthwaite. She'd dashed out to do a bit of shopping, leaving her next-door neighbour to keep an eye on Ray, though with luck she'd be back before he woke and missed her. He could be very difficult if he found her absent, as if she had nothing better to do than sit with him all day.

James asked after him, naturally wanting to know if he was showing any further signs of movement. Lizzie shook her head.

'I doubt he will now. He can move his left arm and one foot. That's about it.'

'I'm sorry, Lizzie.'

'Aye, so am I.' She bobbed her head, anxious to be gone, but he caught her arm, staying her.

'Does he talk much?'

'He shouts a lot,' she said, with a wry smile. 'Never was the patient sort, my Ray.'

'I mean about the accident, about how it happened?'

'No.'

'Has he said what we were arguing about?'

She looked at him, clear-eyed and uncondemning. 'Why should he? I know what it was about. It was about those daft bairns of ours running away. All because of some silly swim in the tarn with no clothes on. Nine days wonder, that's all it would've been, only they were too young to see it.' She made no mention of their running off into the forest because of James Hollinthwaite's decision to send his son away to school, on the grounds that it was really none of her business and a part of her agreed with him. It might do the lad good, instead of being mollycoddled at home.

'Yes, that was it,' he agreed. 'The swim. Lot of fuss about nothing.' There was a small awkward pause in which neither of them knew quite what to say next.

'Has the lad settled then?'

'Yes, eventually.' Another pause. 'Though that first school wasn't quite the right one for him. We're moving him to a new one.'

'Oh, I see.' Lizzie made a mental note to mention this fact to Alena. It didn't sound as if Rob had settled at all. And she'd want to know if he had moved. 'Anyroad, he'll be home for the summer holidays in no time, I dare say. Olivia will be looking forward to that.'

'He may stay at my sister's, in Edinburgh. For the sake of his education, you know, since it is such a fine city. We haven't quite decided.'

'I see,' Lizzie said again, and indeed she did, very plainly.

'And your own family?' he finally, and rather stiffly, enquired.

'Very well, thank you, but I must...'

'Of course.' James doffed his hat. 'Mustn't keep you. Give Ray my best regards.' And he turned and marched away, leaving Lizzie frowning after him.

Hard-hearted old devil, she thought. Did no one give a tinker's cuss for that poor lad, shifted from pillar to post? Why didn't Olivia put her foot down? Lizzie tried to imagine what it must be like being married to James Hollinthwaite and failed completely, inwardly admitting that nobody should have to endure such torture. But why had he stopped for a chat? What had it all been about? James Hollinthwaite certainly wasn't a man to waste time in conversation without trying to do some good to himself.

—

James was not a happy man. Nothing in his life was going quite as it should. He'd thought that sending Rob away to school would solve everything, but so far it had proved to be a complete failure. The boy was upstairs even now licking his wounds, and where James would send him next he hadn't the first idea.

'Don't unpack his trunk,' he'd instructed Olivia, who had immediately started fussing round her son, hugging and kissing the lad as if he were a hero.

'Can't he have a short holiday? Aren't you at least pleased to have him home for a while? Your own son,' she'd asked, taunting him in that way which always set his blood pressure rising.

'This isn't the time for holidays. He's in disgrace, and will do as he's told.'

It was all to do with some rag or other, which Robert hadn't coped with very well. James hadn't been given the full details, nor had he asked for them. Couldn't handle discipline, the headmaster had said, didn't fit in. James would like to have denied it, dismissed the matter as a load of nonsense and argued that the boy hadn't been given a proper chance to settle. Unfortunately, in his opinion, the boy had been too long tied to his mother's apron strings and it would take a major effort to put some real spunk into him. But, by gad, one way or another, he would do it.

No, nothing had gone quite right lately. And James seemed to be carrying the can for everything that went wrong. Even talking to Lizzie Townsen in the street filled him with guilt. But then he hadn't reckoned with that damned fight dragging open old wounds that he'd long since thought healed. Not that he considered himself responsible for Ray Townsen's condition. That was the man's own stupid fault. He'd started the fisticuffs in the first place, hadn't he? Thankfully, Lizzie didn't see anything untoward about their quarrel, so that was all right. Ray always did have an unreliable temper.

Business too was far from satisfactory. What with unemployment being the way it was, there was precious little spare money around for spending on fancy goods, or even on staples. And women's clothes had gone so short, they barely needed any fabric in them at all. All quite shocking, in James's opinion, from every point of view. Not least that such fashions badly affected the textile industry, which in turn meant they needed fewer bobbins. Add to that the rise of cotton imports from India, challenging their own home market, and the threat that Britain might soon come off the Gold Standard, and matters were dire. It wouldn't surprise him if there weren't a General Election soon; most certainly a financial crisis was in the offing, which meant interest rates, even taxes, might rise. He'd have to make sure his own interests were safeguarded. No doubt about that. No good standing by and letting things happen.

Which brought his mind back full circle to his errant son. If the boy thought he could slip back into his old layabout ways with that young lass, he'd another think coming. James set aside his account books for once, and spent two long hours on the telephone. By the end of it, he had secured a place for Rob in a school that might not have quite the reputation of the first, but had the advantage of being firmer on discipline. Which, apparently, was exactly what the boy needed.

When Alena got home from the mill that evening, Lizzie broke it to her as gently as she could that Rob was to move schools and it was unlikely that he would be home in the summer. Alena stared at her mother, stony-faced, for a long moment, then turning on her heel went at once to her room, where she remained with the door shut fast, not even coming down for supper.

But whatever Alena suffered in those bleak hours would have been a thousand times worse had she known that but a few hundred yards away Rob himself sat in abject misery with his family. They faced each other across the dining-room table in silent and grim sufferance. Olivia kept her eyes on her plate, casting only occasional anxious glances at each of them while Rob pushed his food about uneaten, gazing from time to time through the window, wishing he was as free as the wind that shook the treetops – as he knew his father would very much like to shake him.

'Eat up, lad. It's not the end of the world. There are other schools.'

He looked across at his father then, obstinacy flaring in his hazel eyes. 'I don't want to go to another school. I want to stay here, in Ellersgarth.'

James filled his mouth with partridge pie. 'Rubbish,' he said, spitting crumbs about the table. 'You're not fifteen yet. How many times must I say it – you'll not get to university if you don't have a proper education.'

'I don't want to go to university.'

'Aye, you do. Every young chap does. Wish I'd had the opportunity. I had to start work when I was twelve, nay eleven, working in the boys' home where I was brought up. How would you feel if I asked you to shovel cow muck from five in the morning, at eleven years of age? You don't know you're born, lad. You're lucky to have a home, not to mention a caring family.' Caring? Rob thought. Don't make me laugh. He'd heard these phrases repeated so often they no longer made any impression.

Obstinately he stated, 'I'd do it, if I could stay at home with my family,' glancing across at Olivia as he said this. But they both knew he had no wish to farm, or learn to run the bobbin mill, so the mockery in his father's eyes only diminished him further.

'Eat your supper. We can't afford to let good food go to waste because you're having a bit of a tantrum.'

'I'm not having a tantrum, I just want you to hear my opinion.'

James's face was growing red, eyes bulging as much as his full cheeks. 'Your opinion? What sort of *opinion* can a boy of your age have?'

Rob knew that his expression must be one of utter misery and he struggled to sound calm and adult, to organise the carefully planned phrases which threatened to scatter like stray leaves beneath the onslaught of his father's contempt. 'I have a brain which you're always telling me to use. Must you always reject me? Don't you care what I want to do with my own life?' He watched spellbound as a trickle of gravy ran from the corner of James's mouth.

'Don't talk daft.' The gravy splattered in tiny telling spots all over the damask tablecloth. 'You're too young to know what you want. You'll do as you're told and be grateful for it. Now let your food stop your insolent tongue. I've had enough of this.'

'But I won't…' He got no further as Olivia put out a hand to rest it gently on his, a look in her eyes that beseeched him to stop.

Rob could take no more. He staggered to his feet, all the carefully worded explanations of how he wanted to serve an apprenticeship in the forest, then perhaps go on to college and qualify as a forester, dissolving like mist in his head. He watched his father stuff yet more pastry into his mouth and chew on it with the calm assurance that he was in complete control and there was nothing anybody, certainly not his own son, or wife, could say or do to alter that fact.

Even so, Rob had one last valiant try. 'You can't make me do what you say,' he cried. 'Send me to a new school if you must, but you can't make me learn, or obey your every bloody command!' And he ran from the room to hide the shame of tears in the privacy of his room.

Later that night, when the house was in darkness, despite the howl of the wind in the eaves and the spatter of rain on the windowpanes, Rob crept from his warm bed still fully clothed and let himself quietly out of the kitchen door. It was a daunting walk through the eerie stillness of night, beneath the whispering blackness of the beech trees that lined the long drive, but his mind was made up. He didn't trust his father, and knew he must grab this opportunity while he could.

It took only a scattering of shingle against her windowpane to bring Alena from her bed. Rob saw the twitch of her curtains then in seconds she was beside him, her blue eyes glinting with excitement in the moonlight, the warmth of her body seeming to enfold him even though she did not touch him. Her hands thrust deep into her pockets and her voice quite matter-of-fact, she asked him how he was.

Only then did he find all the words he wanted to say to her had vanished from his head. They sat on the garden wall, kicking their heels and gazing at the moon sailing high above a bank of clouds as they struggled for explanations and descriptions of the difficulties in their new lives. Alena too seemed scarcely able to look him in the eye, let alone take part in her usual bold teasing.

She shied away from talking about her father's illness, knew better than to ask him questions about his own father. And all the gossip she'd so often longed to tell him, about Tom and Dolly, Sandra and her crush on Harry, Jim getting married and Kit's latest girlfriend whom he'd promised to take to Windermere and then forgotten and left standing in the rain, seemed suddenly small and insignificant. Not at all the sort of thing which would be of interest to this public schoolboy in smart grey trousers and blazer. He seemed more like a stranger to her and Alena could find no way to bridge the yawning gap between them. Only when he jumped down from the wall did the words burst from her.

'You'll come back for me one day, won't you?'

'Always.'

'You won't forget?'

'How could I forget? You make me who I am.'

It was enough and said everything that needed to be said between them. Which was just as well for the next morning, almost the instant dawn broke, Rob was called from his bed and taken by his father in the motor to the station at Lake Side, where he was packed on to a north-bound train with his trunk, a five-pound note, and instructions to make it work this time.

'I want no namby-pamby in this family,' James informed him as he slammed the carriage door shut. Then he walked from the platform without another word or a backward glance, failing entirely to see the stark hatred in his son's eyes, or the grim set of his young face.

-

James's fears were proved entirely correct and by August a coalition government had been formed. In September Britain was indeed forced off the Gold Standard, prices rose, a means test was introduced, and in October a hasty general election brought the Conservatives into power on a landslide. The only businesses that had more customers than they could cope with were the soup kitchens which sprang up the length and breadth of the land.

There were, however, new industries coming, of which James was only too aware. The electric grid was spreading fast; cinema, motor cars, and domestic products of all kinds coming to the fore. But what good would they do him? He knew nothing of such things.

He sat in his study for hours on end, reading his account books until he could have recited them like psalms. If the bobbin mill wasn't going to make his fortune, there must be some other way. What other skills did he have? What else did he own? A farm, too small to make anyone rich. A patch of woodland, and some land. How could he best use his resources?

It was exceedingly vexing to be disappointed in his business as well as in his son.

And then he remembered George Tyson. George had done very nicely for himself. Made a fortune in shares, on top of the one he already had. But then, James had no liquid capital to speak of. George had also become a local councillor, and was canny enough to keep his ear to the ground and have a good idea where the money was being made these days, no doubt about that. With that fact in mind, it might be worth telling Olivia to invite George over for another of her famous dinners. Aye, that might be the very thing.

Chapter Eight

1933

With her seventeenth birthday in sight, Alena decided that Hallowe'en mischief and climbing trees were no longer the kind of activities she should be interested in. She'd grown taller, her curves had filled out to a slender gracefulness, her face matured to a fine beauty, shedding some of its soft plumpness without losing any of its natural allure. Her eyes still glowed with a glorious brilliance, laughter never far away. And although she'd persuaded Lizzie to trim and bob her hair, it still reached to her shoulders and curled as haphazardly as ever. Alena liked the more grown-up style, and spent happy hours brushing and curling it.

She'd worked at Low Birk Mill for nearly three years now, and though she still constantly thought of Rob and his promise to return, deep down she no longer believed it. She found that it simply hurt too much to devote time and emotion to longing for a lost friendship.

Since that poignant moonlit night, Rob had never again returned to the valley. Even their correspondence had, if anything, grown more sparse and painfully polite. Sometimes she thought he only wrote to her out of duty, and he never said anything which remotely encouraged an exchange of confidences. He sent her cards on her birthday, of course, and at Christmas, but she had learned not to reveal quite so much of her feelings in her more frequent letters to him. What was the point, when it only left her weeping into a damp pillow all night?

She'd tried not to blame him. Yet a part of her railed and raged at his quiet acceptance of his lot, telling herself that if he really loved her, he would stand up to his father and insist on coming home, at least for a visit.

But in the end she'd been forced to accept that she must make a new life for herself, and in the years since their final parting, had found many friends amongst the girls in the mill.

She'd also learned that aching legs and back from the hours of standing and carrying swill-loads of bobbins, not to mention cold feet and chilblains, were all part of the job. But not for a minute would she have changed places with anyone. The girls were a cheery bunch, always ready with a joke and a friendly smile. Alena was as happy as she could be, in the circumstances.

Edith, who had been there the longest, would often be seen clutching her aching back and complaining, 'Eeh, I'm that worn out. I wish I were in heaven wi' t'door locked.' No one took this declaration very seriously.

Then there was Annie Cockcroft, giggly Deirdre Swainson, Mary-Jane Linklater, who suffered from rheumatism and chills on her chest, moaning Minnie Hodgson and her group of stalwarts, quiet pretty little Sandra, and Dolly. About a dozen girls altogether, including Alena herself. A small but merry band, as Edith was fond of saying.

The men weren't bad either; not that they ever offered to help the women lift a heavy swill, or to load a sack of finished bobbins into the wagon for them. Every man and woman for themselves, that was the unvarying rule, and one that Alena approved of. She certainly never asked for help.

'You've to pull your own weight here,' they'd shout, if anyone dared to complain.

'I'm not carrying you.' Or, 'Fetch it yourself, I'm not your donkey.'

Only the foreman, Stan Renshaw, was a bit of a trial. If he took a dislike to a girl, he could make life very difficult by leaving her on the same machine for months on end.

'He left me on the boring machine for nigh on two year,' Edith told her. 'And right boring it was too. When I asked for a change, he says, "All reet, you can change with Annie sitting next to you."' She shook her head in disgust. 'So I spent another two year doing the same soddin' job, only on a different machine. Bloody man!'

'Time he was put out to grass,' Minnie agreed, and a few days later, to everyone's astonishment, Stan Renshaw did indeed declare his intention to retire. The girls excitedly discussed who would take his place.

'I hope it isn't Alex,' Deirdre groaned.

'Or that awful Arthur who's always giving little homilies about the devil watching us while we work. Gives me the creeps!'

'Happen it'll be your Harry, Alena,' Sandra suggested.

'I very much doubt it.' Somehow Alena instinctively knew that for all he had little to do with the day-to-day running of his mill, James Hollinthwaite would never favour a member of the Townsen family with promotion. Though after that fight with her father, he surely, as her mother so often remarked, owed them one. Yet still Alena guessed it would not be forthcoming.

Harry, however, could talk of little else that evening as the family sat down to eat supper around the big kitchen table. Since two of her brothers, Tom and Jim, were now married men, there was more space and less laughter at the kitchen table these days. Lizzie watched with pleasure as her eldest son talked of his dreams.

'If I was made foreman, we'd be laughing. I'd get a good rise then, and Ma wouldn't have to worry ever again. Why not? I've worked in that mill for twelve years, since I was fourteen. I know what's what.'

Lizzie scooped out a ladleful of steaming stew that had as much mutton in it as her Christmas puddings had sixpences. 'Who decides? James Hollinthwaite, or Bill Lindale, his manager?'

'Both. Either. I don't know. Does it matter?'

Alena suggested that perhaps it might and was told, very firmly, that she knew nowt about owt, so would she for once keep her opinions to herself?

Lizzie frowned at her son as she filled his plate to overflowing with potatoes, onions and carrots swimming in gravy, searching out a few extra pieces of precious meat for him. 'Alena might have a point, things being the way they are between our two families. You're happen best out of it. Anyroad, they'll give it to one of the older men,' she warned.

'Who? Old Joe, who's sat on the same machine for thirty years? He couldn't organise a tea party, let alone a mill full of workers. Good relations between men and their employers is an important issue these days, Ma. And work is hard to come by so I mean to apply for the job, come what may.'

–

Sandra thumped at the dough, wryly admitting to herself that at least her anger would result in lighter bread.

It had been a perfectly simple request. Many of the girls had bicycles, certainly Alena had ridden one for years, so why shouldn't she? Walking the length of the village, and then out up that long winding lane every morning and evening, was wearing to say the least. And it added hours to her day, which she could ill afford. Sandra had rather hoped that her aunt would have taken to the idea, since she liked her to get home from the mill in good time to cook supper. But she realised now she should have known better than to ask.

'Do you think I'm made of money?' Aunt Elsie had predictably remarked. 'It would be a complete waste. You can't even ride a bike.'

'I could learn.'

'Want, want, want, that's all I hear from you these days. Haven't I given you enough over the years? Gave you a home and devoted my life to your care, since my poor darling

Georgie died. Oh, dear, and now you've brought on one of my headaches. I shall have to retire to my bed for the afternoon, and you must make supper. I'll have a little of that haddock, lightly poached in butter, dear. And do cut the bread thin for a change.'

Sandra sighed as she recalled the painful conversation, and slapped the dough some more. Aunt Elsie, a maiden lady with a strange musty smell about her and a small moustache, had been left with the task of raising Sandra from childhood after her father, Elsie's brother George, was killed on the Somme. Sandra's mother had not survived her birth. Even that had produced guilt in her as a child.

Sandra lived at Grove House, a tall Victorian terraced house, hemmed in by huge pieces of mahogany furniture, violent flock wallpaper, aspidistras, and almost permanently closed paper blinds because, as Aunt Elsie frequently commented: 'Curtains are such a fire hazard, dear, and the sun does dreadful damage to the carpets.'

But the effort of bringing up a lively young girl had, as her aunt constantly reminded her, taken its toll. Elsie Myers had been told by a doting mother when she was quite a young gel herself, that she was not strong and her heart might very well fail to sustain her into adulthood, and certainly not through the rigours of matrimony. Elsie had readily agreed. Nor did it sustain her through ordinary household chores, for all it had flouted her mother's dire prediction by carrying her through the long years since with remarkable tenacity.

It was Sandra who cleaned the house from top to toe every Saturday afternoon, since the mill closed early that day. Sundays she spent cooking the stringy meat her aunt wheedled out of the butcher at a knock-down price, baking a selection of breads and cakes to see them through the week, followed by an hour or two digging the garden and tending their small vegetable plot. Add to that all the numerous chores, errands and interactions necessitated by caring for an elderly aunt, due to the sad state of her health, and Sandra was usually quite glad to be back in the mill on Monday mornings. And usually she knew better than to complain, for that only resulted in one of Elsie's 'bad turns'. But today, for once, she'd made a stand.

'If I had a bike, I'd be able to cycle to the market in Kendal and pick up a few bargains every Saturday. There's a wonderful fish stall there, I believe.' It was all she could think of by way of persuasion. Her aunt was very partial to a nice bit of fish, and the prospect of enjoying the freedom of such outings was heady indeed to Sandra.

In truth, she had watched Harry on his bike, and dreamed of him noticing her at last if she bought one too. She saw them cycling alone together deep into the forests of Grizedale, picnicking by Lake Windermere or beneath a peaceful beech tree, where he would kiss her and say how he had waited all his life for a girl like her. Or he might treat her to tea and cakes in Hawkshead and she would say hang the expense and risk wearing a pair of those new Bear Brand stockings, so he could admire her legs as she poured his tea. Then they would ride home together, laughing at some remark she had made and Harry would beg to see her the following weekend, and then every single day as he couldn't bear to be parted from her.

A dream soon dashed.

'Don't be silly, dear. The fishmonger calls every Thursday with a freshly caught selection. What could be better than that? And no one in this village would dare overcharge me. I simply wouldn't have it.'

And the truth of both these statements was such that Sandra, stricken with the guilt her aunt always managed to produce in her, could only urge her to rest as long as she pleased, and agree to bring up supper on a tray, the moment she had cooked it.

'Thank you, dear. And do bake the bread light. Last week's quite gave me indigestion.'

Serves you right for eating so much of it, thought Sandra, thumping the dough some more. It would be light today, all right.

One of the best places to work was in the barrel house. The temperature was higher than in the rest of the mill because of its proximity to the boiler. Here the small bobbins were put in a barrel with shavings and bits of sandpaper. The door was shut and the barrel turned by the turbine. When they came out, the bobbins would be all smooth so that thread would not snag on them. It was a noisy job, since these small wooden reels made an unholy row racketing around the barrels, but a good place to be in winter, the only place where there wasn't ice inside the windows.

The larger bobbins, however, had to be sanded by hand, a task that required nimble fingers and expert timing. It was one morning a week or two later, shortly after her seventeenth birthday, that Alena was working on this job.

She wore gloves, to stop her fingers from getting skinned as she held the sandpaper to the bobbin spinning rapidly on its spindle, first the rough sandpaper, and then the fine. When the bobbin was smooth, Sandra would be ready to knock it off with the next. The machine was never stopped for this, so she too made very sure she kept her own fingers clear of the spinning spindle. It might take ten minutes to do a swill-load, which usually contained about a gross of bobbins, so they'd hope to do six gross an hour, thirty-six gross a day, at least, which left little time for conversation. Besides, the two girls had grown tired of attempting to communicate over the racket of the tumbling bobbins and had become almost mesmerised by the warmth in the barrel house, and the ceaseless rhythm of the spinning bobbins. So it came as a shock when a voice spoke close against Alena's ear.

'I can see you're an expert at this job.' It made her jump, and she turned round in a fury, ready to berate whatever fool had made her lose her rhythm and nearly skin her fingers as a result, to meet the grinning face of Mickey Roscoe. She could hardly believe her eyes.

Mickey Roscoe here, at the mill? The last time she had seen him was years ago in the forest, but she would have recognised him anywhere. Same black hair flattened to his round head with the same Brylcreem, rust brown eyes sparkling with laughter, and, if anything, even better looking than she remembered. He was certainly tidier in a spanking clean shirt, with a knotted silk scarf tucked in the neck, which made him look as if he should be attending Cartmel Races instead of a bobbin mill.

She must have said his name out loud, for he grinned that old quirky grin, making him look more like a wicked elf than ever with his winged brows and curling mouth. 'We'll talk later,' he mouthed, and strolled away with his powerful shoulders thrust back, rolling on the balls of his feet in that well-remembered gait, pleased with himself and the effect he'd produced.

Alena looked into Sandra's startled eyes and both girls erupted into a fit of giggles. 'Daft bugger!'

Later, when the day's shift was over and Alena stood buttoning up her coat, he walked right over to her, bold as brass, grasped her by the shoulders and kissed her right on the cheek. Blushing hotly, she could only gasp.

'Good to see you again. Alena. I'd forgotten this was the mill you worked at.' It was such a blatant lie, since she hadn't told him any such thing, or even where she lived, that had he not robbed her of breath and half her wits already, she certainly would have given him a piece of her mind on the matter. Instead, to cover her embarrassment, and acutely aware of the other's girls' curiosity, she tugged her red tam o'shanter firmly down over her hair, making unsuccessful attempts to tuck her wayward curls into it in preparation for the cycle ride home.

'You remember me well enough though, don't you?' he stated, with arrogant assurance. 'Knew you would, Alena. Are you glad to see me?'

She heard a snort of laughter from one of the girls behind her. Oh, lord, she thought, they'll never let me hear the last of this. 'It's certainly a surprise,' she managed, amazed at her own coolness. 'You're the last person I expected to see.'

He shrugged on his jacket, flicked on his neb cap, and then taking the bicycle from her and tucking her arm firmly in his, calmly informed her, 'I'll walk you home. Give us time to catch up on old times, eh?' And without waiting for her agreement, that was exactly what he did. Sandra and the other girls stood and watched them go, open-mouthed at his audacity.

Only Dolly managed to find her voice in that moment. 'If you can't have one man, you'll have any. Ain't that the way it goes, Alena Townsen?'

Her cheeks burned with embarrassment all the way home. But when she protested to Mickey about his behaviour, he only laughed.

'I reckon you and me'll become great friends, don't you? On Saturday we'll go for a drink, or to the pictures, or a walk in the woods if you've a mind. I'll pick you up at seven.'

Finally coming to her senses, Alena folded her arms, tapping one foot in indignation. 'Don't you think you should ask, and not tell a girl what she's doing?'

'Why?' The corners of his lips curled bewitchingly upwards. 'I thought you girls liked masterful men.' He looked upon her with benign tenderness, giving no hint of the steel tenacity of his resolve to have his way in this. Through the years, unbeknown to her, he'd waited for the right moment to move, much as a stalker might view his prey. The comparison made him smile. But then, as a natural hunter, didn't he possess the necessary patience?

He'd struck lucky by meeting up with Bill Lindale in the Stag. A few pints and a bit of necessary larding on Mickey's undoubted skills, and a job had been offered. He'd given up life in the forest, finding himself a poky room in the village and quarrelling with his father as a result, so he wasn't about to take no for an answer now, not after all his trouble.

'Women don't like to be bossed,' Alena was saying, sounding scandalised yet, he was sure, secretly delighted by his outrageous behaviour.

He grinned at her again. ''Course they do. Nothing pleases them more than a strong man. You'll come, won't you? You must know that there's hardly been a day when I haven't thought of you. I would've come sooner, only I made myself wait until you were all grown-up.' He touched her cheek with the blunt tip of one finger. 'It was worth the wait. You have grown quite beautiful, Alena.'

She knew she should refuse. Oh, she wanted to, she did really, but was entranced by the thought of his not forgetting her, of his waiting for her to grow up. Mickey Roscoe was far too full of himself for his own good, of course, but even as the refusal formed in her head, she was looking into his laughing eyes and thinking what fun he was. What a devil! And though she was sure he used his charm on all the girls, it was nonetheless endearing.

'Wasn't I good to you when you were in the forest?' he asked.

'Of course.'

If Rob had been here, or if she'd seen anything of him at all during these last years, then maybe she would have found it easier to refuse. But beyond their stilted and unsatisfactory correspondence, there'd been no contact between them of any kind. For all she knew, Rob had forgotten her. Anyone would think they'd never been friends at all. Every holiday she'd waited and hoped for him to visit, but he never had. If Robert Hollinthwaite couldn't be bothered to come and see her, even once, why should she make herself miserable for him?

She might still grieve for him deep down, perhaps always would, but Alena was young and lonely and bored. Christmas was coming, and standing in front of her was a good-looking bloke wanting to take her out. Why shouldn't she accept and have a bit of fun for a change? Not that she would have him think her cheap. Oh, dear me, no. She unfolded her arms and flicked back her bouncing curls.

'I'll think about it, and let you know before Saturday.' And with a lift of her chin she clicked open the small gate and marched up the path straight into the house without a backward glance. Mickey only smiled, for he knew he had won, and her back view was, if anything, even more delightful than her front.

–

The girls at the mill were agog to hear all about him.

'Where did you meet?'

'Bit pushy, isn't he?'

'By heck, what a nerve. Just went right up and kissed you, without a by your leave.'

'Cheeky bugger, I'd've slapped his bloody face.'

'No, you wouldn't, Minnie Hodgson. You'd've chucked your Percy out and welcomed him in with open arms.' And so the ribald banter continued.

Mickey, for all his cheek and flashy ways, had charm and good looks. He was, after all, the most eligible young man they had seen in a long time and proved to be popular with the other bobbin girls, even with the older women. He behaved like the perfect gentleman he certainly wasn't, and all Alena could do was laugh at his effrontery.

It was only to Sandra she told the full story. Their fingers busy, and without pausing in the production of the large hand-sanded bobbins, Alena told her friend over the noise of the rattling machinery how she'd come to meet Mickey Roscoe, and something of his grim-faced father. Sandra listened wide-eyed.

'And will you go out with him?'

'I don't know,' and then more defiantly, 'I very much doubt it. He really isn't my sort. Far too pushy.'

When Friday night came and everyone had collected their wages, looking forward to the weekend ahead, Mickey reminded Alena that he would call for her at seven the next night. And he did so right in front of everyone, as if making sure she had no way of retreat.

'By heck,' Edith said, half under her breath. 'He's a fast worker this one. He'll have her wed by Christmas.'

'And in the family way by New Year,' put in Dolly.

Perhaps it was this last comment which decided her. Offering him her warmest smile. Alena said, 'Yes, thank you, that would be lovely. All right if I bring Sandra along? Only she's my best friend. Never go anywhere without her.'

This was stretching the truth considerably; for all Sandra's doglike devotion, she was rarely allowed out from under her aunt's thumb. Alena, ignoring such niceties, felt somehow that she'd no wish to be left alone with Mickey Roscoe just yet, certainly not in the woods where she had walked with Rob. 'Perhaps you could bring one of your friends too? But not on Saturday. We'll meet you at the bottom of Lake Windermere by the steamer pier at two o'clock on Sunday. Sandra can come and have dinner with us first, then you can take us both for a lovely sail. That all right with you?' she said, addressing this last remark to her startled friend.

'Yes,' Sandra said, without a thought as to how she might achieve the freedom to enjoy this much longed-for treat, but her heart missed a beat at the prospect of seeing Harry in his own home at last.

'That's settled then,' said Alena, not even waiting for Mickey's approval.

Mickey was angry at this unexpected change in his plans, and the intrusion of a third party. He wasn't used to being told what to do by some slip of a girl, and wouldn't have taken it from any but this one. Then he looked at the mouse-like Sandra, decided she was no threat and was only too aware that he might not get another chance if he played it wrong this time. Consciously he unclenched his bunched fists, shrugged his shoulders and smilingly agreed with what good grace he could muster.

'Very well, but next time I choose,' he said lightly.

'If there *is* a next time.'

'Oh, there will be. You can count on that.'

'By heck, he's a right one, this one,' said Edith, much impressed by the little byplay she'd just witnessed. And Mickey did not disagree.

–

Sandra Myers was the kind of girl any mother would like her son to bring home. She was quiet, polite, had obvious good manners and a tendency towards shyness, so Lizzie made her most welcome.

All the family were squashed around the big wooden kitchen table, it being a Sunday tradition, except for Ray, who remained confined to the front parlour. And, as usual, they spent much of their time squabbling over who had the salt, more space than they were entitled to or their elbows on the table, which was strictly forbidden.

In all of this, their guest added little to the general buzz of conversation, beyond a very few essential details about her background and how her poor aunt suffered from a weak heart. Lizzie privately thought that Elsie Myers always sounded robust enough to her in her weekly ding-dong battles with the butcher over the price of his cuts. But it sounded a sad sort of upbringing for any young lass.

'She only let me come here today,' Sandra explained, 'on the strict understanding that she'd have to send for me if she had a bad turn. Though I've left her kipper ready.'

'A kipper? For her Sunday dinner?'

'That's all she says she's fit for, today.'

'I see,' Lizzie said. Playing the martyr and making the lass suffer, no doubt, for daring to step outside the front door of that mausoleum. Kippers for Sunday dinner, whatever next? My word, it was no wonder the girl looked so pale and thin, living with that old skinflint. She wore her mouse-brown hair in a short bob, which did nothing at all for her but the huge grey eyes, prim nose and small pointed chin all added up to a fragile prettiness. Slim as a colt, though not half so co-ordinated, she seemed all arms and legs with an anxious smile pinned to her face that spoke volumes about her eagerness to please.

By heck, Lizzie thought. One breath of wind, and she'd blow clean away.

She sat her next to Harry, at Alena's insistence, and from time to time noticed how the girl would lift expressive eyes from her plate to gaze up at him with what could only be described as spaniel-like devotion. Not a soul seated at that table missed the meaning of these glances, except perhaps the recipient himself, which unfortunately resulted in a good deal of covert hilarity. Alena was soon biting down hard on her lower lip. Kit, Jim and Tom exchanged many knowing winks which Lizzie, equally covertly, attempted to control. Jim's wife, Ruby, seated at the end of the table so she could keep an eye on her sleeping son, was bright-eyed with delight. And Dolly had her hand clapped over her mouth as if she might explode.

Not that Lizzie really minded, so long as the girl didn't notice. There was nothing she loved more than to have her family about her on a Sunday. Just like the old days it was, only she had even less control over their waywardness now than when they'd been small. The small terraced cottage shone with beeswax and loving care, a bright log fire burning and not a sign of clutter anywhere, despite the fact that five adults still lived in it. Ray had made many of the pieces of furniture that stood against her carefully papered walls, even the sycamore ladle she used to serve the soup. Being the corner house, it was larger than most in the row with three good bedrooms and even a wash basin upstairs, though the lavatory was still out the back. Bought by Ray soon after he came home from the war, she'd always considered herself lucky to be able to bring up her family here. What more could any woman ask for?

And they all looked so well, every one of them. Jim, of course, so full of himself since he'd become a father. Alena, getting over the moodiness she'd suffered when Rob had gone away to school. Tom, hopefully settling into life as a husband.

Even Dolly was mending, and though no one could call her an easy girl to get along with, she was at least learning to keep her caustic tongue a bit more in check these days. It was sad about the bairn she lost, but though there'd been no sign of another since, there was plenty of time to try again. She was a healthy enough young woman. Lizzie thought, watching her daughter-in-law tuck into the beef and Yorkshire on her plate. She certainly had a healthy appetite.

And if the food was simple, being a piece of brisket that barely stretched to feed the nine of them, never mind an extra mouth, at least there were plenty of vegetables, grown by Kit on their allotment out the back. Lizzie had encouraged him in this interest; would've liked him to do it full time in order to get him out of the dusty atmosphere of the mill which was so bad for his chest, if only they could afford it. Not that he ever listened to her advice. But even this beloved son looked well, and wasn't coughing so much. She still hoped that one day he'd find himself a nice lass and settle down too. As for Harry, well – Lizzie did a quick calculation of his and Sandra's ages; at twenty-six there must be a good eight years between them. What of it? It wasn't too great a difference, and he could do worse than little Sandra here.

Aye, she was fortunate indeed in her family.

The only sadness was that Ray, the man who had provided so well for them over the years, and been a good husband to her despite his volatile nature at times, was now deep in depression and could barely manage to feed himself. She'd have to go into the parlour shortly and give him his soup, which was all he ever seemed to want these days. But just for a few moments longer, she'd enjoy this lively family of hers.

Chapter Nine

Jim said, 'You must show Sandra your letter to the manager after dinner. The one asking to be considered as foreman.'

'Oh, I should like that,' she eagerly agreed. 'I'm sure if anyone deserves it, Harry, you do. You should mention how many times lately you've reached the bonus. He's sure to be impressed. You make far more bobbins a day than old Alex.'

Harry looked down upon her with new eyes. 'You're right. I never thought of mentioning that. Thanks, Sandra.' And Kit spluttered into his soup, earning himself another reproving glare from Lizzie.

''Course, I shouldn't make the letter sound too boastful,' Harry conceded.

'Why not?' Sandra quietly asked. 'It would only be the truth.' Dolly chose that moment to have a choking fit, needing to be patted on the back by Kit, her own husband apparently too occupied with wiping tears of laughter from his eyes.

Sandra looked about the table, glancing from one to the other of them with a puzzled frown creasing her brow. Could they, she wondered, with dawning horror, be making fun of her? Surely not? What had she said that was so funny?

She really liked Alena's family, and had adored the big, blond eldest son for years. She always made a point of saying hello to him at work, and had on two occasions managed to be invited by Alena for a cup of tea and a bit of crack after their shift. But she still rarely got more than a passing nod out of Harry for all her efforts. She'd patiently waited for the long-promised invitation to family dinner which seemed to have been forgotten, and would ever be grateful to Mickey Roscoe for making Alena remember. Now Harry had actually welcomed her advice, more than she could ever have hoped for, so Sandra had no wish to mess up her best opportunity to date by making silly remarks. She bit her lip and vowed not to say another word, in case it was the wrong one.

'Pay no attention to this lot,' Alena hurried in with excuses. 'Irreverent rogues, the lot of them.'

'She's right there,' agreed Lizzie. 'Can't bear to think one of their own might have some go about them.'

'No Townsen will ever be promoted if James Hollinthwaite has anything to say about the matter, which of course he does, being the owner,' Alena remarked.

Lizzie frowned. 'I think you're being a bit hard on him.'

'Huh, am I indeed?'

'But surely he can see that Harry would be ideal?' Sandra said, anxious to help and be accepted into the teasing warmth of this family, and was surprised by another spurt of suppressed laughter erupting around the table from everyone except, to be fair, Harry, Alena and her mother.

The moment of awkwardness was saved by a shout from the parlour, and Lizzie for once got thankfully to her feet. 'His Lordship wants his soup.'

'I'll go,' Alena offered, ready as always to save her mother from a heartbreaking and never-ending routine.

'No, you won't, lass. While I give him his soup, you lot get on with your dinner before it goes cold.' She wagged a finger at the gathered company. 'And Sandra is talking a lot of sense. Listen to the lass.' Having placed her own dinner over a pan of boiling water, and covered it with a plate, she half filled a bowl with soup and carried it away in the direction of the still bawling voice.

Later, Harry showed Sandra his carefully worded letter, and she made a few hesitant suggestions which he gratefully accepted. Then she sat by him while he wrote out a fair copy, put it in an envelope and set it on the mantelpiece ready to be delivered personally to the manager's office first thing Monday morning.

Harry could then optimistically hope for promotion, and Sandra that he would remember who helped him get it.

–

Alena felt oddly nervous as they stood on the Lake Side pier at two o'clock that afternoon. Both girls were warm and smart in woollen skirts and jolly sweaters, long scarves wound about their necks, and Alena was still tomboy enough to have one of Kit's old slouch hats pulled down over her curls, since it was a cool if bright autumn day.

Lake Windermere lay before them, a ten-and-a-half-mile sheet of water, the largest lake in England, and at its edge the steamer, patiently waiting for its next trip. Since it was a Sunday there were a few families with children on the pier, laughter and chatter all around. Alena was glad of that. She wasn't ready to spend time alone with this man, not yet. But most of the summer visitors had gone; only the stalwart few and the genuine lovers of the Lake District knew this was the best time to visit, when the colours in the surrounding hills and woodland glowed with molten gold, crimson and a rich bronze.

The girls, however, had stopped admiring the view and were thoroughly chilled by the time Mickey arrived, twenty minutes late. He brought no one with him for which Sandra, at least, was secretly relieved. But he was still agreeable to taking both girls out on the lake, if with less than the expected enthusiasm.

Blue skies and bright sunshine might beguile the unwary into peeling off extra layers, but the autumn breeze was brisk, the kind known as a lazy wind since it went through, rather than round you. Even the swans and coots scurried hither and thither, feathers ruffling as they were slapped by razor-sharp waves. Yet the clarity of the air and the brilliance of the surrounding mountains, made it hard not to take pleasure in the outing. And it felt good to be out in the fresh air after the confines of the dusty mill and overcrowded cottage.

The three of them sat close to the boiler for warmth, and whenever Alena pointed something out, such as a flock of geese heading south, a pair of mute swans, or even a particularly attractive shape of cloud, he listened with great interest to what she had to say. It was really most flattering.

She told him how Harry was putting himself forward for the job of foreman and Mickey listened keenly, saying it was the right thing to do.

'I'm sure he'll get it,' Sandra put in, loyalty shining in her pale eyes. 'Bill Lindale, the manager, likes him a lot.'

'That's always supposing that James Hollinthwaite doesn't squash the idea,' said Alena, and explained how he didn't much care for the Townsens.

Mickey expressed his sympathy. 'Why is that, I wonder? Seems a bit unfair.'

'Of course it's unfair. Something to do with the war, and not keeping Dad's job open for him. They've been in a state of feud ever since. It's ridiculous.' She was shaking her head in disgust, as if to imply despair of adults and their mysterious ways.

Lost for any other small talk, they sat in silence, enjoying the scenery and the very welcome mug of scalding hot tea made for them by the boatman from hot water boiled in the Windermere kettle that sat on top of the steam boiler for exactly that purpose. It was all so pleasant that when Mickey slipped one arm about her shoulders, Alena pretended not to notice. In a way she quite liked it. At least she imagined she must, else why would she allow it?

She slanted a sideways glance at him from under her lashes, and in that moment wished with all her heart that it were Rob sitting here, so close beside her. She could almost see him as she willed the face to be his, could trace the straight line of his nose, the curve of his jaw, the way he would turn and smile at her, making her heart do a little somersault of pleasure.

But the texture of the skin was rougher, the eyes darker than Rob's, the weight of the arm against her shoulder felt different from Rob's arm, even the smell of this man was wrong.

She closed her eyes for a moment, gently easing herself away from him. What was the point of torturing herself? This was not Rob. He was not here. The last she'd heard of him, he was at a school in Northumberland. At least the Hollinthwaites pandered to his love of hill and woodland, even if they refused to heed his desire to return home. She still saw Olivia from time to time, who told her he was settled now, and that James meant him to go on to university if his examination results were good. So perhaps he no longer wished to return. It was months since she'd had even a postcard from him. Every morning she hoped for a letter, but more often than not she was left with only an empty place in her heart. It seemed he'd finally forgotten her.

'Are you warm enough?'

She jumped guiltily as Mickey's soft voice brought her back from her reverie. His warm breath against her ear caused a shiver to trickle down her spine, though not in any unpleasant way, she noticed, or was that because she'd been thinking of Rob? The two faces fused in her mind and she grew confused. Whose company had she been enjoying? The reality or the dream?

'Yes, thank you.' She was surprised her voice sounded so cool and in control, and met his gaze unwaveringly. He was really quite an attractive young man, and most attentive. In that moment she very nearly, but not quite, wished that she hadn't brought Sandra along, that she could put Rob out of her mind for ever and end her pining. But to what purpose? Becoming Mickey Roscoe's girl? Heavens, no, surely not?

Feeling the familiar heat rise in her cheeks at this traitorous thought, she deliberately turned her gaze to the distant mountains and began to chatter about having walked up this one or that, yet afterwards couldn't remember a word she'd said.

Sandra didn't help, simply sat beside them, quieter than ever, apparently lost in thoughts of her own.

At the end of the sail, Mickey bought them tea and cakes at the Lake Side Hotel, which must have cost him a pretty penny, Alena decided, impressed despite herself by the white damask tablecloths, shining mahogany and the musical accompaniment as they tucked into tiny scones and Sandra poured tea from a silver pot in her dainty, ladylike way.

Afterwards he insisted on walking them both home. It was pleasant, idling along the lanes through the undulating countryside, the mountains already wearing their pale winter cloaks, though the first fall of snow had still to come. They took a shortcut through the forest when they reached the two-hundred-year-old avenue of beeches. It was as they neared Ellersgarth and turned the corner by Hollin Bridge that Alena spotted a figure beneath the limestone arch that had once been a route for pack ponies. Or rather two figures. The pair seemed locked together on a patch of grass left bare by summer-starved waters not yet augmented by winter floods.

'Don't look,' said Mickey, chuckling as he put a hand over her eyes, doing the same for Sandra. 'Not fit for a decent girl to see.'

Alena laughingly allowed him to shield her vision, though it was already too late. It had taken only a glimpse for her to see that one of the figures had been Danny Fielding, a good-looking ne'er-do-well her brothers kept well clear of. And the other was Dolly.

—

Low Birk Mill had never suffered a major calamity, not even a serious fire. It was a regular task for the men to damp down the sawdust and shavings every morning and night. But there were no safety guards on any of the machines so it was important not to lose concentration for a second. Small accidents, in particular lost fingers and damaged thumbs, were common in a bobbin mill. They always said you could recognise an old bobbin worker merely by looking at his hands. The task of foreman necessitated keeping production high and workers at their machines despite the hazards.

He needed to have a strong character, be able to manage people in a fair way and yet be disciplined. A good foreman, for instance, couldn't risk wasting valuable production time by allowing a machine to be stopped for adjustment or cleaning. This task, and the sharpening of tools, was normally done on a Saturday morning after the required number of bobbins had been produced for the week, and not a moment sooner. Since it took all of four hours to do it properly, it was virtually impossible to produce the required number of bobbins on the same day a machine was cleaned and stripped, so the canny wood turner made sure that he produced a few extra each day during the week and secreted these away for Saturday's batch. Otherwise he would have to come in on a Sunday to do the cleaning and tool-sharpening.

It was likewise the task of a canny foreman to notice that if so many extra bobbins could be produced each day, then the turner was reaching his bonus too easily and the figures to achieve it needed adjusting. But since it was such common practice, and a man needed his Sunday off, a more sympathetic foreman would have the sense to turn a blind eye.

Harry had always been good at reaching a bonus. Lizzie had become so used to the extra he brought in as a result of his hard work, that she came to think of it as part of his normal wage.

Mickey Roscoe, more concerned with his own advancement than Harry's, needing to impress Alena and understanding little of the Townsen family situation, made it his business 'accidentally' to bump into James Hollinthwaite one evening.

'Do I know you, boy?' he barked, irritated at having his way blocked by a mere mill worker yet seeing something vaguely familiar in the stocky figure. Mickey politely introduced himself, reminding James how his own father, Frank Roscoe, had once done him the favour of finding his missing son, and how he too was in a position to do him a similar service. And seeing the sharpening of interest in the man's narrowed eyes, calmly informed him how it was that some of the men were taking advantage of his generosity.

'Reaching the bonus is too easy for them, they can still make enough each day to store a few extra and save themselves a half day's work come Saturday,' Mickey explained to the glowering mill owner.

James Hollinthwaite knew little about bobbin production. He'd never shown more than a cursory interest in the day-to-day running of the mill. He didn't even wish to live in the mill-house that went with it, leaving that to his manager, Bill Lindale. All he wanted out of the mill were profits, and was infuriated by the very notion of being robbed of some of them by his own workers.

'Who are these men?'

Mickey slyly adopted an expression of fear. 'Nay, I can't name names, not me own work colleagues. Too risky. Who knows what they might do to me?' He half glanced over his shoulder, as if fearful he was at this moment being followed. 'I mean, it's not as if I had any right to watch them, particularly with me being a newcomer.' He let that thought sink in before blithely commenting, 'And what if I were wrong? Though I'm certain I'm not.'

'That's for me to find out. You did right to warn me, young man. I appreciate it.'

Mickey smirked with satisfaction. Oh, yes, this little encounter would do him a lot of good in the future, he was sure of it. 'It was just that one of them has put forward his name to be the new foreman, claiming he deserves the job because he reaches his bonus so often.' He put on an expression of outraged innocence. 'Well, that seemed like cheating to me, which I didn't think was quite right. I thought you'd want to know the truth about him.'

Hollinthwaite clearly remembered the letter from Harry which Bill Lindale had showed him, and his brow cleared. 'Ah, so that's the way of it. I should have known. Thank you, I shan't forget this.' As Mickey turned to go, he added, 'If you've ever anything more…' And their eyes met in perfect understanding.

—

Harry was not promoted to the job of foreman and was, in consequence, bitterly disappointed. Everyone in the mill had been certain he would get it. Even Bill Lindale, when he walked into the lathe shop to make the announcement, cast a sorrowful glance in his direction by way of apology.

Boring but safe Arthur Thistlethwaite was given the job instead.

'Well, he might save our souls,' Edith dryly remarked. 'But that's about all.'

'Which will do naught to put any more bread on our plates,' Minnie grimly agreed.

'Right, Arthur, what we need is better wages and shorter hours,' Annie Cockcroft informed him. A stocky, determined little person with a fiery temper, she was not a woman to be ignored.

'And a new lavatory,' Deirdre giggled to a chorus of approval. They all hated the three closets, only one of which was functional since the middle one hadn't worked for years and the end seat was covered with a board and piece of sacking for the girls to enjoy an illegal break if they wanted a cigarette. It had been known to hold as many as five girls, all gossiping and smoking in that one cubicle.

'Nay, that ain't my job,' he mourned. 'I'm on t'side of management noo.'

'Whoever told you that rubbish?' Edith scorned. 'And see if you can get Lizzie back. We need her to make our dinners. I'm fair sick o' sandwiches. She looked after us, Lizzie did. Put plasters on our cuts and injuries. We need her. She'll happen come back part-time, if she gets enough money to help pay someone to mind Ray.'

Alena didn't hear any of this for she was taking very little interest in the conversation at all. Her troubled eyes were fixed on Dolly, who was even now casting languishing glances in the direction of Danny Fielding. Had it really been her wild sister-in-law under the bridge? Up to God knew what with that no-good piece of work. How could she, when she was married to Tom? And what should Alena do about it?

'Got dust in your eye?' Dolly remarked, coming to stand by her while the list of tasks for the new foreman continued to lengthen, and the debate heated up.

Annoyed she'd been caught out in her curiosity, Alena hissed furiously, 'Are you quite mad? What do you think you're playing at?' At which Dolly pushed her face close up to Alena's and spat the words back at her.

'What am *I* playing at? I'm minding me own bloody business. Which is what you'd best do, if you know what's good for you.' Annie Cockcroft's booming voice rang out again. 'And ask for a new first aid box while you're at it, lad. We've naught left in this one bar an eye bath and a bit o'bandage and sticking plaster.' Poor Arthur began to look bemused by this growing list of requirements, quite changing his mind about his good fortune and wishing that someone else had got the foreman's job. It didn't seem to occur to him to exercise the new authority he'd been given and send them all back to their machines.

Mickey didn't join in the conversation either, half his attention being on Alena, the rest on Bill Lindale who remained in the lathe shop, frowning at the fracas resulting from this management decision which had been made in spite of his advice to the contrary. Mickey kept his head down, wanting Lindale to see how hard he was working, but he made sure he took in the gist of what was being said, in case it should come in useful later.

Out of the corner of his eye, he saw Alena grasp hold of her sister-in-law's arm and heard the fierce hiss of her voice. 'If you were to mend your ways, then maybe it would be easier for me to mind my own business.'

Now what, he wondered, was all that about?

If Alena's voice had been a touch overloud, it was not to be wondered at, she thought. She was so infuriated with Dolly. How could she be so cruel to poor Tom? First trapping him into marriage and then betraying him. What sort of wife would do such a thing? It made her heart ache to think how differently she would behave with Rob, given the chance. At least Sandra, she noticed with some satisfaction, was the first to offer sympathy to Harry.

'They'll realise their mistake,' Alena heard her say, as the girl reached out to touch his arm. 'They've picked the wrong man. You are by far the best man for the job.'

'In your opinion.'

'Of course.'

And Alena couldn't help feeling pleased to see the two smiling into each other's eyes. They'd been seen walking out together once or twice since the Sunday Sandra had helped him with the letter. And even though his application hadn't paid off, this new friendship might be doing them both a world of good. Alena knew that her friend was tired of living with her aunt, who apparently found the responsibility of bringing up her brother's daughter something of a chore. Most of all, she longed for someone to love and cherish her for her own sake, and not out of duty. A feeling Alena could sympathise with entirely. Didn't everyone long to be loved?

Where was Rob? Did he still love her? If so, why didn't he come home?

A question being asked at precisely that moment by his own mother.

–

Olivia sat at her dressing table, one hand clenched tightly around a silver hairbrush, the other clutching the nightgown to her throat.

'It's all right, don't fret,' her husband snarled. 'I'm not about to ravish you. If you won't come to me willingly, I'll certainly not make you. I came to enquire if you've done anything yet about my request for one of your dinner parties?'

'Yet another scheme to dupe some poor fool into doing you a favour? And using my services to achieve it, without a care as to what I really want from life.'

'What can you possibly want from life that I haven't generously provided?' he tetchily responded. 'You could try being equally generous with me.'

'Generous? *Generous!* Why should I be generous when you've robbed me of my precious child? Why won't you allow him home? I thought you loved him.'

'I do love him. He's my son.' James said it with the kind of possessiveness in his tone that he might use over a horse or piece of land.

'Well then.' Olivia felt quite light-headed with nervous energy, and what she recognised in herself as lonely despair. There were days when she could feel depression settle upon her like a suffocating shroud. She'd long since given up on her marriage, accepting its stultifying limits with dull resignation. She was expected to be grateful because James didn't have affairs or, if he did, with such supreme discretion she'd certainly detected no sign, apart from that little fling with a housekeeper years ago. Though even that hadn't lasted long, for he'd quickly come to regret it and dispensed with the woman's services without any prompting from his wife. But then James was quite unable to express love and tenderness, so perhaps the woman left of her own accord.

Olivia stared at her reflection in the mirror, mentally tracing the fine lines around the eyes and droop of discontentment at the corners of her mouth. Where had her youth gone? When had she grown older? Life is passing me by, she thought, fear joining the tumult of emotions surging inside her, together with a righteous anger.

She needed warmth in her life. Love. No one should be expected to live without it. And if her husband had none to give her, then where else could she find it but from her precious son? She wanted – *needed* – Rob. Why had he driven the boy away? Was James so blindly arrogant that he didn't realise they risked losing him entirely? Not once in all these years had the boy been allowed home on a proper visit. She said as much now. 'Your sister in Edinburgh sees more of him than I do, and you've only allowed me to visit the school twice. It won't do, James, it simply won't do.'

Recognising the rising tension in her voice, and the way she had become so agitated she was picking up brushes and perfume bottles and clattering them down again in that agitated manner he had come to detest, he attempted to defuse the situation. 'Very well. I'll buy you a train ticket tomorrow. You can go and visit the boy at school. Take him out to tea. Then go on and stay with my sister for a while in Edinburgh. Perhaps the change of scene will do you good. We can postpone the dinner until you get back.'

At which point he left the room and Olivia threw the silver brush at the closed door, for once entirely losing control.

Days later, she stood at Lake Side station, calm and almost regal in an emerald velvet travelling suit, very much the squire's lady. And if, with the matching hat which cost more than all of Birkwith Row spent on bread in a month, and a cluster of fashionable luggage at her feet, she appeared to have everything in the world that a woman could ask for, then that was only because no one could see into her heart. Except perhaps Frank Roscoe who, suddenly appearing from the huddle of station buildings by the lake, found some aspect of the forlorn figure made him catch his breath, not least the pale beautiful face.

Thanking his lucky stars that he had on his best blue serge suit and wore a tie today in place of his usual muffler, it being a Saturday and he on his way to a hound trail meeting, he politely doffed his neat checked cap and introduced himself.

'Of course, Mr Roscoe. You found our two naughty runaways.' Her beautiful eyes lit up and, without hesitation, she shook his blue-stained hand. 'I'm on my way to see Robert now as a matter of fact, at his school in Northumberland. And then I go on to visit my sister-in-law in Edinburgh, if she'll have me.' She gave a tinkling laugh, suddenly feeling delightfully light-hearted at the prospect of the next few weeks away, almost like a holiday.

Oh, and she was undeniably glad to be going! But what she wanted more than anything was to bring Rob home. Then why didn't she do that? Why didn't she disobey James's hard-hearted rules and fight for her son? Even as she considered the impossibility of this dream she felt the tears start, right there on the station platform. Utterly shaming. But then she became aware of Frank Roscoe watching her, not with criticism but kind concern, and dabbed at her eyes with a scented handker-chief.

'Mothers,' she laughed. 'So soft where their sons are concerned.'

'Indeed, I remember him as a son to be proud of. But what a coincidence! I'm heading over the border myself, by way of business.' Frank lied with such smoothness that he almost believed it himself. Olivia, looking into the velvet brown eyes in the weathered face, hadn't a single doubt.

'Oh, how splendid.' And as the train rushed into the small station, making everyone laugh as they tried to cover their ears against its whistle, whilst shielding their eyes and noses from the belching steam and smoke, Frank gathered up her smart luggage with careless ease and stowed it safely aboard, with himself beside her on the plush leather seat.

Chapter Ten

Sandra's mind was fully occupied as she worked on the blocking machine. She desperately prayed that his lack of promotion would not impede her growing friendship with Harry. But then she also prayed that something more than friendship would grow between them.

In the days following the appointment of the new foreman, the atmosphere at the mill became strained, as if no one quite knew what to expect or what was expected of them. Arthur did his best but often became confused and uncertain, left in no doubt that most of the workers would have preferred Harry in the job.

Sandra liked to think that he appreciated her support at this difficult time. He'd never yet asked her out, but then he understood her difficulties with Aunt Elsie. There were times when Sandra hated her aunt, which was really quite dreadful. Almost a sin. But was he serious, or simply enjoying her company as a friend when he walked her home a couple of evenings a week? She longed to know but didn't dare ask, for fear of scaring him off.

If only she had more confidence in herself, could dazzle him with her wit and charm and enchant him as Alena had plainly enchanted Mickey Roscoe. Not that her friend noticed or even seemed to care half the time, what effect she had on that young man.

Sandra struggled to keep her mind on her work. On this machine she had to push the tops of the thinner poles against a saw which sliced them into suitable lengths for bobbins, though still of differing diameters at this stage. These rough blocks would become the 24s, used for sewing and consequently very small. It was a monotonous job that grew ever more taxing as the hours slipped by and feet and fingers grew colder. The most difficult part was holding the final inches of pole when fingers were dangerously close to the saw which, on this machine, had to be constantly sharpened to be safe.

Driven by a fast pulley, there was no safety guard and it was impossible to lock off the pulley while the blade was sharpened as this would have wasted time, and time was money, so it was left to run loose. Sometimes everything went smoothly; at other times, like this morning, her fingers felt clumsy and nervous. The blade never seemed sharp enough, and the pulley did indeed seem to be playing fast and loose with her. For this reason, out of all the machines in the mill, Sandra hated this one the most.

It was very nearly twelve thirty and her thoughts were already straying to a half-hour break with her feet up, a mug of tea and the potted meat sandwiches she'd made for herself. The bread would not be fresh, and certainly there'd be more jelly than meat between the slices. Even so, as soon as the hooter sounded, she thankfully left the machine and hurried to the canteen.

Many of the girls were already seated at the trestle table with Lizzie once more installed in the kitchen, for at least a few hours each morning, from whence came the tantalising aroma of vegetable broth. This would also contain her famous suet dumplings, Sandra guessed, as light as they were warm and filling. Without hesitation she bought a dish of the broth with her last few pennies and ate the food with gratitude, feeling the welcome heat of it spread through her stomach, her fingers and toes tingle as life returned to them.

'You were ready for that,' Alena teased, laughing at the speed with which she'd cleaned her plate. Sandra told her just how cold it was in the outer workshop, how she hated the blocking machine, how she was all fingers and thumbs this morning.

'I can't seem to get it to run smoothly. Perhaps it's simply too difficult for me?'

'Don't run yourself down all the time, Sandra.'

'Why not? Doesn't everyone see me as stupid, a silly creature who is the butt of all their jokes?'

'No, of course not.' With shame Alena recalled her own laughter at the girl's doglike devotion to Harry and instantly offered, 'You can change with me, if you like?'

'Really? Oh, do you think Arthur would agree?'

Seeing him seated at a corner of the table, Alena said, 'Let's ask.'

He had no objection to the girls making the swap. Unlike his predecessor, so long as the work was done, he didn't much care who did it. So it was Alena who went back to the dreaded blocking machine when the half hour was up, and Sandra to one of the pressing machines, upon which Alena had been working.

Alena picked up the first pole, a good four feet long and little more than three inches in diameter, and while Sandra sat down with a sigh of relief, feeling much more able to manage, she started work with some trepidation. She really didn't like it any more than Sandra did, but had wanted to prove her support and friendship. She set the pulley to run fast and as she pushed in the first pole of wood towards the rotating blade, Sandra happily pulled down the lever on the pressing machine, which instantly slipped from her grasp. She laughed as, with the pressure released, it sprang back – whereupon a block of wood flew free and at 4,000 revs per minute, struck her right in the eye.

–

No one, not even Alena when she was informed of the accident, was allowed to go with Sandra to the local cottage hospital where she was taken, still unconscious, in Bill Lindale's old Ford motor.

To be one girl short was bad enough, he said, he certainly couldn't afford to have two off work.

Silent and grim-faced, the rest of the workers stayed at their machines, taking perhaps more care than usual.

At the end of the shift, Edith drew Alena to one side. 'I had a look at that lever on the pressing machine and, as I suspected, it were covered in fat. Someone meant her hands to slip.' The old woman sagely nodded her grey head. 'A common enough trick, often played on newcomers for all it's a dangerous one. But in this case, I don't reckon it were meant for poor Sandra at all. No one expected you to change machines at dinner time. I'd say it were meant for you, Alena. You should look to your back, lass. Someone's out to get you. And I reckon I know who it might be.'

'You've no need to tell me, Edith. I already know.'

Alena tackled Dolly on the subject at once, catching her before she had time to make her way home. 'Why? What's your game? I thought we agreed all the jokes were over.'

The mill yard was quickly emptying as workers turned up coat collars, tightened scarves, pulled out bicycles and hurried to avoid the first spatter of icy raindrops that was being flung at them in a funnel of wind from the hills that hung above the valley. Dolly, looking as if she'd like to hurry after them, did not offer her usual smirk. In fact, she appeared pale and shocked by the incident. 'Why blame me, Alena Townsen? Why would I hurt Sandra?'

'Because you meant it for me, not her. You didn't expect us to swap, did you? Nobody changed machines under Stan, but Arthur is new and a bit soft. And I know why you did it. It's because I saw you under the bridge with...'

'We were only talking,' Dolly interrupted, fearful suddenly that the very trees around them might have ears, and the information somehow reach Tom. 'It were just for a laugh, anyroad. What's wrong wi' a bit of a joke?'

Alena drew in her breath slowly, appalled by the direction her relationship with Dolly was taking and desperately determined to say nothing that would make matters worse, for Tom's sake at least. Yet her head was buzzing with words she'd like to use, given half a chance. 'Some joke! That "accident" was too dangerous to be funny. And you and me are family now, so why the campaign?'

Dolly's lip curled and, spinning on her heel, she flounced off along the path by the mill leat that led up to the sluice gate at High Birk Tarn, her feet slipping in the mud. It was in quite the opposite direction from both their homes but neither girl felt ready to face anyone else yet. The sound of the rushing water muffled their words, and the smell of sweet earth and damp moss, strong in their nostrils as they walked up through the woodland, perhaps calmed their tempers somewhat.

As Alena caught up with her, Dolly was saying, 'Me in the same family as you? That's a laugh. You'd never think so, the way you all go on. My God, I'd nearly given birth before any of you lot took enough notice of me to let us get wed. And you're the worst of them all, Alena Townsen, wrapped up in your own troubles. You and your precious Rob. As for that brother of yours, my bloody husband...'

Alena stopped, appalled by the expression of hatred on the other girl's face. 'Leave Tom out of this. This vendetta appears to be between you and me for some reason, though for the life of me I can't imagine what that is.'

Dolly's face had grown ugly and, cruelly mimicking Alena's voice, she repeated the words and tone of voice, 'You can't imagine why, can you not?' In that moment her jealousy of Alena, which she'd suffered from ever since they'd been at school together, became utterly unbearable. Even in the mill Alena had picked up skills quicker than any other newcomer Dolly could remember. She hadn't particularly wanted to hurt her, let alone Sandra, but certainly she'd meant to give her a bit of a fright. Why not? Had things too easy, that lass. It didn't seem fair that the girl should have so much, and Dolly so little. Alena Townsen had looks, charm, brains, could tie you in knots with her clever arguments, and had a family who adored her. Tom, for one, never stopped comparing his wife with his wonderful sister.

Dolly had thought she'd fallen in clover catching Tom Townsen and marrying into a proper family, but then she'd lost the one thing that had held him to her. He barely spoke a word to her these days, and kept what felt like a clear two feet between them in bed. He'd made it plain that if he could find anywhere else to sleep, he would do so. Selfish, like the whole bloody family. She'd tried respectability and it hadn't worked; now she'd look elsewhere for comfort. But she wouldn't have it that the failure of the marriage was her fault. She was the victim in all of this, she'd convinced herself of that fact long since.

'You don't think I have a fair grievance?' Dolly stabbed a chubby finger into Alena's chest. 'I'll tell you summat. A woman's wedding should be the happiest day in all her bloomin' life. Not some hole-in-a-corner affair with no guests and not even a plate of pie and chips at the pub to celebrate.'

Alena wiped the rain from her face as she mustered all her strained patience. 'In case it escaped your notice, my father was very seriously injured and had been at death's door for months then. None of us felt quite in the mood for a wedding celebration.'

Dolly's eyes glittered. 'And whose fault was that, I wonder? Not mine. *I* wasn't the one who ran away and caused his accident, now was I?'

Alena reeled for, in a way, Dolly was right. She *was* to blame for her father's state. If she hadn't persuaded Rob to run away, if she hadn't persuaded him to go swimming in the tarn on his birthday, then Ray would never have thought to go looking for her by it. There wouldn't have been a fight between their two fathers, and Ray wouldn't have been half drowned as a result.

'Even then I had to keep bloody working till I dropped it.' Dolly's voice was rising over the drumming of raindrops as she relived past grievances. 'A woman should have her first baby safely, not delivered by some old hag of a neighbour who hasn't the first idea what she's doing.' She could still see the look of satisfaction on Betty Thoms's face when the child was found to be dead, as if it were some kind of twisted justice. 'Not one of you Townsens gave a damn whether the bairn lived or died.' She slapped at a nearby branch, causing a shower of rain to soak them both.

'Oh, that's not true, Dolly. It wasn't our fault you lost the baby. What's got into you? It was desperately sad, but just one of those things. A terrible accident.'

'One of those things?' Dolly's lip curled. 'Oh, aye, and so was that accident Sandra had today.'

'I don't think so. For goodness' sake, she might lose an eye!'

'What is it you want, for me to apologise?'

'It'd be a start. Listen, Dolly…'

'No, you listen to me for once.' Again the finger stabbed Alena's chest. 'If your family had given me a bit of money, I could've stopped off work and looked after meself proper. Then happen I wouldn't've lost me baby.'

There was petulance in the voice, and bitter resentment, but no sign of real anguish. Not even a single tear for the lost child, nor any sign of regret for poor Sandra, both of whom were surely the innocent victims in all of this. Alena felt a surge of sympathy for Tom in that moment, and sincerely wished that he'd never married the silly girl, yet managed against all the odds not to say so. She must make allowances for Dolly's loss. Everyone grieved in a different way. The rain was soaking through her coat now and she shivered, rubbing her arms and shoulders for warmth. Fighting words roared in her head but losing her temper wouldn't help either of them one bit. Again she drew in a deep, calming breath and, for Lizzie's sake, attempted to build bridges.

'I can understand how awful it must have been for you to lose the baby, particularly since it was your first, even so…'

143

'*He*, not it. He was my *son*, remember.'

Alena felt worse than ever. 'And Tom's, I know. But we didn't have any money to give you, I'm afraid. We were all sorry though, really we were. Now we must hope that Sandra makes a full recovery.'

'You'll blame me if she doesn't.'

Alena's sigh sounded as weary as she felt. 'No, Dolly, I won't blame you, and Sandra won't hear of your part in this from me. But think before you act in future, and get rid of that chip on your shoulder.'

With a toss of her head, Dolly strolled back down the path with an air of unconcern. 'I can't stay here gossiping with you all day. I have a husband to feed. Trouble with you, Alena Townsen, is you look down on me, allus have done, because I'm a bastard wi'out a dad.'

'Oh, Dolly, that's not true.'

'Aye, it is. And my bairn too might have been a bastard, had Tom not done the decent thing and it'd lived, poor mite. Everyone hates me for losing it.'

'No one hates you.'

'Tom does.' And something about the bleakness of Dolly's expression, and the painful quaver in her voice, made Alena feel a rush of pity for the girl, despite everything. Whatever was wrong had more to do with Dolly and Tom than herself and Sandra. He blamed his wife for trapping him into marriage; she was trying to cure her grief by seeing other men, perhaps in the hope of making him jealous. But Alena knew she could do nothing to help. Marriage was a private affair and so, for the sake of family harmony, she pressed her lips together, resolving that she wouldn't be the one to make further trouble between husband and wife.

'I won't say anything to him, about what I saw the other day.'

'There's naught to tell.'

'Let's hope so.'

For a long moment Dolly fixed Alena with a glare so cold and hard, it made her shiver. Then it was as if a dam had burst.

Her knees seemed to give way and she sank down into the wet grass, tears pouring down her cheeks together with the rain, sobbing about how she'd never meant to hurt Sandra, how nobody cared about her. How lonely she was, how miserable, and how Tom ignored her.

'Oh, Dolly,' Alena said, putting her arms about her. 'What are we to do with you?'

Sandra was lucky and did not lose the eye but, damaged beyond repair, the sight in it was quite gone. From now on, her life would never be the same again. Aunt Elsie, for one, was far from pleased.

'Just when you were old enough to be of some use, you go and do this!' As if the accident had been deliberate.

The message from James Hollinthwaite was even worse. He considered her virtually useless in the bobbin mill. He was not prepared to take back a half-blind worker, nor offer any compensation for the loss of employment over an incident that was not his fault. Sandra's wages to date were delivered to her aunt's door, which was, in his opinion, the extent of his responsibility in the matter. Unfortunate for the girl, no doubt about that, but also an inconvenience to him. He now had the task of finding a replacement, a young school leaver no doubt, who would not work at Sandra's capacity for some months. Exceedingly irritating.

Fortunately other aspects of James's life had taken a turn for the better. George Tyson had given him some valuable information on how to make real money out of his land by growing conifer crops. The government, it seemed, was paying good prices for such timber in order to replenish the nation's stocks in case of war. James did not believe war would ever come again, but was himself already in possession of a sizeable larch plantation which would bring in a healthy sum, and could easily plant more.

He set in motion enquiries over the possible purchase of other parcels of land in various parts of the Lake District. A man couldn't have too much land, and he knew now what he could do with it. Besides which, he'd been reliably informed that the Forestry Commission were buying up all they could find. Of course he had known that they first acquired land for forestry back in 1919 with Whinlatter Pass; now it seemed they were after more. And anything that was good enough for the Forestry Commission, was certainly good enough for him.

Olivia too was in a much sunnier mood. Her trip to Edinburgh had done her good and she had returned looking almost as she used to when she was young, all bright-eyed and smiling, ready to forget their differences. The relief was substantial. He loathed her depressions and sulks. And the last thing he needed at this delicate juncture was a bothersome wife making his life difficult.

She had taken up walking, good healthy exercise which brought the roses back to her cheeks, and was even taking an interest in her garden and events in the village again. If she continued in this vein, James might permit her to have the boy home for a few weeks this summer. So long as Robert promised to behave. Though he doubted he need have any more fears about his friendship with the Townsen girl.

According to Mickey Roscoe, who had proved so useful that James took care to speak with him on a regular basis, Alena was now walking out with him. Mickey expected them to wed before too long. James did not much care for the young man, but what concern was it of his whom the chit married, so long as she kept away from Robert? And it would admittedly be pleasant to have his son home on a visit. James puffed out his chest, rubbing his hands together in self-congratulatory style. Everything was working out exceedingly well, and their differences were perhaps not insurmountable after all. The boy had always declared an interest in trees. This new forestry project might be the very thing to bring him to heel.

Mickey had lied about his success with Alena. Apart from ordinary day-to-day contact at the mill, and walking her home occasionally after work, he saw frustratingly little of her. A state of affairs he believed he could change, given the right mix of patience and manipulation.

For her part, Alena was more concerned with helping Sandra come to terms with her new situation. The two girls spent hours together, Alena patiently nursing her through the pain of debilitating headaches, helping her get used to the unsightly eyepatch, and consoling her over the loss of her job. She was always ready to listen to Sandra's fears and help her relearn actions she'd performed all her life without a second's thought.

'Everything's in the wrong place. I try to put a cup on a table, miss it entirely and it smashes to the floor.'

'Give yourself time, you'll adjust.'

'And I can't find work anywhere. Aunt Elsie says she can't afford to keep me for nothing. Oh, Alena, what am I going to do?' Then she would weep and anger would burn deep within Alena at the way Dolly's wildness had brought about this terrible state of affairs.

On one of the rare occasions brother and sister were alone, Alena broke her own rule and tackled Tom on the subject of his marriage. 'I know it's none of my business but you and Dolly – are things any better between you?'

He looked at her for a long moment. 'You're right, it's none of your business.'

She did not mention it again, nor did she mention seeing his wife in close contact with another man, reminding herself to keep her nose out of other folk's affairs. It was far too dangerous. Except, that is, in one respect.

Alena and Edith mutually agreed that no good would come of Sandra's learning it had not been an accident.

'It'll be hard enough for the poor lass to cope, without having that burden to bear as well.'

147

Which seemed to be true since the hardest part for Sandra lay in picking up the threads of her life again and overcoming a whole new set of insecurities. Although Harry was anxious, even eager, to continue his friendship with her, she perversely refused to have anything more to do with him. 'He feels sorry for me, Alena. I know he kindly visited me in hospital, but I can't bear to see his pity, or to have him saddled with a useless woman like me. What if I were to lose the sight in my other eye? I'd be blind then, wouldn't I?'

'You aren't going to lose the sight in your other eye. It was a terrible accident that you lost the sight in one, but the other is fine and will remain so. You have to tell yourself that it might have been worse. You could have been killed, Sandra. Don't you realise that? And Harry doesn't feel sorry for you, no more than anyone else anyway, and he really likes you, honestly he does.'

But Sandra would only shake her head and the moment she heard his step at the front door, would rush out of the back, leaving Alena to make excuses for her.

Such time as Alena didn't spend with Sandra, was devoted to helping her mother. Now that Lizzie was back at work, for all it was only part-time and she was glad to have it, she seemed to compensate for leaving her husband to a neighbour's care in the morning by doing more and more for him in the afternoon. As a result she soon became overtired, and it seemed even more important that Alena should share the load and help care for her father.

–

Ray was not at all interested in food these days so it was a slow business, rather like feeding a child. Shovelling in a spoonful, scraping the dribbles off his whiskered chin and waiting while he masticated it. Not a pleasant occupation and Alena felt guilty that her one desire was to get the task over with as quickly as possible. Her days at the mill were like a sanctuary to her now, not only away from the guilt of Sandra's 'accident' and a handicap which should by rights have been her own, but also far from the smell of her father's sickness.

This morning, as she offered up the next mouthful, he grabbed the spoon with a grip that was astonishingly strong, as if all the energy of his once fit and now wasted body was centred in that single limb.

'You're a good girl.'

'Don't talk, Dad. You have to eat.'

'Be a good lass to your ma – when I'm gone.'

He often talked in this way, all maudlin and sentimental. Alena sighed, taking no more notice of it this morning than any other. 'I will. Dad, don't worry. Come on, eat up. The porridge is good and hot with a bit of salt, just how you like it.'

He was still nodding, as if satisfied he had solved a great problem. His mouth twisted as he spoke, the words often coming out all funny and mumbling, sometimes back to front. At other times, like today, he was surprisingly lucid. Either way, Alena had to lean close, not always sure that she had heard correctly. So it was now, with his next words.

'She had to fetch thoo hersel, tha knows.'

While he paused for breath, Alena patiently scooped up the last dribble. 'What did you say, Dad? Do you mean Ma had me on her own? Is that it? She never told me.'

'Nobody wanted thee, a puny wee bairn. Not me, not anyone. 'Cept Lizzie. She allus wanted a li'le girl, as a change from all them girt lads, she said.'

Again an achingly long pause after this major effort while he drew a long rasping breath followed by a coughing fit. Alena sat waiting with the spoon hanging in her hand, porridge dripping from the end of it, as she tried to take in exactly what her father was saying.

'When I got back from t'war, I had to mek sure.'

'Make sure of what?' That he truly didn't want her? What was he talking about? *Nobody wanted thee, a puny wee bairn.* Oh, dear God, what a thing to say! Except for her mother. Her mother had longed for a girl and, as Alena already knew full well, Lizzie had always loved her. If anything, the two of them had grown closer in recent years. Her mother had patiently listened to her worries and fears over losing Rob, showing every sign of understanding. There had been many lonely nights when Alena was sure she couldn't have coped nearly as well as she had, without her lovely ma.

But Alena was less sure of her father, for they'd never been close. Now she could see why. *Not me, not anyone.*

She swallowed the lump that had come into her throat. To hear from his own lips that he had never wanted her, perhaps had never loved her, was almost more than she could bear. She could feel her heart pounding and a dizziness creep in so that she felt as if she were about to faint.

'Look what thanks I got,' he continued, glaring at her in his old way for a moment before the blankness came again into his eyes. Then, energy spent, eyes closed, his mouth drooped open and there came the familiar, sonorous sounds of his snores.

–

Lizzie stood at the sink, washing up the breakfast dishes. She was in a hurry, her mind busily planning what she could make for the mill workers from the few ingredients she had in her store. It was a bitter spring day with a cold wind rushing up the valley so they'd need summat warming, as long as it was cheap.

Despite the uncertainty of the weather, she'd walked as usual yesterday afternoon as far as High Birk Tarn, looking out over the misted tops of Coniston Old Man and Dunnerdale. Then back through the coppice, seeing the first spikes of the short-stemmed wild daffodils sprouting beneath the shelter of the huge trees. In a few weeks would follow a haze of bluebells, and in the meadows a flurry of blossom to herald the promise of another summer. Lizzie sighed, recalling days when she'd had time to linger on her walk, or share it with Ray, his arm clasped firmly about her waist, telling her how lovely she was, how she was the only girl for him. Now he lay in bed a broken man, and she spent the time wishing for a bit of meat to liven up the potato pie she could make for the mill workers. But he'd been a fine man once, that he had. A loving man. And she chuckled at sweet memories flooding back even as her hands scrubbed the porridge pan.

Alena burst into kitchen, interrupting her thoughts, and though she saw the smile on her mother's face, wasted no time wondering at it.

'Dad's just told me that he never wanted me,' she announced, dropping the dish and spoon on the draining board with a clatter.

'Oh, God. What has he been saying now?' Lizzie said, with half an eye worriedly calculating the small amount of porridge her husband had eaten.

'Enough. No wonder we never got on. He never really loved me at all, did he?' Alena couldn't disguise the hard edge to her voice.

Lizzie looked upon her daughter with anguished eyes. 'Don't be silly. He's ill. He doesn't know what he's saying half the time.'

'He knew very well. See if I care,' she said, tossing her copper curls and making them bounce more wildly than ever. But when, two days later, Ray was found to have died in his sleep, it was Alena who cried, not Lizzie.

Chapter Eleven

Afterwards Alena could remember little of her father's funeral.

The Townsen family standing together in the churchyard; all four brothers, two daughters-in-law, one child and Lizzie and herself, not forgetting a collection of aunts, uncles and cousins who hadn't set foot in the house since Ray had been struck down. Now they all gathered, apparently united in their grief but showing nothing of their feelings to any of the curious onlookers who had come, some to pay their last respects to Ray as a friend, others for the spectacle, or because it was expected of them as neighbours.

Sandra was standing by Harry's side, her concern for him overcoming her own sensitivities at this time. He seemed pleased to have her there, for he had her hand firmly grasped in his own and didn't look as if he meant ever to let it go. For that, at least, Alena felt gratitude and happiness for her friend.

On her own behalf, she felt nothing but anger. All her life she had striven to gain her father's love, even some small show of interest. In these last years, while he'd been ill, she'd fooled herself into thinking that he appreciated her care. But in the end he'd rejected her, as she should have known he would.

Alena was surprised to see James Hollinthwaite present at the little service, and even more surprised that her mother should go right up to him to thank him for coming. She could see how he patted Ma's hand and offered her his handkerchief when she looked upset.

Mickey was there too and afterwards, when all the relatives had eaten Ma's larder bare but seemed too well settled in her front parlour to consider leaving, Alena had been glad of his invitation to go for a walk.

He was calm, quiet and kind to her on that sad occasion, and on all their other walks thereafter, letting her talk without interruption, asking no questions, never intruding on her grief. And he made no attempt to touch her, so Alena's gratitude and respect for him grew.

Perhaps, in the days and weeks following, it was to prove that life was still strong in her that she welcomed his attentions, as well as in a kind of rebellion against the new and terrible knowledge that her father had never loved her. However many times Lizzie denied it, claiming that she must have misunderstood, Alena believed not only that Ray had never loved her, but that he had despised her.

This would explain a great deal. In addition to being hard and distant, he'd often struck her mother if she'd taken Alena's side in a quarrel, so Ma's sufferings too should be laid at her door. The misery of this new-found knowledge brought a torrent of guilt and confusion, and with it the realisation that she couldn't even decide whether she had ever loved him. Throughout her life, despite his bullying, Alena had ached for Ray to show some sign of affection and offer her the chance to respond. But he never had, and now she was simply glad he could no longer hurt her.

She took to going out every night. She pinned her hair into flirtatious curls, visited Ambleside and spent more than she could afford on a new dress and shoes with a higher heel than she was used to wearing. She even bought lipstick, and a powder compact with loose ivory powder inside. It made her feel very grown-up to dab it on her nose with a powder puff dampened in cold water. As if she were a woman instead of a young girl, in charge of her own destiny at last.

Her mother called her fast. 'Where is it you go every night?'

'Where I please.'

'Oh. Alena, don't do this to yourself.' Lizzie was watching as she applied a thick layer of scarlet lipstick to the cupid's bow of her mouth. 'This isn't about your father, is it? Of course Ray loved you. He may not have wanted a girl at first, as I always did, but he was never sorry we got you.'

'He didn't show it.'

'That was just his way. He always liked to talk tough, and he hated to show any sign of emotion. He was the same with the boys, but inside he was soft as butter.' She took the brush from her daughter's hand and began to coil the copper curls, feeling them spring back with a life of their own as she tried to pin them in place. 'It's true he was a bitter man, bitter over losing that good job he once had with the Hollinthwaites despite... despite fighting in the war and everything. But he loved all his children, you included. Never think different.'

But Alena did think different, very different, basing this new knowledge not only on memories of her cold, impatient father, but on Ray's own words as he lay dying. She took the brush from Lizzie with a gesture of impatience, and finished the job herself. 'A man doesn't tell lies on his deathbed,' she said, closer to tears than she was prepared to admit.

Lizzie gazed upon her daughter in exasperation, yet with deep sadness in her heart. 'I wish I could say something to put it right,' she said, knowing that if she said the wrong thing, she might only make matters worse.

'Well, you can't.' Alena was dabbing far too much powder on to cheeks and nose, so that she looked rather like a child who has been in the flour bag. Keenly aware of waves of disapproval emanating from Lizzie, she compounded the felony by applying a dark pencil to her eyebrows. 'Don't wait up for me. Mickey's bought a second-hand Baby Austin and he's taking me to the pictures. There's a new Fred Astaire movie on at the Royalty.'

'Do as you like then. I'll not stop you. But plastering make-up on your face, and behaving like a cheap trollop won't solve anything, Alena Townsen, and you know it.'

Alena's blue eyes glittered. 'What have I got to lose?' She could feel the sting of tears, but not for a moment would her pride allow them to fall, so she cultivated anger in their place. 'So far as I know, you might all feel the same way. Perhaps none of you ever really cared a jot about me?'

'Oh, Alena.'

But she was too far gone in her own anguish to pay any heed to her mother's despair. 'No wonder I always felt like the odd one out. Maybe it wasn't because I was the only girl at all. Maybe I was just unwanted. A mistake you all wished hadn't happened.' Through the wave of pain in her head she heard Lizzie gasp, but in her pent-up state all she could do was stalk from the room, head held high, slamming the door so hard, she didn't even hear her mother's voice calling after her.

'I always loved you. I loved you when I first clapped eyes on you and I've never regretted fighting to keep you, not once, not even when others said you'd've been better off born dead.'

Perhaps, Lizzie thought afterwards, that was just as well.

—

It was the first week in July that Rob came home. The heat was oppressive, the sun burning hot, the sky so blue and clear you could barely see the far mountains for the heat haze rising from the valleys before them.

His father drove him from the station in a brand new Morris motor, very much the man of property talking to his son about some forestry project he was engaged in. Rob wasn't listening, he was far too busy looking through the windows for his first glimpse of the white cottage at the corner, of Finsthwaite Heights, the beech avenue, Hollin Bridge and Ellersgarth itself, to take notice. In the end, even James realised he was wasting his time and, laughing, told him they'd talk later, when he'd settled in.

Ellersgarth Farm looked the same as ever; shabby but homely, a clutter of Wellingtons in the porch, great vases of roses, lilies and delphiniums in every room, and the smell of Mrs Milburn's cooking lingering in every dusty passage. Oh, but he was glad to be home. He hugged and kissed his mother, teasing her about the tears she shed at the return of her prodigal son, but then could barely spare the time to take off his coat and dump his belongings in his old room before he was off out into the forest, seeking to reacquaint himself with old, favourite places. And perhaps, if he were lucky, with favourite friends.

Dolly, hearing the news from her mother, who had in turn got it direct from Mrs Milburn's own lips while they waited to be served in Mrs Rigg's Village Shop, hurried to number 14 Birkwith Row with the good tidings, knowing that Alena would want to be told immediately.

Since Sandra's accident the relationship between the two girls had warmed somewhat, as if Dolly had realised that she'd gone too far and should try to make amends. But since it was a Saturday, Alena was not at home. She was out with Mickey, Lizzie told her, and she'd no idea when her daughter would be back.

As luck would have it, Dolly met Rob himself on her way back home and he too asked if she knew where Alena might be. So changed was he, so much taller and broader, certainly more mature and far better looking than she remembered, with his light brown hair falling disarmingly over his brow, that Dolly answered with particular care. 'Alena is out, but she'll be mad as blazes that she's missed you.'

'Will you give her a message for me?'

'I will if I can.'

'Tell her to meet me in the usual place. Tomorrow at two. I'll be waiting.'

'Right.' And as she watched him stride away, it occurred to Dolly that she held the happiness of this pair in her own fair hands.

–

Mickey had parked his little car and, at that moment, he and Alena were walking by Esthwaite Water, not exactly entwined but certainly hand in hand. He'd promised to treat her to a pot of tea and a toasted teacake in Hawkshead afterwards, despite her protests that he spent too much money on her. He assured her that as a skilled man he earned a good wage and there was nothing he liked better than to spoil his girl. But he was wily enough to look upon the money he spent as a good investment in his future. He meant, as usual, first to take payment for it in the shape of a kiss. He'd like a bit more than kisses, since he was a normal red-blooded male, but knew that rushing her would be a mistake. Now he'd driven out to a suitably remote spot, where there was a romantic view of the sun flaming over Helvellyn, tinting the grey clouds to lavender and rose pink.

'Shall we sit here for a minute?' He indicated a patch of grass and without waiting for her reply, spread his jacket for her to sit on. 'I'm glad I came to work in Ellersgarth.'

'You like working at the mill then?'

'I'm good at my job, but then you know that. And I'm good for you. You know that too.' He cocked his head to one side in that cheeky way he had, making her laugh.

'I know you think a lot of yourself.'

'You wouldn't like me so much if I were a fool, now would you?'

'I suppose not,' she admitted.

'Most of all, I'm glad I met you.' He softened his voice, disarming her with its suddenly serious tone. 'Nothing's too good for you.'

Not quite knowing how to reply to this, Alena smiled absently, keeping her eyes on a chaffinch as it pecked at fallen grass seed. Mickey might be a bit flashy but, as he so often told her himself, he had devilish charm and his heart was in the right place. It was certainly true that, for all his boasting and pushy ways, she did quite like him.

'We make a good pair, don't you think?' he persisted, stretching out flat on the grass, hands clasped behind his head, feet crossed, as he relaxed in the warmth of the sun. But he did not trouble to survey the beauties of nature all about them, the pale grandeur of the mountains or the shine of the lake. Mickey had eyes only for Alena. She was the centre of his universe and nothing and no one else existed so far as he was concerned.

Again she smiled. A second chaffinch had arrived, challenging the first. 'We're good friends, certainly,' she agreed.

'Robert Hollinthwaite did us both a favour then, eh?'

Now she did look at him, and frowned. 'What do you mean? In what way did Rob do us a favour?'

'If you hadn't run off with him into Grizedale, I might never have met you.'

Alena flinched, having no wish to be reminded of that time, nor hear Rob spoken of in that casual way. Mickey, seeing that he'd overstepped some invisible mark, instantly apologised. 'Sorry, I only meant…'

'I know what you meant.' She turned her attention back to the chaffinches, now fighting over a worm, both tugging so hard the only certain loser was the worm itself.

'I remember you had a fancy for him once, and that you missed him when he left. You were nobbut a lass, and him little more than a boy, still wet behind the ears. A childhood friendship, that's all it was.'

She wondered if that were true, if that were all it had been. It was so long since she'd seen Rob, how could she know? Perhaps, like her father, he had never loved her either.

'Now you're a woman and you've got me, so you don't need him any more. He allus was weak, not able to stand up to that bully of a father of his.'

'James Hollinthwaite is a difficult man to stand up to.'

'He'd not have kept me from you, though, if I'd been in the lad's place. Anyway,' Mickey continued, skilfully redirecting her attention to the present as he saw her lovely face begin to cloud over, 'you like me now. Bowled over by my masterful charm, you are.' He leaned upon one elbow and ran his fingers through the slicked down curls of his black hair. 'It's my good looks you've fallen for. You can't get enough of me. But then, you and me are good for each other. We have fun don't we? So there you are, he did us a favour.' And there was such audacity in both words and gesture, such a glimmer of wicked good humour in the foxy brown eyes, that she found herself laughing, even agreeing with him that, yes, for all his big talk, they were indeed having fun.

She'd never told Mickey of her correspondence with Rob. His letters had grown ever more rare over the years but were all the more precious for that. She continued to write to him without fail, though only once a month now, and in none of them had she mentioned that she was seeing Mickey Roscoe. Alena liked both young men, and since they lived in different places, where was the harm in befriending the two of them?

'You're not sorry you chose me, are you, Alena?' Mickey leaned closer, taking her chin in his hand. 'You can't be, or you wouldn't come out with me so often. You and me belong together, we're like that.' And he crossed two fingers, indicating their closeness, before suddenly and without any warning sliding one of his strong hands about her neck and pulling her face down to his. As his mouth closed over hers Alena felt the familiar surge of panic she experienced whenever Mickey kissed her, mingled with a strange excitement, as if she knew she courted danger and didn't care.

She put her hands flat against his chest, anxious to stay in control. But ignoring her feeble efforts, he expertly twisted round so that he was pushing her down on to the grass, his arms tightening about her as his mouth moved over hers. Sensuous and gentle, almost calculated, the kiss went on and on while Alena concentrated on showing him how very grown-up and daring she was. She could feel his body trembling against hers, testifying to the heady sensation of her power over him.

When he drew back his head to grin down at her, she found herself grinning back. But as she moved to sit up, he caught and kissed her again, sliding open the buttons of her dress so swiftly

159

and sneakily that before she realised what was happening his cool fingers had grasped her soft breast. Alena put a stop to that nonsense with a sharp slap.

'*No!*'

At once he was contrite. 'Sorry, I got carried away. By heck, Alena, there's nothing I wouldn't do for you. I'd never hurt you, believe me. You're my girl.'

A little shocked by his daring, she pushed him away and sat up in a fluster, patting her skirt down over her knees. 'I never said I was your girl. When did I say that?'

'You don't need to tell me, I know.'

'Do you indeed?'

'Aye.' Then he laughed, a deep throaty chuckle that sounded so richly seductive it almost made her forget she was cross with him, and she found her lips curving once more into a ready smile. 'Anyway, why else would you get all dolled up, if not to please me?'

'Dolled up?' She stared at him, genuinely perplexed.

He lay back again, pulling her half on top of him so he could closely study her face. 'Aye. Lipstick, hairdo, new frock. A chap can read the signs.'

'That was for my pleasure, not yours.' The wounded outrage of her tone seemed to cause him even more amusement.

'Never will admit what you feel, will you? I like that in a woman, an air of mystery.' He raised one eyebrow. 'Adds a spice of danger, don't you reckon? Only there's a time and place for mystery, eh? Come on, lass, how about another kiss, or happen a bit more? Don't be coy. We've known each other long enough, and a chap needs a spark of affection to light up his life. I've been patient, wouldn't you say?'

He had indeed been patient, Alena couldn't deny it. He'd been kind and consoling, given her a strong shoulder to cry on and sympathy in her troubles. And of course he deserved a spark of affection in his life. Didn't everyone? But was she the right one to give it to him? More important, what did she, Alena

Townsen, want from life? And could Mickey Roscoe provide it?

'All right,' she told him finally. 'Just one more kiss. But I'm watching your hands this time, make no mistake about that.'

–

Dolly was sitting in the kitchen peeling potatoes for Lizzie when Alena got home. It was less of a surprise to see her sister-in-law thus occupied than it might once have been, so Alena took very little notice beyond wishing them both good evening. She sank into a fireside chair and propped up her feet on the brass fender. But then something in the resolute pursing of her mother's lips and glimmer of suppressed impatience in Dolly's eyes, told her all was not quite as it should be, that the pair were holding something back.

'What?' She looked from one to the other of them. 'You look like the cat that's swallowed the cream, Dolly. What is it? What's happened?' Alena was hoping that her sister-in-law might be pregnant again. She knew that Dolly desperately wanted another baby yet, perhaps because of the troubles in her marriage, none seemed to be forthcoming. 'Come on, why are you looking so pleased with yourself?'

'It's not about me,' Dolly said hastily, as if reading her thoughts. 'It's you who should be preening yourself.' She folded her plump arms and set her head to one side to deliver the message with a knowing smile. 'Tomorrow at two, in the usual place which, apparently, you will know. Or so he says.'

Her mind still on Mickey and whether she had permitted him to be a little too bold, Alena looked blank. 'Who said? What are you talking about?'

'He were right disappointed that you weren't in when I saw him this afternoon, and most particular that I give you his message.'

'*Who?*' Alena was frowning, not understanding the enigmatic remarks, and then as the pair started to giggle, instinct brought her to her feet as if she'd been scalded. 'Rob?' Her voice was barely above a whisper. 'You've seen *Rob!*'

Then she was reaching for both her coat and the door handle almost in the same instant. It took their combined efforts to hold her back. 'Not now, love. Tomorrow, he said,' Lizzie gently reminded her, staring at her daughter's mouth now bare of lipstick, then lifting a lock of wildly curling hair that had broken free from its pins. 'Just as well, it'll give you time to smarten yourself up. Where have you been today? Through a hedge backwards? And you've got grass stains on your new frock. They'll never come off.'

But Alena wasn't interested in grass stains, though she did rush to the kitchen sink to splash cold water over her face. 'What does it matter what I *wear*? He's *here*. At last.'

Lizzie offered her a towel to dry herself. 'You look a bit rumpled, that's all.'

'Oh, for goodness' sake, Ma, I'm not a child any more. Neither is Rob. He wants to see *me*, not my frock.' She turned to the mirror that hung over the fireplace, whipped out all the hair pins and began vigorously to brush the stiff curls.

'Happen because you're a young woman now, and not a child, you wouldn't want him to ask too many questions about *why* you're looking so rumpled, would you?'

Alena paused only momentarily before slamming down the brush that seemed to have made scant difference, perhaps even added to the wildness of her hair since she hadn't the patience to put back all the pins. 'Oh Ma, don't.' And she gave her mother a quick hug. 'I must go to him. *Now.*'

'Nay, lass, think.'

'He said tomorrow,' Dolly quietly put in, pausing as she reached for another potato to consider Alena with a thoughtful frown. 'Ma's right. Happen it'll be difficult if you go barging in before then. He might not be too pleased.'

Alena actually laughed at that. 'Don't be ridiculous. Of course he will be pleased. He'll be delighted.' She was halfway out the door when her parting words clinched the argument. 'We haven't seen each other *for four* years, for God's sake!' Then the whirlwind preparations were over and the house reverberated with an echoing silence.

'Dear God,' Lizzie said, staring at the closed door. 'What have you done now, Dolly?'

–

Alena's heart was beating twenty to the dozen, and not simply from the exertion of running all the way to Ellersgarth Farm. There was a pain in her side, her mouth had gone dry and she felt sick.

What if he wasn't there, after all? Or if Dolly was right, and he wasn't pleased to see her? Or if his feelings about her had changed? Mickey said that Rob was weak, not simply quiet and thoughtful.

Could that be true? Perhaps he did give in too easily to James's strictures. Was that why he'd stopped writing?

Perhaps he only wanted to meet her tomorrow in order to tell her they must part for good? Alena's heart sank at this dreadful prospect and she slithered to a halt, becoming aware of a prickle of sweat between her breasts. Oh lord, why did she never listen to anyone? She should at least have changed her grubby frock.

By the time she reached the last corner of the long drive which led up to the farmhouse, Alena had quite convinced herself that either he would not be there, or that he wouldn't want to see her. Then suddenly there he was, leaning casually against the trunk of a beech tree. The shock of seeing him was so great that at first she couldn't believe her eyes. How different he looked, how splendid.

This tall, sophisticated, good-looking young man in open-necked shirt and slacks simply couldn't be Rob, could he? Where was the harum-scarum boy with tumbling curls and grubby knees? She had once been familiar with every single freckle on his fine skin, even with the way the silken hairs grew on his strong young arms. But she knew nothing of this man. He seemed a stranger to her.

And he was not alone.

On this warm summer evening, Olivia had arranged a small supper party outside on the lawn. A long table had been set up, covered in a lace cloth, upon which lay an assortment of cold meats, salads and desserts. Dressed in beige silk and looking even more stunning than usual, she seemed relaxed and happier than Alena could ever remember seeing her. She was laughing as she handed round plates of food to the few assembled guests, clearly delighted to have her son home at last. James was deep in conversation with a portly gentleman and neither they, nor Rob himself, noticed Alena for some moments, which gave her ample time to collect her breath.

And then he pushed himself away from the tree, swung round to face her, and she knew he'd become aware of her presence as if by instinct. She saw then, with a breathless lift of her heart, that he was smiling at her, as he always had.

Rob saw a beautiful young woman in a blue summer dress marked with grass stains and mud on the hem. Her hair was as wild as he'd remembered it, her eyes even more blue, and he saw that she was breathing heavily, as if she had been running. Alena. Who else could look such a scarecrow and tear his heart in two?

Yet almost in the same instant that he pulled his hands from his pockets and took a step towards her, his father was beside him, firmly grasping his arm and preventing him from taking another.

He saw her hesitate, her lovely young face revealing a heart-breaking picture of fading hope, delight turning to dismay. Perhaps she saw his frown, heard his fierce whisper to James, but despite the fact that a deathly silence had fallen upon the assembled company and everyone was staring at them, she took a half-step towards him, his name on her lips. Brushing aside his father's restraining hand, Rob strode purposefully forward to meet her.

Dear God, thank you, she murmured, releasing a breath she hadn't been aware she was holding, for in that moment she knew that everyone had been wrong. The long empty years and endless lonely nights were vanquished by that smile, and he was a stranger no more. Rob was still hers.

They stood and simply looked at each other, not touching, not smiling, not even speaking. Nothing that needed to be said could be expressed in that magical moment of reunion. It was enough that they were together.

Then, as of one mind, they turned and walked back up the long drive, seeking the privacy of the woods. Several pairs of eyes watched them go, but no voices called to them, no protest came from Olivia or James, nor any sound from the fascinated guests. Not that either of the young people would have cared, or even noticed.

By instinct they chose the right path. Walking with the setting sun at their backs, their feet unerringly followed the way to the heart of their private childhood paradise. Yet each was only too aware that they were no longer children, that they had grown to adulthood, and that this might be the start of a journey for a man and a woman.

Chapter Twelve

The oak still stood, proud and noble. The rope they had swung from as children still hung from the crooked bough. Protected amongst the thick crown of leaves and branches, birds nested and reared their young, grubs turned into butterflies, beetles scurried and fungi bloomed. High in the trunk a red squirrel peeped at them before leaping to a branch and scurrying away in fright. It caused them both to laugh, but didn't quite break the tension that was building between them.

They sat between roots which spread out over the green turf of the woodlands, like arms embracing them, exactly as they had done all those years before. Alena curled her feet beneath her and leaned back against the sun-warmed bark to gaze at Rob in wonder, unable to believe that at last he was here beside her.

'I thought you'd forgotten Ellersgarth existed,' she said, reminding herself how he'd clearly become so engrossed with his new friends and his new life that he couldn't even find the time to write, let alone come and see her. She longed to ask why, but was too afraid of what the answer might be. Instead she pursed her lips, lifting her chin in that pert way she had, attempting to fool him into thinking she really didn't care one way or the other. For a moment that was exactly what he did believe, and all his insecurities rushed to the surface as he hastened to defend himself.

'It's not my fault that it's been so long since I came home on a visit. I longed to come.'

'You were too busy playing on your new rugger pitch, or swimming in your new swimming bath, I suppose,' she mocked.

'No. I kept asking all the time, but the more I asked, the more Father refused to allow me. He thought it would unsettle me, that I was better off staying at school.'

'I dare say you were – better than bothering to stand up to him.' They were quarrelling again. This was their first moment together after nearly four years and they were squabbling, only the light inconsequence of their bickering had quite gone, leaving hurt and a dull emptiness in its place. If someone else had come along and made these accusations they would have united as allies. Now they seemed stuck on opposite sides of an insurmountable fence.

Rob was shaking his head. 'I hated being away from the hills, the lakes and the forest, and from Ellersgarth.'

'But not from me?' she couldn't resist provoking him.

'Most of all from you.' His voice was low and sounded suddenly angry. 'You must have realised that, Alena. You said you'd wait. And I've written.'

'I barely received a postcard this last year.'

'I had exams and…' He paused, not wanting to explain how there was little privacy in a boys' school. 'I thought you'd forgotten me.' His father had taken great pleasure in telling him she was seeing Mickey Roscoe. Rob had hidden his hurt by pretending he was no longer interested. But looking at her now, at the smear of dust on her nose, her wayward curls, her wide defiant eyes, he knew he could never lose interest in her. Ever. But he had his pride.

'You've made new friends too, I hear.' Alena's heart quickened as she recognised in the dullness of his expression that he knew she was going out with Mickey Roscoe. *Had* gone out with Mickey Roscoe. Past tense. Still, she hadn't forgiven him, had no intention of letting him off the hook for his neglect too easily.

'You don't expect me to sit at home and mope, do you? Don't make me laugh.' But there was something in her eyes that told a different story from the words she was speaking and, not for the first time, he began to doubt his father. For it came to him then, the reason for her coolness. It was as if she had actually spoken her fears out loud or he could read them in her mind, and at last he smiled.

'You look exactly the same, Alena.' He wanted to say 'only lovelier than ever', but couldn't quite manage it.

'Huh, how would you remember what I looked like?'

'With a fish-face like yours? How could I forget?'

She cast him a quick, startled glance and saw how he grinned, the flecks of gold that she remembered so well dancing in his eyes. And suddenly it was all right again. He was the old Rob, ready to tease and squabble, but his love for her clear in every word, every gesture.

'Well, I can't say I missed your horse-face either.' And they smiled into each other's eyes with perfect understanding.

'I pictured you every night, Alena, but maybe I did forget that you would have grown up and changed from the young girl I once knew.'

'And you are no longer a boy,' she added, a slight breathlessness in her voice, for it was true. This Rob, sitting so relaxed with arms resting on his knees, seemed different. The broad maturity of his chest and shoulders, the way his fair hair fell across a wide brow, the absence of freckles, and the shadow of stubble on his chin, all told their tale. He was a man.

On that first evening they talked as if they were in the midst of a conversation that had been interrupted for four minutes, instead of four years. The awkwardness between them vanished as if it had never been, and the time apart was forgotten as stories were told, news exchanged, agonies shared. Rob finally admitted to the way he'd been bullied at his first school, and how in dealing with it he'd been suspended.

'Father hated that. It hurt his pride that a son of his should be picked on in that way.'

She was outraged. 'How utterly stupid! He should have been proud of you sticking up for yourself, not blame you for being bullied. How *unfair*! It's like blaming a poor hedgehog for being flattened by a great farm tractor.'

'Hardly, I'm still in one piece, see?' But he was laughing at her anger, loving her enthusiasm, her fervour, her outraged sense of justice. He'd forgotten how very wound up and emotional she could become. Yet it was one of the things he loved most about her, her enthusiasm, the way she lived life to the full, and felt everything so keenly. Now he carefully reassured her, saying he hadn't meant to complain; hadn't liked the school much in any case. 'I'm glad I left. He did find me a better one, I'll give him that. Nobody attempted to bully me there.' Which mollified her a little.

A small silence fell, in which Alena suddenly felt oddly shy. 'So now you'll be looking for a job?'

He pulled a face. 'Yes, though Father still favours university. Battle lines will no doubt be drawn up yet again before I get my way, as I fully intend to this time.' Which caused them both to smile.

'Good for you. Do what you want to do.'

'I mean to be a woodsman. I might go and see Frank Roscoe again, see if he knows of anyone looking for an apprentice. How about you? Are you happy, Ally?'

She felt her heart contract at the use of his pet-name for her. ''Course I'm happy, though we've had our own troubles here.' She told him then about her work at the mill, about Dolly losing the baby and Sandra's accident, though glossing over its cause.

'But the best thing is, I think Harry and Sandra are walking out together. Isn't that wonderful? Ma had almost given up hope of his finding a girl. Now we just need to find someone for Kit.'

'Which, for all his good looks, with his father's temper, won't be so easy,' Rob added, then saw her face fall. 'Sorry, I didn't mean to be rude.'

'No, it's not that. You're right, he is like Dad.'

When Rob heard the true reason for her reaction, he expressed such sorrow at Ray's death that tears sprang glittering to her blue eyes. But she decided this was not the moment to tell him why, exactly, she grieved so deeply. She might break down entirely then. Alena dashed the tears away and asked him to tell her more about his future plans and ambitions, and they became so utterly absorbed in their conversation and each other, that it was only when the distant church clock struck ten that she scrambled to her feet in a panic.

'Heavens, I shouldn't be here! I've got work tomorrow. I have to be up at six.' The long summer day had beguiled them into thinking it might never end. As she turned to go, he grasped her wrist and pulled her back to him.

'I'll see you tomorrow, won't I?'

Alena looked surprised, as if it were a foolish question to ask. 'Of course.' Then before she could change her mind, or think better of it, she kissed him full upon his mouth, soft and warm and sweetly beguiling, and for all it was fleeting and light-heartedly done, it came as no surprise to either of them that seconds later she was in his arms, and he was at last kissing her as she had always longed to be kissed. Childhood was over.

–

Following supper with Lizzie that evening, Dolly and Tom walked home in complete silence. This was such a common state of affairs between them that neither of them remarked upon it, or made any attempt to break it. The Lakeland night was warm and soft, a gentle breeze whispering in the boughs of the beeches, and Dolly tucked her arm in his, wanting any passers-by to be sure of whose wife she was. Relations between them may well have fallen into a distant, lacklustre tolerance, but that was no reason, she believed, to broadcast their problems. They'd developed a sort of truce in which each intruded as little as possible upon the other, but it made neither of them happy. This wasn't at all how Dolly had imagined married life with the much sought-after Tom Townsen.

As they reached The Golden Stag, Tom jerked a nod vaguely in Dolly's direction and, shrugging free of her arm, headed towards the open pub door.

'Here, where you off to?'

He stopped, surprised. 'For a pint, if it's aught to do with you.' And something in the casual way he disregarded her, brought out all her carefully suppressed misery.

'I'm your wife, in case you've forgotten. But then, I'm surprised you bother to stay married to me at all, since most of your time these days is spent in that bloody pub.'

'And where is *your* time spent, Dolly? Or perhaps I should say, with whom?'

She stared at him, a sudden shaft of fear making her heart thump. Dolly knew she was losing him and hadn't the first idea how to get him back, or even if she wanted to. She'd longed for the security he could give her, and the child she'd carried, within the respectability of marriage. They'd certainly been good together once, but she realised now that to make a marriage work there needed to be more than sexual gratification, perhaps even more than a bairn. There needed to be love. Did she love Tom? Did he love her? She felt she had too little experience to know. Or they'd never had the chance to find out. She certainly still fancied his fine athletic body, as he had once lusted for the round softness of hers. She could still recall the fierce excitement of those heady moments in the woods together. But then sex was easier to understand than love.

She tried to remind him of that now, exuding whatever sexual charm she could still muster, awkward as it felt to be using these feminine wiles on her own husband. She stroked a hand softly over his cheek and down over his broad chest while she pushed her face close to his, pouting her lips seductively. Tom gazed impassively into her eyes. His expression made her feel faintly foolish, yet she persisted, certain she could win back his interest if she tried.

'Look, I know we've not been getting along too well recently, but I'd never – you know – go with another chap.

You're my man, allus will be.' She tried a tremulous smile, then ran the tip of her tongue over her pink lips, flickering it enticingly. Was that a spark of interest in his pale eyes? 'Forget about having a pint, love. Why don't we buy a couple of bottles of stout and go home? What d'you say, eh?'

'Why?' The coldness of his reply stunned her, and the seductive smile slipped a little.

'How do you mean, why? Because we're bloody married, that's why, and it must be months since…'

'A couple of years, actually,' he calmly reminded her. 'But then you wouldn't be able to keep track, would you? Since you don't need my services any more.'

Dolly felt sweat break out beneath the fullness of her breasts. 'For God's sake, who's been telling fibs about me?'

'Nobody needs to, Dolly. I've got eyes in my head.'

Undeterred she rubbed herself against him, put her mouth to his ear and flickered her tongue around the curve of it. She knew, even as she did it, that she was wasting her time, that it was fruitless to plead her innocence, genuine though it may be. She tried another tack. 'If it really is two years since – you know – you must be in dire need. You're a man, after all, love.'

A small, tight silence in which she became aware of his body trembling, though whether with need or rage she couldn't quite decide. Then Tom jerked his head away, brushed her fingers from where they were unbuttoning his shirt and pushed her off, as if she contaminated him. 'Thanks for the offer, Dolly, but if I'm in need of a whore any time, I know where to find one.' And he walked into the pub.

–

Rob and Alena were rarely apart after that first reunion. The days at the mill were an agony of waiting, the evening meal an irritating necessity to be got through before she could tear off her working clothes and, dressed in simple blouse and skirt, or even shirt and shorts as in the old days, would hurry from the cottage and run to the woods to fall into his arms, which was where she most longed to be.

He made no attempt to disguise his need for her. It was as real and as sweet as the wood violets that grew in soft clumps by the great oak, as strong and as noble as the thick branches that spread above their heads. He would kiss her till her face throbbed, trace his kisses along the curves of her throat, over the aroused peaks of her young breasts, and when she was gasping with need, retreat to explore the delights of her mouth once more. They clung together as one, heedless of condemning parents or the curious interest of the world at large. They kissed away each year that had kept them apart, reaffirming the bond that held them.

Alena wondered how much longer she could resist him, how she could continue to bear the passion that burned so fiercely inside her, one that cried out to be fulfilled. This was nothing like the bland, almost insipid pleasure she had felt when Mickey kissed her. Making love to Rob was exciting, thrilling, deliciously painful, and yet so entirely *right*. How either of them managed to hold back from the ultimate union, they could not afterwards have explained.

Certainly not through shyness, since every part of each other's body become as intimately familiar and far more dear than their own. Nor from lack of love or the desire to show it. Each delicious discovery, every new delight, only deepened their love for each other. Perhaps some inner and necessary voice advised the need for caution, or the desire to mark their union in a more conventional and permanent way first was stronger.

The fact that at not quite eighteen they were still too young to marry without permission was, as they both realised, a great stumbling block, and one they dared not explore too closely.

For a whole month this idyll lasted and so beautiful was it, so filled with excitement and the wonder of these new discoveries, that Alena longed for time to stand still so that it could go on like this forever. But, as Lizzie had been so fond of telling her when things were at their worst in the mill, nothing lasts forever. Not bad times nor, unfortunately, good. This was a worry that kept Alena awake at night, and sent her running to Rob with ever greater eagerness, hiding the fear even from herself that one day he might go away again, and this new-found joy would evaporate as quickly as it had arrived.

During these weeks she did not go out with Mickey once. And when Lizzie warned her that he kept on calling, she refused to be troubled.

'I've seen him at the mill and told him I'm too busy just now.' She remembered how he had scowled at her, demanding to know what could be more important than seeing him. She'd simply laughed and walked away, too used to his overinflated sense of self-importance to pay any heed to his sulks. 'Remind him that I see him every day at the mill. He'll have to be satisfied with that.'

'Let's hope he is,' Lizzie said, her heart softening as she recognised the glow of happiness in her daughter, watching how she gulped down her supper in her haste to be away. A quick wash, a peck on her mother's cheek and she was gone. The powder and lipstick had gone too these days. Perhaps Rob didn't much care for them, so that at least was something, Lizzie thought with a wry smile as she cleared the table around Kit, who was still stolidly eating and had taken no part or interest in the conversation.

Yet she felt anxious too. She hadn't been at all keen on Alena's taking up with the likes of Mickey Roscoe, but dropping him might prove even more of a problem. She said as much now and Kit told her not to fret, that Alena was old enough to sort out her own life, and of course it was easier to let her now that Ray was gone. But Lizzie found it hard to let go of her children, particularly this one, being the only girl and the baby of the family.

She heard again the familiar tap at the door and, sighing, prepared the excuses that Alena had instructed her to use. 'Will you go?' she asked her son, but Kit only shook his head.

'Don't get me involved in Alena's mischief.' And folding the evening paper, he slipped out to his precious allotment, leaving her to it.

At least Harry was happy, Lizzie thought with a sigh as she fixed on a bright smile before opening the door. He was seeing Sandra regularly now, though she suspected the old aunt was still creating difficulties for them. Thank goodness Jim at least was settled, with another baby on the way. She opened the door and kept on smiling into Mickey's glum face.

–

Sandra and Harry were, at that precise moment, sitting on the stone wall by Hollin Bridge staring down at the eddying waters in contemplative silence.

Sandra was worried. Harry often took a detour on his way home from the mill, since it was one of the few times they had together and, given half a chance, they'd sit talking far longer than they should. Sandra always made sure Aunt Elsie had her supper early these days, to leave her free to enjoy this time with him. They would laugh and hold hands, talk about the goings-on at the mill, the doings of the various members of his family, and sometimes he would kiss her. His kisses always left her with a pounding heart and a sort of aching hunger. But today Harry was not his usual talkative self. He seemed quiet, more serious than usual, almost morose. What could be wrong?

Had he grown tired of the twitching curtains, of the number of times she'd been forced to refuse his invitations. Apart from the odd invitation to tea or Sunday dinner with his family, they'd never ever been on a proper outing together, to the pictures, on a bus trip, or even out to tea in Hawkshead. Sandra would love, for instance, to go on a steamer ride with him, as Alena had with Mickey. Instead, if they were lucky, they got to walk in the woods or by the lake. More usually they sat here on the bridge because at any moment Aunt Elsie might have one of her funny turns', or need something fetching, and she'd bang her stick on the parlour window to call Sandra in. This then was the sum total of their courting, and never yet had he stepped inside her aunt's house.

So if he'd grown bored and wanted to finish, Sandra wouldn't have been in the least surprised. What man wouldn't grow tired under such restrictions? She held her breath and waited for the death knell to fall on their friendship. He began by telling her how much he enjoyed her company.

'Oh?'

'You know I do.'

As Sandra glanced anxiously up at him, she saw a smile flicker at the corners of his mouth, but all too quickly disappear as a frown creased his brow. 'Does it bother you that I'm so much older than you? I'm twenty-seven and you're, what, nineteen?'

Was that all he was worrying about? A tide of relief flooded through her and she gazed at him with shining eyes. 'Of course not, why should it? What's eight years between friends?' Then he was looking at her so keenly, with such an intensity in his gaze, that she felt a small shiver of delight run right down to her toes. 'You must know what I want to ask you, Sandra.'

'Must I?' She could hardly catch her breath.

Then he said the magical words, and she could hardly take them in. 'I'd like us to wed. There's nothing I want more than for you to be my wife.' And before she could speak a word, he put a finger to her lips and hurried on, 'No, don't say anything yet. I want you to think about it. Eight years is eight years. I need you to be sure. When – if – you are sure, then I'll go and speak to your aunt.'

'Oh, Harry.' She managed a tiny sigh that might have been agreement. He patiently waited for her to marshal her thoughts, not daring to touch her again in case it should frighten her off, Sandra being such a quiet, timid creature for all she was sweet and pretty. He often wondered what she saw in a great oaf like him.

Sandra was struck dumb with shyness, struggling to find the right words. 'What about my eye?'

He frowned. 'What about it? It isn't paining you again, is it? I thought now you no longer wore the eyepatch…'

'No, no pain now, only no sight either.'

Quick as a flash he said, 'I should think you can see enough of me with one. I'm not a pretty sight.' And he grinned disarmingly, making her smile.

'Oh, I wouldn't agree with you there, and yes, I would be honoured to be your wife,' she said, very formally, casting him a sideways glance from beneath her lashes.

Silence followed, her response coming so quickly and with such certainty that both of them seemed suddenly overwhelmed by the magnitude of the moment. And then with an edge of hope mingled with disbelief in his voice, he said, 'You would?'

'I would.'

'Oh, Sandra. Darling Sandra. Sweet, delicious, *wonderful* Sandra, you won't ever regret it.' And cupping her face between his hands, he kissed her softly, and then more fervently as she slid her arms about his waist to press her body as close to his as she dared. Neither heard the smart rap on the windowpane, nor saw the furious pale oval of her aunt's whiskered face.

He was beaming when he finally put her from him. 'Enough of that. I have your reputation to think of. I'd best go and see the old… your aunt, right away.' They both giggled nervously, knowing what he'd been about to say.

'You mean now?'

'Aye, now. No time like the present, and I'm getting older by the minute don't forget. I've none to waste, have I? Not when I can have you for my wife.'

'Oh, Harry.' But as he kissed her again, some of the happiness faded, to be replaced with concern over the interview ahead.

Mickey, slouched behind a hazel thicket, watched them silently cross the road and walk to the door of the tall terraced house. He enjoyed spying on people, listening in to their private conversations. Such uncalled for scraps of information often came in useful. But for once he was too wrapped up in his own problems, too filled with frustration and a sense of disbelief at the way things were going wrong in his own life, to care one way or the other about Alena's brother and Sandra.

Yet again Lizzie had turned him from the door. Either Alena was inside, hiding from him, or there was some more sinister reason and, since Rob Hollinthwaite was home, it didn't take a genius to work out which.

Nor did it take one to work out that something must be done about it. All he had to do was rid himself of this annoying rival. The question was – how? It couldn't be too obvious or Alena would spot his involvement. But there were more ways of killing a rabbit than throttling it. It might take him a while, and need some clever thinking to put a plan into action, but when it was done, it would only be a matter of time before Robert Hollinthwaite was history.

And Mickey did have influential contacts, so that he personally need not be smeared by the dirty work necessary to achieve this blissful state of affairs. At which point he was quite certain Alena would fall into the palm of his hand, as sweetly as a ripe peach.

–

Sandra managed to put Harry off going to see her aunt for a whole week. But come Sunday afternoon, the three of them sat in stiff formality in the front parlour, a strong smell of boiled cabbage lingering from the lunch they had silently partaken of together, dust motes dancing in the shaft of pale sunlight that had been allowed into the room, in view of the visitor and the occasion.

'I hope you will look favourably upon my request, Miss Myers. I have a good job at the mill and a bit put by, and I love Sandra dearly. I assure you that I will endeavour to make her a good husband, and to make her happy.' Harry had, in his humble opinion, said all the right things. He'd told Aunt Elsie he knew of a small cottage he could rent, that he wouldn't rush Sandra into matrimony, in view of her youth, but he hoped her aunt would agree to the wedding taking place sooner rather than later because of their great love for each other. What else could he say?

Yet throughout this long, carefully practised speech, the old lady had not spoken, not even smiled, nor altered her grim expression in the slightest degree. She sat unblinking in her wing-backed chair like some sort of witch from a child's fairy tale, her small, pixie ears taking in every word he said, and many that he didn't, Harry was sure of it.

'Happiness, my good man, is an insubstantial commodity. It can vanish in a moment,' the old lady finally, and coldly, remarked.

Sandra said, 'Of course we'll be happy, Aunt. How could we not be when we love each other so much?' And she slid her hand into Harry's beside her on the horsehair sofa. Aunt Elsie's face froze, then she stood up, tall and regal before the heavy Victorian mantel, the back of her neat grey head reflected in the oval mirror.

'I think you forget, Mr Townsen, that my niece is but a child. She is a good two years from her majority and I see no reason to allow her to venture into the terrors of matrimony before that date.'

'Terrors?' Harry sat stunned, not knowing quite what to say to this. He hadn't expected the old lady to be overjoyed at the news, but nor had he expected this open hostility.

Sandra tried again, struggling to disguise the shakiness of her voice. 'But I love him, Aunt. There's nothing for me to be afraid of. We simply want to be together. And if you don't fancy the idea of being on your own, I'm sure we could find someone to come in each day to clean and make your meals and such. Or perhaps a live-in companion. And I'd still call regularly, of course.'

Elsie Myers gazed upon her young niece in frosty disbelief. 'Allow a stranger? Into *my* house? I think you forget yourself. And they would require a wage, which you know full well I could never afford. Oh, dear me.' And the old lady suddenly clutched at her chest. 'I fear I am about to have a bad turn. I feel quite giddy. Oh, Sandra, Sandra…' And though both ran to offer assistance, Harry was brusquely swept aside with a strength quite surprising from one so frail and on the point of collapse. 'Pray leave, Mr Townsen. I cannot abide company when I am ill. Oh, dear, I need my bed, Sandra. My heart is pounding. I feel quite nauseous. You will have to assist me.'

And stricken with guilt, Sandra hurried a distressed Harry out of the door, before helping her aunt up to bed and doing her a nice coddled egg for her tea.

Chapter Thirteen

Once more he stood watching them, and it was as if time were playing tricks, replaying a scene he'd already lived through. True, on this occasion it was high summer instead of Hallowe'en. No candles stood about the tarn, and they were not innocently swimming in their birthday suits. They were not swimming at all, though the waters were an inviting blue on this beautiful day, coolly refreshing, the surface flat calm, not at all in keeping with the way he was feeling. He almost wished that they had been playing and frolicking in the water as once they had done, for this was far worse.

He almost wished too that Mickey Roscoe hadn't made a point of waylaying him, to inform him what Robert was up to.

'What of it?' Olivia had said, when he'd told her. 'Alena is a lovely girl, and you watched them go off together that evening with your own eyes.'

'I know but...' Why hadn't he stopped them? Surely he couldn't have been moved by the delight mirrored in both young faces? 'I would have stopped them, brought the lad to heel, only I didn't want to make a song and dance of it. Not with everyone watching.' And Olivia had laughed, calling him an old fuddy-duddy.

'Leave Robert alone,' she'd warned. 'If you try to control him too much, you'll lose him.'

'There's no logic in that,' said James. 'We'll lose him if I *don't* control him.' Women, he thought, ruled too much by their emotions to understand what made a man tick. But he surely understood his own son. If the boy was ready to be bedded, so be it, but James would have to make sure he kept him out of the clutches of Alena Townsen. And he'd get him suitably wed though not, please God, just yet. In the fullness of time and to the right person, then the boy might bring some prestige and happen a bit of extra land into the family. 'George Tyson has a daughter, why doesn't he pay some attention to her? A most profitable alliance, that would be.'

Olivia had looked at him then, in that disturbing way she had when saying something she considered of such great importance that she had to spell it out for him, as if he were some sort of idiot. 'You cannot order someone to love where you direct. You above all, James, should know that.'

There it was again, he thought, that implied criticism of himself. What was she referring to anyroad? An affair long since over and done with?

'No one should be expected to marry and live out their life without love,' she finished in reflective tones, the hardness of her gaze emphasising her point. 'I, most of all, should know that.'

'I thought love was a two-way street,' he barked, driven to the limit of his endurance by a disobedient son and a recalcitrant wife who had finally barred him entirely from her bedroom by means of a bolt to the door.

'I'm talking about *love*,' she repeated. 'Not – passion.'

He smirked. 'Sex, you mean. You know naught about passion, Olivia. Not that I've noticed.'

'You don't know everything.'

'Where would you learn such things? If anyone was daft enough to take on a frigid, middle-aged woman such as yourself, you wouldn't have the first idea what to do with him.' And he laughed.

It gave James great satisfaction to see her blush. For once he had discomfited her.

'Anyroad, this isn't about us, is it? It's about our son, who's far too young, in my humble opinion, to be up to what Mickey

Roscoe claims he's up to. The kind of mischief, in fact, that can bring unasked for results and to which I mean to put a stop.'

'Mickey Roscoe told you this?' She put an odd sort of emphasis on his name.

'He did, aye. Said he'd seen them together and they were close. Very close, were his exact words.'

'What else did he tell you?'

James noted with pleasure how the colour had now drained from her face. He'd struck home for once, won a round, had he? Well, that made a nice change. Couldn't bear to have folk gossip about her precious son. This small but gratifying proof of the power he still held over her had sustained him all through his walk up the woodlands by the mill leat. But now, with the confirmation of Mickey's warning before him, his elation vanished.

How could this have happened? How, despite all his efforts to keep them apart, in spite of his not permitting them to see one another for several years, could they still be together?

It occurred to him then, in a rare moment of self-reproach, that his very antipathy to the friendship might have made it more appealing. Perhaps by denying them the chance to grow up and become bored with each other, he'd succeeded only in making forbidden fruit taste sweeter?

Very close, Mickey had said. If they got much closer he'd really have a problem on his hands.

They lay together even now in the long grass which, no more than the trailing willow branches and slender alder stems, did little to hide them. James watched, appalled, as the boy's fingers peeled the girl's blouse from her. The sun glistened on the pale skin of bare shoulders and breasts, the copper halo of hair flying free as she threw back her head in an ecstasy of abandonment.

The very tenderness which his son displayed as he caressed the silken flesh set the heat rising in James's face, partly from embarrassment at playing Peeping Tom, partly from a burning anger he could no longer control. He felt it harden like a knot of steel, bringing with it the familiar pain that clamped his chest like a vice, spreading onward down his arms and making his fingers twitch convulsively.

He should never have agreed to her salvation. It was another's soft heart that had undone him. What a deal of trouble and heartache would have been saved if he'd left the child to die as she'd been expected to do. They'd thought him a benefactor, but what did they know? The guilt of that night had shattered and finally led to the death of one man, and marred the very marriage it should have saved. His own.

The fists were bunched into iron balls of fury that he longed to slam into his son's stupid head. Why couldn't the boy test out his prowess on one of the maids or a stupid village girl, any village girl but this one? Alena Townsen would ruin all James's carefully made plans, if only by playing on his sense of guilt.

But it was too late. The damage was done. He knew he would either have to live with the results of his misjudgement or do something far more radical to put a stop to it, make certain that matters went no further. Well, he'd never been afraid of doing what had to be done in the past. What was stopping him now?

Even as he watched, he saw his son lean over and gently take one dark nipple in his mouth. The girl arched her back, moaning with soft pleasure, her own mouth, with its soft pink lips and white teeth, forming a breathy circle of ecstasy. James could tolerate no more. It was at this delicate juncture that he chose to step out from behind the bushes and, overwhelmed with fury, stifled guilt and frustrated pride, strode up to the young lovers.

'Get away from her!'

The pair sprang apart, their faces a picture of shock and horror. He saw her blench, then flush crimson at being discovered thus, frantically scrabbling to fasten her blouse. He felt no compassion for her discomfiture, not a jot of sympathy for his ash-pale son. Fury at Rob's disobedience had hardened his heart to flint, making him utterly ruthless.

Grasping his son by the collar, he flung him aside, almost instantly picking him up from the ground to hit him again, shouting at the boy as he did so: foul words that rang out over the calm waters, defiling the beauty of the scene. James began to punch him again and again. Rob made no move to defend himself, beyond lifting his arms to shield his face, while the girl's screams sent birds soaring from the treetops in fright. James was beyond listening to her pleas though perhaps an inner voice stirred somewhere, reminding him of an earlier fight that had taken place at this spot, one that had gone terribly wrong. And this was his son.

When he next struck Rob down, he held back, clenching one fist inside the other as he strove to regain control of himself, his breath harsh in his chest.

Rob got slowly to his feet, wiping blood from a cut lip with the back of one hand. Bravely he faced his father, the contempt in his voice cutting short every word as if with a knife. 'Do what you will with me, I don't give a damn. What harm are we doing to anyone? I love her, and she loves me. Do you understand, Father? You can't *ever* change that, no matter what you do or say.'

'Can't I?'

'No. I mean to get work in the forest, find us a little place.'

'Us?'

'Alena and I. We mean to be together, with or without your consent.'

The pause before James answered told its own tale, and then the words seemed to come out of nowhere, or out of the depth of his rage, and nothing could stop them. 'No, you'll not have her. And I'll tell you why. Because she's as much my daughter as you are my son. Which puts you in a peculiarly delicate situation, wouldn't you say?'

He revelled in their stunned silence. Knew they did not recognise the lie. But then, if he was to have his way and remain in control of this son who had already cost him dear, what choice did he have?

–

'*Why didn't you tell me?* Why didn't you tell me you were James Hollinthwaite's mistress?'

In one sentence, he had destroyed Alena's life. Her whole world had been turned upside down and she was reeling from the shock. Now she saw a myriad emotions flit across Lizzie's face. Shock, fear, outrage and despair, and something frighteningly like guilt.

Alena couldn't even recall how she had got home, how her feet had carried her when her entire body was shaking so much her teeth rattled. She could remember the horror on Rob's face, the way he had half turned to her, as if seeking the truth before plunging into the depth of the forest, leaving her alone with James.

Her instinct had been to run after Rob, to deny the terrible words. Why she had not done so she couldn't rightly say. Instead she'd stood rooted to the spot. She could clearly recall, for it would for ever be etched upon her soul, how James had glared at her with cold loathing and simply said, 'I had to do it, Alena.'

'Is it true?'

His smile had been wry, even insolent, and had chilled her to the bone. 'Don't you believe me?'

'I believe you are determined to get me out of his life once and for all. Why did you never mention it before?'

'Sometimes secrets have to be kept, the sensitivities of others considered.'

Who else but Lizzie could he mean? Now Alena folded her arms and confronted her mother. 'Well? Don't tell me you're going to deny it?'

Lizzie at last found her voice. 'Of course I'm going to deny it. It isn't true.'

For a moment Alena looked into her face and hope swelled, compelling her to believe. James Hollinthwaite had simply wanted to drive her away from Rob as he had tried, and failed, to do so many times before. Ma would never have had an affair, had loved Ray despite his faults. She was a good and honest woman, not man-mad like Dolly's mum. Alena felt ashamed for accusing Lizzie of such an unthinkable act, and almost opened her mouth to say so. But one glance at her mother's face, some instinctive awareness of her mood, spelled out a warning, and the heady burst of hope died stillborn. She remembered then the kindness James Hollinthwaite had shown at Ray's funeral, the way her mother always made excuses for him, and the doubts flooded back.

'What is the truth? There's something, isn't there? Tell me.'

Lizzie looked like a woman who had been dealt one blow too many; like an old hawthorn tree bending before the wind in the forest. Alena saw desperate unhappiness in her tired face, and almost welcomed it. For if she herself was hurting, why shouldn't everyone else be hurting too? Neither of them spoke. Alena certainly couldn't as she felt fear close her throat.

At last Lizzie stood up. Moving like an old woman, she slid the kettle on to the stove, going through the familiar motions of brewing tea, fetching the cake tin, setting out plates and mugs. Alena sat tight-faced throughout these delaying tactics. Only when a mug of hot tea was placed before her did she finally find her voice. 'Are you going to tell me?'

Lizzie sat down wearily at the table and sipped at the scalding tea, not caring that it burned her tongue. Then she smiled, the smile that Alena had always loved because it lit up her face and made her look like a happy young girl again.

'I was overwhelmed with joy when I got you.' Her voice grew soft as the memories flooded back. 'Welcomed you as if you were my own, I did. I'd longed for a little girl so much it seemed you'd been sent in answer to my prayers.'

Alena struggled to take in what her mother was saying, but the words were becoming distorted by the sound of blood pounding in her head. Something about never feeling safe, Stella Bird interfering, Ray coming home after the war and being upset. Something shifted and tilted, staying just too far out of reach for her to grasp.

'I know you didn't always see eye to eye with your father but he was every bit as pleased to have you as I was in the end, once he'd grown accustomed to the idea, and couldn't have been kinder.'

'Stop. *Stop!*' Alena fought for breath which seemed to have compacted into a steel ball in her chest. 'Are you saying — are you trying to tell me that although you never were James Hollinthwaite's mistress, neither were you my mother?'

Lizzie looked Alena straight in the eye. 'Yes, love. Strictly speaking, that's exactly what I'm saying.' Unable to bear the anguish in the girl's face, she refilled her mug with a hand that trembled, so that most of the tea spilled out over the table and she had to fetch a cloth to wipe up the spreading pool. Alena hadn't even touched her tea, but Lizzie didn't notice. In her mind she was recalling that long-ago day.

Alena leaned her elbows on the table and covered her face with her hands. A thousand questions burned in her head but the roaring in her ears, the pain in her heart, made it impossible to speak. She could only shut out the sight of Lizzie's face and try to make sense of the terrible words.

'The housekeeper at that time was a Stella Bird. Funny stick of a woman, very well suited to her name. She came to me one day and...'

'Was Stella Bird my mother? Oh, dear sweet heaven, she and James were lovers, weren't they?'

Lizzie sipped her tea. 'There were rumours, aye, but James Hollinthwaite's never been one for hanky-panky, as you might say. Treasures his reputation too much, so I couldn't rightly say it were true.'

But if it were, then Alena could indeed be James Hollinthwaite's child and Rob's sister. Oh, dear God, the thought made her want to vomit. What would she have left if she lost her darling Rob? As it seemed she'd already lost Ma.

Her voice thick with tears, she said, 'I see now why you never properly answered any of my questions. No wonder Dad never loved me. No wonder I sometimes felt the odd one out, as if nobody understood me.'

Lizzie was shaking her head, a deep sadness in her soft grey eyes, and a pain in them which stated she would have done anything – *anything* – to have saved her lovely daughter from this agony. 'Everyone feels that way when they're growing up. And in a houseful of men, how could you not? But I never shut you out, love. Never. I always loved you as me own, whether I gave birth to you or not.'

Alena tossed her head, angrily sweeping the tears from her cheeks. 'How do I know that? Why should I believe you, when you've told me nothing but lies all my life.'

'Oh, Alena.' Lizzie looked stricken. 'Don't say such a cruel thing, lass. Don't say anything you might regret.' But Alena was suffering too much anguish to hear the soft words, or respond to the warmth of the loving embrace she needed so desperately. If ever, she thought, she could find it in her heart to forgive the deceit, it was certainly not at this moment while the wound was still raw. The woman she had loved as a mother now sat at the familiar kitchen table with her hands clenched tightly together, as if in supplication. Alena turned her face away, refusing even to look at Lizzie as she fired out questions.

'You admit, though, that I'm not your child?'

'Not in the way the boys are, that's true, but nonetheless precious for all that. Still mine in my heart.'

'Yet you kept it a secret all these years. Why? You should have told me. You should have.' Alena was on her feet now, anxiety making her voice climb with rising hysteria as she desperately fought to keep herself under control.

'You're right, I should have told you,' Lizzie admitted. 'I meant to. when you were old enough to understand, but then...

I kept putting it off – left it too late.' Silence while Lizzie confronted the reality she had avoided for so long. How she'd lived in dread of Alena learning she was not her ma after all. 'I suppose a part of me hoped I might never have to tell you, that you might never find out. But, of course, that was too much to hope for.' She'd thought Alena might be too naïve, too passionate, seeing things only in terms of black and white, right and wrong. How could all the emotions and complications of that time be properly explained?

Now the girl had heard in a way which was a hundred times worse.

Somewhere, deep inside, Lizzie confronted a memory of Ray as he carried out his own investigations after the war, behaving coldly towards her, not wanting to talk properly about the situation. Coming home to find an infant not of his making had caused a great deal of trouble between them. She'd had a hard time convincing him of the truth, and he'd gone to endless lengths to confirm the validity of her story. And then, out of the blue, James Hollinthwaite had told him there was no longer a job for him, and naturally they'd been more concerned with finding somewhere else to live than establishing the identity of the parents of the lovely child whom Lizzie, at least, now called her own. Yet the whole affair had left her with an abiding sense of guilt. Even seeing the two youngsters grow up so close had added to that guilt; their friendship keeping the link with the Hollinthwaite family and serving as a constant reminder of the high price Ray had paid. There had been times when it had felt almost like a betrayal to her oversensitive husband, and sorely tested Lizzie's loyalty. But how to explain any of this to Alena, without making her feel even more rejected than she already did, was beyond her in that moment.

Alena could feel her heart hammering against her rib cage; anger boiled within her, knotting her up in a torment of distress. She could taste blood in her mouth after biting her lips in her torment. Lips that would never again taste kisses from Rob's sweet mouth. Illegitimate. A *bastard*, Dolly would call her. The realisation of this alone was enough to dismay her, but she could live with that gladly if there could still be hope, still a chance that she and Rob may not be related. If only she could be anyone else's child but James's.

'You must know something. All my life has been a *lie*. How could you do this to me? Who am I then if not Alena Townsen?'

'You are Alena, and always will be. My Alena. I think it was fate. We were meant to be together, you and me.'

'*But who am I?*'

Lizzie heard the pain and fear in her voice, saw the hardening of the young face, and instinctively got up and held out her arms, dropping them helplessly to her sides when Alena made no move towards them. 'All right, I'll tell you what I know; what Stella told me. But you have to remember that you're my lass. Nothing will change that.'

'Tell me everything.' Oh, please don't let this unspeakable thing happen to us!

Lizzie was moving to put on the kettle. 'I don't know about you, lass, but I need more tea.'

–

The tea made, and a mug warming their hands, mother and daughter sat quietly together as they had so often done over the years. The story took surprisingly little time to tell.

Alena learned that her real mother had not been Stella Bird, as she had feared, but some young girl who had got herself into trouble, perhaps with a soldier who never came back from the front. She'd turned up on the doorstep of Ellersgarth Farm one wild night at the end of October 1916, obviously in labour and suffering from having been on the road for some time. There was mud on her clothing, but a fine silk dress and good worsted coat, not fitted for the harshness of a Lakeland winter, indicated that she came from a good family.

'She was young and unused to hardship.' Lizzie's voice grew soft, filling with sadness as she became gripped by the tale she related. 'Happen they'd turned her out because of her shameful condition. Or perhaps the family had an argument and the girl left in a huff before they had time to be reconciled. We'll never know. There was nothing on her to give a clue, Stella said, not even a purse or change of clothes. The girl claimed to have walked out, taking nothing with her, and never gone back.' Lizzie didn't need to remind Alena of the time she had done very much the same thing.

The birth had proved to be a difficult one which the girl had not survived.

'You were so small and weak, everyone thought you would follow her before the night was out. But you didn't. Against all the odds, you lived.'

Despite herself, Alena found her curiosity irresistibly stirred by this sad tale. 'So what happened then?'

'Stella came for me. We were living on the estate then, in the gamekeeper's cottage, and since I already had four children of me own, I was an obvious choice to look after a sickly bairn, until your future could be settled more permanently.' And now Lizzie reached out and grasped her daughter's hand between her own, giving it a little squeeze. 'Only when I went to fetch you, I took one look at you, like a little peg doll in the laundry basket, and fell in love with you on the spot. You were the daughter I'd always longed for. I made up my mind, there and then, to keep you for meself.

'Stella didn't like it, said the minute you were well, she'd find another home for you. But I kept putting her off. You had jaundice, weren't suckling well, suffered a lot of colic and were weakly. And then she left and, what with a war on, no one else had time to bother about one small infant.'

Tears were frighteningly close. Even now Alena could feel them running down her cheeks as if she no longer had any control over her own body. What was she supposed to believe?

'Ray came home on leave and found me with a bairn. That really put the fat in the fire.' Lizzie pulled a wry face. 'But in the end I convinced him I'd been faithful, and how it had all come about. So he set out to settle the matter, to make you safe. But when he came home for good, after the war, he'd lost his job with Mr Hollinthwaite.'

'Why was that? Was it because of me?'

Lizzie sipped at her tea, taking her time. What good would it do for Alena to hear of the disputes and recriminations of that time? She'd no wish for the guilt to live on into the next generation. 'Ray was late coming back because of an old wound that had flared up, and Mr Hollinthwaite hadn't the patience to wait. There were more men than jobs in those days, so he'd already tekken on someone else. Ray never forgave him, though, for all he found work quick enough at the mill, and earning more money too. The mill didn't belong to James Hollinthwaite in those days. He bought it later. And Ray had put by enough to get us this grand li'le cottage. Then he had everything put on a proper legal footing, so no one could take you away from us.'

Lizzie smiled softly. 'So, you see, life has its ups as well as its downs, and you haven't had too bad a life with us, now have you? Or happen you think so. Happen you'd rather have been tekken on by someone else?'

'Oh, Ma. How can you say that?' And somehow it was no longer a question of forgiveness. Alena knew that she could never have hoped for a better mother, nor one who would have loved and cared for her more. In a strange way, she felt even closer to Lizzie now, as if she were the only certain thing in a topsy-turvy world. She was still her ma, always had been and always would be. Tears were running down her cheeks again, soft tears of love, and she wasn't even bothering to wipe them away.

'What's this? Crying? And you my tough little tomboy?'

'Not any more, nor so tough as I like to pretend,' Alena confessed, the sad fate of the poor unknown girl filling her with such poignant sadness that pride no longer seemed to matter.

193

'We're none of us that, love. Are we still friends? Am I forgiven?' And Alena didn't even protest when her mother wiped her nose for her as if she were a baby still, and then wrapped her close in a great big hug.

''Course we are. For ever and always.'

'I'll say this. Your mother, whoever she was, would be proud of the way you've grown into such a fine young lady.'

'Did you see her, this young girl who was my mother?'

'Nay, like I said, she were dead when I collected you.' Lizzie dabbed away the tears from her daughter's cheeks.

'But you saw the coffin, went to her funeral?'

A small silence, the hint of a frown. 'I don't reckon I know aught about any funeral.' And now the silence between them lengthened and grew.

Alena kept her brilliant blue gaze fixed upon Lizzie, willing her to say more, to offer some definite information concerning the existence of this young girl. Her thoughts churning, she plucked one out of nowhere. 'Is that why you were writing those letters that time?'

Lizzie flinched at the realisation that Alena knew of this, must have picked it up from an overheard conversation. Was that one of the reasons she had run away? The pain she felt for her beloved child deepened. 'I was trying to find out summat about her. I thought you'd want to know. But I'm afraid I failed, love. I could find neither the vicar who buried her, nor Stella.'

'Then you've no absolute proof that she existed?'

'I have Stella Bird's word for it.'

'But that's all?'

And now they both saw the implications. If the rumours were true about the affair and a child had been the result, this was exactly the sort of fanciful tale the housekeeper would need to tell, to divert suspicion away from them both. 'I'd no reason not to believe her. I'm not one to give credence to gossip-mongers and, as I said, James Hollinthwaite is a cold fish with a high opinion of hissel.'

'What about Olivia? Do you think she might know anything?'

'Nay. James'd make sure of that.'

'Oh, Ma. Do you think it's true? If we can't find out one way or the other then what of Rob and me?' She'd finally managed to say his name.

Lizzie stroked back a damp curl and met her daughter's pleading gaze unflinchingly. 'Nay, I don't know what to think. But happen you'd best not see him again, lass. Just to be on the safe side. Not till we know for sure, anyroad.'

Chapter Fourteen

The tensions at Ellersgarth Farm were even greater. Olivia was frantic. Once more her darling son was leaving and no one would tell her why. Rob was clearly suffering from some terrible agony that he would speak of to no one, not even to his mother. Particularly his mother. She begged and pleaded with him not to leave, but he packed a single bag, kissed her tenderly and told her he would write when he'd got settled. Then he walked out of the house and, for all she knew, out of her life.

She turned instead to James, but he was no more forthcoming. He'd had a long talk with the boy, man to man, spelling out a few facts about life and marriage and they'd had something of a disagreement. But it was a private matter between father and son and really nothing for her to worry over. The boy would come round, he told her, given time to get over his sulks.

In fact he'd finally made a suggestion for Rob's future which had proved acceptable. It had been a climbdown in a way, but perhaps would be for the best in the long run, the way things were shaping up. But James certainly had no intention at this juncture of divulging any of this to his wife, for she would only start asking too many questions. James had always taken the view that the less Olivia knew the better. And he certainly had no wish to risk any exchange of views between herself and the Townsen girl, or the whole silly business could blow up again, despite the pains he'd taken to drive them apart. So he patronisingly suggested she take a short holiday. 'Italy perhaps, or France. You like France, my dear, being so well versed in the language. Shall I buy you a ticket?'

'*No*,' she screamed, beside herself with misery. 'I couldn't take a holiday when my son, my own darling boy, has walked out and gone we know not where.'

'Don't start on your hysterics, Olivia, the boy said he'd write.'

'Letters? What good are a few letters? I need him here, where I can see him, touch him, talk to him. Why do you always drive him away? You must find him for me, James. Apologise for your quarrel, whatever it was. Make him come home!' And of course, to appease her, James patted her shoulder and promised that he would do everything he could, while having no intention of doing any such thing.

For a week Olivia languished, weeping and railing by turn, all her carefully nurtured forbearance finally crumbling away. Love. Was that too much to ask? For years she had endured the stultifying confines of a loveless marriage. She'd done her duty by James, hadn't asked for passion or excitement, only warmth and kindness, a feeling that she was cared for. She'd tolerated her husband's frozen heart because of Rob, and perhaps for the sake of propriety. Now, if she was to be denied these essentials even from her beloved son, who had been driven from the house, her life seemed pointless.

One morning she woke perfectly calm, as if a storm had passed. She dressed in sensible warm clothing, packed a bag of essentials and, without asking James's permission, drove his new motor up the drive, along the lanes and headed in the direction of Grizedale. She drove at a reckless rate, uncaring of what or whom she might encounter on the way, the wind whipping her hair into disarray. When the road ended she abandoned the Morris and walked, nearly ran, the rest of the way to that secret place in the woods she knew so well.

Here, Olivia found her lover, rested her cheek against the hard expanse of his chest, stroked his beloved weathered face and cried, 'Find my boy for me, Frank. Find him!'

But they did not find him. Frank Roscoe because he did not know where to look. James because for all he could easily guess, he had no intention even of trying. And neither of them, for their different reasons, greatly minded that he was lost or wished him to be found.

–

By the time Alena sought out Olivia at Ellersgarth Farm, Mrs Hollinthwaite had, according to a dour-faced Mrs Milburn, 'Packed her bags and done a moonlight flit. Run off God knows where, with the Lord knows who. Seems to be a fashion in this house.'

There was only one person who could answer her many questions, and that was James Hollinthwaite himself. And Alena knew he was unlikely to oblige. Even so, she meant to ask him. Every day she called at the house, varying the time in her determination to gain admittance, but was always denied entry. James insisted that he had no wish to see or speak to her. In the end Mrs Milburn convinced her to stop trying. 'He's that cut up about the missus leaving, I reckon the poor man'll run mad if you pester him too much. Leave him be, lass. He paces the rooms of this empty house night after night. You wouldn't believe he'd feel her going so keenly, and the boy too. What a pandemonium!'

And although Alena was of the more sceptical opinion that James Hollinthwaite grieved the loss of his family as he might his sporting gun or his favourite cherry-wood walking stick rather than for their own sake, she ceased to call on the embattled housekeeper. And then one Sunday she met him coming out of church, and bravely followed him along the lane until he was forced to turn and face her. Alena felt a loathing for this man that shamed her. Never had she experienced such hatred for another human being. For all the difficulties she'd had with her father (she still thought of Ray as such), and for all his casual brutality, it paled into insignificance besides this more calculated evil.

'I will not have you hounding me, Alena Townsen. Pray desist.'

'I want the truth.'

'You have it. Would it make you feel better if I were to repeat it?'

'I'd be more likely to believe you, if it weren't for the fact I know how determined you were to separate us.'

He stood watching her, saying nothing. Alena experienced a surge of desire to fight him, to shout out her denial, to run and find Rob and make him come back to her no matter what the cost. Her emotions swung from hope to fear and back to hope again. But what if she were wrong? What if it were not a lie? Could she afford to ignore this worm of a doubt and perhaps, suffer terrible consequences?

'It was a lie, wasn't it? Ma has told me all about the girl who arrived at your door that night. Why won't you admit it?'

Again that unnerving smile and Alena felt heat rise up her neck and flood her cheeks. But she really mustn't lose her temper with him. No good would come of that. Nor would she let him see how she feared his answer. Chin up, face set, every line of her graceful body showed a raw and desperate dignity. 'Where is he?'

'Where you won't find him.'

'You'll not keep us apart. He'll never stop loving me, nor I him. You can't *ever* take that away from us.'

And callously, cruelly, he laughed. The sudden sound brought a chill to her heart as if a cloud had blotted out the sun. Then just as quickly it died, his face closing in like the weather darkening the tops of the Furness Fells, and where formerly had been sunshine and the happy song of the thrush in the peaceful quiet of the lane, now there seemed to be only silence and a deep, shivering cold despite the fact that the sun still shone warm on her back.

'Much good may it do you both. Love cannot be deposited in a bank. It won't build a man a house or make his fortune. In fact, it has no value. And whether you believe me or not is really quite irrelevant. Rob does. And because of that belief, my son may have your love, if he feels so inclined, but he can't have you. Ever!'

It was then that she saw the extent of his victory. Her views on the subject were really of no account. Rob believed what his father told him. And Rob had gone.

–

James had little time during the next twelve months to worry too much about his disobedient son or straying wife. Not for a moment did he doubt that his actions had been justified, so why should he concern himself? It didn't even trouble him that there were rumblings of war in distant Germany. If war ever came, and hopefully it wouldn't, he'd make sure he was on the winning side and make money out of it. He'd got a good price for the larch he'd already sold. And he had more to offer, which the Navy would undoubtedly need.

The bobbin mill might do well enough, but who knew what the future might hold? James Hollinthwaite did not believe in keeping all his eggs in one basket.

He noted with interest the public outcry over the purchase by the Forestry Commission of 7,000 acres of land in Eskdale, the Duddon Valley and Ennerdale. He studied the reports and letters in the press, pumped his friend George Tyson for every scrap of information he could muster, listened to news of questions in the House, of petitions and arguments from people in every walk of life from the lowest to the highest in the land. Keenly, he mapped every detail of the campaign.

Eskdale, a magnificent curving fellside of broken crag and bracken, possessed without doubt a noble loveliness which made it one of the finest of the Lake District valleys. Duddon Valley, which ran from the stepping stones below Grass Gars to the head of Mosedale and as far as Wrynose, was uniquely remote and unspoiled with breathtaking views of Scafell. The fells of Ennerdale were surrounded by some of the finest peaks of Lakeland: Pillar, Windy Gap, Great Gable, Haystacks and Steeple to name but a few. These, then, were the areas under threat.

The Council for the Preservation of Rural England and the Friends of the Lake District were the ones fighting the plans, holding conferences and meetings, negotiating, making demands. The Commission reminded them that afforestation actually began back in 1919 when Whinlatter, a part of Thornthwaite Forest near Keswick, missed by a single day the distinction of being the first planting of larch by the Forestry Commission. Eggesford in Devon held that record. Even then they were only following a fashion begun by private landowners: the Curwens of Belle Isle, the Spedding family of Mire House. Even the Brocklebanks of Liverpool had planted larch, calling them 'exotics', in the grounds of their famous mansions. Later they'd turned to commercial production for the lead and copper mines of Derwent Water and Coniston.

It was this last argument which was of most interest to James. He believed in following in the steps of fine families and the traditions of their noble houses. Except that he, not being constrained by their more conservative principles and tender hearts, could do even better. Sitka spruce was a better tree to plant than larch, his research informed him. It was fast-growing and well suited to a damp climate. Not for a moment did he doubt that the Commission would win, or that his own plans, when he put them into operation, would be equally successful.

-

Life was hard for Rob in the upper reaches of Grizedale. He'd spent months working on these heights, planting in all weathers, sometimes in conditions so bad he could barely stand against the lashing wind and rain.

But he was thankful for this job with the Forestry Commission, better paid than his previous one with the private landowner his father had put him on to. The Commission had recently bought the estate of Grizedale intact, 2,500 hectares, including the Hall and cottages, from Harold Brocklebank, part-owner of the Cunard Line. The moment Rob had heard, he'd come looking for work and found it.

He worked now in a gang of about a dozen men, planting the young trees in neat rows marked out by stakes and string. He didn't much care for all the square corners and straight lines, but it was so they would know where to find them come summer when the rows had to be weeded out. Weeds could all too quickly choke a young tree to death. Sometimes he felt as if he too were choking.

How he missed Alena still, after all this time. To lose her so soon after discovering the new depth of the love between them was bad enough; if he allowed himself to contemplate the reason for this loss, it tore him in two. The prospect that he loved and desired his own sister filled him with horror.

Yet it must be true. James had spoken of a cold marriage, of his needing the comforts that Stella Bird, and a number of other women in those early years, had offered. Listening to him attempt to justify his actions, Rob had glimpsed an aspect of his parents' life he'd no wish to see. He could still recall the despair of that day, the way his mind had shut down and refused to function. Yet in the inevitable arguments that had followed, for once his father had been sympathetic, and had listened at last to Rob's ambitions. When he'd announced his decision to go and look for work in the forests, James had provided names of prospective employers, saying university could always wait until later.

Now, in the autumn of 1936, Rob felt that he no longer had a home, certainly not one he could return to. Though in many ways he'd not regretted the decision to leave Ellersgarth, he still deeply regretted the loss of Alena. He needed her, he loved her. It was as simple, and as terrifying, as that.

He'd once written, telling her where he was, asking her to visit him. And, of course, without hesitation she had come.

'I couldn't face you before this,' he'd explained as they'd sat together, making a futile attempt to eat sandwiches and cakes in a small tea room in Hawkshead.

'I understand.' She'd looked so utterly beautiful in short skirt and jolly sweater, a long scarf wrapped warmly about her neck, and bright red tam o'shanter tugged down over her wayward curls, his throat had ached with love for her.

'I almost wish I hadn't asked you now,' he'd said, on a half laugh.

'I'm glad you did.' And she'd reached a hand across the table seeking his, only he managed to remove it just in time. He couldn't bear her to touch him. She tucked her own hands out of sight and stared miserably down at her plate, not even touching her half-eaten sandwich.

They talked about insignificant things – village gossip, Alena's family, Rob's new job – and drank endless cups of tea. In the warm tea room there were other people about them and they felt safe. Neither suggested a walk out into the countryside for all it was a gloriously sunny autumn day, for each knew of the dangers being alone could lead them into. Even to catch her eye sent shafts of hot desire pumping through his veins. It was unbearable.

Then she'd leaned forward, her lovely face bright and suddenly alive with hope. 'I came, knowing it would be painful, because I have something to tell you.'

He could still recall the surge of hope he had experienced as she began her tale, and the renewal of intense pain as it faded again. 'You're saying you might not be the child of my father and Stella Bird?'

Alena nodded, blue eyes as bright as the sky shining through the windows. 'It's possible, but there's no proof. I could be the daughter of this young girl, a perfect stranger, who apparently arrived in great distress, soaking wet and about to give birth.'

'An orphan from the storm?' Amused disbelief in his voice, with a hard edge of disappointment to it. 'Sounds like a Colbert movie. You'll be telling me your stepfather beat you next.'

'Of course he didn't,' she said crossly, resolving not to mention the spats Ray had had with Lizzie. 'I'm only repeating what Stella told my mother.'

'But she offered no proof. Your mother never saw this – supposed girl.'

'No. But I'm sure that what James told us was a lie, Rob. Can't you believe that?'

'Why should he lie?' He was growing annoyed, she could hear it in his voice, and frustration mounted in her. Why wouldn't he listen to her argument? He always had when they were small. What had changed?

'Because it's in his interest to lie. He's borne a grudge against my family for years, ever since my father complained over losing his job after the war. He wants to control everybody, that's what this is all about. Your mother, for one, has had enough. She's run away, did she tell you?'

Anger flashed in his eyes. 'My mother tells me everything. She left because she felt he'd driven me away, but I went of my own accord. I've accepted it, Alena. So must you.' He stood up and started fumbling in his pockets for change. 'We can't all live in your fairy-tale romantic world.'

'*Damn you!*' she said, and stormed out of the tea room, heedless of the curious onlookers.

He hated the fact that he'd upset her that day, but still woke at night in a lather of sweat over what might have happened between them if he hadn't been so strong. He was forever tormented by the memory of the silky smoothness of her skin, the vivid beauty of her hair which sprang from her forehead as if with a life of its own. Even her carefully disguised feminine fragility, hidden beneath a more robust tomboy image, and the sheer athletic grace of her slender body. Oh, how he had wanted her then, in that silly little cafe, and now, over a year later. His own sister!

Their volatile friendship had reasserted itself by the time he'd walked her to the bus, but even now he could plainly visualise the plea in her ashen face as she begged him, one last time, to deny the terrible facts and alter reality in some way, to accept that his father had told a mischievous falsehood. Yet how could he? He'd looked into James's face that day and believed him. Nothing Alena had told him could alter that fact.

They'd stood for a moment in awkward silence, a light breeze ruffling the curls he longed to touch, the sun kissing her cheeks with gold, where his own kisses should be. The shadow of a smile tugged at the corners of her rosy lips, then she had turned and climbed into the bus, waved, and was gone out of his life for ever. He had wished that day, to die of the pain.

Now he thrust his spade into the cold wet soil, made four cuts to form a square, turned the last turf over, split it in the middle and pushed in the young tree. Then he stamped it firm. The rain was running down his neck, leaking inside his muffler and soaking the collars of the two warm shirts he wore beneath his pullover and thick jacket. His fingers felt like ice-cold sausages and his feet, in their several pairs of socks and soil-caked boots, hardly seemed a part of his own body. But for all the cold and the wet, and the back-breaking discomfort of the job, not least carrying heavy bundles of young trees up the fell, he enjoyed working out in the open. He felt a surge of pride whenever he stood back and viewed the result of the gang's labours, the rows of transplants stretching for miles. Their ganger, a fair man for all he was a tough disciplinarian, encouraged this sense of pride in his men.

'You'll be able to show this forest to your bairns and your grandchildren one day,' he would say. 'It'll be growing tall and strong by then, bursting with life. Now that'll be summat to see.'

But Rob knew that he would have no children. Any hope of marriage and a family had died on that tragic summer's day. A life in which he could never have Alena seemed bleak indeed.

Every morning when he woke, he told himself that he would not think of her this day. But he always did.

–

Alena was attempting, with some difficulty, to settle again to the humdrum life of the mill. At first each day had been a living nightmare, as if she were not in control. She felt as if she were outside her body, watching it go through the everyday motions of life without actually being a part of it. She saw herself cycle to the mill each day, join the throng of workers who piled off the buses, coming from as far afield as Ulverston, Coniston, Dalton and Haverthwaite in their search for employment, make her quota of bobbins and then cycle back home each evening.

Many of the smaller bobbin mills were having difficulties finding enough orders to keep going since the cotton mills were suffering badly from the depression. Some had even closed down. Much as she would have liked to tell James Hollinthwaite he could keep his job, Alena had no choice but to hang on to it.

It was only the company of the other girls which made life tolerable. They'd sit in the canteen each dinner time, tossing scrap bobbins and bits of waste into the old black fire-range to keep themselves warm (though it was strictly forbidden since all waste was meant to go in the boiler to run the machines), and exchange endless jokes and stories. Alena tried to match their good humour, but her heart wasn't in it. And she told them nothing of her own troubles.

They were aware Rob had left, and that Alena had been to see him to persuade him to return, but were unaware of the reason he'd refused. They saw only her resulting depression.

But once she'd heard Lizzie's version of events, Alena had been buoyed up by the certainty that if only she could find him, she would easily persuade Rob to believe in it. To receive his letter of invitation had been a joy, though Lizzie had warned her against going.

'But I have to *do* something. I'm certain James Hollinthwaite *lied*.'

'You can't turn a boy against his own father. It wouldn't be right. Give it time. Happen we'll find proof one day.'

'One day. When I'm old?' For once Alena had ignored Lizzie's advice and had raced to Rob with a heart filled with hope. When he hadn't believed a word, had even mocked the story as fanciful nonsense, the quenching of the final glimmer of hope had been dire indeed. Now a small seed of anger had begun to grow. Why did Rob always believe everything his precious father told him? Why couldn't he see that James meant only to exercise control over his son? It was some small satisfaction that the man no longer controlled his own wife. Olivia had escaped his cold-hearted tyranny, though it was frustrating that she'd done so before Alena had the chance to discover what exactly she knew of that long-ago night.

Following the futile visit, rebellion had set in and Alena had again taken up with Mickey Roscoe. He'd waited for her one day after her shift and simply informed her that it would be a good idea, in his usual arrogant, audacious manner. And Alena had agreed. Perhaps that was why she needed him, because she wasn't capable right then of making decisions?

She almost wished she could hate Rob, but she could never do that. Alena knew she would always love him for he was a part of her. Even though she now accepted she could never have him.

–

When they had finished their quota of planting for the day, the men made their way wearily back down the fellside, glad of the promised comfort of their respective lodgings. Rob was paid twenty-five shillings a week, ten of which went to his landlady, Mrs Blamire. If his room was small and bare, and never quite warm enough, she at least fed him well, though she charged extra for meals. Nevertheless he was grateful. A man needed a full stomach on this job, and not all of the foresters were so fortunate.

On days when it was too wet or wild to climb to the peaks, he would receive no pay at all. Then he would sit alone in his room, reading or writing letters to his mother. Dull as it was, it seemed infinitely more sensible than playing cards with the other men and running the risk of gambling or drinking away the hard-earned money he'd gained thus far that week.

But he was desperately lonely.

For this reason, if for no other, the letters he received from Olivia were of vital importance to him. The days when he found one of her envelopes beside his plate, crisp and white and smelling faintly of her perfume, were glorious indeed. Over the years, mother and son had developed their relationship into one almost entirely based upon correspondence. Their meetings were so rare, and so far apart, that it was largely through the words they put on paper that they had come to understand each other; at times pouring out their hearts in the way people can only do in a letter. In the past, as now, being able to talk to her in this way had proved a great solace to Rob, counterbalancing the grim times, the heartache, and the loneliness.

Today as he sat down – scrubbed clean and at last warm – to a supper of spicy Cumberland sausage and pickle, he saw the square envelope with a jolt of pleasure. He slid it into his pocket to read later in the privacy of his room, but the anticipation of it kept him bright and cheerful throughout the hearty meal. He enjoyed teasing Mrs Blamire, who had a passion for cats that she fed on brown trout, saying if ever he came back in another life he'd choose to be one of her cats, since she looked after them so well. And she would blush and preen herself as she always did when this delightful young man teased, for didn't he make her feel like a girl again?

Instead of going down to the local pub for the single evening pint he allowed himself, Rob hurried up to his room, eager to read his letter and perhaps sit down and write an immediate reply.

He'd been sorry, if not surprised, to hear that his parents' marriage had ended. Olivia was now living in a small cottage near Thornthwaite and claimed never to have been happier. He guessed she was not alone, but since she had not yet chosen to tell him with whom she lived, he did not enquire too closely, for fear of seeming to intrude.

He ripped open the envelope and read: 'My darling Rob'. He could almost hear the light, musical tones of her voice. There followed the usual expressions of concern for his well-being, instructions for him to take care, stay warm, and eat his greens. Some everyday tittle-tattle about walks she had taken, visits to Keswick and Derwent Water that she'd enjoyed, and her own inadequacies on the domestic front. He could sense how much she loved it, her enthusiasm for her new life almost leapt off the page. But then the tone changed.

> *Darling, I have some important news for you. Since you finally confessed to me the terrible reason why you left home, I've hardly been able to bear the thought of your unhappiness. I know nothing of any girl coming to the house, pregnant or otherwise. Even so, it is true that your father and Stella did have an affair. It didn't last long and, as Alena says, the whole tale could just as likely be one of James's lies. As you know, he is entirely ruthless when it comes to getting his own way in anything. But I can understand why you feel the need for further proof. I shall do some investigating. Who knows? Perhaps I shall have some real news for you soon.*

And she closed with her usual expressions of love. Rob folded the letter and stored it with the others in a leather folder. He did not allow himself to hope. Even so he read his mail with increased eagerness over the following weeks. No further mention was ever made of the subject. Meanwhile, back in Ellersgarth, Mickey announced to Alena that it was time to consider a date for their marriage.

Chapter Fifteen

Lizzie said that Alena could do worse; that although she herself hadn't much cared for Mickey's bragging when she first met him, she'd come to see this as a harmless part of his nature. And he was a useful bloke to have around, calling regularly to offer to do jobs about the house which her four boys never seemed to have time for these days.

Mickey himself had explained to Alena that he was a hard-working, canny sort of chap and would make her a good husband. 'And you can't deny I'm handsome.'

She'd laughed at that. Mickey could always make her laugh. Then he'd gently taken hold of her hands.

'Not having had much of a family life myself, it's important to me to marry and make one of my own. Can you understand that? I never knew what it was to be loved by a mother, but there's no doubt in my mind, Alena, that you will make a good mother to our children. And I mean to be a good father.' Aware of her soft heart, for all her tough exterior, Mickey considered this to be his trump card.

And indeed, put like that, how could she refuse? He'd been such a good friend, Alena almost felt she owed it to him to marry him. Her own family life had been so warm, and the love from her mother and four brothers so strong, it had helped her cope with the remoteness she'd felt from Ray.

Her brothers, of course, offered varying forms of advice. Harry, though anxious to wed himself, suggested she take her time, saying she was still young. Jim agreed he was more than ready to be an uncle as he jiggled his latest offspring on his knee. Kit, teasing as always, said he was surprised she'd found anybody willing to have her. Only Tom warned that she might live to regret it.

'Marriage isn't always easy,' he told her, in that gentle voice of his and her heart went out to him for, of course, it was his own situation he was thinking of.

'Oh, Tom, I do wish you and Dolly could be happy. I wish I could help to put it right. But she has had a hard time, you know.'

His face twisted with bitterness. 'Nobody seems to realise that it's been pretty hard for me too. That bairn was my son too.' And he walked away, shoulders slumped.

But if she didn't marry Mickey, what would she do with her life? There were no other eligible males she liked half so much, and she'd no wish to end up a sour old maid like Sandra's aunt.

–

Sandra's reaction, however, went right to the heart of the matter. 'Do you love him?' A simple question with no simple answer.

They sat beneath the oak, still a favourite place for thinking things through. Sunshine glimmered in the glade in brilliant waves of light, as if washed by a sea of green and russet. From the depths of the wood they heard the cough of a deer, while high above their heads red squirrels darted from branch to branch, showing off their acrobatic skills. Somehow, the intense beauty of this place, and Alena's sweet memories of it, made the ache for Rob more painful than ever.

'I don't know.' It was the only honest reply.

'Then you mustn't marry him until you do know.' The two girls had yet again bemoaned their respective difficulties, to come up, as usual, with no solution.

'But if I can't have Rob, what does it matter who I marry?'

'It matters because marriage is a decision to spend your life with one person. Your entire life!' Sandra propped her chin on her hand, her face solemn. 'That's why Harry and I are so sure. Even though I'm half blind, he still wants me. A lifetime wouldn't be long enough for us.'

Alena was ashamed to feel a surge of jealousy. Harry and Sandra would eventually be able to achieve their dream, and sooner rather than later. There was no such possibility for her.

'I can't bear to think of spending my life alone. I always expected to marry, didn't you?'

'Doesn't everyone? But that's not a good enough reason.'

'I do like Mickey. He's a bit cocky, yes, but I think that's a cover-up really, for shyness. Frank Roscoe, his father, is such a larger-than-life character, and he left Mickey to his own devices when he was a boy. It must have been an odd sort of life being brought up in the forest, moving from place to place and never being settled. I think that's why he longs now for a real home, a place to call his own. And he's always been good to me.'

'Then compromise,' Sandra suggested. 'Let him buy you an engagement ring and promise to marry him when you've both saved up.'

'He's adamant I should make up my mind soon.'

'But you're even younger than me. If he wants a date, give him one twelve months from now, when you've reached twenty-one. That's fair enough.'

'I hadn't thought of that. Oh, Sandra, you are clever.' A long engagement seemed the perfect solution.

Sandra then spoiled everything by asking about Rob, since she was privy to the whole, tragic tale. 'Will you invite him to the wedding?' And Alena's qualms came rushing back as the familiar pain pierced her breast. But, like it or not, life must go on and she must learn to live it.

'No,' she said. 'I won't even tell him.'

–

Mickey was not in favour of a long engagement but astute enough not to allow his irritation at the delay to show.

'We need to save up, find a place of our own to rent. I don't want to get married and find I'm still living at home with my mother. What would be the point?' And since Mickey himself occupied a single room in fairly cheap lodgings, he could find little argument against that. He heaved a weary sigh, adopted a woebegone expression, put his hand to his breast as if his heart were broken, and gazed at her with huge soulful eyes in a way that set her giggling.

Their courtship continued as it always had. He became a regular visitor to the house, almost one of the family. He was always ready to sit and argue with her brothers on whether Carlisle would win their next match and go up in the league, or whether the unions could take action against the government for the huge rise in unemployment.

'There's talk of a march from Jarrow. They've been hit hard in the north-east. Lot of hunger there.'

'It's bad enough here. I wouldn't like to cross Hollinthwaite,' Jim admitted, with the caution of a married man. 'Where else would we find work?'

When Mickey and Alena were alone, they talked of more personal matters. Of where they might live after they married and how many children they might have. Mickey loved to plan, and Alena was happy to sit back and let him. Talking saved all that undignified tussle in the back seat of his car. But he remained impatient, constantly dreaming up schemes to bring the wedding forward. When she felt his plans needed to be curbed, Alena would point out the benefits of delay, how she was still very young, and didn't want to rush into anything. 'And I'd need Ma's permission, after all.'

'Your mother likes me, no problem there.' And since this was true, she tried another tack.

'We need more time to get to know each other.'

He pulled her close at that, running his hands over her slender body. 'We've been friends for years, so we know each other pretty well already, but I'd be willing to get to know you even better. Haven't I told you so a thousand times?' And, laughing, she'd slap his hand away yet again.

Sometimes he accused her of being too missish, in spite of all the kissing and the way the windows steamed up in the little car.

'Come on, Alena,' he'd plead, sliding his hand inch by inch over her knee. 'You know you're panting for it really.'

'Mickey Roscoe, I am not!'

He once suggested she should ask for a diaphragm. 'It's all right for us to go all the way now, since we're to wed, and it would save all this silly business of you trapping my hand every five minutes.'

When she'd expressed shock at discussing such a thing with the family doctor, he'd told her to find a clinic. He'd read about them in some newspaper or other, said they could supply everything necessary. But Alena flatly refused. She wouldn't even consider discussing the matter with Lizzie.

'You don't mind if I keep trying?'

'You really are a rogue, Mickey Roscoe.'

'That's why you like me.'

It's true, she thought, I do like him. He was strong, even masterful, with an impish sense of humour, and quite attractive for all his flashy style. And he carried about him a slight air of danger and promise of excitement, as if he were still a wild creature whom no one could ever truly tie down.

'We'll wait till we wed. Till then we'll just go for long walks,' she told him, settling the matter once and for all. Petrol was expensive and Mickey was saving hard, first for an engagement ring, and then a place of their own. So if there were evenings when he didn't call at Birkwith Row, Alena wasn't surprised, was almost relieved, assuming he was doing overtime, or helping Jack Turner at the Stag which he sometimes did. He was his own man, after all, he told her, not chained to her leg, lovely as that leg was.

Even so, she was surprised how dull life became when he wasn't there. She found she missed his enthusiastic chatter and positive way of looking at things. Perhaps, after all, he was a man after her own heart.

But then she'd given her heart to Rob, hadn't she? He'd always been there, her dearest friend, his quiet strength and thoughtful ways becoming an essential part of her life. Though, as Mickey constantly reminded her, she was a woman now, not a child, and perhaps he did have a point when he said that Rob was still blindly following his father's dictate, still believing every word James Hollinthwaite said. A part of her felt bound to protest at the unfairness of this accusation, yet she nursed it to herself like a defence, in the fight against a very real sense of confusion.

–

Sandra now helped Mrs Rigg in the village store, thanks to that kind lady's generous heart. On a Saturday, which was Mrs Rigg's day off, or sometimes after Alena had finished at the mill, the two girls would sit together behind the counter and gossip, when Sandra wasn't weighing out little blue bags of sugar or cones of sweets for her customers.

The pay was abominable, the hours erratic, but at least Sandra's lack of complete vision was not a problem and if she should suffer a headache, as she often did, Mrs Rigg would pack her off home with exhortations to go to bed with an Aspro. She rarely managed to do that immediately, having first to prepare Aunt Elsie's supper, but with luck she'd at least get a quiet sit down and cup of tea, followed by an early night.

Her kindly employer also permitted her a special discount on groceries, which pleased Aunt Elsie enormously, and Mrs Rigg would often give Sandra a bag of broken biscuits or a twist of tea to take home.

This afternoon, as with every other, the two girls had talked through Alena's problems: how much she missed Rob, how she understood his feelings but a part of her felt despair, even anger, at his refusal to believe Lizzie's version of events. If he loved her, as he claimed to do, why couldn't he take her word rather than James Hollinthwaite's?

But then, if he did truly love her, how dare he take the risk?

It was a depressing merry-go-round that eventually stopped when Alena grew too tired or upset to continue with it. Fortunately Sandra was openly sympathetic and in perfect accord with her friend's misery, for wasn't she suffering similar emotions over her own dear Harry?

'To think we could be sisters by now, if it weren't for Aunt Elsie.'

'Will you marry when you turn twenty-one?'

'We hope to wed on my birthday next month. We have it all planned.'

'And what does Aunt Elsie think of that?'

Sandra's pretty mouth turned down at the corners. 'She refuses to discuss it, except to say that she will not be coming to the wedding.'

'Why? I know I'm prejudiced because Harry is my brother, but what on earth has she got against him?'

'If you want my honest opinion, it's got nothing to do with Harry.' Sandra concentrated on cutting a slice of cheese, mouth tightly pursed for a moment before she continued, 'It wouldn't make any difference who it was, she'd still be against him. She needs me at home, you see. Aunt Elsie isn't at all well and is afraid something dreadful might happen to her if I am not there. I do worry about that sometimes.'

'She isn't your responsibility.'

'Yes, she is. Aunt Elsie gave me a home and brought me up. I'd have been sent to an orphanage or something awful if she hadn't.'

Alena nodded, understanding the sensitivity of the situation.

'I can only hope she doesn't have one of her bad turns on the day, or I'll never get to that wedding.' Sandra added the carefully wrapped packet to Mrs Bradley's order.

Alena was outraged at the idea. 'Don't let her walk all over you, Sandra. She's as fit as a flea really, if she would but admit it. And it's time you stood up for yourself and told her so.'

'I could never do that,' Sandra said, hands poised over the blue sugar bag she was filling, shocked by the very idea. 'What if she were to have a heart attack? It would be all my fault.'

'That's what she's banking on, you thinking that.'

But Sandra shook her head, and her voice went all dreamy. 'I can't take the risk. I keep looking at the frock I've made. Peach-coloured satin. It's hanging in my wardrobe, and I wonder if I'll ever have the chance to wear it. The wedding might never happen.'

'It will if you make it happen.'

'And the nearer the day comes, the more I long to – you know – do it. I mean, how we've managed to hold back this far is a miracle. Or sheer willpower, more like.' Sandra dropped her voice, in case someone should come into the shop and overhear this shocking admission. 'But I do wonder what it's like, don't you?' This was a familiar conversation that would bring on either giggles or tears, depending on their mood at the time.

Alena was not, strictly speaking, in a position to offer advice on the subject, since it was one she preferred to avoid. The fact that she and Rob had never consummated their love had been both a relief and source of regret to her, as if by making love they would have proved they could in no way be related. But the prospect of doing *it* with Mickey Roscoe had not, as yet, been fully explored in Alena's mind. Only in Mickey's. She still needed time.

Sandra said, 'Do you think it hurts?'

'Can't much, can it, or people wouldn't keep on doing it.' And they both collapsed into a fit of giggles, propping each other up on their stools and mopping tears of laughter from their eyes.

Their hilarity was interrupted by the arrival of Mrs Milburn in a fine lather of excitement which she barely managed to contain while purchasing a slab of Fairy household soap and some dolly blue for her next wash day. Her lips were clamped tightly together, her movements quick and angry as she slapped down halfpennies and pennies on the shiny mahogany counter top. Alena, watching her behaviour with close attention, could finally bear the suspense no longer. 'What is it, Mrs Milburn? Are you quite well?'

'If I am, it's a wonder, what with all the comings and goings I've had to put up with lately. It wasn't like this when Mrs Hollinthwaite was at home. Her dinner parties were allus elegant, polite affairs, not raucous gatherings of noisy men.'

'Oh, dear.' Alena and Sandra exchanged barely suppressed grins, struggling not to dissolve into giggles yet again. 'What has he done now?' Knowing that there was nothing Mrs Milburn liked better than to gossip about her employer, for all she might maintain otherwise.

'He's only gone and decided to turn the whole area into forest.'

'The whole area pretty well is forest already, Mrs Milburn,' Alena tactfully reminded her.

'Not conifer forest, it isn't. We have beautiful woodland here where once the King himself could come to hunt deer and have sport if he'd a mind to. We've grown fine, regal hardwood in this valley for centuries. Wonderful beech and oak that James Hollinthwaite means to cut down, though what right he thinks he has...' Mrs Milburn set down her basket on the nearby bentwood chair and leaned across the counter, propping her capacious bosom comfortably upon its polished surface as she punctuated every word with a tap of her finger. 'He means to plant up every acre he owns in this valley, and then on Longmire, Thwaite Head, Rusland Heights and Finsthwaite Heights, with Sitka spruce and larch. What he doesn't own already, he means to buy.' And she jerked her head in a fierce nod, as if to say, 'Now what do you think of that?'

Sandra and Alena didn't know what to think. Mrs Milburn was known for her tendency to exaggerate and both girls guessed even the greedy James Hollinthwaite would have difficulty in purchasing every acre of land he wanted. But they considered this piece of new information with some alarm, for all they both had enough worries of their own.

Then Alena remembered Mickey saying something about the Forestry Commission planting conifers in Ennerdale, and how he felt that kind of intense forestry threatened his own greatly loved and, in his opinion, more natural coppicing industry. How the smallness of the area could be thrown out of balance by these great towering trees, better suited to Scandinavian mountains than cloaking the miniature mountains and fellsides of the English Lake District.

'Choke this whole valley to death it will,' Mrs Milburn was saying. 'We don't want great dark plantations here. This isn't the place for bloody Christmas trees, pardon my language.'

It was so unheard of for Mrs Milburn to swear that both girls were struck speechless, unsure how to respond, but equally disturbed by the pictures she was painting.

'He wouldn't do that, surely?'

'Wouldn't he just, if it made him a deal of brass.' And they all realised that this must be true. James Hollinthwaite had never considered anybody but himself before. Why should he change now?

—

It was a week later, and Dolly had decided she'd grown tired of marriage. Respectability was not all it was cracked up to be, so far as she was concerned. And Tom was a bore. They lived such separate lives these days, you'd never think they were man and wife.

Every evening she made supper which he ate, usually in silence, and then either he went out to the pub, or she put on her glad rags, as he called them, and went out to enjoy herself. They both usually ended up at The Golden Stag, for where else was there for a bit of fun in this village? But, as with their journeys to and from work and the nights in the big wide bed, each completely ignored the other.

Tonight he'd insisted on eating early since he was going out, first to a meeting with his brothers and then on to the Stag, and Dolly certainly had no intention of sitting in waiting for him, it being a Saturday.

She spent an hour getting ready before the fire, aware of his surreptitious gaze as she rested each foot on the arm of his chair while she rolled on her stockings. She positively drenched herself in Essence of Violets, then pulled on her underwear with languorous care. Tom kept the newspaper sturdily before him throughout this performance, but Dolly sensed his attention by the way his hands clenched and ripped a page as he turned it, or the number of times he moved his chair and fidgeted. He did glance at her once, his face scarlet with anger, then snatched up the paper and turned away from her as she flounced about in her dressing gown, letting it slip off bare shoulders to reveal her plump breasts.

She stood before the mirror wearing only a pink brassiere, French knickers and her stockings and suspenders while she slapped a thick layer of pancake stick on to her face, pressing it in with a damp sponge. The tension in the small living room was so strong she almost forgot to breathe. She rubbed rouge into her cheeks and, pouting her lips with conscious seductiveness, applied the most vivid red lipstick she could find. With anyone else the result might have been catastrophic, but whether it was her skill, or because make-up actually enhanced her natural prettiness, by the time she'd pencilled her eyebrows, blackened her lashes with a dab of vaseline and soot, and pinned up her thick brown hair, she looked every bit as glamorous as one of the screen goddesses she worshipped so ardently.

She stepped into her dress, fastened it slowly, button by button, then asked with feigned innocence, one hand resting on the provocative thrust of one hip: 'Wouldn't you say I look a real corker?'

Tom cast her a contemptuous glance, taking in the voluptuous curves of her figure, the new red dress and high-heeled shoes which suited her so well, and must have cost a pretty penny.

'Where did you get the money for those?'

Dolly merely shrugged, telling him it was really none of his business, and he'd no right to be so disapproving since he'd shown no interest in her for ages. There was no doubt at all in her mind that marrying Tom Townsen had been a terrible mistake. Now he was accusing her of letting other men buy her drinks.

'You never offer, so why shouldn't I accept?'

'Because you're my wife. It only makes you look cheap.'

'Oh, that's it, is it? You don't want to be seen out with me, your own wife, but neither can I go out with anyone else. What am I supposed to do, twiddle my thumbs here all night?'

'You could come to this meeting with me.'

'Why the hell should I?'

'There's something up, something to do with James Hollinthwaite. Harry wants to tell us all about it.'

Dolly examined her lips in the mirror and dabbed at a smudge with the tip of her little finger. 'And I've told you, I've made other plans.' Then she collected her smart new coat, but didn't put it on until she got outside the door so that he could get a good view of her silk-stockinged legs. Tom watched her go with burning eyes.

–

It was quiet that night in the Stag with the place half empty. So quiet in fact that Dolly almost wished she'd gone to Harry's daft meeting. She found it hard to imagine what could be so important as to empty the pub. There was hardly anybody there at all that she knew, apart from a few old men, and she certainly had no wish to sit with them.

Then, as luck would have it, she saw James Hollinthwaite come in. He bought a whisky and took it to the table by the window. Dolly considered him. He was old enough to be her father of course, but then she didn't have a father, and he wasn't bad-looking for his age. And certainly very rich. A fact which no girl should ignore, particularly one in her situation with a useless husband and no reason to stay married to him.

She finished her glass of stout, said her goodnights to Jack Turner, then slid off the bar stool and made her way to the door, 'accidentally' knocking against James's elbow as she passed. Most of his whisky spilled all over the table and dripped on to the slate floor. Dolly put her hands to her pretty pink cheeks, dark eyes wide with dismay. 'Oh, what have I done? Let me buy you another.'

But of course, being a gentleman, he wouldn't hear of such a thing and, since she was so very distressed and all alone because her husband really had very little time to spare for her these days, he bought her a small port as well as another whisky for himself, and asked her to keep him company while they drank it. It was quite by the way that the conversation turned to his son, and a great surprise to Dolly that he hadn't heard Robert had been visited by Alena.

'Oh, dear,' said Dolly, putting the tip of one finger to her scarlet mouth and biting it with her pretty white teeth. 'She'll kill me when she finds out I've told on her.'

James Hollinthwaite covered her hand with his own and gave it a reassuring squeeze. 'Don't worry, my dear. She won't hear it from me. Do you think your husband would mind if I bought you another?'

-

Tom might very well have minded, had he not been so thoroughly engrossed in the meeting. Outraged by the prospect of their valley being swamped by conifers, all in the name of progress, the kitchen of number 14 Birkwith Row had never been so full of folk. Fierce argument raged to and fro while Lizzie tried to keep everyone's mug topped up with tea.

Sandra listened with pride as Harry warned them all of the unsightly square blocks of uniform dark green trees that had already blighted Ennerdale; of the severe unnatural edges of the plantations; the gloomy black interiors, and how the countryside lost all the usual elements of the changing seasons. No rich colours, no berries and therefore fewer birds, not even any bluebells come spring as there'd be far less sunlight on the forest floor.

'Even the nationals picked up the hot potato last year,' Harry said.

'You can't halt progress,' Bill Lindale placidly pointed out. 'If done sympathetically, I dare say the trees have a sort of beauty of their own.'

Harry thumped the kitchen table. 'They do hell as like. The Commission has made damn' few concessions. They march ahead regardless, planting when and where they like.'

'They've agreed not to touch the upper part of Kentmere, and 440 acres in Eskdale.'

'Aye, if the public purse will make recompense for the favour of not planting land that was probably implantable in any case, since it's too bloody steep.' He thumped the table with increased fervour, making it quiver. 'So, why shouldn't greedy landowners like Hollinthwaite follow suit? Who knows where it could end? Every inch of the mountains could be smothered in bloody spruce.'

He was becoming so upset that Sandra went to stand by his side and rest a hand upon his shoulder.

Alena said, 'So what do you intend to do about it?' And as one, everyone looked at her.

'What can we do?' Bill Lindale asked.

'Fight, of course,' said Harry. 'We can't let him win.'

'We could get up a petition?' Sandra suggested. 'Send a deputation?'

'Aye, we could,' Harry agreed, grinning at her with pride. 'So, are you with me or not?'

'So long as it's done in a proper manner,' said the more cautious Bill. 'I'm with you if everyone else is.'

And the shouts of the men packed into the small kitchen echoed their approval.

Chapter Sixteen

It was, without doubt a beautiful valley. A wilderness not quite tamed by man in which could be found prime sessile oak, lime, ash, alder – in fact as many as twenty different species of tree, including the famous beeches. And here too was the breeding ground for some of the finest free-ranging red deer in the land who came each autumn at rutting time. The more sedentary roe moved quietly through the forest, secure in the peace of the place. Otters bathed in the river, buzzards soared in the thermals over the fells, and badgers and red squirrels had their own secret places in the woods.

Surely a valley worth fighting for?

Harry led the deputation to present their case. They marched up the long drive to Ellersgarth Farm and offered up a list of names protesting against the plan. Many of the men with him were Hollinthwaite's own mill workers, a fact not missed by James.

Alena and Sandra hovered on the fringes of the group. Mrs Rigg, Maggie Sutton, Lizzie and some of the other women were present, looking uncomfortable and out of place amidst the heaving mass of male bodies. Even Dolly was there, for once, standing beside Tom.

James stood on his doorstep and answered their criticisms by claiming that the scheme would bring more jobs to the area, for their own sons as well as his. He denied he meant to cut down perfectly sound trees. 'No more than is necessary.'

'And how many would that be?' Harry yelled.

'Aye, go on, tell us,' put in Tom. Dolly tugged at his sleeve, warning him not to get involved. He shrugged her off.

'Some space must be cleared where trees are mature.'

'And can be sold for a profit, eh?' The mood was growing ugly.

'Trees are meant to be felled.'

'Not ad hoc, Mr Hollinthwaite,' Bill Lindale politely pointed out. 'What worries us is how this type of forestry blankets out everything else. It's not really suited to our land and climate, let alone our small valley here.'

James held on to his patience while coldly pointing out that nothing they could say or do would change his mind. He had every right to plant as many of his own acres as he wished. 'If there's ever another war,' he warned 'they'll need all my current crops of larch for lining trenches, building gun emplacements and such like, not oak for sailing ships. Those days are gone. And I shall need to replant.'

As a result of discussions with his councillor friend, George Tyson, he had made his preparations well. Since the Forestry Commission had been his role model, he too had bought land, quietly and without fuss, from farmers greedy for a bit of hard cash. And if George considered it a sad day for the Lake District to blanket it with conifers, James did not. He saw it as an opportunity. Anything the Forestiy Commission could do, he could do better.

'These woodlands were once well managed,' he pointed out in a voice rich with reasonableness for all he had to raise it over the growing tide of discontent. 'Apart from a few remaining gangs of coppicers, sadly outdated now, the forest is going to rack and ruin. Many trees are falling, they're so dangerous. Better we replant than see it disintegrate. In any case, the open fell land, which is where most of the planting will take place, is useless for anything else.'

'The sheep farmers might say different,' one voice called out.

'The government evidently don't think so, since they've allowed a grant for the Commission to carry out their plans.

Think of the relief they could to bring to unemployment in a depressed area.'

He told the men gathered before him how the Forestry Commission meant to bring in workers from West Cumberland, men perhaps more used to mining than planting trees on wild open fellsides, but it would be a job, so they'd be unlikely to complain. Why shouldn't he do likewise on his own land? Who was there to stop him? And he would be doing them all a favour by bringing work to the area, if they could but see it.

'If you make a fuss,' he warned, 'I'm not above bussing workers in myself from Workington and Whitehaven, and anywhere else I can find strong men who aren't afraid of hard work.'

'You bloody try it!' somebody shouted.

James refrained from shouting back. 'Far too much of the Lake District is being ruined by overgrazing. The planting of conifers would hold the thin soil together, enrich it for future planting.'

'You'd be bound to take that point of view, since it's in your interest,' Harry responded.

'These are the Forestry Commission's findings, not mine.' A flicker at the corner of one eye betrayed James's growing irritation.

'Aye, well, they would say that, wouldn't they? And happen in some areas it's true. But we don't have thin soil in this valley, it's rich and good. This is about brass, not trees, and we'll not let you ruin our forest in order to line your own pocket.'

Glaring down upon Harry's broad stubborn face, James felt yet again that his entire life seemed to have been blighted by interference from the Townsen family. Whatever he did, whatever he planned they disapproved, disagreed or put obstacles in the way of his achievements. The feud between the two families had worsened to such an extent that he never let himself consider how it had come about, no longer allowed himself to feel in any way responsible. They were a permanent sore in his side, an itch he couldn't rid himself of by scratching.

He turned on Harry with such venom in his tone that the whole assembled company of men were struck into silence. 'And how will you stop me doing what I please on my own land, Harry Townsen? You who are willing enough to line your own pocket at my expense, by robbing me of my profits.'

Harry took a step forward, his towering frame rigid with fury. 'What exactly are you accusing me of?' The men were almost eyeball to eyeball, a stand-off that could only end one way.

Bill Lindale stepped quickly forward, attempting to take a firm grip of Harry's solid arm and jerk him back, but Harry's iron strength made this well-nigh impossible. Before anyone else could move they were all left gasping at James's next words.

'Stealing my profits, Townsen, by claiming a bonus to which you weren't entitled. I'm not the fool you all take me for. But targets can be changed, and then you won't find it so easy to make money out of me.' He flung out an arm in an expansive gesture that indicated the entire company. 'None of you is irreplaceable. If you value your jobs in my mill, every man jack of you, then you'd best shut up and go home.' Faced with this bleak alternative, after a moment or two spent whispering and shuffling feet, many of the men seemed willing enough to do as he suggested. Work was hard to come by after all, with half the country unemployed, and they all had families to feed, rent to pay.

'Not worth losing our livelihood over a few bloody trees,' muttered one, and his mates nodded their agreement.

They began to trickle away in twos and threes, some of them wishing they'd never got involved in this argument in the first place. Who knew what repercussions there might be?

James was still talking, thumbs hooked into his waistcoat, rocking on his heels, very much a man in control, a man filled with an inflated sense of his own importance. 'You can collect your cards in the morning, Townsen. I've had enough of your sort in my mill.' And then surprisingly – though perhaps not, in view of his well-known short temper – it was Kit Townsen who surged forward and clipped Hollinthwaite's chin with his fist.

Catching him off balance, it sent him reeling backwards but, unfortunately, although it broke a tooth and produced a satisfactory flow of blood, the blow was infinitely weaker than any Ray might have inflicted in the past. Hindered as Kit was by his recurrent chest problems, his temper might be keen but his strength was not what it might be. And, in turn, with the back of one clenched fist, Hollinthwaite swatted the young man to the ground like a bluebottle batted out of the way for being a nuisance.

A subdued group of villagers gathered up a semi-conscious Kit, tightened their grip upon his furious brother and returned down the long drive, a thoroughly bedraggled bunch now, showing far less spring in their step than when they'd walked up it. James watched them go. Laughing softly to himself, he dabbed at the trickle of blood on his chin. It was only then that he noticed movement by the porch door.

'What the hell…?'

'I thought your wounds might need some attention.' And Dolly stepped out of the shadows where she'd been hiding and stood, all softness and womanly concern, in the pool of light spilling from the door. He considered her for a moment in silence then, stepping back, allowed her to precede him into the hall.

–

Alena couldn't understand why Mickey hadn't been at the meeting or joined in the deputation. He'd been the one to rouse her interest in forestry in the first place, and he, as much as any of them, would hate it if huge swathes of their woodlands were torn apart. He had spoken passionately of the freedom of the wildlife, and said how much he was against every acre of open fellside being filled with plantations.

When she asked him, he said he'd had to go and see a bloke about a bit of business.

'What sort of business?'

'What's this? Checking up on me?' And his rust brown eyes flashed, not quite meeting her shrewd gaze but glinting with satisfaction at her interest.

Alena found herself flushing. It seemed odd to feel this wave of uncertainty. He claimed to adore her, and was desperate for them to marry, so why this prickle of unease? Surely she couldn't be jealous? Of whom? And why?

Yet in the following days she found herself anxiously biting her lip if he hadn't appeared at her door by eight, afraid he might be losing interest in her because she'd insisted on waiting till they wed. And Mickey, aware of the effect of his strategy, continued to keep her guessing about when he might call. If she asked why he hadn't come to see her, he would laugh and say that surely she hadn't missed him? She decided it was because she couldn't bear the thought of being alone again. To lose Rob had been painful because she loved him so much and, despite claiming only to feel fondness for Mickey, she couldn't bear the thought of losing him as well.

Little by little she began to allow him greater freedom with her. Sometimes, when they walked in the woods, she became quite daring, might even let him lift her blouse and fondle her bare breasts. But never for a moment did Alena permit herself to lose control; for all his kisses might please her a little, they did not excite her as Rob's had done. And afterwards, alone in her room, she would curl up in her bed and feel ashamed.

It was more prudent to engage him in conversation, but whenever the question of James Hollinthwaite and his forestry plans cropped up. Mickey would shrug his shoulders and claim the planting would go ahead no matter what they did, so it was not worth risking his job over.

And perhaps he did have a point. Fighting to save the valley had cost Harry his job and Sandra all hope of a wedding next month. What would be the eventual price?

Sandra herself had similar bleak thoughts. Bad enough that Aunt Elsie had stood in the way of their marriage, but the loss of employment was far more serious. How could they marry now?

Would Harry find another job? Certainly not before the end of November. Perhaps not for months, she thought bleakly. And she would remain well and truly under her aunt's thumb, stuck in this shop weighing potatoes for the likes of Maggie Sutton forever, if she wasn't careful.

No one would dare to stand against James Hollinthwaite ever again, for fear they'd be next in line for the sack. The chances were he'd get his way now and the whole valley would change because of his greed. It made her so angry, she wanted to go right up to him and give him a piece of her mind. She, Sandra Myers, who usually never said boo to a goose. But how could she? For all she no longer worked in Hollinthwaite's mill, she was lucky to have a job of any kind, and a mere girl could never dare to set herself up against the powerful James Hollinthwaite.

Even if she could find half the confidence that Alena and, most of all, Dolly seemed to have, Sandra reminded herself of her handicap. She no longer wore the eyepatch but was always nervous of doing the bad eye more damage, or, worse, harming the other.

Yet for that very reason she, more than most, had reason to stand up against him. James Hollinthwaite had never attempted to hold her job open, nor shown any inclination to offer her an alternative. Utterly ruthless, all he ever considered were his own profits. Yet if he'd had safety guards fitted on the machine, or if the lever had been better designed, the accident might never have happened and she would still have her full sight, and be in good health. He must be partly responsible, at least. Who else could she blame?

She was filled with a sense of outrage; against Hollinthwaite, against her aunt, against all those who thought they could rule with an iron rod, and the first streak of rebellion was lit within her. It flared and glowed like a beacon, and Sandra felt a new resolve.

'I said two pounds of potatoes, not a ton.'

Jerked back to reality, she smiled an apology to Maggie Sutton as she removed several potatoes from the heap on the scales. 'Sorry. How's Dolly? I haven't seen much of her recently.'

'Neither have I. Little slut!' And Dolly's mother handed over a few coppers and left Sandra to ponder on this remark, before again weighing the odds for a solution to her troubles, almost as if they were potatoes.

–

'And what do you mean to do about it?'

Sandra slid her hand into Harry's as they sat on the horsehair sofa before her aunt, ensconced like a queen in her wing-backed chair with its antimacassars and arm protectors, anxious to show him her support.

He appreciated the gesture but it offered little comfort. In his present situation he found Aunt Elsie, who had always looked upon him as entirely unworthy of her niece in any case, even more daunting. Whenever he was in her company, he could see himself through her eyes as she critically assessed his old serge trousers, patched brown boots and jacket near worn through at the elbows.

'I'm a skilled wood turner, Miss Myers,' he said, as he strove to put a case for the marriage to go ahead regardless. Though strictly speaking Sandra would soon no longer need her aunt's permission, she still felt the need for her blessing so he had agreed to this little meeting. 'I'm a solid enough working chap, and I'm sure I'll get tekken on again. Though I realise you were happen wanting summat a bit better for Sandra.'

Elsie Myers took her time answering as she clicked her long rope of jet beads with tapering pale fingers. The sound echoed in the high-ceilinged room, seeming to emphasise everyone's awareness that she held the power. 'Sandra is very special to me, being my late brother's only child. And he left her in my care.

'You must see, Mr Townsen, that she is a gentle girl, never really suited to work in the mill which, in point of fact, was a temporary state of affairs until some better form of employment could be found, or she had become suitably affianced.' Implying it would be highly unlikely that she'd ever consider him to be a suitable candidate for the post. 'She is very nicely placed in the village shop and, as you know, I always had my doubts about this match for, as an invalid myself, I fear for the poor dear girl. Sandra may prefer to make light of the accident, but only I can understand how she must suffer.'

Sandra looked at her aunt in some surprise at this show of sympathy, since the accident had made little difference to the regime of chores she was expected to carry out. Not that she minded the work, for she was thankful still to feel useful, have some way of earning her keep in the home her aunt had kindly offered. But she did hate to be described as a 'poor dear girl.'

'She needs someone very special. And you must admit that your own situation is far too precarious now. What sort of care or security could you offer? Very little, I fear, Mr Townsen.'

Sandra felt her heart sink at the sight of the bleak expression in Harry's face at these words. Even so he did his best, stoutly informing Aunt Elsie that he considered himself a caring enough sort of bloke though he confessed to few ambitions, no political convictions beyond that of common decency to his fellow human beings and was, as he'd be the first to admit, a simple countryman born and bred, no more nor less. And again he promised to do everything in his power to make Sandra happy.

He'd spoken with such a firm conviction, as if that should be enough for anyone, that Sandra loved him in that moment, so desperately, so completely that if he'd asked her to, she'd have gone and lived with him without the blessing of matrimony, let alone the permission of her straight-laced aunt.

Yet what was the use of such dreams? Aunt Elsie got to her feet and stood regally upon her hearth rug, spine rigid. She informed Harry that although by the end of November, when Sandra reached her majority, she could by rights marry whom she wished, though such action was not to be recommended.

'I sincerely hope Mr Townsen that as a skilled man you soon find alternative employment. Until that day I shall advise my poor dear niece to wait. I am sure the last thing you would want is for her to suffer even more than she has already?'

Harry began to offer assurances that no, indeed he would not, and how he was certain he would find work soon, had in fact set many enquiries in motion. Sandra, anxious to win over her aunt, her mind on her lovely peach satin frock and the hope of lying at last in Harry's strong arms, went to stand before her. Recklessly she clutched at a hand that was dry as paper.

'We hoped, at least *I* hoped, that we could still marry next month, as arranged, and that Harry could come and live here with us. We've plenty of room, after all, and he can earn his keep by doing odd jobs about the village until something more substantial turns up. There are a few jobs he could do in the house for a start. The porch has been leaking for months. And with my job at the shop, we'd get by,' she finished rather breathlessly, her heart sinking to new depths as she saw the thunderclouds gather upon her aunt's thin face.

'My dear child, what can you be thinking of? I can't have a *man* living in *my* house! Let alone one without employment. And I'm certainly not prepared to find him any odd jobs to compensate for his being sacked. He must live off somebody else, not me.'

Harry was on his feet, face beetroot red. 'I've never asked for charity in my life, Miss Myers, and I'm certainly not asking for it now. Sandra had no right to ask such a thing. If I'd known... I'd rather we never married at all, than for me to live off her earnings.' And, stiff with pride, he walked away. The door banged behind him so hard it flew open again and a flurry of dried leaves gusted in and scattered across the floor.

'There, didn't I tell you he was using you?' Aunt Elsie said, and Sandra ran to her room to curl up in a ball on her bed and wish she'd learned to keep her mouth shut.

–

Coils of smoky mist laced the trees as Dolly ran through the woods. Each silver skein, breaking and reforming about the fragile stems of alder and birch, created a picture as delicate and colourless as a sepia print. The moon seemed to hang from a tree like a pale lantern when, her stomach knotted with excitement, she hurried through a green tunnel of overhanging branches, feet slipping on the carpet of mossy grass in her haste, knowing he would be waiting and that tonight, at last, it might happen.

Marriage? You could keep it. No, far more exciting was this secret life she lived. A life of which no one but herself, and the other person involved, was aware. What did you call it? A tryst? A rendezvous? Even the strange words excited her.

She crept through a gap in the hedge, droplets of the soft Lakeland rain that had fallen earlier dampening her hair. But she paid it no heed, edging her way along, not wishing to walk out in the open in case someone should see her. This was only her third visit to Ellersgarth Farm. On the first, the night of the deputation, she'd dressed James's wounds and listened sympathetically to his sad tale of a runaway wife and an ungrateful son. Dolly let it be known, by hint and innuendo, that she wouldn't be averse to offering him a little comfort.

'A lonely life has to be filled in some way, hasn't it?' she'd remarked, seeing the glimmer of interest when he'd thanked her, and feeling the way his hand had lingered upon her shoulder as he'd shown her to the door.

The second time she'd called at the farm with a home-made fruit cake she'd slaved over for hours, since baking wasn't exactly her strong point but was the only excuse she could come up with to see him again. James had invited her in and offered her sherry in the parlour. He could have told her that Mrs Milburn was an excellent cook and made a superb fruit loaf; instead the messages they'd sent each other over the rims of their crystal glasses had set Dolly's heart thudding with the danger of it all.

She didn't think of Tom. So far as she was concerned, any way she could hit back at her husband for his neglect was surely fully justified.

Today, James had actually asked her to call, waylaying her on her way out of the mill. He rarely came anywhere near the mill yard or his workers, so she was flattered. She'd put on a pretty rose-print frock with a deep vee neckline and now hurried along under cover of the hedge on soft feet. Perhaps he would offer her champagne before he made passionate love to her? And although she felt nervous, unsure even, she also felt rebellious. This was a man of experience, of wealth and power, and he wanted her. That would show Tom Townsen!

The sudden grip on her arm caught her off balance and Dolly found herself jerked to the ground before she'd realised what was happening. Winded by her fall, she felt the sharpness of stones like blades of steel against her backbone.

'What the hell...?'

'I might ask you the same question. What exactly are you up to, Dolly Townsen? What the hell do you think you're doing, creeping about James Hollinthwaite's place? Or need I ask?'

Her lip curled with contempt, even as she struggled to free herself. She could have lied, told him anything, even that she was gathering wood for the fire, and he'd be fool enough to believe her. Instead she said on a note of triumphant defiance, 'Visiting my lover, what else? At least he's man enough to do what you're not.'

'If that's what you want, then we'd best not disappoint you.' She thought he meant to let her go then and started to laugh, but found both her wrists held in one cruel grip as if in a steel trap, while Tom's other hand was pulling up her skirt, searching for the button that held up her camiknickers.

'God Almighty, what d'you...' But she got no further as she needed all her strength now to fight him, though she had little

236

in her armoury. She tried feet and knees, kicking and scrabbling in the mud and leaves in her efforts to hurt him. She even used her teeth, feeling the sting of blood run over her tongue as his mouth grated against hers. Dolly could smell the beer he must have drunk, taste it in her mouth, and somewhere deep inside a memory stirred.

He was glaring down at her with the kind of expression that brought a bolt of excitement shooting right through her, shocking her by revealing itself in a groan of pleasure as his fingers discovered the soft core of her. 'You're my bloody wife. Have you forgotten that? Not man enough, you say? We'll see about that, damn you. If anyone has the right to have you, Dolly, it's bloody me.'

Her protests now were weak. It was already too late. Her underclothing now hung shamelessly upon a nearby holly bush and Tom was thrusting inside her, grunting and sweating and groaning, still holding her arms pinned to the ground above her head. But no longer did she resist him. For all her seeming helplessness, Dolly was arching her back and moving with him, her body instinctively responding to the rhythm of his, greedy to capture the full force of his manhood. Then it was over in a cataclysm of emotion and he rolled off her, adjusted his clothing and walked away, not even turning back when she called his name, nor paying any heed to the sound of her sobbing.

Chapter Seventeen

Dolly lay staring up at the leaf patterns playing in the shafts of moonlight upon the dark ceiling, her eyes hot and dry.

She was frantic with worry. Tonight she'd hurried home at the end of her early shift and prepared a tasty mutton hotpot for supper, put on the rose-print frock, dabbed a bit of ivory powder on her face and outlined her full lips enticingly with a matching pink lipstick. Maggie was out, staying overnight with Mr Turner at the Stag, which meant they'd have the house to themselves for once. Smiling over her plans, Dolly fluffed out her hair and settled to wait for her husband to come home and be bowled over afresh by her charms.

Now it was past ten and he hadn't been in all evening. Where on earth could he be? He'd been behaving more oddly than usual this last week or two, if that were possible, ever since he'd taken her so roughly in the woods. Perhaps he was ashamed of treating his wife in such a way? But to Dolly, that moment had been a revelation.

'I don't blame you,' she'd told him, when she'd finally followed him home that night and, just as if nothing untoward had occurred, climbed into the big bed beside him in her mother's front room. They'd lain side by side, like a pair of logs she thought, all silent and stiff. 'Did you enjoy it?' she'd softly asked. 'Reminded me how we used to be so good together. Do you remember?'

He had not replied. Whether he had indeed been remembering, or simply going to sleep, she never knew.

She did know how much she loved him, and could only hope his taking her like that meant he still had some feelings for her. Oh, dear God, what had she done? She'd worried over how to convince him she was sorry, that she would behave better in future. Vowed to talk to him, to explain properly how she felt and how much she really cared for him. But the following morning and every day since then, the subject had not been mentioned. Even now, weeks later, he still refused to discuss their problems, for all she was trying so hard to be a good wife to him.

Dolly hadn't been near the pub for weeks. She sat in, good as gold, night after night, determined to show that she had changed. And although Tom still went out as much as ever, she didn't complain, not once. She just kept on hoping he'd notice. The effort was almost killing her, but she'd decided to save her marriage, no matter what the sacrifice involved.

–

Harry and Sandra sat on the drystone wall staring into the swirling waters of the beck as she struggled to understand what he was telling her.

'So, taking everything into account, I reckon it would be best if we didn't see each other for a while.'

'Not see each other?' Sandra was staring up at him, her face a picture of disbelief. 'Why? What are you trying to say, Harry?'

He shifted uneasily. 'I think you can guess.'

'No, tell me. Look at me.' She grasped his arms and gave him a little shake. His usually bright, laughing face looked all tight and cold and angry. But he would not look at her. He kept his gaze fixed somewhere over her left shoulder.

'It's because of my eye, isn't it? Because I'm half blind.'

'No, don't ever think that.' He did look at her then yet still not quite seeing her. There was a vagueness to his gaze, as if it were fixed on some distant place. Only the anger in his voice, harsh and grating, revealed his pain. 'Your aunt's right. There's naught I can offer you. I've no job, no house of us own to live in, a few quid in the Post Office and that's about it. You deserve better, Sandra. More than I've got to give.'

'You gave me your love. I don't need anything else.' There were tears in her voice, on her cheeks, splashing on to his hands where they hung between his knees, but she could not stop them.

He took her hands gently between his own and set them on her lap. folding them together as if setting her free. 'Let's just leave it for now. Consider the engagement at an end, Sandra love, at least until I... Happen I'll find work next week, tomorrow mebbe, but I can't just sit here and starve, and pull you down with me.'

'We won't starve, there's my... We could go somewhere else. Start again. Together.'

'Where could we go? I'll not risk uprooting you till I've summat decent to offer you. Work'll be hard to find, I'm not fooling myself over that. Everywhere's as bad these days.' There was an edge of bitterness to his anger now. 'Haven't you heard of the hunger march from Jarrow, the soup kitchens opening the length and breadth of the land? The three million unemployed?'

'What about the Public Assistance Committee?' she asked helplessly, knowing his pride wouldn't allow him to take help from anyone.

'They won't do aught to help, since I were sacked. It's up to me.'

'But I'll wait for you, Harry. I don't mind waiting.'

'I'll not hold you to it. If you should meet somebody else...'

'I won't. I don't want anybody else.' She felt frantic with anxiety, wanting to cling to him but not daring even to touch him as he seemed so different, so remote and formal. Already he was getting to his feet, had moved a foot away from her. It felt like a mile. He thrust his hands deep into his pockets and then, on a note of bravado, lifted his chin, winked at her and walked away. She thought the sound of his boots echoing on the stones of the packhorse bridge would stay with her for ever.

Alena held Sandra close and let her sob out her pain and misery unchecked. Miss Myers was 'having a lie down to ease a troublesome headache', and the two girls were free to sit before a fire of half a dozen small coals that gave off little, if any, heat in the cold parlour. But it was painful to witness her friend's anguish. Hadn't she suffered enough? She'd given her love so joyously and unselfishly to Harry, patiently waiting for her twenty-first birthday and her dreams to be realised. Now she felt let down, cheated, overwhelmed by despair.

When the storm of tears subsided, or there were none left to shed, Alena went into the neat little kitchen, turned on the gas and set the kettle over the flame, feeling a righteous burst of anger towards her brother for all loyalty made her able to understand his point of view. Unfortunately, Aunt Elsie, though a difficult and selfish old woman, did have a valid point. Harry could not, in his present circumstances, afford to keep a wife.

Setting a steaming cup of tea in front of Sandra, best China of course, as befitted the Grove House, Alena attempted to say some of this. 'It's probably only temporary. Harry's right, he's a skilled worker. Some other mill will be glad to take him on. I don't know what Hollinthwaite was thinking of to sack him, let alone over a trick that every bobbin worker plays. But then, who can understand that man?'

But Harry didn't find any work, not that week or the next. Every day he caught the workers' bus and went round all the bobbin mills he could think of, asking for work. There was none to be found. In desperation he went as far afield as Workington and Barrow, returning each evening increasingly demoralised, the situation there being even worse. If he wasn't careful, all his meagre savings would be used up in travelling while he looked for an elusive job. He'd even gone against his principles and asked the Forestry Commission for work, but all their jobs were taken.

There were times when Sandra saw him in the village, some-times waiting for his mates to come out of the mill at the end of their shift. He would look so dejected, hands thrust deep into his pockets, shoulders hunched, that all her instincts cried out for her to run to him, but she never did. She thought he was aware of her passing by, but he would always half turn away, as if to discourage any action on her part. Sandra understood that it was his pride that had made him end their engagement, not lack of love for her. One day, perhaps, that love would bring him back to her, if she waited.

It was on her twenty-first birthday, a dull, rainy, lonely day at the end of November 1936, that she decided to fight James Hollinthwaite. Alena came for tea: tinned salmon sandwiches and a jam sponge with a single candle to celebrate the auspicious day. Aunt Elsie ate her fill then retired to bed early after all the 'excitement'. And as the two girls sat toasting bread by the fire on the end of a long toasting fork, and enjoying the two bottles of stout that Alena had secreted in her coat pocket, Sandra made her decision.

What did she have to lose? She would start a campaign. Alena might have laughed at the very idea of quiet, mouse-like Sandra campaigning for anything, let alone setting herself up against the formidable James Hollinthwaite, had she not seen the glint of resolve in her friend's eye.

'He'll destroy this place as surely as he tries to control the people within it. Someone's got to stop him. Why not me? Are you with me or not? What have you got to lose, except your job?'

Alena laughed, thought of all she had suffered at James Hollinthwaite's hands, and a kind of recklessness raced through her. Sandra was right. He did need stopping. Job or no job. And she had no intention of being afraid of him. 'What indeed?'

Sandra set about her campaign with a diligence that surprised even herself. Aunt Elsie was appalled by the activity and resulting mess in her kitchen but, for once, Sandra did not allow this to deter her.

She painted posters to advertise the public meeting she planned to hold, and pinned them up all over the village. The vicar agreed to her using the village hall, and Mrs Rigg provided a selection of biscuits to go with the tea Sandra had bought. She asked Lizzie if she would make it, but the expression of panic that came into the woman's troubled face told her this had been a mistake.

'Nay, I'd love to help, lass. But what with our Harry out of work, my wages are important, for all they're little enough. You'll have to find someone else.' But this proved surprisingly difficult. Everyone had some reason why they couldn't help. Few promised even to attend. They'd something else on, family visiting whom they hadn't seen in an age, or else they had a cold, a headache, didn't feel quite up to the mark. The more honest openly confessed, as Lizzie had done, that they daren't take the risk. Even so, Sandra was determined to go ahead with the meeting, as planned.

–

Another supper kept warm in the oven, another night in alone for Dolly. She couldn't even face eating so sat in misery by the burned-out coals in the empty grate, all her merry plumpness falling away and she didn't even care. Where was he tonight? Surely he wasn't going to risk attending Sandra's meeting, not after what had happened to Harry?

Jack Turner at the Stag had told Maggie that young Tom rarely showed up there any more. He'd been seen on long walks, spotted in the woods, but whether alone or not, Dolly couldn't say. Tom wouldn't be with some other woman, would he? The thought made her feel all queasy and sick inside. He surely wouldn't do that to her, he wouldn't. Nevertheless jealousy was born in her. She even, for the first time, began to wonder how he had felt when the rumours had gone around about her and Danny Fielding, for all it had only been an innocent bit of fun.

Reaching a decision, she tipped the dried remains of his meal into the bin, put on her coat and went looking for him. She'd give him a piece of her mind, that she would. But, as she'd feared, he wasn't at The Golden Stag. Nobody had seen him all evening. Nor was he at Sandra's meeting, as one glance into the village hall confirmed.

Dolly walked the entire length of the lane right through the village as far as Hollin Bridge, but still hadn't seen him by the time she reached the end and turned despondently, to head back home. Could he be in someone's house? Whose? She knocked on a few doors only to see heads shake and hear their denials. No one knew where Tom was.

Shivering with cold and emotion, she decided to call it a day, and set out along the path through the woods that fringed Ellersgarth Farm. It would save at least half a mile. She thought nothing of the rustling in the undergrowth, or the crack of a twig, thinking it a deer or rabbit. And then she almost fell over him.

He was lying in the shadows beneath a sycamore but she knew at once that it was him. She recognised the sound of his groans. And Dolly, being Dolly, assumed it to be a woman that caused him to gasp and moan in such a way. Hadn't she heard the sound often enough before? Hot rage, fuelled by the bitter disappointment she felt in her marriage, flooded through her and she flew at him, hands flailing, ready to slap him about the ears for his betrayal. But they weren't groans at all that she had heard, but sobs. Her husband lay on the damp grass with his arms wrapped about his head, crying his heart out.

–

Alena had made a point of arriving first, so she could turn on the gas and set the big kettles to boil. It was cold in the village hall and she kept on her coat and hat while she did it.

Sandra arrived five minutes later, dressed in a smart navy blue costume with a short belted jacket and calf-length skirt cut on the bias. She'd made it herself from a worn out jersey wool frock of Aunt Elsie's and was reasonably pleased with the result. She'd pinned a large daisy just below the shoulder as a note of defiance, but felt far from brave as she spread the tablecloth and set out cups and saucers and plates of biscuits. The short speech she'd prepared lay upon the table, and, as the fingers of the village hall clock crept towards seven o'clock, her nervousness increased accordingly.

'I must be crazy, taking on James Hollinthwaite. What am I thinking of?'

'I wouldn't worry.' Alena told her, a touch of asperity in her voice. 'No one will come. They are all too afraid of him. There'll be you, me, and Mrs Rigg's biscuits. Will she give us a refund on the uneaten ones, do you reckon?'

Sandra giggled. 'Oh, Alena. How would I do without you?'

'Very well, by the looks of you.' And Alena hugged her friend. 'I admire you. Your campaign has at least given you something else to think about besides Harry.' And got you out of the clutches of dreadful Aunt Elsie for a while, she might well have added.

'And stopped you thinking about Rob, or whether to marry Mickey?' As she saw Alena's face, Sandra hurried on, 'But it isn't just that I need something to do. I'm serious about this campaign. What if you're right and only a few people do come, the old and the unemployed probably? What then?'

'You'll give your speech and I'll move from chair to chair around the hall, applauding madly. Or you could do a rendition of "The Biggest Aspidistra in the World", and hope you get paid for it as well as Our Gracie.' And they both fell to giggling again at this delightful notion.

But for all their hilarity they were relieved when, at five to seven, the door opened and old Joe Pickthall walked in, leaning heavily on his walking stick. He hadn't worked for James Hollinthwaite for years, so had nothing to lose by opposing him as he fiercely announced to the girls. They exchanged a speaking glance.

'He'll not rape oor valley wi' them gaunt giants,' the old man said with spirit.

His arrival seemed to start a small rush. Three other old men followed him in and one woman, a Mrs Simpson, who had lived alone since her son and husband were both killed in the last war. She promptly sat down and got out her knitting.

'She probably thinks she's come to a parish council meeting,' Alena whispered, and suddenly felt so nervous she had to bite her lip hard to stop herself from laughing. Sandra looked almost ethereal, her thin face gaunt with worry. Then just as the clock started to strike seven, Harry walked in and, nodding to them by way of greeting, sat on the end chair nearest the door on the back row, twisting his cap in his lap but not speaking to anyone.

No one else came. Sandra gave her talk in a small high-pitched voice and when she had finished there was a brief flurry of applause. She'd hoped that Harry would come over and congratulate her, but he got up, hooked his cap back on over his thatch of blond hair and slid quietly out of the hall. She watched him go with raw agony in her eyes.

Alena made a pot of tea, which the seven of them drank. Old Mrs Simpson said she'd really enjoyed herself and had got twenty-two rows done. The three old men had a good moan about trees, the lack of employment for the young, and the weather, not necessarily in that order. And Joe compared James Hollinthwaite's high-handedness with the antics of: 'That chap Hitler who reckons he can decide who does what and when and with who. Stopped marriage between Germans and Jews he has. You should go and start a protest there, lass. If we don't stop him, we'll have another war.'

But none of them laughed. It suddenly wasn't funny any more, and somehow put things in perspective.

–

'We have to talk.' Dolly and Tom sat together in a heap of fallen leaves. Cocooned in the soft dusk and quiet rustlings of the forest, perhaps now at last they were free to speak of their pain.

'I've missed one of me monthlies, Tom.' Silence. 'What if I've fallen again after – after – you know? That would be summat, eh?' And Dolly realised her mistake at once, for he turned his back on her with a snort of derision.

'And how would I know it were mine, if you did?' His voice was so hard and bitter, she couldn't believe she'd heard right.

''Course it would be yours!' She was outraged by the accusation. But no matter how hard she tried to convince him that he was the only man she'd ever actually done it with, she could tell by the frozen stiffness of his back that he didn't believe her. 'Since we were wed anyroad,' she acknowledged, wanting to be honest.

'There you are then. You're cheap, Dolly, that's your problem. Anybody's for a farthing. How do I even know if that bairn you lost were mine?'

Her throat felt tight and swollen and she could hardly get the words out. 'Oh, Tom, 'course he was. He was the spitting image of you. How can you say such a thing?'

'Well, you didn't seem to care much about him.'

'Are you saying it were my fault that the baby died? I wanted him same as you did. I just wanted him to have a father. Fathers are important to a child.'

'But not a husband to a wife, eh? You were back at work days after he died, without a care in the world. I was the only one of us to grieve.' He was facing her now, punching himself in the breast with his fist, and Dolly was waving her hand to quieten him, afraid he'd storm off and leave her before they'd made their peace.

'That's not true, it's not true!'

She could see his eyes glittering angrily in the darkness. 'It's true all right. You tarted yourself up and went back to work as if naught had happened. You didn't give a damn our baby had died. Never have. And while I grieved, you threw yourself at any pair of trousers that came within hailing distance. Now, apparently, you've decided to go for summat a bit older. Not to mention richer. Well, you're bloody welcome to him!'

She hadn't realised Tom had grieved so much for the baby. He'd never said, keeping his feelings all bottled up, showing only anger. She'd thought he was annoyed with her for making him marry her, and he'd thought she hadn't cared about their child. Now he believed she bothered with other men, and as a result no longer trusted her.

Deep down Dolly knew his suspicions to be justified. She had flirted with and chatted up quite a few blokes in these last few years, usually in the Stag, and also under the bridge with Danny a time or two. More to flatter her own vanity than anything really serious. Though things might have got a bit out of hand, admittedly, if Tom hadn't followed her to Ellersgarth Farm that night. She could feel her cheeks burning with shame in the darkness. Just as well he had, really. She'd been a right daft fool. The question was, though, could she explain all of this to Tom? Was it too late for her to save her marriage?

–

On Monday morning, Alena was working in the drying room, just off the barrel house. She was sewing the tops of the sacks with a curved needle and string, using blanket stitch and finishing off with a pair of 'pig's lugs', one at each corner. When the sack was ready she would use these lugs to lift it on to the bogey, and when they were all done, push it to the loading bay where she'd fling the heavy sacks of bobbins through the big doors on to the truck in the yard below.

The men in the yard shouted up to her. 'How did your meeting go? Have you saved the world yet?'

Incensed, she shouted back, 'At least we're trying, which is more than can be said for some folk.'

'We've more sense. Listening to you Townsens can get a bloke in trouble. Mind, there's some forms of trouble I wouldn't mind getting into with you, Alena, if you'd only say the word.' And there followed the kind of ribald joking she could only deal with by closing her ears and pinning a smile to her face. But, still with a touch of the tomboy in her, she managed to fling down the sacks faster than they could catch them, and never quite where they expected, so that minutes later they were begging her to slow down and she was the one laughing.

Mickey came to her during her dinner break and sat next to her at the trestle table to eat his sandwiches. 'You'll be giving up this campaign nonsense now, I take it?' he said. 'Now that it hasn't worked and the meeting was a failure.'

She looked at him aghast. 'Who says it hasn't worked? We've hardly started yet. Sandra's really got the bit between her teeth. She's planning more posters, letters to the newspapers, all kinds of things.'

He snorted with laughter. 'I suppose it'll keep her mind off her troubles, but you have better things to occupy your time.'

'Such as? Making bobbins for James Hollinthwaite?'

'Planning our wedding, I don't like my girl chatting up men in the yard.' He sincerely hoped too that those men would never let on it had been he who had actively put them off attending the meeting, warning of likely reprisals from Hollinthwaite if they did. He might care deeply about the Lake District, and the coppicing industry in particular, but Alena was more important than anything else in his life. Mickey did not intend to lose her, or let her go on playing fast and loose with their plans.

'Chatting up?' She couldn't believe what she was hearing. 'If there was any chatting up being done, it was by them, not me. Don't be so touchy, Mickey.'

'I won't be made a fool of. Time I put a ring on that pretty finger of yours, and let them see who you belong to.'

'I don't belong to anyone.'

'Aye, you do,' he said and, grabbing her to him, kissed her full on the mouth right there in the canteen in front of everyone.

The girls giggled while the men roared with laughter, stamped their feet and cheered as the kiss went on and on. Alena couldn't move since Mickey's embrace was tight about her, trapping her arms to her sides. When he finally let her go she was all hot and flushed, and utterly speechless.

'When's the happy day then?' a voice called out.

'Soon,' Mickey grinned. 'And you're all invited.'

And unless she was to look even more foolish, Alena could do nothing but sit and smile at the ensuing saucy remarks. The mill canteen was not a place for oversensitivity. But as the men got up to go back to work, she called out to them: 'Not that any of you deserve an invitation since you're all cowards, the lot of you. You'd roll over and play dead if Hollinthwaite told you to, while he strangles your valley to death. Haven't you considered that you and your sons could be out of work in a few years' time. He'll be making more money out of harvesting his spruce than he will out of bobbins then.'

There was a momentary silence while this was digested. Even Lizzie paused in pouring out a cup of tea for a latecomer. The whole room seemed to hold its breath for a long moment, then one by one the men shuffled off back to work. It hadn't escaped Alena's notice that not one of them had argued with her.

Lizzie raised her eyebrows, a twinkle in her grey eyes, before continuing with her pouring. Mickey, however, looked less pleased and told Alena sharply that they'd get down to details about the wedding when he came round later that evening, and hadn't she better get back to work?

'I'm going,' she said, and walked away from him with the kind of swaying athletic grace that made his mouth go all dry.

When she reached home that evening, Alena flung off her coat and flopped down at the kitchen table as if she carried the cares of the world on her shoulders. In a way she felt as if she did. 'Why do I feel so strange?' she asked Lizzie. 'I know Mickey wants to get married as soon as possible. He never stops going on about it, and I am fond of him, so why do I keep putting him off?'

'Nay, don't ask me. I'm only your mother.' Lizzie folded freshly ironed shirts while she listened to her daughter search her heart.

'I suppose I don't feel ready.'

'You're young yet. But if you've any doubts, lass, you can postpone it, or even call it off. You don't have to wed Mickey Roscoe.' Lizzie's eyes were soft. She longed to cradle this precious daughter in her arms while knowing it would not have been the right thing to do. Alena was a woman with a mind of her own who had to make decisions for herself. Sometimes such decisions were hard. Lizzie was beginning to think that full-grown children were more of a problem than when they were little. If there wasn't one of them to worry over, it was another.

'Oh, but I want to marry him, really I do,' Alena was saying. 'We get on well and he's such fun.' She could never admit to her mother how his lovemaking fascinated her. If she enjoyed his kisses and didn't mind him caressing her, it surely meant she must be growing to love him? 'It's only that he's anxious for us to be together. Mickey is the impatient sort, greedy for life. He wants everything to happen quickly, which is usually my problem so how can I blame him for it? And I know we'll be happy.'

'It's just cold feet then?' Lizzie queried, and Alena agreed that it must be. She was certain that once they could truly afford to marry, she'd be more than ready. 'We haven't even a home to call our own yet.'

She was startled therefore when Mickey arrived later that evening in his best brown serge suit, and announced he'd been promoted to foreman. Arthur, it seemed, had been pensioned off as he never did anything but ask for favours from the managers. 'Mr Hollinthwaite says he was too much on the side of the workers, which isn't the point of a foreman at all.' He also told Alena he'd had a bit of luck and found them a good house, quite close by, and saw no reason, if Mrs Townsen were agreeable, why they shouldn't get wed on the first day of spring.

—

Much to Dolly's disappointment her period arrived the following week. It caused her severe stomach cramps and when she went off to bed early, Tom brought her up a cup of tea. Since their long talk he hadn't been out once to the pub, which gave her some cause for hope. She'd caught him looking at her once or twice in a thoughtful sort of way. Perhaps he was softening, which helped her remain resolute in her determination to make a go of things.

'We've not struck lucky this time,' she admitted with some shyness as he slid a hot water bottle in beside her. 'But happen we could try again. If you wanted to?' And although he said nothing, Dolly noticed how he went off downstairs again with that thoughtful look on his face.

The following day he came home with a cut lip and a black eye. 'It's all right, don't panic. You should see the other bloke.' And he grinned. 'I've just given that Danny Fielding a piece of my mind. Told him not to interfere with my wife in future, if he knows what's good for him.'

'Oh, Tom, you didn't! But Danny Fielding and I never...'

'Aye, so you said, but it'll do no harm for him to know I choose to believe *you*, and not him. I'll stand no more nonsense. I wanted to make that clear.'

Dolly had the sense to keep her mouth shut and be grateful, for it seemed that some sort of male pride had been salvaged by this boyish display of fisticuffs. And if Tom were championing her again, it looked as if he meant to keep her.

Then his face softened slightly as he hunkered down beside her chair and very tentatively rubbed the tip of one finger over her hand.

'We didn't get off to a good start, you and me, eh?'

'No.'

'But if you're serious about trying again, I wouldn't be against the idea. If it isn't too late.'

Dolly could scarcely breathe for pleasure. 'Do you think it is?'

He was very nearly smiling, and there was in his eye that familiar glint, the one which always set her heart racing. 'Happen not. Now you sit there and put your feet up. You still look a bit washed out. I'll make tea tonight.'

Chapter Eighteen

On the twelfth of December 1936, King Edward renounced the throne for the sake of the woman he loved. The papers were full of it and since everyone had been gripped with the romance of it all for months, no one was without an opinion on the subject.

Sandra believed he should be allowed a morganatic marriage. Alena considered he should put duty first and give her up, and Mickey insisted that he would never give up Alena, so why should the king give up Mrs Simpson?

Alena gave a light laugh. 'Never? That's a bit drastic, isn't it? What if something happened – you lost your job for instance, as Harry did, and could no longer afford to marry?'

'I wouldn't lose my job.'

She felt her irritation with him growing. 'These things happen.'

'Not to me.'

'All right then, what if I lost my job and changed my mind about marrying you?'

'You wouldn't change your mind. You know I'd always look after you. How could you even suggest otherwise?' And such a wounded expression came into his rust brown eyes that she felt guilty at her impatience, and hastened to reassure him that, of course, she was only teasing.

'You should stop worrying about the king and concentrate on making plans for our wedding,' he gently scolded. 'It will be spring before you know it.'

In a wave of panic Alena went straight to Sandra. 'It's all happening so *fast*. I tell Mickey I'm not ready but he doesn't seem to listen. Oh, Sandra, what am I to do? Why do I feel like this?'

Surprisingly, the first thing her friend said was, 'Will you tell him?'

'Tell who?'

'Rob, of course, about your coming marriage. You still write to him, don't you? What do you think he'll say?'

Alena clicked her tongue impatiently. 'It's really none of his concern. If Rob Hollinthwaite chooses to believe his father's lies, nothing I do can be of any interest to him, ever again.' But the words did not in any way express how she truly felt.

Sandra, close enough to Alena to understand this, gave a sympathetic smile. 'It's rich, isn't it? I long to marry and can't. You could marry but can't quite bring yourself to do it.' And the two girls wrapped their arms about each other and wept.

'I've turned into a silly female,' Alena said, wiping away the tears. 'Anyone would think I didn't want to marry Mickey but I do, really I do. He's kind, and good fun, and quite an exciting lover, you know.'

'Oh, well, that's all right then. You can spend all your time in bed.' And they both fell into a fit of the giggles which for once did not make either of them feel any better.

Alena told Mickey that there was plenty of time before next spring, and she was really far too busy to think of weddings at the moment. The two girls spent every spare moment writing letters to everyone of influence they could think of, as well as to all the local newspapers. Sandra painted huge placards in bold bright letters and walked about the village with them tied about her. The response was more likely to be laughter than support but it didn't put her off trying. She would follow people along the street, bullying them into listening to her.

'For goodness' sake, leave me alone, Sandra,' some would say in guilty exasperation, then take one of her leaflets. Others would rush into their houses and shut the door.

But finding the money for the campaign was a real problem. It was needed to buy paper and envelopes and stamps, which greatly strained their meagre resources. The sealed envelopes would sit on Aunt Elsie's dresser for weeks while they saved up to send them off one at a time. It came as no surprise to either of them that they received few replies.

Mickey spent Christmas with the Townsen family, sharing in their jollity. It felt odd, at first, to have him there as if he were already a part of the family, but Lizzie said it was the right thing to do.

Everyone exchanged gifts, and he gave them all a small present by way of appreciation. For Alena, there was the long-promised engagement ring. It had a single tiny diamond on a gold band. When he slid it on to her finger she almost shouted at him to take it off again, but then her family kissed and congratulated her and she smiled and let Mickey kiss her too.

Getting engaged made her feel suddenly grown-up, as if she must take life more seriously in future. But it was quite exciting all the same. Later that night, as she lay curled up in her bed, warming her toes on the stone hot water bottle, the panic returned and Alena wondered whether she had done the right thing. What would marriage with Mickey be like? Would they be happy? She couldn't always make him out. He was quite possessive and proprietorial, which was flattering in a way, but then could be completely absorbed in his own affairs and scarcely give her a thought.

Deep down she knew she still loved Rob. Her longing for him was like a sickness, but there was also a burning anger that he'd abandoned her, for good this time. How different her life could have been if only James Hollinthwaite hadn't told that shocking lie. She hated him for that. She wished she could hate Rob too for believing it, as if he were to blame for her unhappiness. So many secrets and lies.

Where was Rob this Christmas? Had he spent it with Olivia, or all alone in his lodgings? Would he one day regret his decision to believe James and not her? Or perhaps find himself another girl to marry? A king would willingly give up a crown for the woman he loved, but Rob Hollinthwaite couldn't give up his belief in his father, even when that father lied. No doubt because he'd never loved Alena quite as much as she had loved him.

The sudden bleakness of this thought kept her awake so long into the night that she felt sick and exhausted the next morning. But in the bright light of day, with her mother laughingly scraping the brace of pheasant they'd enjoyed on Christmas Day for any meat fragments she could put into the Boxing Day soup, and her brothers their usual boisterous selves, with even Harry in a jolly mood for once, Alena felt as near to contentment as she ever had since Rob had gone.

Sandra was coming round later, and there'd be Dolly and Tom who seemed much more relaxed, almost reconciled, also Jim and Ruby with their brood, and still a whole day of rest and fun to enjoy. They'd no doubt go sledging, pound each other with snowballs then eat Lizzie's delicious soup followed by her famous mince pies, and play silly games like Blind Man's Bluff and Snap, giggling as much as the children and finishing off with a lusty rendition of carols. Oh, yes, she was very lucky. It made Alena feel guilty to realise just how fortunate she was. She had a loving, happy family about her, and now Mickey as well. She really shouldn't be so selfish as to deny Rob the same. Their friendship was over. A fact of life she really must come to accept.

–

During the cold weeks of January, Sandra seemed to be taking over her aunt's house as much as the campaign was taking over her life. She still worked at Mrs Rigg's shop, still took care of Aunt Elsie's constant needs, but once these essential chores were done, she devoted herself entirely to the campaign. The harder she worked, the less time she had to think.

Papers lay everywhere. A few people had replied, sending their best wishes and support, or making helpful suggestions.

A few even sent money, which was greatly appreciated, for the much-depleted funds. She borrowed material on the subject of afforestation from the CPRE, and from the Friends of the Lake District, and spent hours reading and studying it, trying to understand the long-term implications. The latter organisation had been particularly helpful and had themselves taken up the case by writing to Hollinthwaite and to the *Westmorland Gazette* on the matter.

At one point she followed up their suggestion to ask him if he would be willing to take on the services of a landscape architect to plan how the new softwoods could best be blended in without spoiling the appearance of the present woodlands. Hollinthwaite refused. She wrote again, since he refused to meet her in person, asking if he would at least consider mixed woodland, or staggering the boundaries of the plantations he meant to put on his open land so they were not square blocks. He did not reply.

Sandra understood the reason he did not agree to any of these things: because they would detract from his profits by making the timber more expensive to harvest. Sometimes she became tired and frustrated, wondering if her efforts were getting her anywhere at all, and then one day she heard that a group of contractors had moved in and the first few acres of hardwoods were in the process of being felled.

All the villagers hurried to watch, even abandoning their lathes at the bobbin mill to rush out and stand in horror as beautiful beech and ash trees fell, for no other reason than the pursuit of cash and the need to create space for what Hollinthwaite considered to be more commercial timber. And although the destruction was taking place on his own land, this seemed little consolation as they considered how much of the village and its surrounding area he actually owned. The felling proved that he was entirely serious about his plan.

Pandemonium broke out. Men and women, usually mild-mannered and polite, shouted and ranted at the contractors.

Several scuffles broke out, and people crowded into the wood-lands so that no more trees could be felled without endangering lives. One man's legs were indeed trapped by falling branches but no real harm was done beyond a sprained ankle. He'd been lucky; a more solid part of the tree and it would have been a different matter.

The result of this near disaster was that at last people began to sit up and take notice. Sandra finally won herself an interview with a young and enthusiastic reporter who was eager to take the story back to his editor. He wrote down all her carefully thought out arguments, and described how the women of the village had devised a shift system for watching over the wood-land, since their mentolk must go back to work, to ensure that the felling could not recommence. The piece was published in the local paper together with a huge photograph of Sandra, standing with her arms wrapped about the massive trunk of an ancient oak.

Within days of this appearing she was inundated with offers of help, requests for more interviews, and had become some-thing of a celebrity. She even began to be invited to give talks at various village halls and organisations far and wide in the Lake District. Sandra forgot to be nervous on these occasions, since she was so concerned to spread the word. Her days had never been so full and she blossomed beneath the spotlight of attention, enjoying herself as the campaign gradually gathered steam.

Her finest moment came when the local authority demanded that Hollinthwaite fell no more trees until the matter had been fully investigated. It may well be his own land, they said, but they couldn't allow the lives of village folk to be put at risk or the countryside ruined simply for the sake of his profits. He must present his case properly, then they would look into the matter and report back to him in the fullness of time.

James, as might be expected, was furious, but not even his influential friend, George Tyson could alter the decision. James had no control over Sandra's activities these days, since she was no longer in his employ, but he often wondered why he didn't sack Alena. Ever a thorn in his side, he blamed her for the campaign as much as the Myers girl. But there was something about her confident demeanour, her complete fearlessness when she faced him, that undermined his determination to act against her, and brought out in him only a grudging admiration for her courage.

Sandra couldn't help but think how, if it weren't for James Hollinthwaite's vindictiveness, she and Harry would have been married on her twenty-first birthday. Seeing him at Christmas had brought it all back and, despite her efforts and the success of her campaign, of which she was justly proud, the image of the man she loved was always at the back of her mind. She coped with it by sitting up late, writing letters till her hand hurt, rather than face the prospect of another sleepless night thinking of him. Aunt Elsie kept reminding her how fortunate she was to have escaped the restrictions of marriage, and how agreeable it was that the foolish young man was no longer around to interfere in their lives, which was no help at all.

Sandra watched Alena make a slow start on preparations for her own wedding. At first she was envious and then, taking more careful note of the expression on her friend's face in unguarded moments, whenever she thought herself unobserved, she realised that for all Alena's brightness, things were not quite right.

It didn't take a genius to work out that she still held a soft spot in her heart for Rob. And if James Hollinthwaite really had been lying, then these last few months of Alena's freedom were Rob's final opportunity to discover the truth and put things right between them.

Perhaps her own suffering made Sandra sensitive to that of her friend, or maybe her constant tiredness from looking after Aunt Elsie affected her capacity to reason. Or perhaps it was simply the fact that writing letters had become so much a part of her routine that she did it without undue thought. But whatever the reason one night she dashed off a letter to Rob, care of the Forestry Commission HQ at Grizedale, telling him of Alena's plans to marry Mickey. She mentioned how quiet and depressed her friend was becoming, not at all her usual lively self, and how as yet she hadn't even brought herself to buy the material for her bridal gown.

The next day Sandra posted the letter along with the rest of her mail, and crossed her fingers for luck. Perhaps he did still care and would be prepared to reconsider the stories James had told, or perhaps he'd already found somebody else and had grown out of his fancy for Alena. Either way Sandra had done her best. Now it was up to him.

–

Rob had little time for romance since his days in the forests were long and hard. But though he might not always agree with the current policy of his employers, he was nevertheless reasonably happy in his work. If he ever thought of home, he tried not to do so with regret. Alena was now a distant and bittersweet memory.

He continued to receive regular letters from his mother. Occasionally they would meet and have tea together in a smart hotel in Keswick. They would sit beside the potted palms and listen to a trio saw away at violin, cello and viola, while they ate buttered crumpets and exchanged news.

To his great surprise Olivia finally confessed to taking Frank Roscoe as her lover, and said she had been living with him happily for some time. The news had shaken him at first, but then he'd looked into his mother's beautiful face, seen how her eyes were bright with happiness, and realised that she was still quite young, still needed love as much as a younger woman might.

'Frank is tender and kind as well as a fascinating man. And he's never afraid to show how much he adores me. Whereas

James will only have realised how he felt about me now that I'm no longer there.' She gave a rueful smile and Rob gained the distinct impression that his father must have shown very little love to his wife over the years, perhaps because of some foolish sense of his own inferiority.

Olivia had cut her hair to a swinging bob, taken to wearing long woolly cardigans and sensible brogues, and sported a cigarette holder. Her long, slender hands now looked work-worn if well-scrubbed, with signs of soil still lurking beneath the fingernails. She seemed a different woman, one free to express her own personality. It would no more have occurred to this woman to hold a dinner party for influential guests than it would to Frank Roscoe to buy a Bentley and employ a chauffeur. They lived very simply but were undoubtedly happy, and Rob was pleased for her.

No mention was made of his request for investigation into his father's revelation, and he couldn't quite bring himself to ask again, fearing that to do so would only reawaken a dormant pain. He doubted she'd discovered anything of interest, in any case. Olivia was careful not even to speak Alena's name, he noticed, and neither did he. Instead, they spent an agreeable hour together discussing inconsequential things, with no knowledge of James's latest controversial project. Finding a newspaper let alone the time to read one, was not a priority for either of them these days.

-

On the day James was defending his trees from a mob of villagers, Rob too was involved in felling. This group of conifers had been planted in the eighteenth century, perhaps one of the plantations that had given rise to Wordsworth's remark that a larch wood was like a sort of abominable 'vegetable manufac-tory'. Rob tended to agree with this sentiment for all it brought him work, and the situation had not been improved by the

Victorian landowners adding acres of Sitka spruce and Douglas fir to their own estates.

But for now his only concern was to choose which tree must come down next. They always cut from the centre of a group so as not to waste any, and deciding where safely to put one down was their chief priority. A very tall tree would be allowed to fall against another, so that it slid slowly down without breaking, for it was worthless if the trunk broke.

Rob back-cut the tree below the throat. This way it fell partway at an angle before the back finally gave, thus slowing its fall. When it was safely down, he wiped the sweat from his brow and had carefully set aside his axe to take a short break while he considered the next, when he heard a familiar voice behind him.

'Not quite the whippersnapper you were, but I can see you've remembered my lessons on how to use an axe.'

He turned to find Frank Roscoe grinning at him, Bracken the dog by his side as usual.

'I keep it sharp enough to cut the hairs off the back of my hand,' Rob agreed, with a grin. 'And never lend it.'

'Good lad.' And, laughing, Frank slapped him on the shoulder. They greeted each other as the old friends they undoubtedly were, Bracken leaping excitedly between the two of them, tongue lolling, barks echoing through the forest, wanting to join in the celebration. But it was not until work was finished for the day that they were able to walk from the forest to the local inn. Here Rob ordered tatie pot and set up a pint of ale for each of them, not forgetting a bowl of water and a ham sandwich for his faithful friend.

As they ate and drank by a roaring log fire, the smell of damp wool, muddy boots and dogs strong in the overwarm room, they settled to a long and comfortable chat. Frank talked about Olivia, anxiously reassuring the young man that he would take very special care of her.

'I'm sure you will,' Rob replied, and the two of them smiled, content with the way things had turned out, though Rob noticed Frank made no mention of Alena, any more than Olivia had. It was as if she had ceased to exist.

Rob asked about Kate and the rest of the coppicers, hearing that they still moved about the woodlands, though customers for their products were becoming harder to find.

'I still maintain that coppicing will survive. If it's going downhill now, it'll come back. The forest itself will demand that it does. Trees are living things and need to be maintained.'

This led to their arguing the toss between softwoods and hardwoods; and whether the Commission would ever agree that it was possible to blend the two without ruining the economy of either the ancient forests or the countryside in the process. Frank maintained they should plant only hardwoods in the Lake District.

''Tis a special area, for leisure and walking, and think of the roads they'll have to build to get the timber out. This isn't Canada.'

Rob could see both sides of the argument. 'They tried mixing hardwoods with the first conifers, but the sheep ate them. In any case, much of the soil on the higher fells is too thin for hardwoods, and oak would never survive in the harsh climate without some sort of protection, so you have to grow that protection first. Planting spruce will prevent loss of soil and put the richness back that's been lost by overgrazing.'

Frank was unconvinced and thumped a fist on the wooden table to emphasise his point. 'I doubt the Herdwick sheep farmers fighting to maintain a traditional way of life that goes back centuries would agree with you, but that's another story to be sure. Aren't I more concerned with me own patch? How much do they mean to plant here in Grizedale, that's what I want to know?'

Enjoying the lively debate, Rob swallowed some beer, acknowledging that he wasn't sure. 'It isn't the Commission's current policy to make forests pretty, only economic. Though I reckon fifty years from now they'll be able to start planting in some hardwoods, once they've had the first crop of soft and the forest has had time to settle. Then a hundred and fifty years after that, they'd have been proved right to plant more forests in Lakeland. Forestry is a long-term project, Frank, as you know. It can't happen overnight.'

Frank frowned, hating to be defeated but nevertheless admiring the way that the lad could hold his ground in an argument these days. 'Aye, well, it's a point of view.' Even so he continued, 'I've heard they're to plant in Eskdale next, that they've already started on the Cumberland side of the Duddon Valley, right along by Bilks Farm and on Harter Fell, aiming to plant as high as Banty Crag. 'Tis criminal to ruin that lovely landscape. Some of the finest scenery in Lakeland being blanketed with square blocks of dark spruce for all time, despite the protests of notables such as Lord Lonsdale himself.'

'At least the work will provide much needed employment, which is more than the coppicing industry is doing right now. Sad really, because I don't mind admitting that's where my heart truly lies.'

'I know that well enough, lad.' And having reached an agreement of sorts, and the conversation come full circle, both men fell silent, amicably sipping their beer.

'I dare say you've heard your father is doing much the same in your own village? Are you agreeing with that too?' Frank said finally.

Rob looked aghast. 'I don't believe you! There's no space for massive conifer forests in Ellersgarth. That wouldn't be right.'

'Try stopping James Hollinthwaite when he's set his mind to something.'

As they left the pub to go their separate ways, Frank suggested that Rob visit his old friend Isaac, the charcoal burner. 'He's working close by here at the moment. Tell him I sent you. Go early enough and he'll give you breakfast. He's the most sociable hermit I know.'

And the next morning before dawn, out of curiosity as much as friendship, Rob set out to find the old man before he went on to where he was working that day. Anything to take his mind off the memories of Ellersgarth that Frank had reawakened, and this news of his father which he didn't quite believe.

–

Built like an oak only, as he himself said, a bit more grizzled on top, Isaac was something of a local character. If he had a second name he never used it, perhaps had even forgotten it for he'd no recollection either of his age, except that it was great. All that was known of him was that his father had been a clever and influential chemist, his mother a delightful and accomplished lady whom he had adored. He'd come to the Lakes on a climbing expedition as a young man while attending Oxford, and had never returned to finish his degree. Only his voice gave away his upbringing, being clear and well-modulated, while his appearance generally made him look like a tramp.

Today he was dressed in his winter garb of an old army greatcoat worn with a sack over his shoulders, for extra warmth, and a wide-brimmed hat with a pheasant's feather. Rob doubted he ever took them off, even when he went to bed. The locals called him 'a well-set-up chap', or 'a good aw roond man at his job', and 'sharp as a razor'.

He was certainly an expert at poaching and setting traps, trout tickling and any other illegal methods of acquiring food which Isaac thought of as nature's bounty. When not working on the charcoal burn he still went climbing, usually alone, and knew where he was from the outline of the fell-tops, or even the sound of a beck. And if anyone wanted to know what the weather was likely to be, or what was happening in the world, they would go and ask old Isaac.

He was sitting in his hut, not a drop of the early morning rain leaking through the turf roof, happily toasting oatcakes in a dry frying pan when Rob stumbled upon him. A few yards away stood the gently smoking dome of the charcoal burn. The stench of it stung his eyes and caught at the back of his throat, but it didn't seem to trouble Isaac. It was the thin spiral of smoke, coiling upwards into a pale lemon sky, which had directed Rob to the clearing. There was a damp chill in the air, and he readily accepted the old man's invitation to share his simple breakfast which, just as Frank had promised, was instantly offered.

'Good morrow, young man. I have neither coffee nor whisky, but you are welcome to share a hot cup of tea and a gasper with me.' Rob grinned, accepted the tea brewed in an old tin can, but declined a puff of the Woodbine. They talked of the ways of the forest as they ate the oatcakes, and of the doings of Mosley.

'The man's gone too far, of course, with his jackboots and brown shirts. Could've had the aristos in the palm of his hand, but he overstepped the mark, don't you know. Never do it now. He's finished, praise be.'

'You don't agree with his politics then?'

'Good God, no. I'm with the rebels, the Commies. How about you?'

Rob shook his head. 'Never really considered the matter.'

'Then time you did, boy. There's a war coming and you'll likely be in it. I'm too old, sad to say. Missed the other shindig too.'

Rob frowned, startled by this talk of war yet not quite able to disagree with this wise old man. After that he kept the conversation to more mundane subjects, and was given a few tips on how to secrete stolen game under a woodpile in case the estate owner should walk by. 'But never forget where you've left your prize, that's the important thing, or on the morrow thou wilst know hunger,' he finished, as if quoting Shakespeare and they both laughed. When Rob had eaten his fill he got up and offered to pay for his breakfast.

'Pay me next time you come by. And make it soon. Any friend of Frank Roscoe's is a friend of mine.'

Rob realised that for all his hermit's ways, little escaped the notice of this old man. 'How did you know I was a friend of his? I should've mentioned that fact, but I forgot.'

Isaac grinned, showing a complete set of healthy teeth. 'People call in. They tell me things. Such as how his son means to marry your girl.'

It was never completely silent in the forest. Always there was the sound of rain dripping from a branch, the cooing of a wood pigeon or the constant twitter of quarrelling birds. Now for once it did indeed seem to grow silent. Rob stared at Isaac for a long time, deep in misery. He hadn't heard of Alena for so long, and now to hear this confirmation of his father's earlier warning about Mickey filled him with despair. Finally he said, 'She isn't my girl. Not any more. She can't ever be.'

Isaac looked at him keenly for a moment, shrugged, then turned his attention to the next oatcake. 'You should never give up on something – or someone – that is necessary to your survival or happiness. That is my philosophy of life, boy, which is why I am here and not in some London office my father had picked out for me. I've never regretted it. Fathers do not know everything. "To thine own self be true." In other words, trust in your own judgement, not his.'

Rob stood nonplussed, unable to think what to say. How could he explain that he was quite unable to disregard James on the question of his relationship with Alena? Not without real proof. It was too difficult, too dangerous – too terrible even to consider. The old man no doubt meant well, but his situation had been rather different from Rob's own. Not wishing to say as much, he thanked Isaac and hurriedly left.

Would the past never let him go? Alena to many Mickey. No wonder neither his mother nor Frank had mentioned her. A wave of sickness came over him and a cold sweat broke out between his shoulder blades. He mustn't think of it, for she wasn't his. She was his *sister*, for God's sake! He must never forget that.

The raw pain in Rob's chest at this thought was a cruel reminder that he had not stopped loving her despite this indisputable fact. But in view of this new information, he decided he would not wish to run the risk of bumping into the pair of lovebirds. To be on the safe side, he decided it was time to leave Grizedale and move to the more remote fells. There was plenty of work to be had in Ennerdale and the Duddon Valley. And so it was that he did not get Sandra's letter, or hear her gently worded version of events.

Chapter Nineteen

January and February were long and cold and bleak. The snow lay thickly in the fields, fierce east winds blowing it over the hedges and piling it up in the narrow lanes so that there were days when Alena had to set out an hour earlier in the blackness of night to reach the mill on time. She hated these weeks when she never glimpsed daylight, except through a dusty mill window, until Sunday came.

Then she and Mickey would walk out in it, revelling in the crystal clear air and the sight of the distant range of ice-tipped mountains all around them. Icicles would hang from the trees, turning the forest into an enchanted place. Here all was serene and oddly silent, the birds and squirrels, otter and deer, conserving their energy till spring came again.

Working in the mill during these winter weeks was particularly taxing, with all the girls coughing and sneezing and never quite getting warm. Lizzie did her best to help by making sure there was a good blaze in the old fire-range each dinner time and hot soup available, but rheumatism, chilblains, influenza, red noses and ice-blue fingers and toes were common complaints. Not that there was ever any question of taking time off to nurse themselves better. None of them would have dared. There were too many people waiting to step into their shoes, and James Hollinthwaite did not have a reputation for being a sympathetic employer.

When they weren't worrying over the continuing depression, the talk was all of the young idealists secretly rushing off to enlist in the Spanish Civil War. Many of them were artists and writers, including George Orwell, and young men quite unfit for war.

Edith said, 'Our chaps in Ellersgarth have more sense than to get involved in somebody else's battles. Hollinthwaite is a Fascist – send him. Give us a bit more fresh air round here.' But for all her black humour, the worry was that the trouble might escalate and concern them all in the end, whether they wanted war or not.

Winter maintained its iron grip throughout March and although Mickey pressed Alena to begin preparations for their wedding, planned for the end of May, she continued to put off the moment.

'There's plenty of time. Ma can make my dress in five minutes,' she airily told him.

'You could at least help me get the house ready.' He had moved into the cottage he had found for them at Burmyre Bottoms, but it had damp peeling wallpaper and hadn't seen a lick of paint in years. 'I seem to spend my life mixing wallpaper paste, or with a paint brush in hand. Even your mother has done more than you, making curtains for our bedroom.'

Alena clicked her tongue with exasperation. 'I'm hopeless at sewing, all fingers and thumbs.' She tried to imagine sharing a bedroom with Mickey. And a bed. But she couldn't. She'd once tried to imagine her mother and Ray making love, or Dolly and Tom, but had ended up shuddering in disbelief. Perhaps sex was something that couldn't be imagined but a fact of life that had to be got used to, like growing older. Now if it were Rob… She closed her mind to this line of thought.

'You could ask her to teach you,' Mickey pointed out.

'Oh, tosh. Don't expect me to be what I'm not.' And, laughing, she kissed him to put an end to his sulks.

She often used the excuse that she was too busy helping Sandra with her campaign. Determined not to let up, and encouraged by their success with the local authority, the campaign work seemed to have escalated. The pair sat up long into the night, talking and planning, making endless lists and writing out copies of their protest letter. Even Dolly had been known to come along and help on occasion, sitting all plumply cheerful in long cardigan and short skirt, talking of how much more considerate Tom was to her these days, as she folded letters and licked postage stamps. And there was still much to be done. The battle hadn't been won yet, only a small skirmish. But Mickey did not approve.

'Why waste time on such things?' he complained. 'You're neglecting yourself badly. Look how rumpled and untidy you are, Ally.'

'Don't call me that.'

He held up his hand, palm out, to placate her. 'I'm only saying that dress looks as if it came out of a ragbag. And red doesn't suit you.'

Flushing with embarrassment, Alena had to admit the dress with its faded fabric and torn hem had seen better days. She hated dresses in any case, and had only bought it in the first place to please him. What with long days spent at the mill and helping Sandra, there'd been little time recently for titivating. She preferred to throw on a sweater and skirt, or better still shirt and slacks like her brothers, shorts in better weather. She hated to fuss about her clothes.

'And your hair is all over the place. Get it cut, for goodness' sake. I can't have my wife looking like a bird's nest when she walks down the aisle.' But as she started to protest at his criticism, Mickey continued, 'I'll drive you to Kendal on Saturday, then you can get some material to make a new dress. Perhaps a box-pleated cream linen would be nice as a going-away outfit, and we can buy satin for your wedding dress at the same time.' For a man, Mickey took an inordinate interest in her appearance.

Alena felt a stir of resentment, but even as she searched for excuses to put him off, he told her how beautiful she was for all there was ink on her chin and her appearance tousled.

Smoothing the curls back from her face, he started kissing her, one hand easing up her skirt and sliding down the tops of her stockings beneath her suspenders. She found herself gasping for breath at this unexpected onslaught but to appease his sulks after she'd fought him off, she guiltily volunteered to ask Ma to cut her hair the very next day, and also found herself agreeing to his proposed visit to the shops.

'That's my girl,' he said proudly.

–

Like the climate, plantation life on the high fells was harsh. Sometimes Rob worked in Ennerdale, other weeks at Whin latter, in the endless progression of planting and weeding, or hammering in fences with a huge maul hammer, in horizontal sleet or driving rain. His first excitement over the job, and belief in the long-term benefits, became tempered by harsh reality. The fences he helped to erect often trapped sheep on the high fells. They strayed from their own heaf, injured or inadvertently driven there by a dog sent to find them. With their way down the fell blocked, the sheep would become pinned against the high new fences and perish there in the next fall of snow.

Rob, along with some of his colleagues, had a hard time persuading their ganger to allow the occasional break in the fenced blocks for lost sheep to find escape.

The screes on Ennerdale were constantly moving. Stones would crack in the frost, clattering downhill, or a loose boulder would topple and threaten the men who struggled to plant small trees in almost barren, stony soil. Sometimes they even had to carry up sacks of fresh soil in which to plant the young trees.

Nor did the promised number of forestry jobs materialise. Men from West Cumberland would often arrive in the early morning, in the hope of finding work, coming by bus if they were lucky enough to have the fare, otherwise on a bicycle and then by foot. But instead of the anticipated high numbers finding work, there were in fact only two others employed constantly besides Rob.

He lived with Phil Gilson and his family. Like men on the other plantations, Phil was attempting to scrape a living from the thin soil of the fells on the smallholding he'd been granted. The aim of the system was that it should subsidise what he earned as a forester. Rob did what he could to help in return for his keep, but they soon discovered that working the holding was a thankless task since little that the family planted survived.

Worse, Phil was an unemployed miner. He knew nothing of sheep and goats, or trees for that matter, and the aching loneliness of the place almost drove his poor wife mad with despair.

It might have sounded a good idea in Whitehall, but the project proved to be far less workable on the ground. It was rare for a family to rise above subsistence level since there were too many days when the snow lay thick on the fells, or the rain and winds were so fierce they'd blow a man down and work was impossible. Then they'd be left kicking their heels at home without pay. Every now and then, Phil would go back to Whitehaven, looking for what he called 'proper work', and his wife would dream of packing their bags and going home to her family and softer climes.

They even considered taking the dole in preference to the kind of back-breaking labour that could lead only to starvation. But Phil was tough, not one to quit, and when the weather was fine, the pay was good.

Rob accepted the difficulties without complaint, almost welcoming the harshness since it kept his mind from dwelling on Alena's lovely face and sent him exhausted to his bed at night. But he too often dreamed of returning home, or even to Grizedale which he loved, and secretly he longed for news of home. Since he worked so hard and moved about quite a bit, at his own request, his mail took some time to catch up with him.

But one day he collected a whole handful of letters. Several from Olivia, a couple from his father, enquiring as to his progress. And one in a strange hand that turned out, surprisingly, to be from Sandra.

–

With April came the first real sign of a thaw. Water dripped like rain from the branches, the beck ran at full flood and pools of snowdrops appeared in the fields and hillsides, making everyone think of spring. And then came the news that Dolly was at last pregnant. It had been a bitter disappointment when the missed period before Christmas had turned out to be a false alarm. But this baby was real, conceived in love. The whole family rejoiced, not least for the obvious improvement in relations between the couple.

'If it's a girl, I shall call her Elizabeth Rose, after our two little princesses,' Dolly said. 'Oh, I do wish we could go to the Coronation in May. Wouldn't that be grand?' Alena agreed that it would, while secretly finding little pleasure either in this momentous event or the prospect of her own wedding, which was now rapidly approaching. The elation common to most brides still eluded her.

Over the last weeks, pressed by Mickey, she had striven to come to terms with the idea, but knew herself to be no nearer. She felt confused and fearful instead of excited at the prospect of becoming a married woman. Acutely aware of a growing sense of panic, she feverishly attempted to quell it by giving her full attention to the smallest detail. She'd avoided the proposed trip to Kendal by pleading a sick headache, a weak excuse when really she should be telling him that she'd very nearly decided to call the wedding off. If only she could pluck up the courage to say the words.

His constant nagging had won in the end, of course. He'd taken her shopping, and a length of satin had been purchased. Lizzie was sewing it at this very moment as Alena cycled home from work one day in late April. The hedgerows were starred with stitchwort and celandine, the sun shone and sparrows dashed from branch to branch in a frenzy of effort to feed their newly hatched families. It was the kind of spring day that should bring a song to any bride's heart. Except this one, who couldn't get her mind off what might have been. Alena whizzed around a corner and almost cycled headlong into a man walking towards her with his head bowed.

'Heavens, I'm sorry.' she cried, skidding to a halt and jumping off her bike to go to his aid. He picked himself out of the hedgerow and dusted down his jacket. It was James Hollinthwaite.

'That's all right. I was hoping to run into you, Alena, though not quite so literally. I hear congratulations are in order at last?' And he actually smiled.

She found her voice with difficulty. 'Yes.'

'I wish you well.'

'Do you?'

'I always did, though you may not have believed so from my manner.'

'No.'

'But you have to admit that my latest efforts on your behalf have been more fruitful.' And his smile sent a chill running down her spine.

'I'm not sure what you mean?'

'It was I who recommended Mickey for promotion, though it was also deserved. He's done well at the mill considering he hasn't been here very long, and I couldn't have my best foreman living in one room in seedy lodgings, not when he intends to marry a fine girl like yourself.'

For a long moment she simply stared at him. 'Are you saying that *you* found the house for Mickey?'

'As for Rob, he's happily settled working in the plantations, which will be of great benefit to me when I come to start planting my own next year.' As if he had planned as much all along. 'I shall put him in charge of...'

'Why?' she asked, ignoring his efforts to present a happy picture of a hard-working son. 'Why did you go to so much trouble for Mickey?' And then it came to her, clear as daylight. 'Of course, why didn't I realise? You promoted him, gave him a rise, made sure he had a house to offer... so that you could be certain I'd accept him. Dear God, you've engineered all of this, haven't you? It's exactly what you wanted, what you've always wanted. For me to be married to someone else, and safely out of the running for Rob.'

He acknowledged her remarks with a casual lift of his dark brows. 'You always were far too intelligent for your own good, Alena. You saw through my ploy, didn't you? But then I'd have done anything to be rid of you. To be rid of your whole damned family.' And as he walked away from her along the lane, he called back over his shoulder, 'Do at least send me an invitation to your wedding. I'd hate to miss that.'

As she stood and stared after his departing figure, those few short sentences, even the arrogance in his swaggering walk, reawakened her fury. Alena recognised his words were as near an admission as she was ever likely to get. James Hollinthwaite had as good as told her that he'd lied.

—

Lizzie didn't see it as a problem. 'You've known all along it could be a lie.'

'But now he's as good as admitted it.'

'He said he'd do anything to be rid of you? That's not quite the same thing,' she reasoned, much to Alena's vexation. 'And you still don't have the proof you would need to convince Rob who, if you recall, is out of your life now. You're to marry Mickey, remember. As for that other business, why shouldn't Mickey accept promotion when it's offered, or a house for that matter? It's very good of Mr Hollinthwaite to be so generous. Mind you, he owns enough property in this village, so why shouldn't he help you? He owes you that much at least. You've either got to put the past behind you, Alena, or call this wedding off, once and for all. Now which is it to be?'

Alena considered Mickey's likely reaction to being jilted, thought of how touchy he was and how he hated to be made to look a fool, and her courage failed her yet again.

Lizzie's heart went out to her confused daughter, but she merely remarked in rousing tones, 'Right then, are you going to try on this frock? I need to pin the darts.'

And meekly Alena stood on a chair while her mother crawled about on hands and knees with pins in her mouth, tucking and tacking the dress which was to make her into Mickey's bride.

Sandra arrived, and sat on a stool to watch and offer advice. 'Will we have a bit of a party afterwards? Down at the Stag perhaps? They've got a gramophone now so we could play some records and dance. You know, "Dancing Cheek to Cheek" and "Red Sails in the Sunset".' She crooned softly, wrapping her arms about herself, then grabbed Lizzie and began to waltz about the room, the pair of them struggling to sing through their laughter. Even Alena found herself giggling.

Harry walked in and found them. 'So this is what you get up to when we menfolk are out?' He grinned at Alena, smiling down at him from her precarious position on the chair, all pink-cheeked and clean and tidy for once, in pieces of pinned satin. He did not acknowledge Sandra's presence at all, nor she his.

Lizzie shooed him into the front room. 'We've no time for waiting on you this evening.' But she did take him in a cup of tea when Sandra refused to do so. Lizzie put it in her son's hands and asked, 'Any luck?'

His silence answered her question and she knew, without asking further, that he'd done his best but no one was keen to take on a sacked man, particularly one who'd been accused of dishonesty. 'Will you be walking Sandra home later?'

A short pause, then he picked up the evening paper and shook it open. 'I don't think so, Ma.'

'Men! Never know when you're well off. You'll be sorry one day that you didn't hang on to her.' And she closed the parlour door with a firm click, leaving him staring sightlessly at the paper in his hands.

Back in the kitchen she found Sandra had gone and Alena was ripping off the pattern pieces with little regard for the tacking or pins. 'Take care, lass, you'll ruin it.'

'I don't care. I *hate* satin anyway.' Whereupon she burst into tears and ran from the room.

With a resigned sigh, Lizzie picked up the discarded pieces of wedding dress and began to inspect the damage. No more than wedding nerves, she hoped. And poor Sandra still suffering. If it wasn't one thing, she thought, it was another.

–

Alena put on slacks and a sweater, pulled on her tam o'shanter and escaped, as she always did when she was hurting, to their special oak in the forest. She shinned up the trunk and propped herself upon a crooked branch, pressing her face against the roughness of the bark, hoping this would stop the tears. A wood pigeon cooed, its monotonous call soothing her nerves. She felt as unsettled as the weather. Clouds were gathering ominously, the wind veering round to the east with a hint of rain in it. But at least the days were longer now, so she needn't hurry back. She might even take a long walk before supper. She needed to be alone for once. Most of all she needed to think.

Ever since she'd bumped into James Hollinthwaite, half her mind seemed to be taken up with thinking of Rob: of how he was, where he was living, and if he ever thought of her. Though, as Ma said, she shouldn't really be thinking of him at all, not as an affianced bride, a mere few weeks from her wedding to another man. It was just that the nearer the day came, the more she worried over it, and the more that small kernel of disquiet grew.

She asked herself questions all the time. Did she love Mickey enough to spend the rest of her life with him? And why did she feel as if he'd talked her into it? Or as if everyone had taken it for granted that they would marry and she'd had no say in the matter at all, which was nonsense of course. She was a grown woman, surely old enough to make up her own mind. Even so, she'd once tried suggesting they might postpone it and he'd been aghast at the idea.

She knew Ma watched her, aware of her confusion and disquiet but Alena felt unable to explain how she felt because she didn't fully understand it herself. She couldn't describe the sense of uncertainty, the dizzy fear of being out of control of her own life. She'd made the decision readily enough, giggling with Sandra over the anticipated joys of her wedding night as if it were all a lark. So why didn't she feel happy? Because it wasn't a lark, or because every bride felt this way? Perhaps it was simply the wedding day itself that she dreaded. She'd always hated a fuss, and knew she wouldn't feel comfortable in a fancy frock with everyone looking at her. So, if she was now experiencing doubts, or cold feet, as her mother put it, surely these would pass once the day itself was over and done with, everyone had thrown their confetti, played their little jokes and she and Mickey were alone in the little cottage?

Oddly enough this prospect did nothing to lighten her mood and Alena felt a flare of irritation at herself. What on earth was the matter with her?

Dolly and Tom had suffered their share of problems, after all, losing the baby and very nearly their marriage. But they'd pulled through and it was lovely now to see their obvious happiness in each other which, at one time, would have seemed impossible to achieve. They'd got themselves into such a muddle of misery and grief that they'd both quite lost sight of the fact that they were really very fond of each other. Perhaps that was what was happening to her.

If only as happy an outcome could be found for poor Sandra. Harry now planned to take himself off to Liverpool or Manchester, some place where he hoped to find better luck in his search for employment. Lizzie doubted he'd be successful even there, but then she wanted him at home. At least she and Sandra had become quite close in their shared, if different, love for Harry.

The wind tugged at her tam o'shanter and Alena grabbed it, chewing on her lower lip as these thoughts raced through her head.

Mickey was working late, and had told her that he couldn't come round this evening. This was happening more and more, and sometimes she wondered how it was he managed to find so much overtime when the mill was supposedly not doing as well as it should. Oh dear, there she went again, mistrusting him when he was really only trying to save hard for their life together. Why did loving someone have to be so complicated? Love should be freely given, joyfully received, and not hindered by awkwardness, jealousy and pride, or ruined by secrets and the interfering lies of other people. A lie to which James Hollinthwaite had as good as admitted. What was it he had said?

'*You saw through my ploy, didn't you?*' What was that if not an admission of guilt?

It was just as the first drops of rain started to fall that she made her decision. Alena saw exactly what she must do. She must take control of her own life. She must make up her mind, as Lizzie had suggested, if her feelings for Rob were truly in the past. Only then could she decide about Mickey.

—

The next day at work Alena feigned stomach pains, and the moment her shift was over she packed a bag and persuaded Jim to give her a lift in his small van.

'I'll be back in a day or two. Tell Mickey I'm sick,' were her parting words as the van set off, bumping and rattling up the rough track into the woods. He deposited her at the Forestry Commission's offices, wished her luck and set off back home at once, Alena assuring him she could get a lift from someone when she was ready. She knocked on the office door but no one answered. When she tried the handle, she found the door locked.

'They'll be out inspecting the work. There's a sign on the door, see. Back later. Only they didn't come back later, and probably won't at all now, not till tomorrow.' This information came from a man leaning against a stone wall, smoking a cigarette. He wore the familiar work clothes of a forester and Alena tentatively approached him with her questions.

Rob, it seemed, was not in Grizedale. The man told her he was either at Ennerdale or Whinlatter, he wasn't sure which. Depression settled upon Alena as, with night coming on and no arrangements made for where she was to stay, both places seemed as far distant as the moon. Then she had an idea. 'It's really Mrs Hollinthwaite, his mother, I'm looking for. I was hoping he could tell me where I could find her so she can help me with – with a little matter.' The little matter of her future happiness.

The forester had no knowledge of Rob's mother, and Alena knew that if he had met Olivia he would certainly have remembered her. But he did direct her to some good clean lodgings at a cottage nearby where a Mrs Blamire, who remembered Rob well since he was so tolerant of her cats, made a special fuss over this lovely young girl who had come looking for him. Alena accepted a hot drink then went straight to bed to avoid answering further questions.

Refreshed after a night's sleep, she enjoyed a good breakfast of porridge and a platter of ham and eggs any forester would welcome. As she settled her bill, she asked the landlady, 'I don't suppose you know a Frank Roscoe?' It had come out of nowhere and she didn't quite know why.

The woman laughed. 'Doesn't everyone? Follow the smoke signals and you'll find him not far away.'

'Smoke signals?'

'Where the charcoal burner is, sitting beneath his crab apple tree, you'll more than likely find Frank.'

Alena did not find Frank. But she did find an old man chewing on a bent Woodbine, and he was indeed sitting beneath a crab apple tree beside what appeared to be a smoking beehive. He looked so disreputable that for a moment she almost turned and ran away, but he interpreted her silence otherwise.

'You are admiring my tree?'

'I was wondering how my landlady knew I would find you beneath it.'

'Ah, charcoal burners always have a crab apple on their pitstead.'

'Why?'

He laughed, then tapped the side of his nose. 'One of the mysteries of the forest. And very often an adder too, but I do not care for the creatures myself.'

'Have you seen Frank Roscoe?' She really had no wish to discuss snakes.

'Good gracious me, you ask a great many questions, child. My mother told me that curiosity is ill manners in another house, but since we are not in a house mayhap I will forgive you. Frank is a will o' the wisp, here today and gone tomorrow.'

'I see.' She couldn't disguise her disappointment.

The old man stood up, lithe and tall, lifted his hat and swept it before him, the pheasant's feather making an arc of colour as he did so. 'Pray allow me to introduce myself – Isaac, at your service. And you are?'

'I beg your pardon. Alena Townsen.' She thrust out a hand which, obligingly, he lifted to his mouth and kissed. She giggled.

'Ah, yes, indeed. I have heard him speak of you.' He replaced the hat gently and tweaked the feather.

283

'Have you?' For a moment she was surprised and then smiled at her own foolishness. In a matter of weeks Frank Roscoe would be her father-in-law. It was hardly surprising he had mentioned her. 'What about Kate and the other coppicers. Do you know where they are? Kate might know where he is and I *must* speak to him.' She heard the pleading note in her voice, like a soft young girl which, she supposed, was exactly what she was.

The old man was packing gaps in the stack with sods of earth to keep out the air and stop his charcoal from burning up and turning to ash, but he cast sly glances in Alena's direction from beneath his wide-brimmed hat.

'The coppicers are working about two miles away, in the next clearing, I believe.' A glimmer of hope but then Alena recalled that Kate had never known where Roscoe was before, so why should she now? It was as she offered her thanks and turned to go that the old man casually remarked, 'Not that he sees much of Kate these days. He gets home more regularly than he did. He's a changed man is Frank, since he found the love of his life.' Isaac smiled his knowing smile, 'name of Olivia, as in *Twelfth Night*. A good, sweet lady. I had the honour to meet her once. But you'd have to travel to the forests of Thornthwaite to find her, and perhaps the trip would be too far for you, dear child?'

'Oh, no,' Alena said, eyes shining. 'It wouldn't at all. Do you, by any chance know of anyone going to Keswick who could give me a lift? Or the location of the nearest bus stop?' If she had to walk every step of the way she would find the place. Suddenly it didn't seem any distance at all.

Chapter Twenty

She found Olivia kneeling on the lawn in her small garden, planting out bright-eyed pansies beneath a silver birch. When she saw Alena, she dropped the trowel and ran to envelop her in a bear hug. She smelled of warm earth and flowers, and the soup she must have eaten for lunch. When the greetings were over, she insisted on warming some up for Alena. Olivia carried it out to her on a tray, together with a plate of her famous scones.

'I must have known you were coming,' she said, shooing off a few cheeky sparrows so she could place it on a rustic table.

'As delicious as always,' Alena told her when she'd finished every last drop. 'No wonder Mrs Milburn was always so grumpy, you were a much better cook than she ever was!'

'I wasn't then, but I am now,' Olivia said, laughing. They sat in companionable silence, saying little but content to be together again, enjoying the pale spring sunshine. Alena worried over how to broach the subject so close to her heart. Later she was shown over the tiny cottage to admire the white-walled rooms, rustic furniture, a small untidy kitchen with inglenook and ratten crook from which hung the griddle. But most of all she loved the glorious views from the tiny windows: Skiddaw and Blencathra lifting their magnificent heads above their fellows to gaze imperiously down upon the slate calm of Bassenthwaite. Alena was entranced.

'No wonder you love it here.'

Olivia knelt again on the lawn and picked up her trowel. 'You've come about Rob and those dreadful lies, haven't you?' She slid a pansy into place and patted the soil firmly about it.

Alena took a deep breath. 'I wondered if you knew anything – anything at all to help me? My mother has told me what she knows, which is very little, but there must be more. Who was this girl? Where did she come from? *Who am I?*' She met Olivia's gaze, sensing a sympathy and understanding she had not expected to find.

Olivia sat back on her heels, a slight frown marring her brow. 'I never saw her, of course, or even knew she existed until recently so I can add little to the tale on my own account. I once promised Rob I would investigate and I did, in a perfunctory way, but failed to locate either Stella or the vicar. I didn't pursue the matter further. Couldn't bring myself to, I suppose. Afraid of what I might find. But then Rob, more determined than I, has finally taken up the case and he...' She stopped speaking to look up as they both heard the click of the garden gate. When she turned back to Alena, she was smiling. 'But he can tell you better himself.'

And suddenly there he was, tall and bronzed and more handsome than ever. He strode up the garden path towards her but although his eyes were fixed upon her face, he wasn't smiling.

–

'I'm getting married on the last Saturday in May.' She hadn't meant to be so blunt, but the words sprang from her lips as if they must be spoken. Olivia had suddenly found something terribly important to do in the kitchen and Alena and Rob sat awkwardly, side by side, on the garden bench beneath the spreading arms of a sweet chestnut, not even looking at each other. Over the Skiddaw range the clouds gathered into a swirling mass, a frosting of snow still lighting the jagged peaks, reminding them that summer was still some way off.

There'd been an attempt at polite conversation, desultory and hesitant, as if they were strangers.

'Olivia seems happier than I've ever seen her,' Alena remarked. 'She deserves it. Oh, I'm sorry.'

'No, don't be, it's true. My father never made her truly happy. Too busy telling her how to behave and filling in her diary, I think. Whereas Frank seems to have found the knack. She's changed. She gardens and smokes, dresses in the kind of unfashionable clothes the old Olivia wouldn't have been seen dead in and she laughs a lot, even tells jokes. All that tightly wound up emotion that made her so impossible to live with seems to have gone, or found an outlet. She's so relaxed now, so obviously enjoying life.' He picked up a soggy leaf and began to tear it into little pieces. His fingers were still long and slender, for all they were now weathered and hard. Alena wanted to kiss them.

It was in the silence following this statement that she blurted out her news.

'So I heard. I'm glad for you, if it makes you happy.' His voice sounded hollow and she tried to find hope in that fact.

'Who told you?' she asked, keeping her tone deliberately light, and she knotted her fingers together in her lap when really they longed to caress his face, to brush back the damp curls from his brow. 'Was it Sandra? She kept threatening to write.'

'*Threatening?* Strange choice of word. Didn't you want me to know?' And she saw him frown, felt the undertow of anger.

'Perhaps not,' she admitted. An awkward silence fell, then Alena cleared her throat. 'Olivia says you've been making enquiries?'

He laughed, without any trace of humour. 'I'm not sure that my efforts were such a good idea. It's all rather too late now, isn't it?'

'What is? Tell me, Rob. If you don't, I shall – I shall *burst.*' And he almost laughed out loud at her vehemence, fondness softening the tight lines of his face at last.

'It's true, I did get a letter from Sandra. It finally spurred me into taking action myself. She said you were having second thoughts.' He waited a moment for her to correct him. When she kept her gaze fixed upon Olivia's pansies, he continued, 'I traced the old vicar's widow through the good offices of the Church of England and she put me in touch with Mrs Bird, Stella's mother. Apparently he'd kept in touch with Stella, who is now dead, out of a sense of guilt. Mrs Bird is in a rest home at Lytham St Anne's and she was surprisingly helpful.'

Again he paused, and then continued more quietly, 'You were right. James did tell us a deliberate lie. We are not brother and sister.'

She stared at him, utterly unable to speak, a part of her mind wondering why on earth she hadn't thought to follow the same line of enquiries, yet she felt stunned by her confused emotions. Joy, hope, utter panic and despair. In one sentence her whole life had changed. But had it?

The nation was preparing to celebrate the coronation of a new king but Mickey Roscoe could think only of their coming wedding, just two weeks after that. He'd even bought railway tickets and paid for a week in a hotel in Scarborough following the ceremony.

Rob was saying, 'You realise what this means, Ally? For us.'

She found she was shaking, suddenly feeling the coolness of a spring breeze on her skin.

'It means...' He grasped her by the shoulders and pulled her gently into his arms, warming her with his own body as she leaned against him. He kissed her then, and there was desperate hunger in it, the fierce igniting of a long-held passion at last finding release. A kiss in which all their differences, all the years apart, seemed to melt away. Yet there was restraint there too, a sense of disbelief that they might, at last, be able to find happiness. When it was over he let her go with reluctance to keep his gaze upon her moist mouth. 'I can't find the words to express what I feel. All these years apart for no reason. All that anguish, that guilt...' He closed his eyes and threw back his head, hands clenched into fists. 'If only I hadn't been so stubborn. If only I'd believed you instead of my bloody father.'

She put out a hand to halt the words, unable to bear his agony. 'Don't – don't torture yourself, Rob. Of course you had to believe him. How could you not? He is your father, and I couldn't prove…' She stopped. 'Rob, how do you *know* that what Stella's mother says is true? What exactly did she tell you?'

He slid an arm about her, hugging her close to his side, stroking the tears from her face, kissing her again and again as if he could never have enough of her. Neither of them now spared a thought for the fact that barely three weeks from her wedding, this wasn't perhaps the wisest situation for her to be in. They were both too absorbed in this new discovery, the delights of being together at last.

Then he related the story Mrs Bird had told. So many secrets and lies, it was a relief to hear the truth at last. Alena learned how Stella, when she was in service as a young girl, had found herself to be pregnant. She'd tried to get rid of the baby and apparently did herself great injury. As a result, she was unable to bear any more children.

'So that proves you couldn't be her child, hers and James's.' Rob's voice was tight with excitement. 'Before Stella died, she related the whole sorry tale to her mother. What Lizzie told you was absolutely true. A young girl did indeed come to the house that night, gave birth to a child – you – and then sadly died. They buried her in the woods that same night, without even a proper funeral. A poor, unknown girl, little more than a child herself, put in unconsecrated ground with nothing even to mark her existence, though apparently with a vicar officiating. Typical of my father, if you think about it; giving the appearance of doing the right thing, while really being utterly ruthless and self-seeking.'

Alena was gazing at him, enthralled.

'He had the poor girl quietly buried because he was afraid of being accused of not doing enough to save her, of being blamed for her death. She, and you too, I expect, were a nuisance to him, no more than a problem to be addressed. Your very presence could damage his carefully nurtured reputation. All his life he's been desperate to avoid any hint of scandal. Everyone around him has to behave with perfect obedience, doing exactly as he orders – like some bloody dictator.'

Rob stopped speaking for a moment until he had his voice back under control, then shook his head in disbelief. 'Mother knew nothing, of course, since she was in labour at the time, with me. Everyone else involved was under strict instructions to say nothing and keep the matter a secret.'

Alena frowned. 'But the vicar knew?'

'Vicars, or some at any rate, can be bribed. And my father made certain that this one was soon moved on to another parish.'

'Ma tried to find him once, but Dad wasn't pleased.' Alena recalled the slap she had witnessed that day, and her father's anger, perhaps because he had indeed lost his job for prying. 'James sacked him, perhaps bribed him with money to keep quiet. So he bought a house and brought me up as his own daughter but, not surprisingly, he always nursed a secret resentment.' She gave a wry smile. 'Perhaps that's why we never really got on.'

They sat now with arms wrapped about each other, Alena's head resting comfortably on Rob's chest, both engrossed in their own thoughts for a long, long time. It was she who finally broke the silence.

'Now what?'

He kissed the top of her head. 'That's rather up to you.'

–

They stayed with Olivia for three days. Frank came home and listened to the tale too. He showed surprisingly little resentment of the fact that she intended to call off her wedding to his son, claiming he'd always thought the marriage would not work.

'We've never got on that well. Mickey thinks I neglected him when he was young, for all I did the best I could in difficult circumstances. But me own son or no, he's too brash and pushy for you, and you're too independent.'

They'd all laughed at this, then Olivia and Alena cooked a huge meal of pheasant and roast potatoes and they ate together as if they were a real family. Everybody laughed and told jokes, making a celebration of it for, in a way, that was what it was.

Alena and Rob spent every moment of every one of those precious few days together. They walked by the lake, explored the woodlands, exclaimed over pale yellow daffodils, white garlic flowers and wild hyacinth as if they had never seen them before. They helped Olivia in her garden, touching and kissing and laughing as they dug and weeded and talked endlessly. Their happiness was so infectious that Olivia sang as she worked, and even Frank Roscoe went about grinning from ear to ear. It seemed like a glorious holiday that would never end.

Yet Alena knew she must go home, not simply because she needed to keep her job but to explain to Mickey that she could not, after all, go through with the wedding. Rob offered to come with her and help but she refused, thinking it best she do this herself, in her own way.

'But you'll come soon, won't you?'

'Just try and stop me.'

She arrived home to a barrage of questions except from Mickey who, thinking she'd spent the time in bed, believed it was wedding nerves that had laid her low.

The dress hung ready in her wardrobe, Sandra was to be bridesmaid and Dolly matron of honour since she wasn't showing very much yet. Half the village seemed to be coming and Lizzie had been baking for days. The whole thing had gathered a momentum of its own and Alena no longer felt she had any say in the matter.

She knew she should tell Mickey right away. She practised what she should say. She would explain she couldn't go through with it, that she was sorry she'd agreed to marry him in the first place because she didn't truly love him. But that didn't sound quite right. The days slipped by and still she hadn't found the right words. There was something so single-minded about Mickey, something so overwhelming about his confidence, that it was hard to persuade him to see anyone else's point of view.

The Coronation also served to delay Alena. How could she explain everything that needed to be said with excitement over the national celebration running so high? Ellersgarth was trimmed with red, white and blue bunting for the big event, street parties planned, Coronation mugs bought for the children and a day's holiday promised for everyone. And with Alena's wedding still to come, best frocks were being ironed, hats bought and trimmed, the whole village looking upon May as an entire month of jubilation. How could she spoil it for everyone?

Perhaps, she thought, it would be better to wait until Rob arrived, again putting off the moment of truth as she waited and hoped he would come to help her, for all she had told him she'd deal with the matter herself. And he had arrangements of his own to make. The high plantations were no place for a woman, he'd told her, so he was anxious to find new employment, which wouldn't be easy.

And then finally, seven days before the wedding, she stood before Mickey, barely able to speak for nervousness. Lizzie had gone to see Sandra, ironically for a final fitting of her dress. Kit was at the Stag, and Alena had made up her mind to have the whole matter settled before they came home. She made Mickey sit in her father's chair while she told him, noting how his face tightened, almost aged before her eyes.

She reached out a hand to him, then let it drop to her side. 'So you see why I can't marry you? I'm sorry, Mickey, but it wouldn't be right. I don't – feel towards you as I should, so I must call the wedding off.'

He glanced at her as if he didn't quite see her. Then he got up, pulled out a chair and sat at the kitchen table. 'How about that cup of tea you promised me? And some of your ma's ginger cake wouldn't go amiss, if there's any going.'

She was stunned by his calmness. 'Mickey, did you hear what I said? I'm asking you to release me. Rob's come back and everything's changed.'

'I don't see why.'

Alena smothered a sigh and, sitting in the chair opposite him, she laced her fingers tightly together, striving to keep her patience and explain things properly, and kindly, as he deserved. 'You can't pretend you don't know how I feel about Rob, how I've always felt about him. Ever since we were children together he has been a part of me. But as I've just tried to explain, James Hollinthwaite *lied*.

'He deliberately created a feud between our families, all because he wanted to save himself from awkward questions about the death of that poor girl. He's so utterly ruthless when it comes to his own reputation that he thought nothing of lying in order to keep it, or of driving us apart because of the festering hatred he had developed towards the Townsens over the years. Now we know there's no reason why we can't – can't – get back together,' she finished, her voice faltering as she saw the anger clouding Mickey's face.

'And so goodbye, Mickey, and thanks for the memory, eh?'

Alena winced. 'Don't put it like that. I know I must have hurt you and I'm sorry for that. Truly sorry. But I can't help it. I...' She paused, and drawing in a deep breath, continued, 'There's no easy way to say this, Mickey, but I love Rob, and really can't live without him.'

'And you no longer love me?'

She leaned across the table, anxious to make him see her point of view in as gentle a way as she could. 'You always knew that I didn't feel quite the same about you as you did about me. You said it didn't matter, but it does. It matters a great deal, so it's all for the best really. It wouldn't have worked. You'd only have regretted it.'

'I think I'll be the judge of that.' He flung back the chair in a sudden expulsion of violent energy, as if he'd like to fling away this piece of unwelcome information she was bringing him in exactly the same way. 'Thanks for being so honest, Alena. But you know that I hate to be told what I must or must not do and, as you say, I knew all along that you weren't head over heels in love with me. So what?' He shrugged, the corners of his mouth twisting upwards, making him look more puckish than ever. 'We'll do all right, and I know you'll come to love me in time. The fact that Rob Hollinthwaite has returned like the prodigal son is naught to do with us. Now, I've had enough of this talk and would really like that cup of tea, so put the kettle on. The subject is closed.'

She was aghast. He didn't seem to have understood a word she had said. 'Closed? How can it be closed? Don't you understand what I'm saying to you? The wedding is *off*.'

He took a step towards her and very slowly brought his face down till it was just inches from her own, his voice low and soft, the menace in it unmistakeable. 'No, Alena, you are the one who doesn't seem to understand. This wedding is not off. It is still very much *on*.' For the first time all the disquiet and unease and irritation she had felt lately crystallised into a very real fear of Mickey.

'You can't mean that?' She gave a short high laugh of disbelief. 'You can't *make* me marry you.'

He put his head to one side and smiled at her but his next words were spoken in a voice that was ice cold. 'Do you reckon the rest of the village will believe James lied? They've only your word for it, yours and Rob's, and you'd be bound to say so, wouldn't you?'

'Don't be silly, we've got proof now.'

'People believe what they want to believe. And don't forget, Alena, that you've accepted my ring and made a vow to marry me. If you attempt to take up with him again, I'll make sure everyone continues to believe the worst. I'll make both your lives impossible. Is that clear, Alena? Do you understand that, my precious?'

She backed away from him, her face paper white. 'I think you'd best go, Mickey. I'm sorry you've taken it so badly but I'm not going to change my mind. I can't marry you and that's flat.'

Smiling, he picked up his cap from where he'd flung it on the sideboard and sauntered to the door. 'We'll see about that, shall we? I've certainly no intention of giving you up. You are *mine*!' When he had gone, Alena ran to the kitchen and vomited into the sink.

—

Mickey stormed the length of Birkwith Row, down the main village street, cut across Hollin Wood and minutes later was hammering on the back door of Ellersgarth Farm. But for once his mentor was uninterested in assisting Mickey with his problems. James Hollinthwaite stood four-square in his kitchen doorway and blamed him for the fact his son had returned, evidently with the intention of taking up with the girl again; saying Mickey had allowed Alena to delay the wedding too long, that he should have got her to the altar quickly.

'How could I, if she wouldn't come?'

'How do you think? For God's sake, do I have to spell it out for you?'

For all he'd been unsure of her love, Mickey had been certain that he'd won her. He'd pushed their lovemaking as far as he dared, while being enchanted with the fact that his wife would be coming a virgin to his bed on their wedding night. A part of him had relished that prospect, so he'd always been ready to back down when she'd refused him. Now, for the first time in his life he, the invincible Mickey Roscoe, had lost all confidence and control of the situation. And who else could he blame for that but Alena?

'So what do we do now? Give in?' he asked, mouth drooping into a pettish sulk.

'You'll have to use some of that cunning you claim to have.'
And the door was shut firmly in his face.

Mickey punched his fist into the door jamb, making blood
spurt from his knuckles. Drat the man! James Hollinthwaite
could whistle for his favours in future. There'd be no more
coming from Mickey. But he wasn't done yet. He'd get her back
in spite of them all, see if he didn't. Nobody robbed Mickey
Roscoe of what was rightfully his and got away with it.

–

Each day he called at the house but Alena, her desperation
increasing, refused to see him. Lizzie, distressed by this turn
of events, for all she felt a sense of relief and happiness for her
precious daughter, didn't dare leave the house for fear of what
might happen. Sandra explained to everyone that the wedding
had been called off, but then learned a day or two later that
Mickey had also called round to say it was very definitely on.
The whole village was buzzing with the excitement of it all,
and the girls at the mill were agog for more information.

'Is it on or off then? My best frock is getting dizzy from being
brought in and out of the wardrobe.'

'Did you fling his ring back at him?' Annie Cockcroft asked.

'Or keep it to pawn?' Deirdre smilingly enquired.

'Aren't we going to have our hen party then?' Minnie
wanted to know.

Edith said, 'There are other considerations besides a glass of
stout for you, Minnie Hodgson. Leave the poor lass alone. She
has to mek up her own mind on summat like this.'

If it hadn't been for the thought of Rob, Alena felt sure she
wouldn't have survived. It wasn't that she cared a jot what folk
thought, but she hated the increasing pressure still being put on
her by Mickey. He even arranged for the vicar to call and calm
her 'wedding nerves'. Unable to be rude to the man, Alena
invited him in and brewed a pot of tea, listening to him politely
as she warmed her perpetually cold hands around a mug of

scalding tea. She even managed to smile when he told her that he'd suffered much the same phenomenon, and hadn't he been happily married to his dear Doris for twenty-eight years? She saw him out with relief.

–

A day or two later Alena came out of the mill as usual, waved to Dolly and Tom as they went off arm in arm, climbed on to her bicycle and swung out of the mill yard. Great fat drops of rain started and she turned up her collar. It was then that she saw him.

She skidded on loose stones and almost fell, gazing at him spellbound, hardly able to believe that he had come at last, that this time he would never leave her alone again. He took her rain-washed face between his hands and kissed her, lingering over the taste of her skin. It was the most glorious moment of her life.

'Hello.' His mouth was set in that teasing smile she loved so much. 'Is it still there, do you think? Our tree. Only, rain or no rain, I think we should talk. Will you come?'

Hardly able to look at him for happiness, Alena could only nod. Of course she would come. Wouldn't she follow him to the ends of the earth?

Afterwards, she would always remember the rain. The washing, cleansing, cooling rain. She would remember the smell of mossy earth and the swish of raindrops splashing through the branches. There was no sound in the woods other than the rain. Most of the forest's occupants seemed to be waiting for the sun to break out again, then the birds would emerge, burst into song and perhaps splash and bathe in the small puddles left behind. The deer would continue with their browsing and the squirrels their acrobatics. But for now the two lovers felt quite alone in all the world, sheltered beneath the arms of their tree, shielded by a curtain of rain.

'How long is it since we sat here?'

'Too long.'

'We've missed so much, you and I. All the fun and pain of growing up together.'

'Years and years.'

'Did I say that you haven't changed?'

'I have.'

'Only to grow more beautiful. Oh, Ally, I've missed you so much.'

'Prove it.'

He laughed, shaking his head. A shower of raindrops flicked on to her lips, and she licked them up. 'There is only one way I can do that. I don't think we'd better risk it, do you?'

Her only reply was to smile at him, blue eyes glowing with mischief and a primeval instinct far more alluring. And then the magic of the moment was broken as he asked her the one question she dreaded answering.

'Have you told him, Alena? Are you free?'

–

Why couldn't Mickey see it was all a waste of time? Why didn't he just give in gracefully and accept defeat? She and Rob talked to Lizzie for hours that night, worrying over how they could get it across to Mickey that life for them was impossible to contemplate unless they could be together.

'We've wasted too much time already.'

'Not wasted, lost,' Alena corrected Rob, sliding her hand into his and giving it a little squeeze. 'And not through any fault of our own. We were always meant to be together. It brings us truly alive.'

Lizzie watched them with soft eyes and saw that it was so.

The next day, which was the last before the wedding, Mickey came round yet again. Desperate to have the matter settled, Alena let him in, explaining once more with great care and as much tact as she could muster, that nothing he said or did could change the way she felt. She was very sorry but she couldn't marry him, and there was an end of it.

'It's because I pushed you too hard, isn't it? Because I sometimes criticised your dress, or the way you did your hair.'

Alena sighed. 'It's got nothing to do with that.'

'If I seemed a bit pushy, that's only because you're so very important to me, Ally.'

'Don't call me that!'

He flinched, as if he were a small boy being scolded for being naughty. 'Rob calls you that, why shouldn't I?'

'You're not Rob.'

'No, dammit, I'm not. I'm going to be your husband!' And he drove one fist into the table top. Alena jumped, shocked by the force of the blow, amazed it hadn't split the table in two.

'For God's sake, Mickey, *stop it!*' She was fighting back tears, willing herself not to let him see her fear. If this was to be their final confrontation, she would come out of it with her dignity intact, at least. Instantly he was contrite, reaching for her even as she backed away.

'Please don't be cross with me. It's only because I love you so much.'

'I know,' she said, softening as she heard the pain in his voice.

'I'm sorry I lost my temper. Am I forgiven?'

'Of course.' And she kissed him very quickly on his cheek. It was a mistake. She realised that instantly as she saw the smile spread across his broad face. 'No, Mickey, don't look like that. Can't you see I'm trying to be kind, doing my best not to hurt you? But it's over. Finished. Now please go.' She pulled herself free and watched as he thrust his shoulders back and swung with jaunty footsteps to the door where he turned and winked back at her.

'See you tomorrow then. The big day, eh?'

Less than an hour later, Alena kissed Lizzie goodbye and the pair of them clung together, crying but afraid to let go and accept the inevitable. The decision had been made some time ago, bags had been packed and arrangements made when it became clear to them all that Mickey would never accept that the wedding was off. He would turn up at the church as planned, with the vicar and the organist and the flowers, their friends sitting in the pews. But no Alena.

'This isn't how I wanted your wedding day to be, not my lovely daughter.'

'I know, Ma.' But they also knew that the tensions here had become impossible to bear. However much trouble there would be when Mickey discovered Alena's elopement, it would be far worse if she remained in the village. They had to leave, there was no other way.

'We're not going far,' Rob promised as Lizzie walked with them to the door. 'Just to a forest hut I know of. Not much, but it'll have to do till I can find somewhere better. I'll take good care of her.'

Lizzie put one hand on his arm. 'I know that, lad, or you'd have to climb over my dead body to take her.' And then they were gone and there was nothing but the night wind blowing through the house as Lizzie closed the door.

Chapter Twenty-One

The village was rocked back on its heels by the scandal. What a sight it was! Mickey Roscoe standing at the altar looking a proper dandy in his best blue serge suit and slicked down hair, his cocksure confidence eaten away by a mounting rage that finally erupted as he swung on his heel and strode down the aisle alone, instead of with a beautiful bride on his arm. The poor vicar didn't know which way to turn, but finally pulled himself together sufficiently to insist upon a prayer for the 'poor aggrieved party' before permitting the stunned congregation to escape into sunshine and gossip.

No one could talk of anything else for days. The girls at the bobbin mill reluctantly put away their fancy frocks, but reconciled themselves to the loss of a good party by filling every spare moment with speculation about where the lovers might have gone. Gretna Green, for sure. They'd be over the border by the time Mickey had got his clean socks on that morning. And of course they all kept a keen eye on him as he went about his work in the mill, curious to see how he would cope with the shame of it all. No one could claim Mickey Roscoe was an easy character to deal with. Even so, you couldn't help feeling sorry for the poor blighter.

Maggie Sutton claimed to have seen it coming all along while Mrs Rigg wept copious tears into her hanky, though her sympathies were all with the eloping lovers rather than the deserted groom. Sandra and Dolly, along with Alena's brothers, made no comment whatsoever, preferring to keep their own counsel in the hope that the matter would die down all the sooner.

As for Lizzie, she went about her business as normal with her head held high and her spine rigid with determination to ignore the curious stares and whispered asides that followed her everywhere. Alena was her beloved daughter, and she was proud of the courage the girl had shown. In Lizzie's opinion there were plenty of married couples in this village who would have led happier lives if one or other of the parties concerned had shown similar good sense. She was sad that she'd miss her daughter's wedding, but then what did a ceremony matter? It was what followed that really counted in this world: and she wanted Alena to be happy.

And the words on everyone's lips were. 'Are they really brother and sister or not?' Few had not learned the scandalous tale by this time. Had James Hollinthwaite lied or not? Opinion was divided.

Mrs Milburn reported, to her continuing regret, that James Hollinthwaite had said not one word on the subject. He'd locked himself into his study and hadn't emerged, except when necessary, to her certain knowledge for more than two weeks.

–

James's fury and embarrassment were such that he could not bear the thought of revealing them to anyone. His desk littered with papers and plans, hours spent in conversation on the telephone, he devoted himself with unflagging energy to his conifer project. There was scarcely a moment when he was not engaged upon the matter in some way or another. It had met with opposition, of course. He was aware of the village campaign against him, led by some girl with a grievance over a silly accident that was not his responsibility. Admittedly she was not alone. There were others: land owners, romantics, the local council, even the vicar, who strongly objected to his plans to afforest open fell land, and in particular to his idea of replacing ancient hardwoods with spruce. James ignored them all, brushing them aside as he would irritating insects.

Nevertheless, when he did finally emerge, from self-imposed seclusion, he knew how to turn the scandal surrounding his son to his advantage, how to play for sympathy when the occasion demanded it. Certainly the local council warmed towards him as he politely pointed out that if he could not control the wanton passions of youth, there was little anyone could do to stop *him* from planting whatever he wished on his own land. He said the old hardwood trees were unsafe and would have to be felled in any case, and promised to replant with mixed woodland, whatever the cost. None of this was true but, foolishly, their pity for him urged them to believe him and they raised no further objections. But then, unlike Alena, they did not know him for a dishonest man.

He would prove to everyone, through these ambitious, wealth-producing schemes, that he was still a man in control of his destiny, with not a single regret in his life. A man who could surmount scandal would never tolerate failure. All he had to do was engage the labour and the felling could begin. Knowing Rob's abiding interest in trees, James was certain this would bring his son back to Ellersgarth and his home. If he could but make a man of him, make him forget the Townsen girl and become the son he had always wanted, as ambitious and single-minded as himself, then it would all have been worthwhile.

Now that his plans were made, James felt more able to see the situation as simply a temporary problem, one that could still be resolved. So far as he was aware the couple were not yet wedded, despite rumours to the contrary, though they were probably bedded by now. But then they believed he lied. This made him laugh, but only for a moment as he thought of Olivia, the wife who had deserted him. She was the one most to blame for everything. Her difficulties in producing a son, her cold disregard for his needs throughout their married life, and the way she had crossed his every attempt to guide and control the boy… Now she'd encouraged him to pry.

Fortunately James's own distrust of his fellow men had served him well over the years, in particular when others before his son had gone down similar avenues. It meant they could discover only blind alleys. Unfortunately, he had not legislated for the more intimate effect of that night's events upon himself. Effects that had surprised him. Could he have a conscience after all? he wondered, and snorted with derision at the very idea.

He kicked at a log in the fireplace. How he would like to kick Alena Townsen, and all she represented of his own failures and torment, out of his life and that of his son, no matter what the cost. He succeeded only in making sparks spiral up the chimney, and the room light up their brilliance. It seemed almost prophetic, reminding him yet again of the particular nature of his agony.

Angry with these thoughts, he rose abruptly from his chair and, collecting his hat and stick, went out into the brightness of a summer day and trod the paths of his domain, reminding himself afresh of the tangible evidence of his success.

He came to a small clearing in the woodland close to the back of the house. A wild cherry tree grew here and he frowned ponderously upon a crop of ox-eye daisies that had sprouted defiantly at its root. A shiver ran down his spine. For a moment it was as if the sun had been blotted out and dusk was falling. He felt the cold beat of rain, heard it battering on the cotton canvas sheet, and the wind howling as if with pain through skeletal branches of winter-bare trees. And he smelled yet again the sweet-sour scent of death and damp earth.

What if his son would not come home? All his efforts would then be as dust. For a moment black doubt assailed him as he considered the lost years that he could have spent on the boy, the wasted education that had not resulted in university entrance. Rob's quiet, passive nature and determination to work with his hands instead of his brain, showed only disdain for his father's achievements in acquiring property and wealth. James knew exactly what he would be doing now: living the life of a peasant. Thus his bitter disappointment in his son remained. Even so, an as yet unacknowledged admiration for the way Rob was determined to carve out his own future flickered grudgingly into life.

He heard the piercing sweet notes of a blackbird's song and shook all the doubts and the spectres away.

Once the pair ran out of money, as they soon would since he'd spread the word that no employer in the county who cared for his reputation should consider offering his son a job, Rob would quickly tire of his foolish rebellion, and of Alena Townsen. Perhaps it would have been better to let the relationship run its course years ago. But what did it matter now? So long as no actual ceremony had taken place, then he could hope for victory in the end. All James needed was time and patience, but for all he had these in abundance, he fully intended to play a major role in bringing Rob to heel.

–

He had built her a house. The kind of house the first men of Cumbria might have built, a style perpetuated by the coppicers and charcoal burners. Rob had found the remains of one on his regular treks through the forest, its circular wall still strong and in place. In the days apart, while he'd waited for her to break free from Mickey, he'd built on a chimney, tall and straight, with a fireplace to warm them. A sheet of metal within deflected the flames and heat from the roof, and prevented the fire from becoming too smoky. He'd then cut four long birch poles and set them in the traditional wigwag shape, lashing them together at the top with withies. Further poles had been placed between and the gaps filled with bracken and clay.

Now all they had to do was add a layer of overlapping turfs to the sloping roof to keep out the rain. It took several days of hard work to complete it, but they didn't mind. It had to be done properly, the sods cut as thin as possible to keep weight to a minimum and then pleated together in such a way that not a drop of water could penetrate.

They sang and chattered as they worked, outdoing the birds in their joyousness. A wood pigeon cooed and once, as they ate the food Lizzie had provided, a hare came and sat watching them, before bounding off into the undergrowth. Each night they fell asleep exhausted beneath the blankets she'd also insisted on their taking, a sparkling canopy of stars above their heads, the heather soft at their backs.

They lay untouching, side by side, and for all it was hard to resist consummating their love, yet they were both determined that the first time should be special; a magical moment to remember throughout their lives together, not a hasty coupling beneath a hedge. And after a good night's rest, over a breakfast of oatcakes and tea cooked over a small fire, they would talk excitedly of their plans.

'I can work as a woodsman making sheep hurdles, gates and such like. Perhaps even try my hand at charcoal burning.'

'And I can make besoms and baskets.'

'I'll build you a proper house one day. One to be proud of.'

'I'm proud of this one.'

These wonderfully romantic plans and their love sustained them through the hard labour. Alena swept out the fireplace, fashioned hooks and shelves from branches and hung up the pots and pans that Lizzie had provided. Then she collected wood, stacking it beneath a tree close by, and beside the hearth to dry. Lastly she cleared the ground inside the hut and laid down a layer of dry reeds. She expected them to sleep on bracken, as they had when they'd stayed with the coppicers. Rob, however, had other ideas.

'We may have caused a scandal that will keep the gossips busy for months, and we may have to wait a while before we can make it legal, but I'll not take you on rough bracken.' And Alena could only blush at the promise of this anticipated joy.

As the days passed it became harder to resist the strength of their emotions. Sometimes their fingers would brush against each other, or her hair would graze his cheek and he would smell its sweetness. Then he'd catch her hand and pull her to the ground and kiss her. Work would be forgotten during these times of loving discovery as they lay together, perhaps for hours; then they would guiltily dust each other down and return hot and dishevelled, but secretly smiling, to the task in hand.

Rob made the bed out of birch poles, hammering the sharpened corner posts into the ground, building a rectangular frame and lashing the cross-poles to it. Filled with excitement, and the adventure of it all, Alena stitched up the sheet Lizzie had packed for them and, together, they risked a two-mile trek to a nearby barn, begged for a little straw from the friendly farmer, then dragged it back, singing and laughing at the tops of their voices, spirits high and hearts full of hope and love.

They laid the mattress on the fine birch bed, together with a pillow Alena had also made. When the bed was finished they covered it with the blankets and couldn't help but admire it, standing four-square in the snugness of their hut. Then they smiled shyly at each other.

'What else is left to do?' Alena softly asked.

'Only this.' Rob nailed some sacking across the door, then lifted her up in his arms and carried her inside.

–

That first time was, as he had promised, a tender coming together. They gave of their love generously and with joyful abandon, at last able to express all the feelings they'd been forced to deny for so long. They kissed until their faces burned, touched and caressed with a sensitivity that left them breathless. And when she finally welcomed him inside her, thrilling to his thrusting need of her, glorying in every tremor of his young body, she lifted herself to him and as one they cried out in their ecstasy.

Afterwards they lay entwined together, the new bed strong and firm beneath them, the mattress soft and yielding, smelling sweetly of the coming summer, and Alena cried.

Rob was alarmed. 'What is it? Did I hurt you?'

She hastened to reassure him that he had not, that it was from happiness that she wept, and when words failed her, she told him with her lips, her fingers, the silky touch of her legs against his and her urgent need for him to love her again.

Closeted in the green dimness of the hut, the bed became their sanctuary. They sat on it to eat their meals, they read to each other from the book of poems that Rob had brought with him. They snuggled up beneath the cosy blankets to make their plans for the future, and on each successive occasion that they made love, it was with an increasing passion. This was their world, safe from the dictates of Rob's father and the jealous temper of Mickey.

Alena didn't care if the villagers gossiped about them.

She didn't care that they had no money, or even that the small supply of food they had brought was running low.

She didn't care about a better house, or a grander bed.

She had not a single regret. She was quite certain that Mickey would soon find himself another girl, one who would return his love as she could not. And James Hollinthwaite would accept the inevitable, now that he'd been proved a liar. She had Rob, what more could she ask? She was, at last, supremely happy and safe in his arms.

—

Patience was not something which came easily to Mickey Roscoe. Nevertheless his native cunning served him well.

He couldn't remember ever feeling so humiliated in all his life, and if there was one thing he hated above all else, it was to be made a fool of. No one did that to Mickey Roscoe and lived to tell the tale. But he did not intend to make a hasty retaliation. He needed time to think.

He attempted to rationalise matters by telling himself that it might only be a temporary state of affairs. Who knew what might happen in the next few weeks? Rob would certainly find it hard to get other employment, and love would soon wither on the branch if there was nothing to feed it. Summer would pass and they'd grow cold and hungry. How would Rob's charms appeal then? The excitement would fade and Alena would tire of him.

His own mistake had clearly been that he'd shown her too much respect and hung back too long. A woman should be given no time to think, but be swept off her feet with the joy of love. Though it grieved him to admit it, Mickey acknowledged that Hollinthwaite had been right. He should have made sure of her in the time-honoured way. But it was not too late. So long as she and Rob weren't actually married, there was still hope. And Mickey was certainly man enough for the job, a better man than the one she'd foolishly chosen and would soon come to regret. Then he could forgive her and take her back, and enjoy reasserting his authority over her.

The important thing was first to find out where, exactly, she was living. And what better way to discover it than by close contact with one of Alena's best friends?

Once he'd allowed a suitable period of mourning for his lost bride to elapse, he called upon Sandra, standing on the doorstep of her aunt's house with a woebegone expression that was meant to melt any female heart. He told her that he knew many details concerning Hollinthwaite's forestry project, and explained how, on those evenings he hadn't spent with Alena, he'd attended many public meetings, visited pubs and inns, even got himself invited to discussions in private houses, and generally been the eyes and ears of James Hollinthwaite, bringing him the information he needed to further his plans. But now he would be glad to share all of this with her.

'I owe that man nothing since he has allowed his son to steal my bride.'

'I doubt he could have stopped him,' Sandra felt bound to point out.

'And I desperately need to fill my time with something. Let me help. I'll address envelopes, carry around a placard, stick up posters, whatever you wish, only give me something to take my mind off my troubles.' And he'd looked at her with such moist, beseeching eyes that Sandra, ever soft-hearted, and in dire need of all the help she could get, saw no reason to refuse.

—

If Sandra's judgement in this matter was impaired, it was partly due to concern for her own situation. She was beginning to feel a prisoner in her own home. She gave comfort and succour on a daily basis to her aunt, she worked hard for Mrs Rigg at the village store, and was conducting this campaign on everyone's behalf. She'd certainly stood by Alena through her troubles. It had been her own letter to Rob, apparently, which had sparked his determination to find out the truth, once and for all, and led to his finally coming to claim her.

But who was helping Sandra? Who was offering her comfort and succour, or working to help her find the happiness she craved? No one.

As Mickey put his back into the campaign, she began to feel real sympathy for him. It wasn't his fault that Alena had been in love with someone else and he'd been deprived of his bride. Just as it wasn't her fault that Harry had lost his job and gone away. They were both victims, in a way, like poor King Edward who had now married Mrs Simpson but lost his crown.

She watched Mickey now, seated at Aunt Elsie's chenille-covered table, busily drawing up plans of which sections of the woodland James Hollinthwaite meant to clear and replant. He even sketched out a possible timescale, attempting to explain the process to Sandra. In her chair by the fire Aunt Elsie softly snored, and from out in the hall came the loud tick of the grandfather clock. The huge old-fashioned house seemed suddenly to echo her loneliness, despite Mickey's presence. She wished desperately it could be Harry here beside her. Where was he? Had he found a job in Liverpool? He wrote from time to time but made no promises, never even asked her to wait for him, though she always promised she would in the letters she wrote back.

How different her life would have been if she hadn't suffered that dreadful accident and Harry hadn't led the deputation against Hollinthwaite. Yet he'd been standing up for what was right, and nothing would make her back down from the campaign. What more did she have to lose? The rest of the village, however, was another matter. A few gave her their support, but in a secretive, back-door sort of way; the rest refused even to get involved for fear of ending up like Harry.

Mickey finished his drawing and turned it for her to see. 'There you are. Devastate this village, he will. Quick cash crops, that's what he's going for, and to hell with the consequences.'

'Yes, Mickey, but how do we stop him? How do I persuade everyone to stand against him?'

They were worrying over this problem when there was a knock at the door.

Aunt Elsie woke with a start. 'My house is no longer my own,' she grumbled. 'No wonder I suffer constantly from a headache, with all this activity going on.'

Sandra glanced through the window, to see who was calling so late. 'It's only Lizzie. You like Mrs Townsen, Aunt.'

'I don't think she likes me,' Mickey pointed out, getting up. 'Time I went home in any case. There's not much more we can do tonight.'

Sandra, suddenly anxious that Lizzie didn't see Mickey or interpret her accepting his help as some kind of betrayal, agreed, and bustled him out through the kitchen door. Only then did she let Lizzie in, breathing rather fast and filled with unaccustomed guilt.

'Oh, you are in then. I'd nearly given up hope.'

'Sorry, I was upstairs and Aunt Elsie never answers the door if she can help it.'

Over a cup of tea, Sandra showed Lizzie the maps and plans of the proposed planting sites, without mentioning who had drawn them. Aunt Elsie sat in sulky silence by the fire with her own favourite china cup and saucer, and a plate of Bourbon biscuits, as the two chatted. Sandra prayed the sulks would continue for once, and she'd make no mention of Mickey's having just left.

'I've brought you a bit of news about Harry,' Lizzie said, and Sandra was instantly alert.

'What? Is he all right? He isn't sick or anything?' And Lizzie laughed, patting the girl's hand fondly.

'No. 'Course not. Strong as a horse, my Harry. He's coming home. Only on a visit, mind, but I thought you'd like to know.'

'Oh, Lizzie!'

She leaned close and put a gentle hand to Sandra's cheek which had suddenly grown hot. 'And I'll try and put in a word for you. I know he still loves you, if the fool would but admit it.' And they exchanged knowing smiles. Lizzie shook her head. 'Children, what a trouble they are! Even when they're full-grown and should have more sense.' And she talked for a while about how happy she was that Tom and Dolly seemed content at last, and how she'd felt the baby quicken only yesterday; of Jim and Ruby's brood, and how Kit had finally decided to go into market gardening.

'Told him to do that years ago.' Inevitably the conversation turned to Alena. 'I do worry about the lass. The weather is kind at the moment, being June, but what will happen when autumn comes? They can't stay in that hut, can they? And they could be hungry even now. Perhaps I should take them more food? What do you reckon? Would that be considered interference?'

Sandra raised her eyebrows. 'You know where they are then?'

'Of course I do. I'm her mother. Would it hurt Rob's pride, do you think?' And Sandra smiled.

'Why should it? So long as you take the kind of food that the forest, or Rob's hunting skills, cannot provide. Salt and flour, that sort of thing. They have to eat.'

Lizzie was looking brighter by the minute. 'Oh, Sandra, you've taken a real weight off my mind. That's exactly what I'll do.' And as Aunt Elsie's snores rang out once more, she chuckled and said she'd take her leave so that the old lady could be put to bed.

Taking his ear from the parlour door, Mickey smiled as he slipped quietly back up the passage and let himself out once more through the kitchen and into the back garden to walk jauntily away.

–

Lizzie was excited as she set out with Jim in his old Morris van along the winding lanes into the forest. She had so much news to give Alena. The reaction of the village to the whole scandal would be discussed, of course. But on a more cheerful note, wouldn't she be pleased to hear about Harry coming home, and that he'd found himself a job? Maybe there'd be two marriages in the family and a couple more grandchildren before long. Alena would be as pleased as she if Sandra could escape the clutches of her aunt. But, as yet, these were no more than daydreams.

Lizzie would like to have seen her own daughter safely married, but she wasn't complaining. Everything came to those who had the patience to endure.

'You can drop me here,' she told her son as they rounded a bend and he dutifully drew the van to a halt, only to glance about him with some concern. Beyond the clearing where he was now parked the trees were thickly planted with little light showing between. 'Will you have far to walk? It'll be darker in the forest, particularly later on your way back. Have you a torch?' Lizzie produced one and he grinned. 'You seem to have thought of everything.'

'I hope so.' She indicated the basket of goodies that she carried.

'Why don't you let me come with you? I could at least carry that for you.' But she shook her head.

'I promised to say naught to anyone, not even family. Not till they've had time to get themselves sorted out. You'll come back for me in two hours?'

'On the dot.'

He waited until she was well on her way, smiling at her resolve to keep the lovers' hiding place a secret, before continuing along the road towards Hawkshead. He'd promised to do one or two errands for Ruby and the children while he was out. Had he turned the van around and headed home right away, he might have noticed another vehicle on the road, not too far behind him.

—

Harry came the following Saturday. Sandra met him off the train at Lake Side, her stomach churning with nervousness as she waited. But she was determined to have a proper talk with him well out of earshot and sight of her aunt.

He seemed surprised but, she thought, quite pleased to see her, which came as a relief. She'd taken particular trouble with her appearance, choosing to wear a simple cotton print frock in saffron yellow which, as his admiring glances clearly indicated, suited her fair prettiness. For all the sun was beating down, she carried her straw Panama hat in neatly gloved hands, not wishing to cover her shining hair, which she knew he loved.

They sat on the small pier overlooking the lake and ate ice creams, laughing at a small flotilla of ducklings bobbing up and down in the softly lapping water. It was a perfect June day, a heat haze lying across the lake and making the mountains seem pale and distant.

He said, 'I've found a job, Sandra,' and her heart flipped over.

'Where? What sort of job?'

'In a forest, planting and felling.'

'But you're a skilled woodturner.'

'I know about trees though. Anyroad, I'm young enough to learn new skills. And I'm strong and fit.' He turned to her, excitement written plain in his face. 'It's a grand job, Sandra. In Canada.' It was then that she thought her heart stopped beating altogether.

Chapter Twenty-Two

Harry went on talking, telling her what a fine country Canada was, how the forests stretched from one ocean to the other, more vast than anyone could contemplate. And how it was all going to be a bit of a rush because the ship sailed in exactly three weeks' time. 'Seems long enough but there's all the passport and paperwork to sort out before then, gear to buy and preparations to make, so I'd have to be back in Liverpool by next Friday at the latest. But it'll be a new life, Sandra. A new beginning. What do you think of it, eh?'

She stared at him, misery putting a wobble in her voice when she finally found it. 'I'm not sure what to think. I'm not sure quite what it is you're saying.'

He took her hands gently between his own. 'I'm asking you to come with me, as my wife. I always meant to come back for you if I found a job, and now I've found a good one. The best. There's a house goes with it, and there'll be other young wives for you to get to know. I'll make sure you're not lonely, Sandra.' A hint of anxiety showed in his face now, his voice becoming deeper than usual. 'You'll not refuse me, will you? I've happen behaved a bit daft like, showed a bit too much pride, but I do love you, never doubt that.'

'I never have doubted it, Harry,' she shyly told him, and then his arms were going round her and they were laughing and crying, he smoothing the tears from her cheeks and kissing her as if he might never stop. In that moment there was no room for doubt or fear of any kind, nor need of any more words, for they both felt quite certain they'd discovered that dreams can indeed come true.

It was only later, as they walked home, that the problem at the back of both their minds was mentioned.

Sandra simply said, 'I'll tell her myself this time. And I'll not take no for an answer.'

—

Elsie Myers looked upon her niece with an expression close to hatred. She told Sandra that if she wanted to break her aunt's heart, then of course she must leave; an argument that the girl found hard to swallow. Her aunt had cared for her in a practical sense, but there'd been little, if any, sign of genuine love. Sandra tried to explain she could find someone to take her place, but her aunt wasn't listening.

'It's ingratitude, that's what it is. I've devoted my life to you, madam, opened my home to you, and this is all the thanks I get! If you go against my wishes in this, I shall expect you to pay back every penny I've ever spent on you.'

Sandra went pale. 'You can't mean that?'

'Indeed I do. I'm not a philanthropic society. And he'll not make you happy, this young man. Marriage is a most distasteful business.'

'I think I shall be the best judge of that, Aunt. I'm sorry if you were afraid of men, or marriage, or intimacy,' she bravely and perhaps recklessly added, 'but I am not. I love Harry, and I'm absolutely sure he'll make me very happy.'

Elsie Myers's face had gone quite scarlet. 'How *dare* you! Go and wash your mouth out this minute! Then up to your room and stay there. There'll be no supper for you tonight.'

Sandra was now the one who flushed – with anger. But she was determined not to rise to her aunt's malice. 'No, I'm not a child, Aunt. I'll do as I please. Now, calm down or you'll bring on one of your turns. I'll go and make us both a nice cup of tea and bring you a garibaldi biscuit.'

The arrangement was that Sandra should meet Harry at Birk-with Row at eight on Saturday morning. Unable to sleep from excitement, she was awake and in the kitchen some two hours before that. Aunt Elsie had subsided into one of her sulky silences, finally seeming to have accepted the inevitable. Sandra realised she would not be sorry to be free from her constant demands, or this gloomy mausoleum of a house. For all she was grateful for her aunt's generosity in taking her in, she'd more than paid her way over the years. She certainly did not take seriously Elsie's demand that she repay every penny of her keep. But Sandra had promised that when they'd made their way in Canada, she would send whatever money they could spare.

'Every month, I promise. And you could always come on a visit?' she'd suggested, to no response whatsoever.

She'd also made sure that Aunt Elsie would be well looked after. Mrs Rigg had found a large, jolly woman, a Mrs Hutton, only too willing to come daily to clean the house, prepare Miss Myers's meals and tend to her needs. There'd been so much to do, so many arrangements to make, that the days since Harry's return seemed to have flown by.

She meant to arrive early at Birkwith Row, because she wanted to hear all about Lizzie's recent visit to Alena. It seemed like a miracle that they had finally both found happiness. But then, they certainly deserved it after all the years of patient waiting.

This morning, the last in her aunt's house, Sandra felt too excited to eat breakfast herself, but took a tray up to Aunt Elsie and then prepared a packet of sandwiches for the journey. When she had made them she went about the old house, saying her goodbyes, checking windows and doors were locked, that every room was neat and tidy with not a cushion or a book out of place, just as her aunt liked it.

She removed the old newspapers from the rack, took them to the pantry, then wasted several minutes folding already neatly stacked brown paper carrier bags. Then she checked the plate of sliced tongue and pickle that she'd set ready in the meat safe for Aunt Elsie's luncheon, and finally forced herself to eat a slice of toast and drink a cup of hot Bournvita, in the hope it would calm her churning stomach. She still couldn't quite believe her luck that out of all the girls in the village, Harry should choose her. Her one concern now was to make him a good wife.

By the time the clock struck seven thirty, her strapped brown suitcase and a small carpetbag stood waiting in the hall. She slipped the sandwiches into the pocket of the latter then went back into the kitchen to make a thermos flask of tea. They would arrive in Liverpool around noon and Harry had arranged digs for them. In separate rooms, he said, all right and proper until he'd arranged a hasty wedding for them at the local register office. Sandra had apologised to Lizzie for depriving her of the pleasure of attending.

'Don't you worry about that,' she'd said, kissing them both. 'I don't hold with a lot of fuss over weddings. Can't afford it anyroad. The important thing is that the pair of you are happy.'

Sandra didn't care how hasty, it was all wonderfully romantic and she felt sure she'd burst with the excitement of it all. There was so much happening, so much to be done. A passport to be ordered, various forms to fill in, things to buy. 'Oh!' She suddenly remembered that Harry had instructed her to bring her birth certificate.

She ran back to the parlour and started searching in her aunt's bureau. She found a bundle of papers in an old tin box, dropping several all over the floor in her haste as she rifled through them. Quickly she gathered them up, leaving them in an untidy pile on the open bureau while she searched the box more thoroughly, frantically unfolding each likely document, then having to fold it up quickly again and go on to the next. Why hadn't she thought of the certificate before? Now she would be late. One paper turned out to be her father's will. Barely glancing at it, she tossed it aside. And then she found what she was looking for. Stuffing it in her coat pocket with a sigh of relief, she'd barely set about restoring order when she heard a loud thud. It seemed to go on forever, and then came the scream.

She flew into the hall to find her aunt's breakfast tray on the top step, but Aunt Elsie herself at the bottom of the stairs, one leg twisted very badly beneath the other.

—

Surviving on little but love in the woods was proving to be the happiest time for Alena. She was full of enthusiasm for her new life. She'd been delighted to see Lizzie and grateful for the extra rations she'd brought, but was careful to explain that Rob was a good provider. He caught game and the occasional rabbit, and although strictly speaking she supposed it must be poaching, they had to eat, didn't they? And who would begrudge them the odd pheasant, or trout from the beck, or even notice they were missing? They were learning of many wild plants they could eat, and of course there were mushrooms and wild raspberries, and they'd even found a few early blackberries.

She was thrilled to hear the good news about Harry, and begged Lizzie to call again and bring paper and pen next time, so she could write and congratulate him. And she'd write to Sandra too.

The only difficult part of her mother's visit was seeing Lizzie's reaction to their hut. They might well be proud of it but, with her shining brasses and a kitchen floor you could eat your dinner off, it seemed a poor sort of place to Lizzie for her precious daughter to be living. It had been necessary to calm some of her fears, convincing her that they were not only happy here in the forest, but would do well in it, given time.

'Once we've got a bit of money put by, and we've still a little left from Rob's savings, then we'll rent a proper cottage where we'll live at weekends and in the winter. This is only temporary.'

Their presence on this old pitstead was, in fact, welcomed by the land owner, since it meant the forest would be cleared of dead wood, overgrown trees would be pruned and, through coppicing, the vigour of the woodland would be renewed. Rob had no difficulty in securing satisfactory terms to work this section of the forest and once they'd made their home as comfortable as they could, and Lizzie had replenished their larder, he went again to see Isaac to seek his advice on how best to set himself up in business. The old man took him under his wing without a second's hesitation.

'I'm more than ready to pass on my skills to you. I'll teach you all I know, and more besides,' he declared, as if that were perfectly possible.

Rob humbly thanked him.

'You're right to think of charcoal as well as coppicing. It is a noble craft, my boy, dating back to Iron Age Man when he used to shape his weapons in the glowing embers of the burn. There aren't so many of us about any more, but there's still business to be got. I sell a great deal to industry for fuel, and to seedsmen to mix with bulb fibre and the like. With all this talk of war, even the government is buying charcoal again, though perhaps not for gunpowder these days. Apparently it's useful in the production of gas masks, would you believe?' Isaac gave a resigned shake of his head, making the long feather on his hat quiver. 'And that is a worthy occupation for man and womankind, wouldn't you say? Salvation.'

Rob agreed, interested to hear of this new business opportunity whilst not caring for the reason it had come about. 'When I've learned all I need to know, you've no objection then to my starting my own burn, on the pitstead near our hut?'

'Indeed not, my boy. I'm getting on, though I could not, in all accuracy, tell you quite how old I am. But do not become too attached to your little hut. You'll have to move on, in time.'

'We don't mind.' But although he sounded certain, Rob worried about this. Would Alena mind keeping moving about the forest? Alternatively, would she be too lonely if he had to leave her for days on end while he worked with Isaac to learn his trade? Most of all he worried about the cold. He was under no illusions. Charcoal burning was an arduous occupation, and one that must be carried out, because of the felling, mainly through the winter. How would they survive then?

Alena told him, of course, that she didn't mind at all; that it would all be worthwhile, in the end.

'And I've already started work on my besoms, might even try my hand at making a pole lathe if Isaac will show me how to get started. I could fashion us some bowls and kitchen tools from sycamore, to use for ourselves or even to sell, using the skills I learned in the bobbin mill.'

She kissed him to seal the bargain, and he couldn't help but be comforted and kiss her back, for didn't the happiness shine from her eyes and make her lovelier than ever? He gathered her in his arms and swung her round in a paroxysm of joy and optimism, hardly able to believe that at last they were together.

'And we mustn't forget to plant a crab apple tree.'

'Why?'

'How should I know? It's part of the mystery and magic of charcoal-making, according to Isaac, so let's not take any chances.' And, laughing, they fell on the bed together, kissing and touching and pulling off each other's clothes as if nothing else mattered, for surely it didn't, so long as they had each other.

And if they were apart sometimes during the day, for a little while at least, there would still be the nights when they could be alone in the solitary silence of the forest, and he could stroke her silky skin, find delightful new places to kiss, and bring them both time and again to that height of emotion they could never have dreamed possible. Even now as they snuggled down in their handmade bed, their naked bodies warmly entwined, he could hear a deer snuffling in the undergrowth and the tap-tap of an industrious green woodpecker. What possible harm could come to her in this beautiful place?

If Sandra had felt restricted before, now she felt trapped. She'd called the doctor right away, running to Mrs Rigg's shop in order to use her phone. Then she'd had to race home again, afraid to abandon Aunt Elsie for more than five minutes where she'd left her, propped against cushions at the foot of the stairs. Sandra raced in through the front door and almost ended up with her own leg broken as she fell over a stool lying in her way, so anxious was she to reach her aunt before she succumbed to the oft-threatened heart attack.

There hadn't been too long to wait before the doctor arrived. After a brief examination he declared there were, in fact, no broken bones, only a severe sprain. He gave Miss Myers a stern lecture on how she shouldn't gallop downstairs at her time of life, prescribed a pain killer and ordered her to rest her ankle for a week before putting any weight on it.

Only when the old lady had been comfortably and safely installed back in her own bed did he give a thought to Sandra. In the front vestibule he paused for a fraction of a second, his mind already on his next call.

'You can manage to look after her, I take it. No need for a nurse?'

'No,' Sandra agreed. 'No need at all.' And for some reason she could never afterwards fathom, kept smiling as she showed him out. But then it was too late to do anything else, wasn't it? The train would have gone, and Harry with it.

Sandra had, however, underestimated him. The doctor had been gone barely ten minutes before Harry was there at her door, his bag beside him, anxiously demanding to know what had kept her, telling her he knew he'd missed his train but couldn't bear to leave without her. Falling into his arms, she poured out the whole sorry story. But it was no more than a respite, they both knew that.

'I can't leave her. Not like this. I'll have to speak with Mrs Hutton, see if she can arrange to move in for a while.'

'I'll not go without you,' Harry stubbornly insisted, holding her fast in his big, brawny arms. Tears stood proud in her eyes as Sandra lovingly stroked his face with her hand.

'You go and start getting things organised in Liverpool. I'll sort out everything here and then I'll join you later.'

'Promise?'

A tear splashed on to his hand but Sandra managed a smile, praying for control. 'I promise.'

When he had gone she closed the front door with a quiet click, and the sound reverberated throughout the silent house.

The day was filled with endless hours of running up and down the steep staircase. Kettles had to be boiled and hot water brought for a 'good wash', coffee and biscuits at eleven, poached buttered haddock for lunch, tea and toast with Gentleman's Relish at four, which had to be made afresh three times because the first was too burnt, and the second too cold by the time Sandra had brought it, for all she almost ran up the stairs. Clean nightdresses had to be aired and warmed, the creases ironed out and then aired and warmed all over again. Hot water bottles made, and camphorated oil rubbed on Aunt Elsie's chest, since the shock had brought on her cough.

Nothing Sandra did was quite good enough, and throughout it all was the constant harping on about how it had been her fault; how if she hadn't chosen to run away, none of this would have happened.

'But I wasn't "running away", as you call it. I was simply leaving home to get married. Girls do it all the time.' But she knew her arguments fell on deaf ears.

It was only when she finally fell into bed with a deep sigh of relief that Sandra had time to think of her own situation. She thought about Harry, of how he would even now be alone in the Liverpool boarding house where they should have been together. For some while she could think of little else as the tears flowed, dampening her pillow and making her heart ache with the pity of it all.

For a whole week Sandra endured the sharp edge of her aunt's tongue. Despair and guilt were well set in and she had given up hope of ever managing to join Harry.

Lizzie called regularly on her way home from the mill to sympathise and fuss over Sandra, bringing titbits to make sure she was eating properly, and insisting she should not be a martyr.

'Stand up for yourself, lass. She's only using you.'

Miserably Sandra could only say, 'But she really is ill this time. She had a temperature this morning and was quite feverish. And it's all my fault.'

Lizzie, who wouldn't have put it past the woman to over-heat herself with all those blankets and hot water bottles, was unimpressed. 'She'll mend.'

'But she's the only family I've got.'

'And she took you into her fine house when you were orphaned, I know. But how long an arm has gratitude got? Some time, girl, you have to break loose, mek up your mind to lead your own life, aunt or no aunt.' On her way out, a basket of the old woman's washing firmly wedged against her hip, which was the least she could do for the poor lass, Lizzie promised to call again the next day. 'See you get some rest yourself. I know what it is to act as nurse. We don't want you taken badly, an' all.'

Sandra, agreeing that she was indeed worn out, dutifully went to bed by eight, praying her aunt would not call for her during the night, as she had taken to doing recently. But the moment she'd turned off the light, a querulous voice echoed along the landing.

'Sandra! Sandra!'

Wearily, she switched on her lamp and padded off to her aunt's bedroom in bare feet, then downstairs to reheat a cup of hot milk, left to go cold while her aunt dozed. When she brought it back up, Aunt Elsie handed her two hot water bottles.

'You might as well refill these at the same time.'

Sandra bit back a retort that she hadn't, in fact, mentioned them at the same time, but took the bottles and went back downstairs to fill kettles.

Half an hour later, falling into bed with a sigh of exhausted relief, she tried once more to settle to sleep but her legs were too tired to stay still, and her head filled with worries. Where was Harry now? Had he already left for Canada? If she missed this ship, might there be another? A small pain started at the side of her head and, pressing her fingers against it, she prayed it wouldn't worsen. She hadn't been troubled with these headaches for so long now. Please God, let them not start again.

Sandra breathed deeply, closed her eyes tight, counted sheep, recited nursery rhymes – but sleep refused to come, and the headache worsened. Yet again she went over everything she had done and said during those last few days, wondering whether she could have softened the blow for her aunt, or made it any easier. She went over in fine detail all she had done from the moment she'd got up at six that morning, which seemed like a lifetime ago, till the accident had occurred.

Why had it happened? Why had Aunt Elsie decided, for the first time in her life, to bring down her own tray? Probably because she was going to have to do it every morning from then on, Sandra thought, and guilt struck her afresh.

She remembered taking particular trouble over the tray that morning, since it would be the last she'd have to do, using the prettiest lace tray cloth and silver napkin ring. And instead of the usual blue breakfast cup, she'd poured the Assam tea into Aunt Elsie's best china cup and saucer, as a treat.

Why did the silly old woman have to carry it down while she was still wearing her long nightdress? It was a wonder she hadn't broken her leg, or her neck for that matter. Sleep now far away, eyes gazing blindly at the ceiling, Sandra fought off the debilitating headache by struggling to piece together the picture. Something wasn't quite right, didn't properly add up.

And then it came to her. The breakfast tray had not catapulted down the stairs with her aunt. Afterwards, when the doctor had been strapping up the injured limb, she had picked it up from the top step and carried it downstairs herself. How on earth had it come to be sitting on the top step? And, come to think of it, how had a stool come to be sitting behind the front door?

Stunned by her discovery, Sandra gasped in the darkness. The answer was obvious. *Because Aunt Elsie had not wished to risk breaking her favourite cup and saucer.* And she hadn't hurt herself badly, because she hadn't really fallen at all.

It had been the stool Sandra had heard banging and apparently tumbling down the stairs, no doubt pushed along by her aunt as she had *walked* safely down before deliberately falling the last few stairs for the sake of realism. She'd been prepared to risk minor injury in order to prevent her niece from leaving. Dear lord, but she was a manipulative old witch! Sandra thought with uncharacteristic venom.

But what could she do about it?

Sleep having deserted her for the night, she pulled on her dressing gown and crept downstairs. She made a cup of Horlicks, took two Aspro, and sat for a long time at the kitchen table, slowly sipping the comforting hot drink, turning the facts over and over in her mind. Despite her aunt's having little real affection for her, she was selfishly prepared to destroy her niece's chance of happiness, simply for the sake of her own comfort.

And then another memory from that morning's activities, buried in the back of her mind, began to emerge. Sandra set down her cup and went again to the bureau. The papers had been bundled back inside but were still in disarray, since she'd not had time to tidy them properly. She sat in the winged armchair with a pile in her lap and went through them, one by one, till she came to the one she was looking for – her father's will. Carefully unfolding it, she read every word with keen attention. He had left various small bequests to friends and relatives. Her father, a man of some means as director of a small engineering company in Lancashire, had been better off than she'd realised.

Sandra waded through a longish list and then finally came to it. To his sister, Elsie Myers, he'd left the sum of one thousand pounds and the right to stay on in his home for the remainder of her lifetime.

> *And to my daughter. Sandra Anne Myers, I leave the*
> *remainder of my estate which comprises my home, Grove*
> *House, and all the goods and chattels therein.*

She stared at the will in shock and disbelief. If this was true, the home that her aunt had grudgingly offered from cold charity, had been hers all along!

–

Now Sandra properly understood how Alena had felt. Lies did indeed damage people's lives. Her aunt had told lies, making her feel that she owed even the roof over her head to Aunt Elsie's generosity, when really her father had made provision for her, for them both, all along. The old woman's lies had robbed Sandra not only of her own home and heritage, but of self-esteem and control over her own life, turning her into little more than a skivvy. The damage had rippled outward through the years, with nearly devastating results.

The next day, taking up Lizzie's offer to sit with Aunt Elsie, she caught the bus to Hawkshead and paid a call on the family solicitor. Here she sought, and found, confirmation of the facts. Elsie Myers did indeed have the right to live at Grove House, but the property belonged, in truth, to Sandra.

'Your father was most particular that you be left well provided for. I was under the impression Miss Myers had informed you of this fact when you turned twenty-one. Until then, your aunt was to act as your guardian, of course.' In her anger, Sandra very nearly washed her hands of the whole thing, but the solicitor prudently pointed out that one day, she and Harry might wish to return to the Lake District. In the end, she promised to send him her new address as soon as she knew it, and he to protect her future interest in the property with much closer attention.

It took no more than a short visit to Mrs Hutton to settle matters and secure Sandra's future. Mrs Hutton would indeed be delighted to keep an eye on Miss Myers. She'd move into the spare room at once and act as companion-cum-housekeeper, and it didn't signify that the good lady could afford only a small weekly remuneration, for being widowed and alone in the world herself, Mrs Hutton would most gratefully welcome it.

'I'm sure we'll rub along fine, your aunt and I. I shall enjoy the challenge. Don't you fret, Sandra, I was a nurse during the war. I'm well used to looking after difficult patients. You get off to Canada with your young man and make a good life for yourself.'

Sandra went next to see her dear friend, Mrs Rigg, thanking her for giving her a job when everyone else had written her off as useless. 'You restored my faith in myself, as well as in human nature.'

'Nay, you were allus a good worker. I've naught to complain of.'

'And tell Mickey I'll write as soon as we're settled, to wish him well with the campaign.'

Having taken a tearful farewell of Lizzie, with many promises to write and the hope of a future visit, the final task remaining was simply to inform Aunt Elsie of these arrangements – a chore Sandra despatched with a cool calm that impressed even herself and left her aunt, for once in her life, white-faced and speechless.

Then came Mrs Hutton's firm step on the stair and her jolly voice insisting that Sandra get along. 'Jim Townsen's at the door with his van. your bag's packed aboard and he's all ready to give you a lift to the station. Hurry up now, you'll not want to risk missing another train!' She bustled into the bedroom in a billowing blue dress and apron that crackled with starch, sleeves rolled up over formidable arms. 'And don't you worry none, I'll have your aunt up and about in no time. We'll get started on our exercises the minute you've gone, won't we, dear?'

Sandra almost found it in her heart to feel sorry for Aunt Elsie as she saw panic in her faded eyes.

'Sandra?' The voice was no more than a plaintive croak. But she simply planted a kiss on her aunt's dry cheek, wished her well, then skipped down the stairs, grabbed her coat, and left.

Chapter Twenty-Three

The sun rimmed the hilltops, burning off the morning mist to sail high in a cloudless sky. A Lakeland summer night, Alena had discovered, was surprisingly short. As she stood rubbing the sleep from her eyes while she waited for the kettle to boil for her tea, she watched a herd of young bucks in their foxy red coats grazing in a thicket. How sure of themselves they were, eyes bright, noses shining with moisture in the morning light. Even though it was August, still high summer, she could almost feel their excitement as they sensed the approach of autumn and the rutting season.

But as the excitement of the Coronation had died down, the nation's consciousness seemed to turn more and more to fears of war. On her frequent visits to Alena, Lizzie relayed some of the news she read in the papers to her daughter and Rob.

'There's even talk of building bomb shelters against air raids. Can you imagine? What would we do here?'

They listened politely, but it all seemed too remote, almost another world. Here in the forest their primary consideration was to clear the ground for where Rob would build his first stack, and for them to make as many besoms, clothes props and hurdles as they could, which they must then sell if they were to survive. Through Isaac Rob's contacts were growing, as were his skills, slowly but with a sureness that added to their optimism even if, at times, their very real hunger drove it away again.

This morning, as so many others recently, Alena was alone. Rob had spent the night with Isaac on the burn. The old man usually spent the summers climbing the high fells when he wasn't busy peeling oak bark, but to help Rob he'd started his charcoal season early. They'd been busy for days. Alena understood, but she missed him and would be glad when his apprenticeship was over and Rob back in the glade with her. Even the young stags had moved on, seeking quieter cover as full day approached. The famous Furness Reds were used to peace and solitude and didn't much care for people. Well, this was the right place for them, Alena thought, with a deep sigh of satisfaction.

Sometimes her fancy told her that she wasn't alone, that there were eyes watching her from behind the slender trunks of the coppiced oaks, that she heard unexplained rustling noises. The natural stillness of the forest seemed to awaken all her natural instincts, making her strain to listen and observe. Then she would hear the laughing cry of a woodpecker and she too would join in, laughing at the onslaught of nervousness. Of course she was not alone, how could she be? She shared the forest with a whole variety of animals. She was the interloper.

Even now she could here the cooing call of an amorous grouse, and the rasp of a squirrel's claws against the bark of a tree. Smiling, she went back inside, and brewed her tea, dark and strong, just how she liked it. She spread honey on a thick slice of bread and, taking both outside, sat on her favourite log to watch the sun complete its stupendous climb into a clear azure sky.

–

Over the following days Rob finished clearing the ground on the old pitstead to a diameter of some thirty feet. Any sods that he removed, he saved. They'd be needed later to keep air out of the stack. He checked there were no mole runs, rat holes, or any seepage of water. By the start of September he had enough three-foot lengths, known as shanklings, and a whole stack of two-foot coalwood to begin his burn. During his first season he'd have to fell ready for the next, to give the wood time to season. But to get started, he'd collected wood found lying about the forest floor and friends of Isaac had supplied the rest. He was excited and nervous, thankful that the old man was there to help. Even so, Isaac made sure that Rob did most of the work, as was only right and proper.

He stood, arms folded, in the centre of the clearing, an impressive figure in his long greatcoat, his wide-brimmed hat pulled well down, feather quivering. 'No good building without a firm foundation. So how do we begin, boy?'

Rob smiled at the look of anxiety on Alena's lovely face as he answered confidently. 'We put a thin pole in the centre, then prop the shanklings all around it. You can help fetch them, Alena. We'll place them in the proper position.' For a moment he saw the familiar rebellion flare and thought she'd tell him to fetch them himself, but then she grinned, rolled up her sleeves, and brought the first two poles.

They worked well together, establishing an easy rhythm, stacking the shanklings around the centre pole, called the 'motty-peg', almost vertically at first and then with an increasing slope, layer upon layer. Further layers were added until finally the shorter coalwood was laid on top to give a final height of some five or six feet, the slope of the finished stack gentle. Then Alena brought the green grass and reeds she had collected as Rob began to put on shovelfuls of subsoil, mixed with sand and clay, known as sammel. These were packed into every gap to keep out the air. A blaze must be prevented at all cost. On top of this was laid a tightly packed layer of sods, Rob standing on the dome-like structure while Isaac and Alena threw them up to him.

'And now we can draw out the motty-peg and you can start the burn, boy,' grinned Isaac.

Alena was looking up at him with such pride, shielding her eyes from the sun and thinking how fine he looked up there on top of the stack, so tall and strong and sure, almost noble. She blew him a kiss for luck. 'Go on, this is our beginning. Just you and me from now on.'

Rob drew out the motty-peg and dropped a shovelful of glowing charcoal down the resulting hole, ramming in as much extra charcoal, provided by Isaac, as he could manage. Once he was sure it was alight, he quickly closed the top gap with a wet sod, pressing it in place, then climbed down to stand beside Alena with pride and satisfaction like an aura about him.

And so the vigil began.

'You'll have to watch it carefully,' Isaac warned. 'Restrict the air, stop up draughts with wet sods, reeds or sammel, and keep an eye on the colour of the smoke over the next day or two, as I have taught you. The stack will shift as the wood in the centre is reduced. If you get a fire, you'll lose the lot. I'll call and see how you're faring tomorrow.' Then he lifted his hat by way of farewell and silently slipped away into the forest.

Rob put his arms about Alena and they hugged each other tight. 'It's going to be fine.' she assured him. 'We'll make lots of charcoal which will fetch a good price.'

Rob frowned. 'Isaac often has two burns going at once.'

'One is enough to begin with.'

'I couldn't have done it without you.'

'Yes, you could. But I'd rather you didn't try.'

'You have a smut on your nose.' And he kissed it, before rubbing it off.

'I dare say I'll have a few more before we're done.'

'While we watch, I mean to have a go at whittling tent pegs. If there is to be a war, they'll be much in demand.'

It was as if a cloud had crossed the sun. The delight and happiness faded from Alena's face. 'What will happen to us, if war does come? Will we still be able to stay here, and work in the forest?'

Rob pulled her close, rubbing his chin against her hair which smelled of sunshine and green grass and the first heady hint of smoke. 'You heard what Isaac said. They'll need charcoal for the manufacture of gas masks, tent pegs for the soldiers, ship's fenders, all manner of things. With hard work, and a bit of luck, perhaps we can do our bit here.' And, filled with hope and belief in their own future, their lips came together instinctively and they kissed. But as passion ignited, Rob broke laughingly away from her.

'Not till we have our first load of charcoal. I have to concentrate, and whenever I lie with you, I forget even what day it is.'

'Good.' And she made him kiss her again till he was pleading for mercy and she could feel the strong beat of his heart against her breast.

'Did you let Mickey Roscoe kiss you like this?'

For a moment she was startled, and then unable to resist teasing him for this show of jealousy, pretended to consider. 'Umm, I might have. I can't quite remember.'

He looked stunned then, picking her up, he swung her round till she squealed for mercy. 'You minx! If you had, you wouldn't even need to think about it. You never did, did you? Admit it.'

'Of course he kissed me. Often.' And when Rob threatened to drop her in the beck, she screamed, 'But never like you do. Never, I swear. I put up with his kisses, wet and weak things compared to yours. Utterly dreadful.' And she shuddered, to prove her sincerity.

'I'll show you what a kiss should be like.'

'The burn,' she reminded him. And he instantly tipped her on to the grass where she rolled about in gales of laughter.

–

Utterly dreadful! Wet and weak! So that's what she'd thought of him? Mickey had watched Isaac stroll away, walking with quiet assurance between the lusty growth of young alder, ash and birch as dusk fell. Then he'd turned his attention back to the lovers in time to hear this damning indictment of his prowess. He wanted to leap out of the thicket and knock her to the ground for daring to insult him in such a way. But he managed not to.

They were kissing again, and despite himself he watched, feeling his own hot need curdle somewhere deep in his belly.

She didn't mean it, of course. How could she tell Robert Hollinthwaite the truth? That really they had been entirely happy and compatible. He could still win her back, and knew exactly how to go about it. But he must choose his moment with care. For a while he continued to watch them, saw their happy frolics, witnessed the joy that they found in each other, for all he told himself that Rob was not the man to bring her lasting happiness. When he could bear it no more, Mickey turned on his heel and moved away through the trees, not quite so silently as Isaac, but much fleeter of foot.

He went straight to Ellersgarth Farm and knocked on the door. James Hollinthwaite himself opened it, and almost instantly closed it again when he saw who it was. Mickey wedged his foot in the gap just in time.

'A moment, Mr Hollinthwaite. You allus said, if I'd aught to report...'

Ensconced at the kitchen table – Hollinthwaite's hospitality didn't run to permitting the likes of Mickey Roscoe into his best parlour – a mug of beer in his hand, Mickey took his time. Between sips of the beer, he mentioned how the campaign was running out of steam now that Sandra Myers had left it in his hands.

'It's up to me now, d'you see? Nobody else is willing to cut their own throats by risking unemployment, as she was. Me neither.' James's interest sharpened, but he made no comment.

Then little by little Mickey described the scene he had witnessed in the glade. He gave its exact location, relating the young lovers' plans, almost word for word. 'They're very determined. And they have friends. If you want to stop them, you'll have to call your son to heel.'

James, standing frozen throughout the tale, said nothing.

Mickey took a good long pull on his beer, wiped his mouth with the back of his hand and stood up, ready to depart, measuring the moment for his final and most important piece of advice. At the door he paused, ran one hand over his sleek crop of hair, and half glanced back over his shoulder at Hollinthwaite. 'You'll be starting your felling soon, I shouldn't wonder. Have you planned where you'll start?'

'Close by the mill, then I can easily stack the wood as it comes down.'

'Good thinking. Only...' Mickey paused a moment, making sure he had James's full attention. 'There was a certain ancient oak those two were particularly fond of, somewhere in Low Birk Coppice, I believe. I doubt they'd care for that to be felled, would you? Upset them proper, don't you reckon?' And the two men exchanged a long silent glance.

But for all his seeming complicity with Hollinthwaite, Mickey then went on to warn his fellow workers of the felling that was about to take place. He set himself as firmly on their side as he had on James's, rekindling their anger against Hollinthwaite, setting up shifts to keep a watch on the woodland, instructing them to arm themselves with a good solid branch, warning them that there'd be trouble for sure once the men arrived with their felling axes. With luck, when the two parties came together, there'd be a riot. And he meant Rob Hollinthwaite to be in the middle of it.

–

For the next two days Rob and Alena nursed the burn. As it shifted and sank, they rearranged the remaining stack, added more wet turfs to prevent any hint of flame, blocked each new hole with a spadeful of soil. They constantly moved the hurdles they'd made to screen the stack from the prevailing winds. Night and day they worked, and in the quiet spells they whittled tent pegs, made besoms, or simply lay on their backs and gazed at the stars. Here the Great Bear, there Cassiopeia, and wasn't that Venus, so strong and bright?

They saw the setting sun gild the treetops, the purple shadows of evening turn into soft black night; watched a family of badgers set out on their night patrol, and the first shafts of morning light lance through the high branches, picking out patches of emerald moss and bronze bracken. Everything seemed new and magical, as if they were discovering the world for the first time. Only once did Alena glance covertly into the thicket behind them, as she heard the snap of a twig.

'Those young bucks are on the prowl again,' she laughed.

'I don't blame them,' Rob agreed.

Because heat rises, a stack burns from the top, the wood baking slowly like a cake in an oven. They tried to keep well clear of the smoke which was pungent and no doubt filled with chemicals, but it wasn't always possible, and then they'd cough and choke and their eyes would smart and run with tears. But it didn't matter. Their love of the forest, and each other, saw them through. They laughed and joked, teased and kissed as they went about their work, and if at times they felt pangs of hunger, neither of them complained.

'Now you must "say" it with water.' Isaac had checked the rim of the stack to see if the burn had reached the bottom, studied the colour of the smoke, the grey-brown now turned to a translucent blue, and declared it ready. 'I've arranged for Sam to call and collect your load in a day or two, after he's picked up mine. He delivers the charcoal to Backbarrow and will pay you when he picks up your next lot. Less his own fee, of course.'

Using a special rake for the purpose, Rob removed a small section of the top and poured water down, damping the whole area from the barrel set near the stack. Alena helped by refilling it with buckets from the beck. Judging how much water to put in was a worry. Too much and the charcoal would be dull and brittle, without a good ring to it. Too little and it would turn into ash. Twelve hours later, when the coals were quite cold, they finally removed the turfs and began to pick out sticks of charcoal.

'We've done it!'

'They're perfect. Most of them anyway.' Critically Rob examined them, noting the good ones, the failures, the fine pieces that could be split further to bring a higher price from artists. He was well pleased with their first effort, but celebrations had to wait until all the bags were filled, ready for the carter. Only when this was done, did they stand and regard each other.

'You're filthy.'

'So are you. Black from head to foot. True colliers.'

There was only one solution. It was too far to the tarn, the beck not deep enough; besides, the cold water would barely touch this amount of soot. They boiled water on the fire and filled the barrel Isaac had lent them to stand close to the stack. Taking it in turns, they sat in the hot tub and soaped each other down, washing hair, face, neck, even ears, as well as blackened arms and legs. It was a riotous, noisy ritual, much punctuated with squeals and giggles, tickles and splashing; there was a good deal of running about and chasing, bare feet slipping on the wet grass. Then back in the tub to get warm.

'We need a bigger bath,' Rob complained, after trying and failing to climb in with her.

'Do you remember that swim, all those years ago at the tarn?'

'How could I forget? That was the night I fell in love with you, you minx.'

Alena gasped. 'You never said.'

'Just as well, considering what happened after that. Mind you, I think we're even wetter tonight.'

It took several kettles full of steaming water before they were both clean and dry. Then they tidied away the makeshift bath, checked the sacks of charcoal one last time, and finally went into the hut and pulled the sacking closed.

–

They were paid a good price for their charcoal and, inspired by their success, Alena and Rob soon developed a routine. They worked hard, loved well, and were happy and content.

The coming of autumn had brought woodcock and grouse, pheasant and rabbit. Sometimes they would hear the lion-like roar of a red deer in pursuit of his lady love. The hedgerows were full of fruit and berries, the days clear and bright, filled with sunshine and the sweet scents and rich colours found nowhere as beautifully orchestrated as in the English Lake Country. And overhead, nomadic flocks of grey geese on their flight from the Solway to the milder marshes of Morecambe Bay made them pause and wonder at the wisdom of Nature.

And then one evening as they ate their supper by the fire, Rob told her that before they started the next burn, he must leave her for a little while. 'No more than a day or two. Three at most.'

'Why?' The prospect of being alone again filled her with disquiet. She never thought about the strange rustlings, or the sensation of eyes watching her from the forest, when she was with Rob. Nor had she mentioned these fancies to him, not wanting it to sound as if she were complaining. But now she did think of them, and felt a shiver up her spine.

Rob was saying, 'We need markets for our products. We've a good stockpile of pegs, besoms and hurdles. Now we must find a buyer.'

'Can't we ask Isaac, or Sam the carter?'

'They've suggested one or two possibilities for me to try, certainly, but I need to go and get the orders, Alena. I can't expect them to develop my business for me. It's important I get out and see people myself. And there's a meeting in Ulverston I should attend, concerning ship's fenders. I have to find out exactly what sizes they want, how many the government will buy off me.'

Alena saw his point and began to make suggestions. 'You could try some ironmongers while you're there. See if they would be interested in taking our hurdles or clothes props, or if there's anything else needed. And we could perhaps sell alder for clog soles to the shoemaker.'

Rob nodded. 'Then there'll be the bark for tanning next summer. I need to find out about all these things. After that I must hurry back, because before winter comes we need to build a shelter under which we can work. There's so much to do.'

'Then I shall come with you and help.' She was getting up, tidying away the supper things as if she meant to go that very moment. Rob put a gentle hand on her arm. 'No, Alena. It's difficult enough without our own transport, and we must rely on Sam for the moment. I can go much quicker alone. I'll be back before you miss me, I promise.'

And since there was sense in his argument, she reluctantly had to accept it.

'Go and visit Lizzie.'

She shook her head. 'She's coming to see me tomorrow.'

'Then go home with her. Have a break for a day or two.'

Alena laughed. 'You mean, sleep in a proper bed for once?'

'And enjoy a proper bath. Why not?'

It seemed so much more preferable to staying alone in the forest, that she agreed. When Lizzie came the next afternoon, she found, to her delight, her daughter with a bag packed ready to come home on a visit.

—

At first it felt good to be back in Ma's kitchen with its familiar smells of Lancashire hotpot and ginger cake, and Lizzie enjoyed spoiling her daughter, if only for a day or two. They talked endlessly, not least about Harry and Sandra, now married and settling to life in a new country. They drank gallons of tea, and even had a noisy family gathering with Jim and his family there, Kit – very much a dyed-in-the-wool bachelor now – and

Dolly and Tom, proudly showing off their beautiful new baby daughter.

'Doesn't she have Tom's eyes?'

'And Dolly's cheeky grin.' It was good to see them all so content. But by the third morning of her short holiday, Alena was feeling almost claustrophobic. Missing the openness of the forest and the sweetness of their glade, she began to pack her bag.

Lizzie knew better than to try and delay her, seeing she was itching to be back with Rob again. Alena had scarcely talked of anything else since she arrived. At the door Lizzie enveloped her daughter in one last hug. 'You'll come again if it gets a bit too cold, happen?'

'I will, Ma. But don't worry. We're very cosy in our hut, and we're building up a good business. We'll do all right.'

'The end cottage is empty, the one old Edith had. She's passed on, you know.'

'Oh, I'm sorry to hear that. Edith was a good friend to me.'

'Aye, well, she'd be right glad for you to tek it on. You could get your old job back at the bobbin mill and Rob could still work in the forest, only nearer home.'

'I don't want my old job back. We like it in the forest.'

'Well, work in the forest then, but you can't carry on living in that hut once the bairn is born. Babies need special care, girl. And I'd help you look after it.'

Alena gasped. 'How did you...?'

Lizzie beamed with delight. 'I'm your mother. Besides, I've a bit of experience in that department myself. I doubt anybody would say a word about your coming back to the village. Not even Mickey. All water under the bridge now, eh? He never mentions it. And it would mean we could be neighbours.'

Alena gripped her mother's hand as, for a moment, she was sorely tempted. 'I can't make such a decision on my own, Ma. We'll need to talk about it.'

'You don't mind my speaking up?'

'Course I don't. And I miss you too. Don't worry, we'll sort something out.' And, her mother having put her finger on Alena's greatest concern, they parted on a somewhat subdued note. Jim ran her back as far as the clearing and she walked the rest of the way, almost running and jumping over fallen branches, in her eagerness to be back. She'd stayed longer than she'd meant to but hoped that Rob would be back by now, wondering where she was.

The glade was empty. The pitstead looked stark and cold with no burn in progress. The hut felt damp and smelt of mildew. A lump came to her throat, and in that moment Alena felt so lonely and painfully vulnerable that the thought of a cottage in Birkwith Row had never seemed more appealing. Then she remembered the pat of butter, knuckle of ham, fresh bread and slab of fruit cake that Lizzie had packed. What was she worrying about? Rob hadn't given her a definite time for his return. He could walk into the glade at any moment. And it wouldn't do for him to find the place in a mess, and no supper to eat.

Singing loudly to combat the soft shush of the treetops, she had the fire going in no time and the kettle singing. Outside, night was drawing in and finally she decided that he wasn't coming tonight, so she sat on the bed to eat a crusty ham sandwich, a slice of the fruit cake, and drink a mug of scalding tea and then, tired from the excitement of her short holiday, Alena fell instantly asleep.

When she woke next morning she found a hedgehog had eaten most of Lizzie's butter, a badger had apparently walked off with the bread, and the ham had been knocked to the floor where it was all covered in dust. She'd forgotten to store everything away in their special tins before she fell asleep. It was then that she burst into tears, and found she had to run outside where she was promptly sick over a patch of nettles. Of course it was only the baby, making its presence felt, but somehow, without Rob, living in the forest was no fun at all.

It was as she was washing her face in the refreshing cold waters of the beck, that she heard the crack of a twig and a footfall behind her.

'*Rob!*' She whirled around, ready to run into his arms. But it wasn't Rob who stood behind her. It was Mickey.

'Aren't you going to offer me a cup of coffee?'

She was staring at him as if he were a ghost. 'I've only got tea.'

'That would go down a treat.' He grinned at her, at least she thought he grinned, remembering how his mouth curled naturally upward at the corners.

Mickey Roscoe was the last person she had expected, or wanted, to see here in their forest home, and Alena felt so flustered she could hear her own heartbeat as she went to put the kettle on. What could he want? Why had he come? Her feelings towards him had changed completely since his outburst in Lizzie's kitchen and his refusal to let her go. *His* feelings for her were certainly bordering on the obsessional. It stemmed no doubt from his longing for the stability his unsettled life had failed to provide. Alena had clearly been an essential part of his dream, as if he could possess her as James Hollinthwaite had once possessed Olivia.

He followed her into the hut and it had never seemed more cramped. 'Best if you wait outside. There isn't room to swing a cat in here,' she said, trying to disguise her anxiety with a laugh, but it only came out forced and brittle.

'I can see that.' He eyed the rumpled bed which filled most of the space. Alena expected him to say how he could have offered her so much more, but he simply smiled, and said nothing.

Chapter Twenty-Four

They sat and drank their tea on the fallen log, though it was cool outside in the morning sunshine. Alena, struggling to suppress a shiver in case he should think she was nervous, offered him a slice of toast or Lizzie's cake, anything to cover this increasing awkwardness.

'It's Rob I've come to see, in point of fact,' he said, finally answering her unspoken question. 'I've news of his father.'

For some reason she didn't want him to know that Rob was away, or that she'd no idea when he would be back, so she volunteered to pass on the message. Mickey bluntly and concisely related how James Hollinthwaite had started on the felling. 'I took over the campaign when Sandra left, you know.'

'Yes, Ma told me.'

'Not that anyone was interested in it then. But now even his own bobbin workers are up in arms, willing to risk their livelihoods to fight him. There's dozens of 'em in the forest with clubs, even air rifles. There'll be a riot if something isn't done.' He cast her a sideways glance, noting the shocked expression on her face and wondering if he'd overdone it. 'But then, the woodsmen he's hired have started in the most scenic place.'

'Where?' She hardly dared ask.

'That ancient oak in Low Birk Coppice. Remember it?'

How could she ever forget? The old oak. *Their* oak. James Hollinthwaite had chosen it deliberately, of course, as revenge against them for their elopement. Having imparted his devastating news Mickey suddenly seemed anxious to take his leave. 'You'll tell Rob when he gets home, will you? Only we're hoping he can talk some sense into his father.' He set down the cup, thanked her for the tea and turned to go. She found her voice at last. 'When? When will the oak be felled?'

He frowned, looking anxiously over his shoulder, and she wondered if he was perhaps nervous of meeting Rob, and almost found the thought amusing. 'Soon. Tomorrow, the day after, perhaps even this very afternoon. I'm not sure, but it's vital young Hollinthwaite does what he can to stop it or his father will go through the entire woodland like a knife through butter.'

'But what can Rob do?'

Mickey could feel himself growing impatient. Yet he smiled, for he knew it was important to hold her confidence. 'He's Hollinthwaite's son, for Christ's sake. He must still have some influence. No one else has.' And slicking back his hair in that familiar gesture she knew so well, he added in a softer voice, 'You're looking well, Alena.' Her skin was pale silk against the fire of her hair and his fingers itched to stroke it.

'Thank you.'

'But this isn't the place for you, not with winter coming on. What is that man thinking of to keep you here?' He took a step towards her.

'I'm very well, thank you. I'm sorry, Mickey – for the mess.' He could see the soft rise and fall of her breast with her quickened breathing. Did he still excite her? Dear God, he should have made her his years ago.

He attempted a shrug. 'That's life, as they say. If you ever need help...' He almost reached for her then but stopped himself in time. It was too soon. He must wait a little longer. After a moment's hesitation, he thrust his hands deep in his pockets, pushed back his shoulders, jerked his chin at her by way of farewell and swung away, vanishing into the forest from whence he had come.

–

It took some time but in the end Alena persuaded Rob that he must go. He insisted on hearing, word for word, what Mickey had said, and what she had said to him; how she had felt when she saw him, whether he had commented on their elopement. Alena finally lost patience, not in the mood today for playing on his jealousy.

'What does it matter? We have to stop James from destroying Ellersgarth Woods and Low Birk Coppice.'

'He won't listen.'

'We must make him! We have to save our lovely old tree, and all the other trees that are neither dead nor dying. He can't be allowed to get away with it.'

'Then I shall go and try, one last time, to reason with him But you must stay here.' And when she made to protest, he silenced her with the touch of one finger. 'No, Alena. If there's to be trouble, as there was the last time he attempted this, I want you safely here, not in the midst of a riot. So for once, be a good girl and do as you're told.'

It was only after he had gone, sweeping the undergrowth aside and striding away like a young Lochinvar, that she realised her reason for not disagreeing had been the baby growing inside her, and she hadn't even had time to tell him.

–

James knew he had lost the fight to separate his son from Alena Townsen and to turn him into the kind of man he might admire, just as he had failed in the unequal task of moulding his wife into a woman who would give him the respect and admiration he deserved. He'd no intention of surrendering his ambitions as well. A man found evidence of his worth in his possessions. That had ever been James's creed and he'd no intention of changing it now. He was destined to be rich, and would not tolerate any other course, certainly not one forced upon him by the rabble before him.

The men carried clubs and sticks, faces grimly set, and some of the women had even climbed up into the branches of the old oak, stubbornly refusing to budge. He knew them all. Jack Turner from the Stag; Arthur, who'd been a useless foreman; the Townsen brothers, of course; Bill Lindale, his own manager, for God's sake, heading a crew of sour-looking characters. Annie Cockcroft, Mary-Jane Linklater and Minnie Hodgson and their cronies. Dolly, who'd shared a whisky and other delights with him. Even Mrs Rigg in her floral pinny. The stand-off had lasted a day and a night and James was sick of it. He hated them all, every one.

'Get back!' he shouted, waving his gun with a wild abandon that alarmed even his own woodsmen who stood behind him, axes poised ready to begin. 'Get out of that oak! I'll have it toppled with you all in it, if necessary. Damned if I won't.' Even as he spoke other trees were being climbed by determined villagers. The situation was getting rapidly out of hand. As always it was Lindale who attempted to placate him and cool the situation.

'Noo then, Mr Hollinthwaite, let's keep cool, shall we? It'll do none of us any good if heads get broken.'

'Damn you, yours will be the first I'll break, if you don't get these idiots out of *my* trees.' He swung round and barked instructions to the waiting woodsmen. 'We've wasted enough time, get on with it. Fell any tree you like. It doesn't matter a damn if there's someone in it. Let the blasted fools fall with it.'

'We can't be held responsible for any accident,' the ganger protested, not liking the way things were going at all, for all his men were being well paid.

'I haven't asked you to be. Get on with it!'

A roar went up from the crowd, filling the copse, sending any remaining birds or animals that had not already fled about their business. Several men surged forward and might have grabbed James, had he not once more brandished his gun. They knew he could kill a stag at fifty paces with one shot. No one was taking any chances here. They slunk back, sweating and conversing in angry whispers, and the stink of fear pervaded the woodland, souring the beautiful morning.

But the woodsmen pressed forward, lifting their axes in readiness for striking the tree. One, young and eager and determined to earn the money he'd been promised, attacked a slender ash with sharp steady strokes. Everyone watched, appalled, as he struck it time after time, biting into the sweet white wood. The tree shook as if it flinched with pain.

'Father.' The soft voice seemed to cut through the hubbub of screams and curses, the sounds of cutting and the angry shouts. A hush fell, axes froze, and all eyes turned to Rob. 'May we talk?'

James Hollinthwaite looked upon his son with the same contempt he felt for the villagers. 'It's too late for talking, Robert. Now I need action. I need these trees to come down. *Get out of my way!*'

'I think not.' Rob walked over to the ganger and, with a smile of recognition, lifted the axe from his hands. 'Hello, Joe. Good to see you again. I realise work is hard to come by but I'd rather you didn't find it here, if it's all the same to you. These trees are old friends of mine. I'm sure my father will compensate you for your wasted time this morning. He'll consider it cheap at the price, to have me home again. Isn't that so, Father?'

A gasp rippled through the crowd as the bargain became clear. No one could fail to understand. Rob Hollinthwaite who, above everything else, excepting of course his love for Alena, valued his freedom most and had planned his life accordingly, was offering to give it all up in order to save this section of the forest. The silence following his statement was now so acute, not even a bird dared to sing.

But James didn't seem to be listening. In a sudden paroxysm of fury, he snatched the axe from Rob's hand and attacked the half-felled ash with demented strokes. It creaked and groaned, swayed and rocked, then as it began to fall he swung round to stride defiantly back to his son to show him what he had done. 'There's the first. Your blasted oak will be next. One by one I'll take down this whole bloody forest.'

'*Look out!*' The cry went up a fraction too late. James hadn't stepped far enough away from the ash and as Rob rushed to pull him from its path, its topmost branches hit them both, pinning them to the ground.

—

The exuberant song of a mistle thrush filled the air as Alena stripped the brash and bark from the poles. These would be used to build the shelter they needed, under which they could work out of the wet and windy weather. She remembered how once her hands had been too soft to work with wood. Now they were strong and capable, as she was. There was nothing she and Rob couldn't achieve, if they set their minds to it. Most of all, a deep and lasting happiness, so long as they were together. And inside she nursed her secret, one she ached to tell him and would, the moment he returned.

Alena felt that she too should sing as happily as the thrush, but was too worried about Rob. Would he quarrel with his father, and come back feeling even more rejected? She couldn't imagine James Hollinthwaite giving in, but he must see reason in the end. He couldn't just walk roughshod over everyone else's wishes. He surely didn't have that right, land owner or no.

'I knew you'd send him off on his own so we could be alone.'

The voice, coming out of the thicket behind her, made her jump and she dropped the pole she was stripping to swing about and gaze at him transfixed.

'Mickey? What are you doing here? I thought you'd be helping Rob and the villagers fight Hollinthwaite.' She found herself backing away as he approached, and when he rested his hands upon her shoulders, she flinched.

'I was too slow for you, wasn't I? Too respectful. I expect you mocked me for not proving my manhood. I should have made you mine years ago, then you would never have left me. I certainly wanted to. You are very beautiful, Alena.' His hands were smoothing her arms, sliding over her breasts, and she was fighting down furious sobs of panic, slapping at him in a desperate bid to free herself, but they seemed to be everywhere, clinging to her like limpets.

'Stop it, Mickey. What the hell are you doing? Let me go. Have you gone mad? Take your hands off me.'

She held up her own hands for a moment, then stood perfectly still, as she had once seen a rabbit do to escape the clutches of a weasel, hoping and praying that he would be satisfied with the fright he had given her and let her go.

He stroked her tousled hair away from her face, 'Can you imagine how foolish I felt standing at that altar? I do so hate to be made a fool of, Alena.'

'I didn't mean that to happen.'

'But it did happen.'

She struggled to breathe normally and keep her voice even. 'You wouldn't listen to me. You couldn't seem to understand that I had to end our engagement. I'm sorry I hurt you, Mickey, but I didn't have any choice. I love Rob.'

He leaned his body full against hers, pinning her to the tree, and the hardness of him filled her with terror; mouth too dry to speak, she made no protest as he stroked her cheek. Then he began to unfasten the buttons of her blouse, his eyes never leaving hers, as if he challenged her to resist. But she did not, aware that would only add to his excitement.

This Mickey was not the one who'd joked and had fun with her, the one she had agreed to marry. He seemed so different that she wondered if she'd ever really known him. Perhaps his entire behaviour towards her had been skilfully planned and engineered, his cunning as foxy as his rust brown eyes. While she'd been foolishly flattered by his determination to have her. Was he still? The thought brought fresh fear and she felt herself begin to shake.

'You *imagined* you still loved him,' he was carefully explaining. 'But that was only nostalgia for the past. You're not a young child now, with a fancy for the boy next door.' His smile widened, though his grip did not slacken one bit. 'He isn't the man for you. Alena. You know he isn't. You can't be happy living in a mud hut with that soft idiot.'

–

He was upon her before she realised what was happening, hands squeezing her breast, ripping the fabric of her blouse. She would have screamed were it not for the suffocation of his mouth fastened over hers. Fear rose like bile in her throat as his tongue grazed her teeth, and a terrible helplessness swamped her. She hadn't realised how strong he was, for all he was small and wiry. She gasped out loud with relief when he lifted his head and smiled his puckish smile. Then before she had time to think, he wrapped his arms about her and half dragged, half carried her into the hut, and she was screaming till her lungs ached. This time there was no breaking free. This time his arms were tight around her like a vice. She knew she could do nothing.

'Is this how you wanted it? In the rough and tumble of a straw bed? If I'd known, I'd've taken you years ago, in the open fields. I wanted it to be special for you, for us. I wanted you to come a virgin to my bed. Are you still a virgin? Has that whey-faced bastard proved his manhood yet?' He put his mouth so close to hers that she could taste his breath as he whispered, 'Didn't I explain to you, very carefully, that you're my woman, and always will be? Now I mean to prove it to you.'

She fought to free herself but he tightened his grip, holding her easily. 'I am not your woman. Take your hands off me.'

'You know you like me telling you what to do.'

'*No*, I don't!'

But he only laughed. 'Now you're letting Rob Hollinth-waite tell you, and I don't like that, Alena. I don't like it one bit.'

'You never have listened to anything I've said, in all the years I've known you.'

'You do as I say. You always have.'

'Not any more. It was stupid of me ever to allow it, and all because of my misery over losing Rob. I'm not your woman, Mickey Roscoe. I'm not anybody's woman but my own. And I will make my own choices.'

He stared at her, a look of baffled disbelief in his dark eyes. 'You actually choose him rather than me?'

'I'm sorry, Mickey, but yes, I do choose him.'

For a long moment he said nothing, then he got to his feet, slowly helped her up and painstakingly, almost tenderly, dusted her down. Alena drew in a trembling breath. 'Thank you, I'm truly sorry about jilting you like that, but it was partly your own fault. I hope we can at least still be friends.'

Mickey turned and walked away, hands hanging limply by his side, shoulders hunched, as if all the life had been punched out of him. Then he stopped, put back his head and let out a howl of fury or anguish, she wasn't sure which, to the empty skies. She almost, in that moment, felt sorry for him. Even so she was unprepared for what happened next. He swung about and smacked his open hand across her face, sending her flying so that she stumbled and fell, banging her head against the bed post though she didn't even whimper with the pain of it. Her eyes were riveted upon his, wild and demented, devoid of any humanity.

It was then that something inside her seemed to click into place. It was as if she stepped outside herself to view her own helplessness, saw how he had held her captive, first with his domineering charm and now with his hands and body. And how *she* had allowed it. She recalled seeing Ray treat her mother thus and how she had always sworn she would never allow such conduct towards herself. He *wanted* her to be afraid. And with this realisation, all fear left her. She hadn't been a tomboy all her life for nothing. 'Stand up for yourself,' her brothers had so often told her, and she would do so now. For all the indignity of her situation, her next words sounded the very opposite, spoken in a voice that was steady and firm, and exceptionally calm.

'That's enough, Mickey. It's finished. I'll overlook your behaviour today because I can see you are upset and not thinking clearly. I doubt you'd have gone through with it anyway. For all your domineering manner, you're a decent enough bloke underneath. But I'm not the girl for you. You have to accept that. And I'll not have you hit me, nor allow you to hurt my baby!' There was a stunned silence as, desperately trying to disguise the fact she was still shaking with shock, Alena valiantly continued, 'Just as soon as we can make the arrangements, we mean to marry.'

She saw the fight drain out of him then, heard some pitiful face-saving mumbles about not taking another man's leavings, then the sacking swung back across the door and he was gone. And this time she knew he would not be coming back. Alena's knees buckled, no longer able to support her, and she sank to the ground, weeping with relief.

–

James Hollinthwaite had been carried to his home. One leg was broken, which frustrated him, but would soon mend. The fall had winded him, knocked him unconscious for a while, but it would take more than the felling of a slender ash tree to put an end to him. He sat propped in his favourite chair in his study, the curtains sturdily drawn against the world, the doctor calling daily and Mrs Milburn in her element in the kitchen making beef tea and milk puddings.

And best of all his son was home. Ever since the accident two weeks ago, Rob had remained at Ellersgarth Farm, so it had all worked out right in the end. James smiled at the twists of fate life had dealt him. The boy had always been a disappointment to him, for all his efforts and sacrifices, but despite his obvious inadequacies, Robert was better than no son at all. They had even talked, man to man, for the first time in an age. True, the boy had stood his ground surprisingly well, insisted James shelve his plans for felling, and he had conceded, at least for the present. He'd even agreed not to afforest the fell land he had purchased. But in return Rob had agreed to stay. That was a victory, was it not? Of sorts.

He lay back upon the cushions, pondering what he might fancy for his tea. A double Scotch for a start, to celebrate. So certain was he he had won, that James couldn't quite believe his eyes when the door opened and both Rob and Alena walked in. He had imagined the girl to be still in the forest or else gone back to her mother; hadn't really cared which, so long as he had Rob here, to himself.

'Has she been here all along?' he barked.

'Of course.' Rob looked puzzled. 'Why would she not be? And you may as well know now, Father, that we mean to marry within the next few weeks.'

'Marry?' He could scarce form the word. James struggled to sit up, shock and outrage all over his face, and in a voice that filled the room, exclaimed: '*Marry!*'

The sound was so terrible that Alena slid her hand into Rob's. 'We're to have a child. Your grandchild, Mr Hollinthwaite. And we hope, in time, that you will welcome him or her into the family.'

He stared at her, his mouth working but no sound coming out, the veins on his scrawny neck standing out.

Rob said, 'We mean to live in the end cottage on Birkwith Row. We shall need a warm place for the baby, when it comes. It used to be old Edith's house, if you remember.'

'Are you quite mad? My son, live in Birkwith Row? Is this Lizzie's idea? What has she been saying about me?'

Rob and Alena exchanged a baffled glance. 'My mother suggested it, yes, but…'

'I knew it! She's been bloody poking her nose in where it's not wanted, again. You belong here, boy. At Ellersgarth Farm.

This is your home. And you are to work for me, at the mill. You promised.' James was thumping the arm of his chair with a clenched fist, could feel the all too familiar heat rising in his face, the iron bands tightening across his chest. The boy was as insolent and disobedient as ever. Even now he was shaking his head and smiling, displaying a typically irritating calm.

'I promised to stay here in Ellersgarth. I never said I would work for you at the mill. I have a job in the forest. One I enjoy and intend to pursue. Oh, we'll have to make some adjustments, with the baby and all.' He smiled down at Alena with pride, then lifted his chin in a familiar gesture as he again faced James. 'But you can't control my life any more, Father. I shall make my own decisions in future. I may be your son but I'm also a free man with a mind of my own. Always have, if you had but acknowledged it.'

'Son? Dear God, what an idiot I've been! You're no bloody son of mine. You're a useless lump of baggage who wasn't worth the sacrifices I've made.'

Seeing Rob flinch, knowing how carefully he had prepared his little speech, Alena quickly stepped in with her support. 'Don't reject him again, Mr Hollinthwaite. I know you and Rob have had your differences, that you didn't approve of me or our love, but it's time to put an end to all of that now. We belong together. Rob is your son, and soon he may have a son of his own. Don't you wish him well? You surely don't want to risk losing him, as you have lost Olivia?' And when he didn't answer, only stared at her from eyes dazed with a fury he seemed unable to express, she moved quietly forward, kneeling beside his chair as she struggled to find words to express her own thoughts.

'If trees are not properly tended and cared for, they choke to death for lack of air and sunshine. Love is like sunshine. It makes a person grow and be strong. Can't you give a little to your own son?'

Now his lip curled with cruel contempt. 'I've told you, he's *not* my son. And I've wasted my time trying to make him so. He was the child of some young chit who very nearly gave birth to him on my own clean doorstep. *You* are my child. You, Alena Townsen. All Olivia could manage, after her many failures, was one puling sickly girl whom we doubted would last the night. And I needed a son.'

Alena somehow got to her feet, staggering backwards to find herself leaning against Rob's solid strength, though he was clearly as stunned as she. Gratefully she clung to him, doubting she could have remained upright otherwise. 'What are you saying?'

James's eyes were glazed, as if he were in some distant place, barely aware of their presence. 'All I had to do was swop you for the healthy brat whose mother had so considerately passed away in my kitchen, and then I could have the son I craved. No one would be any the wiser. Not even the doctor since the fool arrived so late. Only Stella was aware of the exchange, and I could trust her. Olivia was too numbed with opium after a difficult birth to understand what was happening. When I gave Rob to her, she believed he was her child. Why should she not?'

The pale eyes focused again upon Alena. 'But *you* weren't meant to survive the night, let alone remain in my sight as a constant reminder of what I had done.'

Rob, his voice barely above a whisper, said, 'Are you saying that was *my* mother you buried in the woods behind the house? Some young girl whose family may still be searching for her?'

'I did what had to be done. I disposed of the body without anyone being any the wiser. The vicar said a prayer over her – that man would do anything for a bottle or two of whisky. What mattered was I'd solved my problem. I had the son I needed, thanks to an unknown girl no one knew anything about.'

'But you gave away your own daughter?'

James shrugged. 'What are families anyway? Who needs them, or love? Olivia was always bleating on about it. Waste of energy which is better spent on more important matters. I managed to survive without either love or a family when

I was a child. Brought up in a boys' home. But it didn't stop me from making a success of my life, did it?' he challenged, expecting their agreement. When it didn't come, he fell into a deep brooding silence and neither Alena nor Rob, still reeling from these revelations, attempted to interrupt. Then James gave an odd sort of smile as he lifted his eyes to his daughter's.

'But you wouldn't go away. Every time I turned round, there you were. In my kitchen, in my garden, with my son, always under my bloody feet. Olivia encouraged you, she was always fond of you, and I...' He put back his head and closed his eyes, fresh pain contorting his features, but whether it was because he still wished to deny a love he actually felt, or wished for a love he could not feel, Alena was unsure.

He addressed his next words to the ceiling. 'You may have your heritage, Alena Townsen. Ellersgarth Farm is yours by rights. You can have it, and the bobbin mill. Everything I possess belongs to you. Through your determination to live, and through the years of your childhood when you plagued me, you managed to make me regret – a thousand times – my decision.'

Alena was holding so tightly to Rob's hand her fingers had gone quite numb. There would be pain later, for Rob more than herself perhaps, with new implications and problems to face, but for now she longed only to make one thing perfectly clear. She drew in a deep shuddering breath.

'I don't want anything from you, James Hollinthwaite. Not your farm, your bobbin mill, your land or your misplaced sense of guilt. All I want is the love of your son, Robert. And he still is your son, no matter what you may say, in every respect that matters. Rob is a fine man, one you should be proud of and accept as he is, not reject or decry because you failed to mould him into the son you craved. *I* am proud of him, and hope that soon he'll be my beloved husband. If he'll still have me?' She turned her face up to Rob then, unaware of the tears streaking her cheeks until he wiped them away.

Then he put his arms about her, kissed her gently on the lips, and led her out of the house.

Acknowledgements

One of the pleasures of writing this book has been the many people I have met who have given so generously of their time and expertise. I express my gratitude to Eileen Thompson, Joyce Wilson and Pat Hogarth for information on bobbin making; Bill Hogarth and Stan Crabtree for coppicing; and Bill Grant for forestry. I also thank the Forestry Commission and the Friends of the Lake District for their assistance. Ellersgarth is a fictitious village in the Furness Woodlands, and Low Birk Mill, if it existed, might bear some resemblance to Spark Bridge, now closed, and Stott Park Bobbin Mill, now operated as a working museum by English Heritage.